BUILT TO FALL

JULIA WOLF

Julia Wolf ♡

Proofreading: My Brother's Editor

Editor: Word Nerd Editing—Monica Black

Model: Carlos Pereira https://www.instagram.com/capereiv/

Cover Design: Amy Queau

To the creators on TikTok who saved my sanity and inspired me to write this story.

CHAPTER ONE

CLAIRE

I REALIZED MY HUSBAND was cheating on me while I unpacked his small suitcase from his latest trip to Chicago. I didn't find anything as sordid as a lipstick stain or a phone number scrawled on hotel stationery. The realization came from a sudden musing.

The last time I'd traveled to Chicago with Derrick, we'd had dinner with Melissa, his best friend from high school. It had been over a year ago, and he hadn't mentioned Melissa since. Not once. Before that dinner, Derrick had been beyond excited to see her again, then nothing.

She'd been lovely too. Petite and blonde—the complete opposite of me. When I'd brought up how pretty I thought she was, my husband had gotten cagey and wouldn't reply.

Then, as I hung up his dress shirt, I wondered why he hadn't seen her since, which was when it hit me. Of course he'd seen her —he just hadn't told me. And he hadn't told me because he was having sex with her. Maybe even falling in love with her. I couldn't say how I was so sure, I just *knew*. Certainty had hit me like a wave and pulled me along in its undertow.

Calmly, I walked into Derrick's office where he was working on his computer. His flop of dark blond hair draped across his forehead, skimming his wire-rim glasses. When we met in college, I had been flattered by his attention and swept off my feet by his all-American good looks and charm. Now, at twenty-eight, most of his youthful boyishness had faded, replaced by hard-lined handsomeness.

"Derrick." I stood in front of him, knowing this was the end of our marriage.

His eyes flicked to mine. "What's up?" He gave me the same crooked grin that had won me over in the first place. Now, it did nothing.

"How long have you been having sex with Melissa?"

For a second, he didn't react, then he shrunk in his chair like all the air had been sucked out of him. "Why would you ask that?"

I shook my head. "I'm not asking if you're cheating on me. I know you are. I'd like to know how long it's been going on." My heart was too frozen to break. I knew this would hurt later, but for now, I was glad for the cold.

"Claire…" He sighed, shoving his fingers through his hair. "A while."

"Since we had dinner?"

He averted his eyes to his computer screen, then brought them back to mine. "Yes. Since the dinner. I'm sorry, babe. I didn't mean for it to happen."

I held up my hand. "No, I don't want to do this."

He stood, rounding the desk. When he tried to touch me, I batted his hands away, which made him frown. "I don't get to say anything?"

"No, you don't. You've been having sex with another woman for a year. I think that's a pretty loud statement." I started to walk out of the room, but he caught my shoulders, yanking me against his chest.

"Stop this. I don't even recognize your voice. Tell me what you're thinking," he soothed.

My voice was flat and devoid of emotion, but Derrick was the one who was unrecognizable. Our marriage wasn't perfect, it wasn't bliss, but it was nice. We made love almost every night, had a tight group of friends, made each other laugh, and still held hands whenever we went out.

"I'm thinking this is over." I turned my head to look back at him, my handsome, unfaithful husband. "You know that, don't you?"

He exhaled a heavy breath and dipped his head to my shoulder. "I don't want that, Claire. I do love you. I love you so much. I just...I messed up. I'll end it. I'll end it right now."

"No, don't bother." I forced his hands off me and spun around to face him again. "If it had been a one-time mistake, I might have been able to get over it. If you'd confessed to me, I might have forgiven you. But this? Me realizing how stupid I've been for a *year* and knowing this would have continued indefinitely had you not been found out? I won't ever get over this. Our marriage is through. I'm leaving."

"Claire..." Derrick lurched toward me, and I jumped back, unwilling to allow him to touch me ever again. "Claire, baby, I love you. You can't leave." His face had flamed to bright red. His blue eyes were liquid behind his glasses.

"I am. I'm going." That was never a doubt. What I was doubtful of was my ability to stand on my own two feet. Derrick had propped me up for so long, I wasn't sure I even remembered how. I didn't have a job or any skills to land on. All I had was a useless college degree and a sister who would take me in without hesitation.

Those thoughts were for later. For now, my focus was on getting out of our home and away from the stranger who called himself my husband.

I made it to the bedroom before Derrick was on me again, trapping me in his arms. He spoke hot, frantic words in my ear while he held me tight. "You have nowhere to go. You can't leave me, Claire. You can't. I messed up, but I'll fix it. This is not the end. I don't accept it."

"Let go of me." I struggled in his hold, turning and twisting, but his arms were iron vises, and his breathing had reached a fever pitch, ragged and rough. I'd been scared of my husband's explosive temper before, but not like this. Fear had cracked my icy veneer, rushing through my veins like venom.

"I won't. You're my wife."

He held me tighter, kissing every part of me his lips could find. "Don't leave, baby. Stay."

I scratched at his arms and hands, yelling for him to let me go, tears filling my eyes, panic taking root in my gut. He only held me harder, kissed me with more fervor. Adrenaline spiked in my blood. If I didn't fight, I'd lose. I stepped on his bare foot with my heel, digging in hard. He grunted in pain and his arms fell away as he stumbled back.

I whirled around while backing toward the nightstand to my cell phone. Never in a million years had I thought I'd need protection from Derrick, but the wild look in his eyes sent chills down my spine.

He started toward me, and I picked up the phone, dialed 911 before I could doubt myself, but hesitated to press send. When his gaze landed on my phone, shock wiped the snarl and anger from his face. His glassy eyes widened, and he sucked in a deep breath.

"Are you scared of me, Claire-bear?" He held his hands out, pleading. "You have to know I would never hurt you."

"But you did, Derrick. You've hurt me."

"I know, I know I messed up. God, baby, you think I don't know? But I'd never hurt you physically."

I rubbed the sore spots on my arms and took another step away. "You did that too."

"No," he rasped. "I didn't mean to."

"It doesn't matter what you meant to do. You did it, and now we're through." Conviction still held strong in my voice, but I'd gotten shakier and off-balance.

His muscles bunched, and I knew, without a shred of doubt, I had to get out of there. The second he came for me, I darted for the door, but I never had a chance. Derrick's arm shot out, and that was the last thing I saw before it all went dark.

CHAPTER TWO

DOMINIC

NAKED AS THE DAY I WAS BORN, I picked up my guitar from beside my bed and laid it across my lap. I strummed a chord idly while staring up at the ceiling. Afternoon light shined in through my open windows, warming my bare skin. It wasn't a bad way to kill some time.

I could have done without the woman rushing around, redressing herself like the open air was burning her skin.

"Slow down."

Stopping, she turned her dark brown eyes on me. I knew that look. I'd lived with that look for years. Nothing good ever came of it.

"This can't happen again." She hopped around, slipping on her heels.

I leaned my head back again, dragging my hand across my forehead. This wasn't the first time we'd had this conversation. "Come on, Iz. We don't need to play that game. It's no fun."

Isabela Ruiz, my former wife and now the ruler of my kingdom, marched to the side of the bed, standing over me. She'd gone from the afterglow to sleek and pissed off in the span of five minutes. Her raven waves tumbled over her shoulders, no worse for wear. Her makeup was barely smudged, although her signature red lipstick had vanished.

Most of it around my dick.

She pointed a French-manicured finger from her chest to mine. "You're right. This isn't fun, Dom. I came here to talk about a press release—not wind up in your sheets."

"Don't act like I had to convince you to be there."

"You didn't, and that's the problem. Every time I'm around you, I forget you're no good for me." She flipped her hair behind her back and worked an earring into her ear. "And then I remember two minutes after I come."

With a harried sigh, she strode from the room, expecting me to follow. Normally, that was reason enough for me to stay put, but I wasn't done with this conversation.

Throwing on a pair of briefs, I sauntered out to my living room where Isabela stood with her arms crossed, waiting for me. The sun was even brighter here, picking up the chocolate hues in her hair and the golden glow of her perfect skin.

Stopping right in front of her, I lifted a wave and brought it to my nose for a long sniff. "Are we going to talk like adults, or am I going to have to keep chasing you all over my house?"

Isabela peered up at me, and there was no mistaking the pain in her pretty brown eyes. The thing was, when she left our marriage the way she did, she lost the right to seek comfort in me. That pain was hers, and I refused to shoulder any more of it.

"How can I move on if I keep coming back here?" she asked.

I scoffed, letting her hair drop. "Aren't you dating that lawyer? The slick, boring one? I call that moving on."

"That ended." She smoothed her hands down her pencil skirt. "But if I were dating him, wouldn't I have just ruined it by fucking my ex?"

I winced. Isabella rarely swore, and when she did, it was most often in Spanish. I was screwed when she cussed in English.

"Then what's the problem? Fucking is the one thing we always got right."

She sucked in a sharp breath. "You see? I'm going to think about you saying that for days, torturing myself with it. I don't want this anymore, Dominic."

I'd said the wrong thing, but I couldn't take it back. I'd add it onto the pile of wrong things I'd said to her over the years.

"So, go. We don't need to have some big breakup scene. We already did that when you walked out on me."

Three years done and gone, and here we were, still in the same place. Maybe she was right. Was it even possible to have casual sex with an ex-wife? It didn't seem like it...at least not now.

"Fine. You're right." She picked up her purse and briefcase from where she'd dropped them beside my couch. "I'll send over the paperwork to terminate my employment with you."

That stopped me dead in my tracks. "What are you talking about?"

She adjusted the strap of her purse on her shoulder. "Obviously I can't continue to do your PR. That means spending too much time together—and when we do, we always wind up in bed. I don't want that anymore. I have to move on."

My brows pulled into a tight line. "That's bullshit, Isabela. I do not accept."

We'd met eight years ago. I'd been in need of new PR, and Isabela's company had come highly recommended. A year later, we were married. Four years after that, we were divorced and demolished. Even after everything we'd been through, the way we hurt each other, we'd stayed friends. Distant friends, but we talked once a month or so...fell in bed once a month or so too.

"It doesn't matter if you accept. I can't work with you. And I certainly can't go on tour with you next month."

She was unwavering, and I thought maybe she wasn't bluffing. She'd put her foot down with me a lot over the years, but I always managed to work that foot back up. Maybe she wanted to truly sever the rest of our flimsy connection.

"So, send one of your underlings on tour with me." I crossed my arms over my chest. "I sure as hell don't trust anyone else to do my PR. Not unless you're in charge of them."

She pressed a finger to the spot between her perfect eyebrows. She always got a headache there, especially when she got pissed at me.

"You slept with the last woman I sent on tour with you. I can't have that, Dom. That is unacceptable. I do not need a lawsuit on top of everything else."

I threw my hands out. "Then send a guy. As long as you're telling them what to do and I don't have to talk to them, I don't give a shit."

Isabella puffed out her cheeks, then slowly released a breath. "Fine. I'll think about our contract." She held up one finger. "But anything physical between you and I is finished. We've been dragging each other along like old baggage the last three years and I'd rather not spend the next three doing the same."

"Drama, woman." I shoved my fingers through my hair in frustration. All I'd wanted out of this day was a really good fuck, some music, a nice meal, and a blunt to round it all off.

"You know," she jabbed a finger at me, "if you didn't make a mess all the time, you wouldn't have such close, personal relationships with your PR people."

I gave her a long, hard look. The mess was telling nosy reporters to go fuck themselves. Flipping off record execs who didn't know their ass from a hit single. Getting in fights with jackholes who didn't know when to stop.

That didn't make me a mess. It made me a man who didn't hold back his reactions. No artist worth his salt felt things in small ways. Insults didn't slide off my back. Injustices didn't fade into the background. Feelings weren't something to manage. I liked my life raw and unmoderated.

"Can't teach an old dog new tricks, Iz. You know that," I drawled.

She rolled her eyes. "Old is right. At forty-two, you'd think you'd learn some self-control."

"I've got plenty." I eyed her in that spicy red skirt, letting her see I was looking at her. "If I didn't, I'd have you bent over, that skirt around your waist, fucking some sense back into you...or fucking you senseless—whichever gets you to keep working for me."

"Not happening." She brushed by me, striding to my front door. "I'll call you, but I won't be by."

"Got it!" I wandered back to my room, threw myself back onto my tangled sheets, and picked up my guitar, shaking my head. I couldn't decide whether I believed Iz, or if her wanting to sever all ties even mattered. We weren't ever getting back together. There was no question about that for either of us. But she'd been a steady source of distraction for so long, my gut protested giving that up.

CHAPTER THREE

CLAIRE

"ANY LUCK?" My sister, Annaliese, peered over my shoulder at my computer.

"It's the same as yesterday. No one waved a magic wand and made the perfect job appear from thin air." I sighed, leaning my head back against her hip. "Why did I possibly think it was smart to be a stay-at-home wife? I can't even tell you what I've done for the last four years."

"Young, dumb, and blinded by love." She stroked my curls and wrapped her arm around my shoulders. "At least you have the internship. If it doesn't lead you to being hired at the firm, you'll have something to pad your resume."

"Unpaid internship." I breathed a heavy sigh, closing my eyes. "But you're right. The internship will at least give my future employers hope that I have an inkling of an idea of what I'm doing. It would just be nice if I could get a cash advance on that future job."

Annaliese circled around me, taking the chair opposite mine at her tiny dining room table. "Obviously you can stay with me, rent-free, for as long as you need...but would it be the worst thing ever to take—"

"Yes, it would be the worst thing ever."

I knew what she'd been going to say without her finishing her sentence. I'd been staying with her for two months and hadn't accepted a cent from Derrick. Maybe it was foolish pride, but I didn't want any type of connection with him, and if he paid me alimony, he'd retain control over me, even if it was court ordered.

That was why I hadn't pressed charges after he gave me a concussion the night I left him. By the time I'd regained consciousness, he'd already called for an ambulance. He'd been repentant, begging me to believe he'd just been trying to stop me from leaving, not hurt me. The stars in my eyes and lump on my forehead said otherwise. But when a police officer questioned me in the hospital, all I could envision were court dates and seeing Derrick's face again and again. I told the officer it was an accident and had Annaliese pick me up as soon as I was allowed to leave.

Annaliese turned contrite, covering my hand with hers. "I'm sorry, baby. You're absolutely right. That douchenozzle would lord his dollah dollah billz over you like he always did."

I snorted a laugh. "Do any of your gardening buddies know you speak like this?"

"Pfft! Chris blasts Travis Scott and DaBaby all day at work. Gardeners can be hip."

My sister, who was seven years older than me, owned a small nursery with her friend, Christine. She'd offered me a job there, but I was still holding out hope of using my college degree, which was *not* in horticulture. Besides, I had the blackest thumb, so I'd probably kill all the plants before anyone could buy them.

I tapped her freckled nose, a feature we shared, although I had about a thousand times more freckles than she did. "Yes, gardeners can be hip, but are you?"

Her brown eyes widened. "Are *you*?"

"I've never made such a bold claim. I accept I'm prematurely middle-aged."

Annaliese stuck out her bottom lip. "That's just sad. You're really young, adorable, and soon-to-be-single. You should be out partying and sleeping with ill-advised dudes."

I forced out a laugh and shut my laptop down. "I can't afford to go out partying. And I've had enough of ill-advised dudes."

"I'm talking sex, not another marriage. God, please don't get married again until you're at least thirty."

Before my wedding, Annaliese had held my hands, told me I looked beautiful, then told me we could escape in an Uber in under five minutes. She'd been neutral on Derrick, but vocally against me getting married at twenty-two.

Like she said, I'd been young, dumb, and stupidly in love.

"You have nothing to worry about on that front." A serious relationship was the last thing on my mind. The very idea gave me hives. "I'm headed to bed now."

She said goodnight, and I took my computer with me to the tiny, converted closet I now called my home. It was a huge step down from the new-construction, bright, and airy condo Derrick and I had shared, but even with a twin mattress on the floor and my clothes hanging above me, I'd never felt more free.

Marley popped her head over my cubicle wall. Her mouth moved, but I didn't hear her. I removed my earbuds. "What was that?"

"All hands on deck. Meeting in the conference room."

My brows drew together. "And that means me?"

"Yes!" She tapped my flimsy wall. "You do *not* want to be the last one to walk into the meeting, so let's go."

Grabbing my iPad, a pad of paper, and two pens, I hurried after Marley, who was the senior intern at the firm. In other words, she actually got paid for her labor. When I'd started here last month, she'd intimidated the hell out of me—especially when I saw the way she treated the other underlings.

Like Marley, the rest of the interns were pretty people. Coiffed and hip, their clothes were perfect, and their hair was always styled and sleek. Actually, that went for everyone who worked here. I sometimes wondered if I was the token plain, chubby girl hired so they wouldn't get sued one day for discrimination.

I'd long ago figured out Marley was nice to me because she didn't see me as a threat. I had a sweet face and quiet demeanor that really couldn't compete with the heat she was bringing.

That was fine by me. I wasn't interested in competition.

The conference room had already started to get crowded. Marley and I found two empty chairs along the edges of the room. Isabela Ruiz, the owner of the firm, stood at the head of the long conference table in the center, sliding her fingers over her iPad.

"She scares me," I whispered to Marley.

"She scares everyone. You can't let it show, though. You can't let anyone see they intimidate you."

"That's a skill I'm still perfecting," I murmured.

Isabela raised her head, scanning the crowd. Every seat was taken, and a few stragglers had to stand in the back, drawing eye daggers from our boss.

"I'm glad some of you were able to be on time. We have a lot to discuss, and I asked for all of you to be here because I need ideas." Her deep, fiery eyes passed over me, then Marley, before returning to me and lingering for a beat. "One of our clients is having a PR crisis, and this isn't the first."

She went on to tell us about a young, brilliant actress who snorted her success up her nose on a nightly basis—which tended to land her in trouble. She was in hot water for punching a homeless man who had asked her for money. That she was in the park where the homeless man slept, looking to score, only added to the heat.

My coworkers threw out ways to rehab her career, and all I could think was this girl needed actual rehab. Ideas like volunteering at a homeless shelter, serving food at a soup kitchen, teaching acting to underprivileged children were all bounced around.

One of the other interns, Steven, raised his hand. "We all know protests are all over the news. What if she went to a few and really got into the thick of them? She could lead chants, carry clever signs, maybe shed a few tears."

Everyone around me nodded, but the idea made my stomach turn. People were protesting real injustices. Using them as a publicity stunt was a true slap in the face to all the legitimate activists.

"Maybe if this girl cared about anyone but herself, she wouldn't need *us* to tell her what to care about," I mumbled to Marley.

Isabela cut Steven off. "What did you say?"

My eyes jerked to hers, and they were pointed squarely at me. "I didn't say anything."

She crossed her arms, her red lips pursing. "I heard exactly what you said. I only wanted to see if you had the guts to repeat it." She turned away from me, addressing the rest of the room. "Claire has a point...as convoluted as it may be. Our client doesn't care about anything we've been tossing around. We need to dig deeper."

The meeting went on, and I tried to disappear into my chair, but it didn't work like I'd hoped. At the end, as I made my way to the exit, Isabela called my name, asking me to stay. Marley's sad eyes said it all: my days were done.

Once the room was clear, she tapped the table beside her. "Come sit, Claire."

How shameful was it to be fired from an unpaid internship? I worked for free, and they still didn't want me around.

I took a seat diagonal from Isabela, arranging my things as neatly as possible in front of me.

"Do you know why I chose you to fill our open intern spot, Claire?" Isabela asked.

My eyes flicked to hers. She was outrageously beautiful in a way I'd never seen in real life. Not simply beautiful, but glamorous and successful too.

"I don't know, no," I replied, surprised Isabela had anything to do with the hiring of interns. But when I thought of it, I shouldn't have been surprised. There were around forty people working here, and Isabela knew everyone's names without blinking. She must have had a hand in each facet of the business.

Her red lips split into a smile. "We went to the same college, and your letter of recommendation came from my favorite professor. How could I turn away a fellow Terrapin?"

I blinked twice before I smiled back. "Go Terps, I guess."

That made her let out a breathy laugh. "Right. Well, my college days are long gone. The point is, I took notice of you when you started working here, and I've seen how diligent you are. What you said in today's meeting really resonated with me, and you voiced one of my frustrations with this business."

"Um...thank you." I had no idea what to say to that.

She shook her head. "Don't say 'um,' Claire. Kill that from your vocabulary right now."

I sat up straighter. "I will."

"Good." She spread her hand out on the table, swiping back and forth. "I want to talk to you about something delicate. This might come out inappropriately, but I promise, it needs to be said. I have a job offer for you."

"I have a job." I pointed to the table. "Here."

"Of course. You would still be working for me, but you'd be promoted to PR assistant and working directly under me for one of my personal clients. You'd have to travel in the upcoming months, and this client can be...difficult."

I waited for the inappropriate shoe to drop. "That sounds okay. I don't mind traveling."

She leaned forward, lowering her voice even though we were alone. "You'd be working for Dominic Cantrell. Are you familiar with him?"

"Yes." I'd been listening to his music just before the meeting. I swallowed hard.

"All right. That's good. Dominic needs around-the-clock PR, and unfortunately, I cannot provide that for him while he's on tour. I'd like to send you as sort of my proxy. I know you're inexperienced, but I think you have a good head on your shoulders, and I'll be guiding you the whole time."

I nodded. "What's the catch?"

She rubbed her lips together, then released a sharp breath. "I need your word you won't sleep with him. Dominic is my ex-husband, so I know him better than most. He's very charming and could convince a nun to drop their habit if he tried. I don't think he'd try with you, but I can't make that promise."

Before I could stop myself, I shuddered. Isabela's hand flew to mine, her gaze intense. "I'm sorry if I misspoke. He would never take anything that's not willingly given. My point is, women have a tendency to be quite willing around Dom. While that's none of my business, what my employees do is."

I relaxed, gently pulling my hand from hers. "That won't be a concern, I can promise you that."

She brightened, her smile genuine. "Are you saying you're in?"

"I don't see how I can possibly turn this down. I'm in."

We sat in the conference room for another hour going over my exact job and the details of the tour. I'd be leaving in two weeks, traveling with Dominic's entourage from city to city, mostly by private jet, for almost two months. While Derrick and I had traveled often as a couple, I'd never done anything like this on my own.

For the first time since my life had shattered into pieces in the middle of my old walk-in closet, optimism shined down. This was a chance for me to advance in my career, and possibly have an adventure too.

I had to set aside the fact that Isabela had said Dominic would seduce a nun, but probably not me. I'd think about that later when I needed to pick at a wound. For now, I marched back to my cubicle where Marley was lingering.

I grinned at her as I approached. "She hired me as a PR assistant."

Marley's smile froze. "You bitch. I'm so jelly! What did you do to deserve that?" She giggled, but she wasn't really joking.

I didn't even care. Nothing could bring me down from this high.

CHAPTER FOUR

DOMINIC

I SAT IN THE MIDDLE OF THE CHAOS SWARMING AROUND ME, wondering how long I was going to keep doing this. I refused to accept forty-two as old—although the gray hairs on my head and chin begged to differ—but touring always made me *feel* old. Even at this point in my career, when I barely had to lift a finger, it was tiring.

My younger self, who'd carried amps on my back and set up my own sound systems, would scoff at how soft I'd gotten. I'd been touring for a long time. Two decades. I'd gone through a few bands, then went solo. Life didn't look anything like it had at twenty-two, but I wasn't sorry for it. I'd paid my dues. Overpaid in some ways.

My assistant, Marta, braced a hand on the back of my seat, her other outstretched with my phone in it. "Isabela," she whispered.

With a groan, I turned it on speaker and threw the phone down on the small, fold-out table in front of me. "Tell me again why you're not here."

"I don't think we need to go over that again." She paused. "Is everything set?"

My jet was steadily filling with some of the people who made my life on the road smooth. I couldn't remember every single person's name, but I recognized everyone.

"What's the PR girl look like?" I asked.

Isabella exhaled heavily through the phone. "Does it matter?"

"It does when it seems she's not here and the plane is supposed to be taking off in a half hour. Pretty bad look for her first day on the job."

It thrilled me that Isabela's plan already wasn't working. She couldn't stand lateness. This girl, this *Claire*, would be out on her ass before the plane took off.

"Are you sure she isn't there? She's young, sort of round, and very plain. She might be blending in with the furniture, so double-check." Isabela chuckled at her own description while I swung my head around to see if anyone had boarded since I'd last looked.

Right behind my seat cowered a girl, red-faced and a little sweaty. Her brown hair did crazy, tangly things around her shoulders, and freckles covered nearly every spare inch of her visible skin. She wasn't as plain as Isabela had described, but I saw why she thought so.

She raised her hand. "I'm here."

I turned back to my phone without a response. "She's here, Iz, and you were pretty unkind in your description."

Isabela ejected a noise that had never been made by a human before. "Am I on speaker, asshole?"

"You are." I glanced back at the girl, and her face was still red. She was either on the verge of tears or seething. If I were her, I'd be pretty pissed to hear my boss say that sort of thing.

"Claire, I'm so sorry. You're lovely, and I'm happy you made it," Isabella soothed.

Claire cleared her throat before she spoke. "My Uber was in an accident a mile away, so I walked, which is why I was running late. I'll be careful when I sit on the furniture, possibly even wear a sign around my neck so no one accidentally sits on me."

Oh, this one had some balls. "You hear that, Isabela? You were worried about me making trouble for you, and here you are being rude to my new PR girl. Tsk, tsk."

When she didn't say anything for a moment, I had a feeling she was doing her breathing exercises—the ones she'd learned during our divorce.

"Claire, I truly am sorry. Are you okay?" she asked.

"I know you are. And yeah, I'm okay. I'm a little sore all over and overheated from walking in the sun, but I'll survive."

I took another glance at her, still standing at my shoulder. Her face hadn't gotten any less red, she was kneading the back of her neck, and didn't look too steady on her feet. I snapped at Marta, ignoring Isabela's questions.

"Marta, this is Claire. She looks about thirty seconds from keeling over. Can you show her to her seat and find her something cold to drink? I need her to work on this tour and that'll be pretty damn difficult if she's dead."

Marta eviscerated me with her eyes, but took Claire in hand, guiding her to the front of the plane where the other staff were seated. I liked to be all by my lonesome in the back.

"Is she gone?" Isabela asked.

"Yep." I tipped my head back, letting the cool air from above hit my face. "I can't believe that happened." My lips curved up in amusement.

"I am the absolute worst. I advocate for other women in the workplace, and then I go and do that. God*dammit*, sometimes I hate myself."

"Ah, Iz, you'll get over it. She'll get over it. It is what it is."

"You know, you should really let someone know they're on speaker."

"Ah, ah, ah, you're not going to turn this around on me." I listened to a few more minutes of Isabela beating herself up before I told her I had to turn off my phone for takeoff.

Maybe her not being on this tour wasn't so bad. We didn't see each other often when I wasn't touring, but when we did, we were either fucking or bickering. While I wasn't old, I *was* getting a little too old for that, and so was she.

When the pilot announced we were prepared for departure, Marta took the seat across from me, shooting invisible daggers out of her staggering green eyes.

"Just so you know, your new employee was in a head-on collision less than an hour ago. Her driver was taken away in an ambulance." Marta crossed her legs and stacked her hands on her knee. "She says she's fine, all while her hands are shaking."

Marta was young, probably a couple years older than the girl. When I'd hired her a few years ago, I'd admittedly been thinking about how nice she'd be to look at more than anything. And she was, in a punk rock, emo girl, black hair, and black eyeliner kind of way. It took me a day to realize she'd kick my ass if she caught me looking at her tits. Another day for me to realize Marta batted for her own team.

"I don't need to know her personal details, just that she'll be able to do her job."

She hissed and leaned forward in her seat. "I know you have at least a scrap of compassion in that hollow chest of yours. Maybe you could take it easy on her, just for today."

That was the thing about becoming friends with an employee: they trash talked like I didn't sign their paycheck. Actually, not 'they.' Marta was the only employee I'd ever befriended, and to be honest, she was the only person I considered to be a real friend. Times like these, though, I regretted the hell out of that fact.

"I have no intention of interacting with her in any way other than professionally. If I should happen to need her professional services at any point today, I'll let her know. I'll even smile if that makes you happy." I bared my teeth, making her shudder.

"Don't try to smile, Dom. It doesn't suit you."

"I won't make a habit of it."

She shook her head and settled back in her seat with her ankle resting on her opposite knee. With the slit in her eyebrow, in her vest and cuffed jeans, I didn't know how I ever thought she was straight.

"How's Izzy?" she asked.

Marta didn't like Isabela, and she'd never even attempted to hide her disdain. Her dislike probably stemmed from the time Iz had encouraged me to fire Marta for no particular reason. Marta thought Isabela was a prissy fake who wasn't out for my best interests.

"She shit-talked the new girl while on speaker phone, so you know, the usual."

She smacked her forehead. "What a cunt. Jesus. Didn't she handpick Claire?"

"No idea how the hiring process went down." I tapped my fingers on my armrest. "How about giving me five minutes of peace?"

She smirked and swung her booted foot back and forth. "Don't act like you don't love me."

"Never said I don't. I love being alone even more, though."

Her eyes slid into slits. "Don't forget I know you, Dom. You're loud and cranky, demanding to be left alone, then you call me over to do some bullshit errand."

"Then you never leave," I groused, my mouth quirking.

Her toes connected with my shin. "Because you ask me to hang out!"

I chuckled and rubbed my beard. "Maybe."

Marta unfolded herself from the chair across from mine and patted me on the shoulder. "Now that we've bonded, I'm going back up front to hang out with the new girl before we take off. I'll let you know whether she's tolerable when we land."

"You do that."

"You'd be sad if I left and never came back." She tugged on my ear like the little brat she was. "But don't worry, you're stuck with me."

Marta sauntered away, and I leaned my head back, resting my eyes and vocals. Our flight to Atlanta wouldn't be long, but I needed all the time to myself I could get. Once the tour swung into full force, alone time would be precious and scarce. In the three years since my divorce, I'd come to realize I craved solitude. At my age, I didn't see that ever changing.

CHAPTER FIVE

CLAIRE

WHAT A SHITTY, terrible way to start a new job. First, I'd been fairly certain I was about to die when my driver ran a red light and plowed into a mail truck. My life had flashed before my eyes, and it was a pitiful showing. Fortunately, I survived, only to have my self-esteem pummeled by Isabela Ruiz, my mentor. And then, the way Dominic Cantrell had dismissed me without even an introduction? Cherry on top of the shit sundae.

I guzzled back the water a pretty flight attendant had given me and chewed on a cracker. My blood pressure had slowed down to normal, and the heat in my face had cooled enough for me to check out my surroundings. Though I'd flown a lot, I'd never flown private before, and this jet was pretty cushy. There were four seats in each row, divided in half by the aisle, and they were deep and wide. Guys with piercings and tattoos and a couple men in suits filled in the available seats. It didn't escape my notice I was one of very few women on board.

Marta, Dominic's assistant, returned, taking the empty seat beside me. She tapped my hand. "Feeling better, kidlet?"

"Yes, much. Thank you for rescuing a complete stranger," I replied.

Marta intimidated me. From her perfect, model-like figure to her exquisite face, raspy voice, and punky hair, she looked like a girl who would have teased me mercilessly in high school while I'd secretly want to befriend her.

"Someone had to." She evil-eyed the men seated around us. "I still can't fathom these dicks didn't see you needed help the second you stepped on board and let you wander all the way to the back."

"It's all a blur at this point." I smiled at her while I massaged my neck. "Have you been doing this long?"

"Years. It feels like decades working for that man." Her words were sharp, but her smile said maybe working for Dominic wasn't so bad for her. I wondered if they were a couple or friends with benefits.

"I take it he isn't thrilled I'm here."

Her smile slid into a smirk. "The only thing Dominic is pleased with is himself, and even that's iffy half the time. I take it you read up on him?"

"I did."

The dossier Isabela had given me had pages and pages of Dominic being surly to reporters, flipping off photographers, close calls with the law, fights that had been covered up, groupies who wouldn't leave the next morning, dropped lawsuits from former band members, ex-employees who'd forgotten the NDA agreement they'd signed when hired. I saw why the man needed full-time PR traveling with him. He was chaos in a very fine, silver fox package.

"Then you know he might not want you here, but he does need you. As long as you do the job you were hired for, you'll get to keep it, cranky rocker be damned."

There was a warning in her tone, which sounded a lot like Isabela's. Why did everyone think I was in danger of throwing myself at Dominic Cantrell? If they knew the last time I'd taken a chance on a man ended with me in the hospital with a concussion, maybe they wouldn't be so worried. *That* I wouldn't be sharing, though.

"I really need this job, so I have every intention of taking it seriously," I replied coolly.

We both grew quiet during takeoff, and Marta scrolled through her phone until the flight attendant brought us drinks.

"To making heinous first impressions." She clinked her soda against mine. "That's on me—not you."

With a half-grin, I smoothed my hand over my wild hair. "I don't know, I'm pretty sure that's on me too."

Her bright eyes flicked over my face. "Girl, you nearly *died*. You had no control over that. Meanwhile, I'm pissing a circle around Dominic." She held up a finger. "It's not because I'm shagging him. Get that thought out of your mind. I've just gotten used to women cozying up to me to get to him and it's tiring."

"Yeah...well, that's not what's happening here," I assured her.

"Good." She nodded. "So, what's your sitch?"

"What do you mean?"

"I mean, do you have a ball and chain at home? Single like a Pringle? A free spirit, never to be tied down?"

I laughed despite myself. "For the first time in a long, *long* time, I'm single...like a Pringle, I guess."

She held up her hand for a high five, and I happily obliged. "Same. That makes this lifestyle a lot easier, I'll tell you that."

"Traveling?"

Her eyebrows bounced up and down. "Traveling with insanely hot musicians. Have you checked out our opening acts?"

"I read their names, but I didn't recognize them."

"Well," she peered at me from over her drink, "The Seasons Change are low-key fire. If Dom lets you have five minutes, you have to watch them with me tomorrow night."

"I'm in." I twisted in my seat to face her fully. "This whole job happened so fast, and I had so much to prepare for, I didn't even think about the *music*."

She swiveled in her seat too, bringing her legs up. "Are you into music?"

"I have it constantly playing. Confession: I love Dominic's early stuff, especially when he was with The Hype."

Her pert nose scrunched. "Don't let him hear you say that. I love their music too, but Dom and the drummer, Eric, had a major falling out a few years back. I'm not allowed to mention that era of his career. It's banned from interviews too."

I tapped my forehead. "Oh god, I remember that now. Jeez, I have some studying to do."

"Forget studying. Tell me what other music you're into."

Marta and I spent the rest of the flight volleying favorites back and forth. Derrick hadn't liked my taste in music and Annaliese listened more to pop, so I didn't have anyone else to talk to about the bands I loved. On the outside, Marta and I had nothing in common, but by the time we landed in Atlanta, I was convinced our insides were plastered with the same band posters. We didn't agree on everything, and she knew more small, indie bands than I did, but we were eerily similar in our taste.

When we disembarked the plane, a passenger bus and a limo waited for us. I headed toward the bus, but Marta stopped me.

"Ride with Dom and me to the hotel. It'll give you a chance to really meet," she said.

My stomach twisted in knots as I waited. It felt like I had an ally in Marta now, but who knew how long that would last. I hoped Dominic and I wouldn't battle, but I really didn't know him yet, not beyond the reports Isabela had given me.

Dominic was the last off the plane. He strode across the tarmac, his eyes hidden behind mirrored aviator sunglasses.

"Miss me?" Marta called as he approached.

He grunted, then completely ignoring me, slid into the car. Marta went next, and I followed, plopping down beside her. Dominic faced us, his long legs spread wide on his bench.

Marta touched my shoulder. "I'm sure you were concerned, but Claire is all better."

He turned his head in my direction. He'd kept on his sunglasses, making it impossible to know the direction of his gaze. "That's a relief."

"It is. Did you enjoy your peace and quiet?" Marta asked.

"As I always do." His face was so expressionless, I snorted a little laugh before I could help myself. "Something funny?"

"No." I should have stopped there, but I didn't. Maybe the sunglasses covering his gaze were making me brave, I didn't know. "It just doesn't seem like you really enjoyed yourself. But I could be wrong."

With that, he slid his sunglasses off and tucked them on the collar of his T-shirt. Black-as-night eyes beneath slashes of ebony brows stared back at me.

"Did you have a nice flight, Claire?" His eyes never wavered from mine, and I was instantly intimidated. He knew exactly what he was doing, and he kept doing it.

"I did." I worked to clear my throat so I would stop squeaking like a damn mouse. My raspy voice was one of my finest attributes, and I'd be damned if this man scared it out of me. "Marta and I talked music for most of it."

"This woman is as much of a music fiend as I am," Marta said proudly. "She's been absent from the live music scene for a few years, but we're going to rectify that."

"Claire's here to work, Marta." Still, his eyes stayed on mine. My cheeks heated, but I wouldn't allow myself to cower. He could burn me to ashes with his coal eyes, and I'd go down with my chin held high.

Marta giggled, which didn't match her all-black exterior. "I'm here to work too, Dominic. But not twenty-four seven. I'm sure Claire will have a few chances to catch the opening acts, or, you know, kick back with me on our days off."

He nodded, his nostrils flaring slightly. "As long as Claire's ready to deal with shit when I need her, I guess it doesn't matter."

Marta opened her mouth to speak, but I was faster. "I've been dealing with shit for a while now, so I've gotten pretty adept. I doubt your shit is anything unique."

It would have been easier to maintain my cool front if the man across from me wasn't so gorgeous in a completely unexpected way. I'd never found a man with salt and pepper hair attractive, but Dominic made it work. Because I had been a fan for a long time, I knew he'd gone gray prematurely. The hair on the top of his head was almost white, and his beard was streaked with silver and the same black of his eyebrows. That contrasted with his smooth, deeply-tanned skin and the tight muscles in his arms and chest beneath his fitted shirt.

Marta clapped and let out a whoop. "You tell him, Claire. If you bust his balls, I'm here for it."

Dominic let out a low rumble from his chest. "I'd advise you not to take Marta's advice to heart. She has somehow wormed her way into becoming my friend on top of being my employee, so she thinks she's allowed to do and say whatever she wants. The same doesn't apply to anyone else."

"No problem." I glanced down at my lap, unable to keep up my ruse any longer. I only had so much bravery in my tank and I'd used a good deal facing certain death on the way to the airport.

Dominic sniffed, and if a sniff could be judgmental, his was. Against my better judgment, I glanced up to find I was still in his sights. He cocked his head, making a slow, rough perusal of me, and I wondered what he thought. I wasn't anything like Isabela, or even Marta, but I had my own vibe. When I left the house this morning, I'd felt almost hip in my rose gold oxfords, skinny jeans, and pinstripe button-up. My hair was much worse for wear, and my makeup had long since abandoned ship, but I wasn't *too* shabby...at least in my opinion.

Dominic sniffed again when he had completed his full sweep of me. It seemed he didn't share my opinion.

Instead of letting his misogyny fly, I perused him, starting at his green suede Adidas sneakers, moving up his long, long, denim-encased legs, over his flat stomach and tattooed arms and hands, to his burning black eyes, and snowy, shorn hair. My eyes flicked back to his, and with precise intention, I sniffed.

My nose wrinkling probably took some of the bite out of it, but no matter. Dominic got the message.

He covered his mouth to hide the upturn of his lips, but I couldn't miss the crinkling around his eyes. My stomach flipped on itself enough to make me nauseous.

Marta jerked her head up from her phone, where she'd been typing away. "What did I miss?"

"Nothing," I rushed out. My bravery was a fragile thing. It came and went as easily as the wind.

Dominic slouched in his seat, stretching his long legs in front of him until his shoes grazed the toes of mine. I refused to draw my legs back, so I left them there as he watched me with interest.

"Just how young are you, Claire?" he asked.

"I'm twenty-six. How old are you, Dominic?" I volleyed back.

"Did you not read my file?" His toes pushed against mine a little more.

"I did, but I must have missed that particular detail." I waved him off, unwilling to bend myself to whatever angle he was headed. "If it comes up, I can always Google. It's not important."

He tapped my toe. "I'm forty-two."

"But a spry seventy at heart," Marta said, wearing her signature smirk.

"That's right." He tapped his chest. "It's all shriveled up and dusty in here."

She stage-whispered to me, "He's so cranky, just like my grandpa."

His dark brows slid together in a solid slash. "I'm beginning to think I shouldn't allow you to influence poor Claire here. Hell, I think you've corrupted me in the time I've known you."

I wouldn't have minded being corrupted a little. In fact, I loved the idea. I'd been the good little wife for so long, and look where that had landed me. Maybe if I were the bad little single girl in my time off, I'd like the view better.

Marta grinned back at our boss. "Groupies have written books about the kind of debauchery you've partaken in. You have ticked every box on the list the bouncers keep at the gates of hell. It's impossible to corrupt the corrupted."

Dominic hummed, then slid his glasses over his eyes again. "You might have a point," he murmured.

Marta rolled her eyes at me and mouthed, "Cranky."

Her plan had been for Dominic and me to get to know one another better, but the only thing I'd learned from this car ride was that Dominic Cantrell made my stomach feel like it was in free fall when he turned the full force of his attention on me—and that he didn't mind being challenged in unexpected ways.

I was still scared and nervous beyond all reason, but like my tiny closet bedroom in my sister's apartment, I could almost taste the freedom I'd be enjoying for the next few months. And after leaving a disaster of a marriage, freedom had never tasted sweeter.

CHAPTER SIX

CLAIRE

MARTA CHECKED US IN AT THE HOTEL, then the three of us, along with two bodyguards, rode the elevator up to one of the floors our tour entourage would be occupying for the next three nights.

When we stepped off the elevator, a group of four stood waiting. They were all dressed in varying forms of tattered T-shirts and skinny jeans. Even the one woman in the group had the same style, and her eyes lit up when she saw us.

"Marta!" She spread her thin arms wide, and Marta stepped into her embrace, squealing as they rocked each other back and forth.

Dominic's low voice vibrated the air beside my ear. "That's Iris. She's the singer for The Seasons Change, our first opener."

I looked up at him, surprised by his proximity and that he actually knew the singer's name for their first opening act. "Marta told me about them on the plane. Apparently they're 'low-key fire.'"

His lips curved, and he dipped his head again to speak in my ear. "I bet she told you about them."

"What does that mean?"

Marta grabbed my hand, pulling me away from Dominic's answer and into the group. She wrapped her arm around my shoulders like we were old friends and hadn't just met a few hours ago.

"This is Claire. She's touring with us. Introduce yourselves to her, you fiends."

I first shook Iris's hand. Her grip was surprisingly strong, and her smile radiated warmth. She was also terribly pretty in a blonde-haired, red-lipped, hipper-than-I'd-ever-be kind of way. I told her I was looking forward to seeing them perform, and she promised to watch out for me in the audience.

Next, I met Callum, the bass player, who looked to be about a million miles away. The drummer, Rodrigo, gave me a high five while he bounced on his toes.

Finally, I was introduced to Adam. With his long, shaggy brown hair and bright blue eyes, he was handsome, but approachable.

"Nice to meet you, Claire." He bit his bottom lip, drawing my eye to the silver ring there.

"You too, Adam." His gaze lingered on mine, and though our interaction couldn't have lasted more than fifteen seconds, his spark of interest was unmistakable.

"Do you have plans tonight?" Iris asked.

Marta glanced over her shoulder to Dominic. "Do we have plans?"

"You know we don't," he answered.

"You should come to dinner with us," Iris said.

"Both of you," Adam added, looking directly at me.

Marta slung her arm around me again. "We're in. Text me the details."

Dominic and his bodyguards moved around us, heading down the hallway. Marta gave Iris another quick hug, then we rushed after them, catching up at the door to Dominic's hotel room.

He held his hand out. "I need the key."

Marta waved it in front of him. "Here you go."

He let himself in, and to my surprise, the bodyguards and Marta followed. Since she still had my room key, I went in too, staying next to the door.

It came as no surprise that Dominic's room was a suite fit for a prince. The living room and dining area were modern and sleek, and from where I stood, I saw two bedrooms, both with king-size beds as the central focus.

Marta moved around the suite, checking things over while the bodyguards did their rounds, presumably making sure everything was safe for Dominic.

He'd already headed to the kitchenette, pouring himself a drink. He glanced up at me as I watched him prepare what looked like a whiskey and soda.

"Want one?" he asked.

"No, I'm good. If I drink now, I won't make it to dinner tonight." I pressed my back against the door, hoping he'd forget I was standing there.

He leaned a hip against the marble counter and took a sip of his drink. "You make friends fast."

There was no point denying it, so I didn't try. "Strangers tend to think I look friendly."

"Are you?"

"I can be. But being friendly doesn't mean I have a lot of friends. My circle is pretty small." And it shrunk significantly the night I left Derrick.

He nodded like he understood, and he probably did. Not because he was especially friendly, but because of his fame. People probably tried to get close with him and ride his coattails, so he had to keep his circle small and tight.

Marta emerged from the second bedroom and brushed her hands off on her jeans. "All clear, boss man."

"Good." Dominic rubbed the top of his short hair with his palm. "I'm staying in for the rest of the day, so you're off the clock. You and Claire both."

She pumped her fist. "Text me if you need anything. My room is next door and Claire's is across the hall."

He dismissed us, opening the door. Marta and the bodyguards went through first, and I trailed behind. As I stepped into the hall, my name was called from behind me. I turned, raising an eyebrow at Dominic.

"Yes?"

His gaze roamed over my face. "Be careful." With that, he clicked the door closed.

After a lot of deliberation, I threw on a pair of tight, ripped-up jeans and a loose, floral camisole. The outfit made me feel cute, but nowhere close to edgy. I would never blend in with this group of rockers, so why try?

When I met Marta in the lobby, she was already with the band having a drink at the lobby bar. She saw me coming and held up a martini glass filled with pink liquid.

"Come here, pretty girl, and toast the start of tour with us," she called, pulling me into the group as she slid a drink into my hand. It tasted cool and fruity-sweet, so no doubt it contained enough alcohol to get me well on the road to drunk. Since I had to work bright and early in the morning, one or two of these would be my limit.

I tapped my glass with everyone else's. When I got to Adam, he leaned in to speak directly into my ear, even though it wasn't *that* loud in the bar.

"Do you know you throw off this incredible vibe?" he asked.

I pulled back, my lips tingling from both my drink and the urge to beam at his compliment. "I didn't know that, but I like hearing it."

He winked. "Anytime."

Rodrigo bounced up next to us, nodding to an entirely different beat than the one coming from the speakers. "So, Claire, what's your deal?"

I sputtered a laugh into my drink. "I don't think I have a deal. I'm doing Dominic Cantrell's PR and I have no idea what to expect."

He sighed, big and heavy. "No, like your life deal. What's that?"

"My life deal? I...um..." I struggled to think of anything to say that didn't involve Derrick. My life deal had completely revolved around him for so long, it was almost impossible to think of who I was now that I'd removed him from the picture.

Adam slipped his arm around my back, pulling me into his side. "Claire's life deal is she's cool as shit and doesn't have to answer your nosy questions."

I jerked my thumb to Adam, full-on grinning. "What he said."

Instead of leaving the hotel bar as originally planned, we decided to stick around, pushed a couple tables together in the back, and ordered a bunch of appetizers to share and another round of drinks. No surprise, Adam and I ended up beside each other again.

I scooped a nacho into my mouth while listening to Iris tell a story about their last tour.

"Nine people were there. *Nine.* And only four were paying any attention." She covered her face with her hands. "And that's on being the first opener for a pop-rock band when you're hardcore punk. I tried to tell our manager and the label we didn't really share an audience, but no one listened. We'd played for more people when we were nineteen and first starting out at house parties."

Adam slapped the table. "It kept us humble."

Rodrigo lifted a fried pickle. "Hear, hear."

Iris dismissed them with a flick of her fingers. "I ate humble pie every day for two years living in a one-bedroom with you fools. I saw enough naked, random girls to last me a lifetime."

Rodrigo giggled, his eyelids drooping. "Like we didn't have to see your randoms."

Tossing her blonde hair behind her shoulder, she hit him with a haughty eyebrow. "I am above reproach."

Adam leaned into me. "She was just as bad as the rest of us."

My eyes crinkled with mirth. "Was? Are you saying this sort of behavior is in the past?"

His mouth hooked in the corner. "I mean...somewhat. I'm no Boy Scout, but I'm nowhere near as crazy as I used to be. It does get old after a while."

I smiled at that, wondering what it was like to have such a crazy life, it became tiresome. My neck twinged from this morning's car accident, so I dug my fingertips into the side.

"You okay?" Adam asked.

"Just a little achy. My Uber crashed on the way to meet the plane this morning."

His mouth dropped open. "Oh shit. You poor, poor thing. Did you get checked out?"

"No." My chest grew warm from his concern. A perfect stranger—a hot, sweet, rock star stranger—was worrying over me. "I'm good, promise."

"Don't try to power through the pain. If you need a massage, or whatever, let me know."

He gave me a crooked grin that was so charming, I imagined he must practice it in front of a mirror.

"Yo, you're handing out massages?" Rodrigo raised his hand. "I'm in need, honey."

Adam gave him the finger. "You gotta be a lot prettier for the offer to apply."

Whoa there. It had been ages since a man other than Derrick had called me pretty, and I was ninety-nine percent sure Adam just had. I felt cute in my new clothes, but pretty? Maybe this was what hot, sweet rockers did to get laid: found the closest chubby girl and doted on her until she spread her legs.

Oh god, that wasn't my voice. That was all the self-doubt Derrick's affair had kickstarted within me. I refused to be a victim to him anymore. If Adam thought I was pretty, I'd take what he said at face value and not question it.

Adam thrust a jalapeno popper toward me. "You have to eat this, Claire. My mouth is spicy, and I need you to be my twin."

I let him drop the popper in my mouth, because who could deny that kind of offer? Then regretted it almost instantly when my tongue caught on fire. I felt like Rodrigo, bouncing in my seat, waving my hand in front of my open mouth.

Adam cackled, laying his head on my shoulder while I tried to figure out how to douse the flames on my tongue.

"Open," Marta ordered. I opened my mouth automatically, and she tossed in a chunk of bread that went with the spinach and artichoke dip. "Tell me when you're ready for another."

It took two more chunks of bread for my taste buds to calm down. I narrowed my eyes on Adam. "No way that was a jalapeno. Did you see me almost die?"

He hadn't stopped laughing during my crisis. "It was! Swear to god. You must have an incredibly sensitive palate. No shame."

"Be nice to Claire. She almost died for real today, you know," Marta announced, her head bobbing in agreement with herself like only a drunk woman's would. She seemed to be having fun at her end of the table, talking with Iris and Callum, but it was nice to know she still had my back, tipsy or not.

"Was it really that bad?" Adam asked, his mouth turning down like he'd just heard a great tragedy.

I pressed my hands to my hot cheeks. "Oh, it was extremely terrible." I launched into more detail of the accident that was nearly the end of me and the moment my life flashed before my eyes. "It was literally only a flash because my life has been so damn boring up until now."

Adam held his hand up for a high five, which I gave him. "Why am I high-fiving you?" I asked.

"Because, my new friend, Claire, you've already succeeded in having a more interesting life. If you died right now, you'd flash on that extremely hot jalapeno popper and know you'd truly lived."

Adam beamed, like he'd really done something. And, I don't know, maybe my two drinks were going to my head, because I felt he had a point. It was only my first day on this tour, and my life had already gotten a little more interesting.

CHAPTER SEVEN

DOMINIC

AFTER ALL THESE YEARS, I had never stopped dreading the first day on tour. I'd spend the day doing interviews in between sound check and resting my voice when I could. Isabela had always complained incessantly that I was terrible with reporters, but I was terrible with most humans, so I wasn't sure what she expected.

Like I kept telling her, I was too old to change. My personality was pretty cemented at this point.

Since I'd be spending most of my time today with Claire, I left my room with the intent to go to hers. As soon as I stepped into the hall, her door swung open and one of the little assholes from The Seasons Change backed out.

"See you later, Claire," he said.

I spotted her over his shoulder, holding the door open and grinning at him. "Bye, Adam."

Adam nearly tripped over his own feet when he spun around and came face-to-face with me. His young, *young* face instantly flushed. "Oh, hey, man. Good morning."

I lifted my chin. "Morning."

He stumbled down the hall after a backward glance at Claire, who waited with her door open.

"Good morning, Dominic. Give me just a second and I'll be ready." She held her palm out, inviting me inside. I probably shouldn't have, considering she was my employee and I'd just witnessed her saying goodbye to her one-night stand, but I crossed the hall to her room anyway.

While Claire slipped a baby pink blazer over her T-shirt, I glanced around, surprised by how neat everything was. No clothes strewn about or trash anywhere. Even the bed was freshly made. I guess it was possible she hadn't slept here last night and that kid had been dropping her off.

"I'm sorry I'm not quite ready. I hate being late, but Adam stopped by with breakfast and I—"

"You don't have to do that." Tucking my hands in my pockets, I leaned against the door. "I don't need an explanation. Though, I do have to say, I *am* both impressed and surprised with how quickly you work."

Claire stopped what she was doing to stare at me with wide eyes and an open mouth. "What? I didn't..." She shook her head. "I just met Adam yesterday. I didn't...I wouldn't...No. The picture you've conjured up is all wrong."

"It's okay, Claire." I held my hands up. "You're young. This is what you *should* be doing. I'm not the morality police."

Claire spent a long beat staring at me from beneath furrowed brows. Her nostrils flared with what I had to assume was indignation, making me chuckle. That only served to make her huff and spin away.

She yanked her phone from her charger and stuffed it in a messenger bag. While eyeing me with annoyance, she slung her bag violently across her chest. "Thank you for your permission."

Claire, the little teddy bear, had some venom in her, which made her slightly interesting. I didn't have time for shy and meek, but this, I could make time for.

I trailed behind her down the hotel hallway to the elevator where my security waited. I liked watching her walk when she was offended. Her curly little ponytail bounced in the same rhythm as the globes of her ass. I bet she looked just as good from the front, with those tits rocking to the beat of her anger.

In the elevator, I glanced at her again, but she kept her attention on her phone.

"We have Rolling Stone first," she said.

"I know."

"Isabela sent them topics they weren't allowed to broach. Me as well." Her eyes slid to mine briefly, then back to her screen. "You have an on-camera interview with Sara Gonzalez from the local ABC News channel."

"I know all this, Claire. Marta sent me my schedule last night."

She rubbed her shiny pink lips together. "I'm sorry if I'm repeating what you already know. Obviously, this is my first day, so there are kinks to be worked out. I'm taking note that you actually read the schedule Marta sends you, so unless you ask, I won't give you a second rundown."

This girl sounded way too uptight for someone who'd gotten laid last night. Though, it couldn't have been that great if her lipstick was still intact. I hadn't seen her reapply it after Adam left, meaning the idiot hadn't kissed her to hell and back. Jesus, maybe the poor bastard really hadn't gotten any last night. I had no idea why that thought tempted me to pump my fist, but it sure as hell did.

As we made our way from the elevators to the private room reserved for all the press, I dipped my head to ask her and caught a whiff of honeysuckle coming from her skin.

"Did that kid really just stop by for breakfast this morning?" I asked.

Her feet came to a halt so fast, I had to grab her shoulders to stop from running into her. She rounded on me, her eyes narrowed and chest puffed, like she was prepared to let me have it. But the second we made eye contact, she contracted, almost folding in on herself.

"That's none of your business," she mumbled.

Claire tugged open the door to our assigned room without sparing me a glance, which I probably deserved. I didn't need to know about the private life of my twenty-six-year-old PR assistant, and she had every right to ignore my probing questions. Neither of those things meant I'd stop asking, though.

The interviews were smooth sailing, if not tedious and fucking boring. The only thing that entertained me was watching Claire flutter about like a nervous mouse. She was fastidious to a fault, making sure the setup was perfect and remained perfect throughout the day. When each new reporter showed up, she double-checked everything, then stood at attention during every single interview, listening intently.

I liked that. I'd gone through a dozen different PR people over the course of my career, including Isabela, and none had acted the way Claire did. Maybe it was because she was new. Whatever the reason, I kinda hoped she kept it up.

"How are you?" she asked once we were en route to the venue in the back of a black limo.

"We've been together for hours, Claire. How do you think I am?"

From the bench opposite mine, she considered me in a slow perusal like the one she'd given me yesterday. I slouched down, stretching my legs to reach her shiny little shoes with my boots.

"I think you're probably ready to be alone for a while. You don't like talking about yourself, and I might be wrong, but it seemed like you were on edge the entire time, as if you were worried someone would bring up a topic you didn't want to discuss." She pushed her foot against mine in a feeble attempt to nudge me away. "That had to be tiring."

I tipped my chin, neither confirming nor denying her summation of me.

She checked her phone. "Once we get to the venue, you'll have an hour before sound check. Marta has lunch ready for you. We'll give you your privacy and the time to rest if that's what you need."

"Sounds perfect. I appreciate the job you're doing."

She dipped her head and reached into her bag like she was searching for something, but there was no mistaking the pleased flush in the apples of her cheeks. Claire Fontana blossomed under praise, and something told me she hadn't gotten enough of it in her life.

My moral compass, which tended to be more than skewed half the time, directed me to cease taking note of the way this girl reacted. If I still needed my attention diverted post-concert, I had no doubt there'd be no shortage of...diversions.

"What does your shirt say?"

Like I said, my moral compass pointed me in the wrong direction all too often, or I ignored it altogether.

She opened her pink blazer to show me the bold black letters on white cotton. "Fear eats the soul. My...friend and I went to an art installation last year where they were printing these. This is the first time I've worn it."

"Do you believe it?"

She tucked an escaped curl behind her ear and rebuttoned her jacket. "Oh yes."

"Do you live by it?"

Again, her cheeks flushed pink, but instead of looking away, her eyes locked on mine. "I'm getting there."

"Good. I'm trying to get there too."

She scoffed and pushed at my boot once more. "I have a hard time believing you have any fear. You're a few hours away from standing in front of thousands of people here to see *you*, and you're as cool as a cucumber."

"Performing doesn't scare me." I opened my palms on my legs. My fears were a lot darker than crowds of people waiting to worship me.

"What does?"

My mouth hitched in amusement. "Now, why would I tell you?"

"You wouldn't." She drew her feet away, tucking them together against her seat and checked her phone again. "We're almost there."

"Claire?"

She paused whatever she'd been pretending to type on her screen. "Yes?"

"Are you scared of me?"

Her plump lips pressed into a thin line, and she touched a hand to her cheek for a moment before dropping it. "Yes, I am."

I closed my eyes and let my head fall back on the rest, releasing a long exhale through my nose. "Good. That's for the best."

Marta waited for us in my dressing room. Her long legs were propped up on my couch, and her music filled the room. She turned the volume down when we walked in.

"Greetings." She jerked her thumb over her shoulder. "Your food's on the table, Dom. Hey, C."

Claire's face transformed from unsure and timid to unadulterated happiness. "Hey, M."

"You have nicknames now?" I picked up my sandwich on a plate and took it to the couch, knocking Marta's legs down to make room.

"Does calling each other by the first letter of our names really count?" Marta asked.

"Hell if I know." I checked between the slices of bread to ensure my order was right. Marta rolled her eyes at me, but she knew the drill.

"Dominic, would you still like that quiet time now?" Claire asked in her soft, throaty voice.

"Yes. You can go."

"Okay." She blinked a couple times, gripping the strap of her messenger bag with both hands. "Marta, do you want to grab lunch with me?"

Marta sat up, her lips twisting. "Oh...well—"

"You can go, Claire." I sucked mustard off my thumb. "Marta's staying."

She nodded, her hand on the knob. "All right. I'll just...I'll be around." Then she hurried out of the room, shutting the door carefully behind her.

Marta's eyes were on me while I ate my sandwich. She knew the drill. We usually ate together before the show—and that didn't change because she'd taken a liking to my new PR girl. Sure, I could have invited Claire to stay, but I didn't want to.

"I could have gone with her," Marta said.

I wiped my mouth with a flimsy napkin. "No. You couldn't have. I wanted you here."

"I get that, but why be so damn rude to her? From her texts, it sounded like press went well." Marta tucked her feet beneath her to face me. "Did something happen?"

"No. She did a good job, which I told her."

Marta gasped. "You did *what?*"

Her surprise had me grinning. "I told her she did a good job, Mar."

She shoved at my shoulder. "Dominic Cantrell, you don't tell *anyone* they do a good job! My yearly bonus is my only sign you're pleased with my performance. What the hell?"

Unbothered, I took another bite of my sandwich while Marta huffed and flailed and called me a bastard. Finally, I pushed her forehead with my index finger.

"You can stop now. I told her she did a good job because she seemed to need it."

Her shoulders rose and fell with indignation. "Maybe I need it sometimes."

I smiled at my sandwich. "You don't."

"Well...fuck off."

My shoulders shook, but I swallowed the laugh. "Nice way to speak to your boss."

She crossed her arms. "That was me talking to my friend. I'm on my lunch break, you know."

I uncapped a water bottle and took a swig. "Any luck with your straight girlfriend last night?"

Marta ripped open a bag of chips and crunched a few in her mouth. "Iris isn't straight."

Marta had been crushing on the lead singer of The Seasons Change since they met a few months ago. While Marta wasn't one to be shy, Iris had thrown her for a loop. Personally, I didn't know one way or another, but if Iris hadn't taken Marta's ample bait yet, I figured she wasn't interested.

"You're one-hundred-percent on that?" I asked.

"No, obviously, you monster." She stuffed more chips into her mouth. "I'll find out soon."

I raised a brow. "Are you...I don't know, going to ask her?"

"I have my ways, and they mostly involve alcohol."

I laid my hand on the top of her head and ruffled her carefully styled hair. "That sounds like a well thought out plan. I'm into it."

She flew off the couch and across the room, smoothing her hair down. "Are we really judging each other's lives now? Is that what's happening? Because I have *opinions*."

I stretched my arms along the back of the couch, my forehead puckering. "Since when have you ever held back?"

She tapped her lip. "There was that week there..."

"The week you started working for me?"

"Shut up. Just leave my game alone and be nicer to Claire."

"I thought you were mad because I was *too* nice." I lifted a hand. "By the way, I saw that kid Adam exiting her room this morning."

Marta paused her manic chip chewing. "*No.* Are you kidding?"

"Nope."

She nibbled at the edge of a chip. "He was looking at her with puppy dog eyes all last night, but she didn't seem to really notice. I'm going to have to get her to spill the damn tea because I thought they went back to their rooms separately last night."

"I'm surprised you noticed anyone besides Iris."

"I've learned from you that prolonged eye contact gives people the creeps."

I pointed to my eyes with two fingers. "This shit is intense, not creepy."

Marta shot me an exaggerated wink and nod. "Okay, Dom, keep telling yourself that."

There was no real, tangible reason Marta and I had become friends. She was a good deal younger, a lot more cheerful, had a wide group of friends, close with her family, and generally functional as a human. But within a week of knowing each other, she'd taken a shine to my grumpy ass, and I looked forward to her antics every day. She took pleasure in calling me on my shit, and...well, I didn't mind it. Not when it came from her.

"Intense," I muttered, eating the last of my sandwich.

"Creepy!" she yelled, then jammed a fistful of chips in her mouth, crumbs falling onto her shirt as she chomped.

I shook my head. From the moment I woke up, I'd been dreading this day, but as I sat in my dressing room with this crazy woman, I realized it hadn't been half bad. Not even close.

CHAPTER EIGHT

CLAIRE

DOMINIC AND I TRAVELED outside of Atlanta into a more rural area of Georgia where he had a radio interview this morning. Even though it was just as easy to do it by phone, he wanted to go in person, and it wasn't my place to ask questions. In fact, Dominic had made it pretty clear where my place was.

While I hadn't expected to become pals with Dominic Cantrell, his callous dismissal of me had stung. Then again, I was still tender all over from my marriage ending, so it wasn't entirely Dominic's fault I had been easily hurt.

Our car rolled into a small town straight out of a greeting card movie. Store fronts lined a dusty main street, a few older people strolling down the sidewalks.

"This is where we're going?" I checked for the station's name on my phone. "KXGA?"

Dominic turned from the window, his mirrored lenses hiding his eyes. "This is it. Good ol' Dublin, Georgia. More peaches than residents."

"Do you have a connection here?" It wasn't my business, but I couldn't help being curious.

"I do." That was all he said before turning back to the window.

The radio station sat at the end of the street, and we were able to pull up right in front, taking one of the slanted parking spots. An older man with tufts of white hair around his shiny skull, wearing a suit that looked like it had fit him two decades ago, stood on the edge of the sidewalk, waiting for us.

Dominic hopped out of the car with a wide smile—the first I'd seen on him so far. The corners of his eyes crinkled from the force, and I...liked it. He was handsome, that wasn't in question, but there was something otherworldly about seeing him genuinely happy, even if it was fleeting.

He shook hands with the older man, who turned out to be the station owner, Dale Lemon. Dominic made sure I was with them and introduced me to Dale, who took little interest in me.

I wasn't from the south, but I recognized a good ol' boy when I saw one. Dale Lemon probably didn't believe women should have roles at work outside of support staff. Thankfully, I didn't work for him and we'd be in and out in an hour, tops.

"How've you been, son?" Dale asked.

Dominic clapped him on the back. "I don't think you can call me son anymore since my hair's about as gray as yours."

Dale laughed, big and rowdy. "I've known you since you were knee-high. You'll always be that kid with skinned knees and a gappy smile no matter how big you get."

Interesting. I had no idea Dominic had grown up in Georgia. Maybe that explained why he'd been willing to come all this way to this tiny station in the middle of nowhere for an interview.

Dale led us through yellowed walls covered with pictures of rock stars who had been famous thirty years ago, then stopped outside of a small room with two vending machines, a cracked laminate table, and a worn black leather couch, the station's broadcast playing over crackling speakers.

"You can have a seat in here, ma'am. I'll take care of ol' Dominic. He's in capable hands." Dale threw me a wink and held his hand out to usher me inside the space that looked more like a prison waiting room than somewhere guests would be shown to.

My gaze focused on Dominic. "Is that what you would like, or would you rather I stay with you during the interview?"

He paused for a long moment, his eyes sweeping over me. I had forgone the message tee and jeans for more professional high-waisted trousers and a purple, short sleeve cardigan, but kept my trusty oxfords. I couldn't tell if Dominic found me wanting or not. He was impossible to read when he wanted to be.

"I'll be fine. Thank you for asking, Claire." He leaned in, speaking low beside my ear. "Keep an eye on the time. We need to make a short stop on the way back."

"Got it. I'll make sure we leave with plenty of time."

He nodded, satisfied with my answer. "You'll be okay in this shithole?"

I snorted a little laugh. "I'll manage."

"Okay. See you on the flipside."

He and Dale left me in the shithole. I didn't really want to sit on the couch, which looked like it hadn't been wiped down since the eighties, so I wandered into the hall to check out the pictures. There was some serious history in these images. Huge bands and smaller ones had visited this little radio station, though it looked like it had been at least ten years since a new picture had been hung.

I stopped in front of a picture of a much younger Dominic from when he was in The Hype. His band members crowded around him, all of them grinning with the lightness of youth and newfound success. Tracing a finger over Dominic's dark hair and easy smile, a pang of wistfulness hit me. He wasn't the same man he'd been in this picture, but I could look back at pictures of myself from a year ago and say the same thing.

"Can I help you?"

Startled, I whirled around to find a guy about my age in a Blue is the Color band tee and ripped-up jeans. His eyebrows were raised expectantly, but his smile was friendly enough.

"I'm good, actually. I just wandered out of the room I was told to wait in to check out these pictures."

"Ah, the hell pit. I don't blame you. Are you with...?" He nodded toward the studio at the end of the long hallway where Dominic was currently being interviewed.

"I am. I'm his PR assistant, Claire."

"Cool, cool. I'm Sam. I do sound engineering here." He waggled his eyebrows. "Livin' the high life."

"It can't be so bad. You probably get to hear new music before anyone else, right?"

"Truer words." He checked his watch. "Have you got some time while Dominic does his thing? I'm about to listen to the new Unrequited release for the first time..."

I couldn't say no to that. Unrequited was one of my favorite bands. I'd begged Derrick to go with me to see them when they were in town, but he'd been completely uninterested, saying they started sucking once they hired a girl drummer. He couldn't have been more wrong. They've killed it more than ever since Maeve O'Day joined.

In Sam's small office, I got lost in the music, but not so lost that I didn't keep track of the time. We still had five minutes before we needed to leave, but I grabbed my bag and phone so I could find Dominic.

"Thanks for saving me from the hell pit," I said.

Sam dipped his chin. "No problem. I wouldn't send my worst enemy in there. I don't think the snack machine has been changed out for a good decade or two."

I giggled. "And the couch, my god."

He tossed his head back. "Let's not even talk about the couch."

I shuddered. "It's unholy."

"What's unholy?"

I whirled around, finding Dominic Cantrell filling the doorway, his eyebrows drawn tight over crow-black eyes, his tattooed hands gripping the frame. The rose on his left hand rippled with tension as he held himself there, suspended between the hallway and office.

I shook my head, snapping into professional mode. "Oh, nothing. How did your interview go?"

"Weren't you listening?"

"Um..." *Oh shit, I'm not supposed to say "um." Thankfully Isabela can't hear me making a fool of myself right now.* "No. I didn't realize you wanted me to. I met Sam in the hallway, and he let me listen to the new Unrequited album."

Dominic cocked his head. "How was it?"

He seemed to genuinely want to know, so I went for full honesty. "It was incredible. Sick. I already know at least two of the songs are going to be on repeat when I download it."

He nodded once. "Nice. I'll have to check it out."

From behind Dominic, Dale clamped his hand on his shoulder. "Ready to do those station bumps?"

I exchanged glances with Dominic, then checked the time on my phone again. Three minutes. "What's a bump?" I asked.

Dominic moved to the side so Dale could answer. "The big guns at KXGA's parent company sent down promo for Dominic to record for their affiliates. We play it between songs and station breaks. Shouldn't take much more than half an hour."

"Actually, Mr. Lemon, Dominic doesn't have time for that today. I'm sorry, there must have been a—"

Dale Lemon went from good ol' boy to angry man in a few blinks. He slammed his hand on the outer wall. "That isn't acceptable. Dominic always records bumps for us."

I moved closer, my knees quaking beneath me. "We'll figure out a way to record the bumps, but it can't be today. If I had known—"

Dale squared off on me. "If you had known what, girlie? If you hadn't been so busy flirtin' with my engineer, you woulda been able to do your job."

This man in front of me was big and full of bluster. He might've been a small-town radio guy, but he didn't seem like the type who took no for an answer, especially not from women.

"I apologize again—"

"Your apologies mean nothin'. You need to make things right."

If I could just get out of this office, I could breathe and think. But Dale had blocked the entrance, trapping me inside. My chin trembled, but I refused to cry, no matter how afraid he made me. He wouldn't hurt me, not with Dominic and Sam as witnesses, but knowing that didn't really help—not when less than three months ago I'd been trapped and hurt by another man.

My mouth opened and closed, but barely a squeak came out. It was then Dominic stepped in, shoving Dale aside like he was kidding around, but using more force than strictly necessary. I took the opportunity to rush out of the room and scramble to the exit.

A minute later, Dominic found me on the sidewalk, convincing my heartrate to return to normal. I held my hair off my neck, fanning my face with my other hand.

He stopped in front of me, looking me over. "He was out of line."

I nodded. "I know."

His warm palm cupped my elbow. "We need to go."

He steered me to the car, allowing me in first, then climbed in after. I took in a shaky breath and attempted a smile. "I'm sorry I messed up. I truly didn't know about the bumps, but I'll check first if a situation like that comes up again."

Dominic scrubbed at his mouth, then released an aggravated groan. "The bumps are no big deal. Dale overreacted. I've known him since I was a kid. He flies off the handle at the drop of a hat." He dropped his hand on his leg. "You need to stand up for yourself, Claire."

"Right." I crossed my ankles and rubbed my damp palms on my pants. "I know. I won't let something like that happen again." He watched my fingers curl into the fabric of my pants, then his eyes flicked to mine. "Won't happen with Dale. I ripped him a new one before I left. No one talks to my employees like that."

"Thank you."

He was right, though. I needed to be my own champion. I'd let people walk all over me for too long, and I was just now seeing it. I had my moments of bravery, but I let far too much slide. What Derrick did to me had the potential to fold me like a flower—I had to be the one to not allow it.

"Don't thank me. I would have put a stop to Dale sooner, but I wanted to see you handle it. Probably a dick move on my part," Dominic admitted.

Our car rolled to a stop at the end of a long driveway, bookended by two overgrown bushes covered in white flowers. Dominic reached for the door. "This is our stop." He left the car before me, offering me his hand. "We'll be quick. Come on."

I let him help me out, then quickly pulled back. "Where are we?" We hadn't gone far from the station. A few turns had led us to a narrow road lined with long driveways and massive trees covered in Spanish moss.

He pointed to the house with peeling blue paint at the end of the driveway. "This was my grandparents' house. I spent my summers here with them. Now that they're gone, I own it." He plucked a white flower from the overgrown bush. "Whenever I'm in town, I always have to get a taste of honeysuckle. Come here."

Pulling the stamen from the center of the flower, Dominic sucked on it, humming softly, then repeated his action.

Curious, I took a flower from the bush. "How do I do this?"

He narrowed his eyes on me. "You've never had honeysuckle?"

"Never. I'm a northerner. I don't think it's really a thing."

Without a word, he took the flower from my hand, slowly pinched the stamen, dragged it out, and held it up to my lips. "Suck, Claire."

I darted my tongue out to catch the nectar and sucked lightly on the flower. The honey sweet flavor surprised me. My lips curved into a delighted smile, and I reached for another.

"I think I can do this one myself," I said.

Dominic followed my movements, sucking the nectar from his own flower.

"Good," he murmured. "What do you think?"

"Delicious." I grinned at him, excited to have been shown a new experience. "Do you ever go wild and stuff the whole flower in your mouth?"

He looked to the ground, kicking up dirt with his sneaker as he chuckled. "Never. Should we try it?"

I rolled the soft, white petals across my bottom lip. "It might not taste very good. Let's not ruin this experience with an imperfect memory. Next time I come upon a honeysuckle bush, though, I'm trying it."

Dominic stood close while I snapped a few pictures of the flowers and then a quick selfie to send Annaliese. My sister surely knew all about honeysuckle since plants were her life, but she'd never believe I sucked on nectar with Dominic Cantrell without some sort of photographic evidence. Plus, I wanted to remember this sweet moment.

"Do you want to go in the house?" I asked.

"Nah, I'm okay. I just like to stop by, get my honeysuckle fix, and make sure the place is still standing. I'm ready to get back to the city."

I plucked another flower. "Do you want to take some for the road?"

His hand tucked in his pockets as he sucked his teeth. "There's something about the location that makes them sweet for me. I've never had the urge to take them with me." He jerked his head toward the car. "Let's go."

This brief glimpse into Dominic Cantrell only made me curious for more. I saw a little bit of his human side, making him less of a rock god and more of an immensely talented, gorgeous man. Still intimidating, but a coating of his shine had dulled a little, which was a good thing.

On the drive back, my curiosity got the better of me. "Was Dale your grandparents' neighbor?"

Dominic faced me, but his eyes were hidden by his mirrored lenses. "His friend and protege. My grandfather owned the station up until about fifteen years ago, then Dale took over."

"Is that where your love of music came from? Hanging out at the station?"

"A mix. I think I strolled out of the womb with a guitar in my hand. I recorded my first demo at that radio station with my grandfather's help. It was a pile of shit, but I was only sixteen. My grandmother...now, she was something else. She was a music teacher and played the organ at her church. The woman had a voice like Janis Joplin. If she'd been born in a different era, she'd have been the rock star of the family."

I almost didn't know what to say. This was the most Dominic had ever said to me. I was so taken aback by how open he was being, my mind had to scramble to keep up.

"They both sound wonderful. I'm glad you had those summers with them."

He studied me for a long time from behind his glasses. Miles went by before he responded. "That's an exceptionally nice sentiment, Claire."

I shrugged. "It's just the truth."

Tapping his fingertips on his knee, he canted his head and stretched his mile-long legs out to my side of the car.

"I won't need you anymore once we're back in Atlanta. You're free for the rest of the day." He returned his gaze to the window and kept it there the rest of the entire drive.

Dismissed yet again.

I wondered what made a man so closed off. Fame probably had something to do with it, but I imagined his locked doors covered caverns filled with reasons.

As curious as I was, I wouldn't be banging down his doors to get inside.

Dominic could keep his secrets, and I'd keep my perfect honeysuckle memories.

CHAPTER NINE

DOMINIC

INSTEAD OF STAYING AT A HOTEL IN MIAMI, I rented a house on the beach. Three nights straight in Atlanta was more than enough for me. Here, I could step outside without being swarmed and surrounded. Not that I was under any illusion photographers wouldn't use zoom lenses to capture my picture, but I had no intention of walking around with my dick out or doing blow by the window. To stay sane, I needed to be able to stretch my legs a little, not hole up in one room unless I was working.

Claire and Marta explored the house we'd spend the next two nights in while I kicked back on the expansive patio by the pool. Florida sun beat down on my face, absorbing into my black shorts and T-shirt.

From inside, Claire's voice carried. "Are you sure I shouldn't stay at the hotel?"

"Nope. It would be such a waste. There are ten bedrooms in this joint. Do you honestly think you'll be in his way?" Marta asked.

"It's hard to say with him," Claire answered.

That had my lips twitching. I hadn't been the friendliest to my new PR assistant, but it wasn't really personal. People weren't my thing, and young, sweet women were so far outside my wheelhouse, I had no idea how to handle them.

Claire wasn't as skittish as I'd first assumed...and maybe not even as sweet. I'd gotten used to her presence. Hell, I didn't even mind it. In fact, I'd told Marta to invite Claire to stay in the house with us.

"Get out here," I called. "Both of you."

They appeared together, a study of darkness and light. Like me, Marta was dressed in all black, but a lot less fabric. Claire wore a white sundress that would have been sweet and innocent if not for the diamond shape cutout below her breasts. When she shifted, I kept catching a glimpse of the under-curve of her tits, which messed up my mind.

I'd dismissed her outright when I first saw her on the plane, and it had been a relief. I didn't want to be attracted to her. Our working relationship would be a hell of a lot simpler if I didn't wonder what it would feel like to slip my fingers inside the cutout and trace the supple flesh peeking out.

"Think you can set up a dinner for tonight?" I asked Marta.

"Sure. Are we doing Cuban?"

"Sounds good. Invite the other guys," I said.

Marta gawked. "Who do you mean? The other bands?"

I nodded, amused by her reaction. "Yes. See if they're up for dinner. I could stand getting to know them, and I'm sure you'd rather have their company than mine."

"Um...okay." Marta swiveled around in a circle. "You're serious, right?"

"Completely."

She went back inside to make phone calls, and Claire started to follow her.

"Claire."

Turning back, she took a step closer to me. "Do you need me?"

"You wouldn't be in this house if I didn't want you here." I cocked my head, allowing myself a moment to look her up and down from behind my shades. "I don't play games, and I always say what I mean. You'd be stashed at the hotel if you weren't welcome."

Her eyes rolled skyward. "Somehow, that wasn't very comforting. But thank you anyway. This is by far the nicest house I've ever been in. A girl could get used to this."

"Well, don't."

It seemed like she could see right through my mirrored lenses, from the startled glare she gave me.

"Enjoy the sun. I'll go see if Marta needs help."

Call me a sadist, but I enjoyed a pissed-off Claire far more than I should have. And from the bounce of her curls as she retreated, she was mighty pissed off.

Only The Seasons Change made it for dinner, but Marta had ordered enough Cuban food for an army. We sat on the patio, drinking mojitos, eating good food, and talking.

Well, they talked, I listened. I didn't often feel out of place, especially not on my own tour, but tonight was an exception. These guys were all in their early twenties, just starting their lives, bright-eyed and fresh. My bright eyes had long ago faded.

"This house is crazy." Iris, the lead singer, shook her head, then lifted her gaze to meet mine from the other end of the table. "Do you still feel awe at being here, or is this normal now?"

Rocking forward in my chair to rest my elbow by my plate, I contemplated her question. "Being able to afford to stay in beautiful places is normal to me and has been for a long time. The house is nice, no doubt. The views are spectacular. But I'm here for the privacy and the sunshine. The rest is cake."

Iris pursed her pretty lips and leaned in like I had. "Why chase fame if privacy is so important?"

"Are you chasing fame? Is that what The Seasons Change is about?" I countered.

"Hell no!" Rodrigo pumped his fist above his head. "We're about the music, baby."

I tipped my chin at him. The kid never stopped moving, but I couldn't find fault in his enthusiasm. "Me too. That's always what I've been about. The landscape becomes more volatile the more successful you become, and the hoops you have to jump through change, but music is always the centerpiece of my motivation."

Iris plucked a piece of her platinum hair. "They made me go blonde. I hate it so much."

The woman was crazy gorgeous, but she was a rocker first. I could understand how being forced into a cupcake image ruffled her leather-and-metal feathers. "Yeah…well, record labels can be dicks." I tugged at the short hair on the crown of my head. "One day, you can tell them to go to hell and stick up your middle fingers as you go gray."

Marta gave my shoulder a shove. "Look at you, being all supportive. Who would have known?"

I returned her shove, chuckling. "I have my moments."

Iris slumped back in her chair, her foot resting on her knee. "I just want to be scary. Who's scared of a sorority-looking bitch?"

Claire raised her hand. "Me. You're intimidating as hell until you smile."

"But you're scared of everyone, aren't you, Claire?" I drawled, raising my drink to my lips, picturing her cowering at Dale. I'd never wanted someone to stand up for themselves more than I had then. At the same time, I'd been close to tearing Dale's head from his shoulders for putting that fear in Claire's eyes.

She turned her head sharply. "There's a difference between being intimidated by how gorgeous and cool another woman is and being genuinely fearful of a man. You know that, right?" There was no anger or admonishment in Claire's words. If anything, she'd said them gently, like I was an idiot who wouldn't understand the difference.

Iris reached a hand across the table, grabbing Claire's. "I'd never want to scare you, you beautiful honey bunny."

Adam, the kid who'd stumbled out of Claire's room in Atlanta, was seated beside her. He gently massaged her neck and murmured something too quiet for me to hear, fading the frown on her face.

The conversation moved on, and Marta slugged my bicep. "I thought we talked about you not being mean to Claire," she hissed.

"I wasn't trying to be mean." Get a rise out of her, yeah. Mean, no. Sometimes, I came across that way unintentionally, though, and I was aware of that—something to work on in my next life.

"We should do two truths and a lie." Adam clapped his hands, finally releasing Claire's poor neck. "Who wants to go first?"

Marta pointed at me. "I think Dominic does."

I slowly opened my palms. "I don't know how to play."

"Dude, it's pretty self-explanatory. You tell us three things about yourself, and we have to figure out which is the lie," Adam said.

I cocked my head, brows pinching. "You better go first. Show me how it's done."

He chuckled and wrapped his arm around Claire's shoulders. "You're more interesting. You go."

Marta grumbled. "Someone fucking go, or I'm going to walk into the ocean."

Claire grinned and lifted her mojito. "I'll go. Don't ruin your cute outfit on my account." She took a sip, her eyes alight with amusement. "All right, here we go. I grew up in Texas and can lasso a calf with my eyes closed. I've been to exactly five concerts, counting the one in Atlanta. I got my very first tattoo last month, and it's as big as my hand."

Everyone started shouting their answers, most agreeing the concert one had to be false.

"What about you, Dom? What's your answer?" Marta asked.

I scratched my chin under my beard, considering. "The tattoo. I don't think Claire has a tattoo."

"Well," she cupped her cheeks, her nose wrinkling, "you're wrong. I do have a tattoo. The lie was about Texas. My parents moved there when I went to college. I've never lassoed a calf, but I went to a rodeo once when I visited them."

Adam tugged her closer. "We've gotta get you to more concerts."

Marta raised her hand. "I want to see this tattoo."

"I'd have to take my dress off, and as much as I like you guys," Claire pointed around the table, skipping right past me, "that's not happening."

The game went on, but I didn't have much interest in guessing the lies from the truth. After a while, I wandered from the table, turning the music up on the speakers. Latin beats hummed through the humid, ocean breeze. Marta pulled Claire to her feet and onto the center of the patio. They danced something vaguely resembling salsa, quick stepping and snapping hips. Claire's dress floated around her legs, and when she raised her arms above her head, pivoting around in a tight circle, her cheeks were flushed and her chest dewy.

I tried to hang back and only watch, but when Adam took Claire away, Marta came for me.

"You'd better get off your old ass and dance with me." She held her arms straight out and curled her fingers to the beat of the song, urging me to come to her.

Marta could be a dog with a bone, and she wouldn't rest until I got on my feet, so I did. With one hand on her back, the other clutching hers, we rocked together through the rest of the song.

"Admit you're having fun." She poked my chest and gave me a mojito-grin.

"I'm having fun." It was a slight exaggeration, but I wasn't having a terrible time. I twirled her twice, then dipped her low. "Why are you dancing with me and not your girl?"

Iris and Rodrigo were hopping around, completely offbeat, while Marta kept stealing glances. It was pretty damn clear she wanted her arms wrapped around someone who wasn't me.

"I'm biding my time, obviously." She spun away from me, breaking out of my loose hold and cutting in between Adam and Claire.

With a laugh, Claire twirled my way. I told myself if I didn't slide my arms around her, it would hurt her feelings—and I'd done enough of that tonight.

Her full breasts brushed my chest, and the warmth of her body seeped into mine, hotter than the Miami sun I'd bathed in all day. Her hands glided up my chest, coming to rest on my shoulders, and her head tipped back for her to see me. She moved like liquid in my arms, smooth and sensual.

"Hi," she breathed.

"Hi, yourself." My fingers splayed on the dip in her back, right above the slope of her round ass.

"Are you being nice now and not poking at my fear?" When I first met Claire, I'd thought her throaty voice didn't match her sweet, soft exterior. Now that I'd spent some time with her, I realized how well it suited her quiet confidence and slowly blossoming sexiness.

"I was trying to tease you like I do Marta, not poke. I'm an asshole, but not that big of an asshole."

Her lips curved into a barely-there smile. "Okay."

"That's it? I'm off the hook?" I pressed her back, bringing her a centimeter or two closer.

"Well...you didn't play."

"Play what?"

"Two truths and a lie. You missed your turn."

I released a short, hard breath. "I don't like games, Claire."

Her bottom lip barely pushed out. "That's a shame. They can be fun sometimes. Do it now."

"Do what?" That pouty lip shouldn't have been tempting, but it was. I could've leaned down and captured it between my teeth. That thought led me to wondering what sounds Claire would make if I did.

Her cool fingertips barely touched the side of my neck. "Tell your truths and your lie."

It took a lot of effort not to allow my muscles to tighten and pull her even closer. Her breath smelled like mint and lime, and the spark in her eyes evoked a lightness in me I hadn't known existed before that moment.

"All right." I tipped my chin and brought my lips near her ear, wanting this game to be ours and ours alone. "I think about quitting the business and living on an island for the rest of my days all the time. When I was a kid, I wanted to be a professional soccer player and even got a full-ride offer to play in college. I don't think love is as real and lasting as everyone tries to convince us it is."

"Oh," she breathed. "That's easy. The first one is a lie. I think you love what you do."

My head jerked back in surprise. "I'm impressed with how quickly you got that."

Her smiling eyes twinkled. "I can picture you playing soccer. And the love thing...well, I agree to an extent, so..." She shimmied her shoulders to the music and spun out of my arms. "Thanks for playing!"

I followed the roll of her hips across the patio, and when she landed back in Adam's arms, my gut twisted in an unfamiliar and unrecognizable knot. I'd be a fool to have any reaction beyond mild interest in any of them. A few weeks from now, the tour would be over, and with the exception of Marta, I'd probably never see any of these people again.

CHAPTER TEN

CLAIRE

THE PLANE RIDE FROM Miami to New Orleans was short and sweet. Marta and I sat together in the front, while the man we both worked for loomed in the back all by himself. As he should. Asshole. Since our dance in Miami, our interactions had cooled dramatically. He'd made a concerted effort to be dismissive of me, and I'd been nothing but professional.

Did he still scare me?

He did. But that wasn't some special Dominic Cantrell attribute. Most men scared me these days. Even Adam, who appeared to be the sweetest man alive, gave me the chills from time to time.

That was what happened when the one man I trusted and loved the most hurt me on every possible level. It made it hard to discern who was real and who was really good at pretending.

I'd skipped Dominic's shows in Atlanta and Miami, though I hadn't missed The Seasons Change's. They were as incredible as Marta had said, and I'd *finally* picked up on the fact that she was mad for Iris. If Iris wasn't mad for Marta, she was a fool.

Marta was a pure delight. Annaliese would adore her, and if this Iris thing didn't work out, maybe I'd introduce them when we went home.

We shared another car with Dominic to the hotel, but he stayed quiet while Marta and I chattered.

"We should go to the pool," she said.

"Ugh. I haven't been in a bathing suit in ages." Our stop in Miami had been so brief and filled with work, I'd managed to avoid it.

She looked me up and down. "And?"

"And if I'm in the sun for any amount of time, I get freckles on top of my freckles."

"And?"

That she was still confused wasn't a surprise. I doubted Marta had been body-conscious once in her life.

"I have to finish writing up a press release and then—"

She sighed dramatically. "All I'm hearing are excuses. You're going to the pool, woman."

"Jesus fucking Christ, Mar." Dominic threw up his hands. "She's telling you she doesn't want to go to the fucking pool. Leave it."

He hadn't yelled, but heat had crept up his face and the crease between his brows had deepened. Marta laughed, and my eyes bounced back and forth between them. After a moment, I noticed the ache in my fingers, and worked to uncurl them from their death grip on my seat.

Yeah, he scared me.

Marta's hand landed lightly on my shoulder, but I jumped anyway. Embarrassed by my reaction, I studied the passing scenery out my window to avoid her probing gaze.

"Don't worry about it. If you don't want to go to the pool, it's fine. We can hang out and see the city, or I can just leave you alone."

In my periphery, Dominic moved to the edge of his seat, studying me. "I'm sorry for raising my voice, Claire." The words came out as almost a whisper, drawing my attention more than Marta's coaxing. I had a feeling Dominic didn't apologize often, so the fact that he had rather instantly worked to put me at ease.

"Thank you." Smoothing my hands over my jeans, I sucked in a slightly shaky breath, then turned to Marta. "I do want to go to the pool. I'll just have to coat myself in SPF."

"That's my girl." She beamed. "I love that you're here. Normally, I have to hang out with Dom or on my own, and neither is very fun."

That made me laugh. "We have to FaceTime with my sister from the pool. She won't believe you've convinced me to put on a bathing suit."

Marta waggled her brows. "And she'll be insanely jealous you're in New Orleans?"

My eyes shifted back and forth, and I shrugged innocently. "*Maybe...*"

She slapped her hands together. "I knew it. Spoken like a true baby sister. When I first started going on the road with Dom, I'd send my brother daily pics and make him so damn jealous. He's a rocker trapped in an accountant's body with three little kids and a minivan. Poor guy."

I winced. "No, not a minivan!"

She picked up her water bottle and tipped it to the side. "Pour one out for Billy's youth."

"Exactly. I'm finally ready to start enjoying my youth. I can't imagine what the minivan life is like. Or entering it willingly." I shuddered, knowing if I'd stayed married to Derrick, the minivan life would have been right around the corner. And though I did want kids one day, it seemed to be somewhere in the far-off distance.

Breathing easier, I let my gaze roam to Dominic's side of the car. He was still studying me. When our eyes met, he nodded once and slouched in his seat, relaxing as he stared. As I turned back to Marta, one corner of his mouth hitched, and a huff of breath left his nose, which he quickly covered by looking away first.

In my room, I tossed my two bathing suits on my bed, debating which to wear. My skin hadn't been kissed by the sun in months, so going conservative and wearing the cherry red, vintage-style one-piece with a skirt that covered the tops of my thighs should have been my first choice. But the rebel inside me wanted to be daring and put on the two-piece I'd never had the guts to be seen wearing in public before.

For kicks, I slipped on the ruched bottoms, the waist stopping just below my belly button. Since that didn't look horrendous, I tried on the matching halter bikini top with a fun ruffle right below my breasts. I didn't look terrible.

When I spun in front of the full-length mirror, I actually thought I looked cute. My stomach was soft, curved, and covered in freckles, but it wasn't offensive to look at. At least I didn't think so. And my butt...well, it didn't matter if I wore a one piece or string bikini—it was *there*.

Before I could stop myself, I threw on a sheer cover-up and my flip flops, tossed a few things in a tote bag, and headed to the pool.

When I arrived, Marta and our friends from The Seasons Change were already there, sitting around a table, shaded by a large, striped umbrella.

"You're here!" Marta announced. "Claire is here!"

Laughing, I held my index finger to my lips. "And now everyone knows it. Quiet, you."

"Claire, you look so cute," Iris said.

"Thank you. And you look amazing."

Iris was even hotter with fewer clothes on, which made sense. Her breasts were high and full, her stomach flat and partially covered by black and gray tattoos, and her legs were miles long. Marta's eyes went wide and a little manic when I looked at her. Apparently, she thought the same thing.

Adam stood, scraping back his chair. "Want to sit?"

"Well, are we actually swimming, or is this a look-adorable-in-our-swimsuits kind of afternoon?" I asked.

"Why not both?" Marta hopped up and tore off her loose T-shirt and cut-off shorts, leaving her in a black bikini. "Let's take a dip."

She hooked her arm with mine, tugging me toward the pool. I kicked off my flip flops as I went and waved to Adam over my shoulder. By the steps, I pulled my cover-up over my head, leaving it in a puddle on the edge, then walked into the cool water.

Marta splashed next to me, submerging without testing the temperature first. She surfaced when I was only up to my thighs. "Get in here, girl. The water's fine."

I took the last two steps quickly, submerging to my stomach. "God, it does feel good."

"I wouldn't steer you wrong. By the way, I can't believe you were trying to hide all this." She drew an hourglass shape with her hands. "Trust, you have *nothing* to be ashamed of."

"I'm not ashamed at all. I don't deny being insecure, though."

"Well, who isn't?" She windmilled her arms in the water, splashing us both. "But I refuse to let my brain hold me back from what I want to do. So, I just chuck off my clothes and hope for the best."

I snorted and fell a little more in love with her. "That's a pretty damn good attitude. I'll remember that if I ever undress in front of anyone again."

She paused her chaotic movements and looked me dead in the eye. "What's that about? I heard a rumor that boy sitting at our table was seen coming out of your room a few mornings back. Are you saying he didn't get to see you naked?"

"I am definitely saying that." I swiped my hair off my forehead. "Who knew Dominic Cantrell was such a terrible gossip?"

"He's awful. Like a little hen, always asking me questions about my love life." Her eye roll was filled with affection.

"Well, here's the truth, which I also told him: Adam brought me breakfast unexpectedly that morning. That's it."

She pressed both hands to her chest and sighed. "Aw, he's got it bad for you, huh?"

I let my eyes drift to the man in question. He wore dark sunglasses, but from the direction he faced, I was fairly certain he was watching us. Or me, rather.

"Maybe? I haven't paid attention to a man in that way for so long, it's hard for me to recognize the signs."

Because I'd been with Derrick for so many years and had let myself feel a lot older than twenty-six, it was hard for me to reconcile a guy like Adam—tattooed, pierced, young, and cool as hell—might be into me. The signs pointed to yes. I'd be stupid not to recognize them, and I refused to ignore signs ever again. But even if he *was* into me, I didn't know what to do with that.

Annaliese would tell me to hit it. Marta probably would too. I just wasn't sure if I was ready for even a casual fling yet.

"I see the signs. I wish Iris would broadcast as loudly as Adam is," Marta said woefully.

Both our heads swiveled in the direction of the woman in question. Her legs were crossed, and she had a beer dangling between two fingers as she laughed at something Rodrigo said. Marta and I sighed at the same time.

"I have to say, I have a little crush on that woman, and I'm ninety-seven percent straight," I said.

With a groan, Marta dunked herself under the water. Giggling, I floated on my back. With the sun beating on my face, I knew my freckles would be intense later, but it felt too good to stop.

It felt too good to pretend I wasn't going through a messy breakup too. Marta hadn't asked, but there'd been times I could have brought up my marriage and pending divorce. I just…

hadn't. I didn't even want to think about what awaited me when I went home.

Floating on my back in the Louisiana sun, I made a decision. While on this tour, I'd live. I'd feel. I wouldn't worry or struggle. I wouldn't say no because of perceived expectations. This was my moment to break out and break free, and if I let it pass me by, I'd regret it more than I regretted Derrick.

Without warning, pool water rained down on me, and my peaceful floating turned to sputtering as my hair flooded into my face. When I swiped it away, Rodrigo popped up beside me, grinning madly.

"Did you see that cannonball, *preciosa*?"

I snapped my fingers. "Damn, I missed it."

He pointed behind him. "You can see the inferior version. Here comes my boy."

Adam flew through the air, pulling his knees up to his chest, and landed in the pool with an explosion of water. After a beat, he shot through the surface, looking like a proud papa of the cannonball he'd just birthed.

"What do you think, Claire? Which splash was bigger?" he asked.

I pushed out my bottom lip in a playful pout. "I missed Rodrigo's, so I don't think it'll be fair for me to judge. You might have to do it again."

Rodrigo headed for the steps before I'd even finished speaking. Adam tugged on the end of my wet hair. "Only because I don't like that sad face on you."

Their cannonball contest went on for three more rounds until the other guests in the pool started giving us the evil eye. Rodrigo went to dry off, and Marta went to flirt, leaving Adam and me in the pool together.

"How's life?" he asked softly.

"I was thinking earlier, before Rodrigo interrupted my peace, life is pretty okay right now." I bumped into the edge of the pool and Adam stopped right in front of me. He looked at me like I was the snack he wanted to eat after an afternoon of swimming —and everyone knew post-swim meals were the best.

I thought he was cute. Handsome. Sexy. I willed some of my parts—aside from my brain—to get that message. He didn't make my stomach swoop or heart go pitter-patter. The area between my legs remained eerily silent too.

He rested his hand on the wall beside my head. "Only okay? How can it be improved?"

"Okay is an improvement over shitshow, which is about where I was before I landed this gig. How about you? How's life?"

"Really good. I get to play my music and meet some pretty cool people. I'm not complaining."

I poked my chest and acted surprised. "Me? Am I one of the cool people?"

He chuckled at my doe eyes. "Gotta say, you're *the* cool person right now."

I looked left and right. "Why is it the first time I'm called cool, no one is around to hear it? Did it even happen?"

Adam splashed me gently, his eyes sparking with amusement. "Since you're new to this whole 'cool' thing, I gotta tell you, people who are old-school cool, don't really talk about being cool. It's just a thing everyone around them acknowledges."

I huffed. "People who grew up cool always think they're better than us new-cools. You make fun of us for flashing our cool around, but you don't know what it's like to grow up without any cool."

Adam cackled so loud, heads turned, making me proud. "I don't think 'cool' has any meaning anymore. Fuck, Claire, you kill me."

Marta sat down on the side of the pool and dipped her feet in. Her interruption was a blessing in disguise. Adam expected me to make him laugh, and while I liked doing it, sometimes I worried I'd dash his high opinion by revealing how truly *uncool* I was.

"So, boss man called," she said.

"Yeah?"

"He needs you for a minute. Normally, I'd tell him to go fuck himself, but since today is technically a workday and he's letting us take it easy in the pool, I thought I'd better relay the message." She kicked at the water, sending waves swirling around me. "You can come back down when you're finished with whatever he wants you to do."

I sighed. "It's fine. I've probably reached my sun limit anyway."

Adam caught my hand underwater. "We should do dinner."

"I'll text you, okay?"

"I'm holding you to it."

He let me pass, and I felt his eyes on me while I climbed out and bent down to retrieve my cover-up. At this point, my confidence was made up almost entirely of bravado, but it didn't feel terrible a guy like Adam was checking me out. Not at all.

Upstairs, I shuffled in my flip flops toward my room. I didn't make it there, though. Dominic's door swung open, and he stepped out in front of me.

Startled by his sudden appearance, I tripped over my own two feet, falling into his chest. His hands gripped my upper arms, steadying me, and then he pushed me upright.

"Hey. Sorry for jumping out at you like that," he said softly. He dipped his head, catching my eyes. "Are you okay?"

"Mortified, and I think I broke my flip flop, but I'm fine."

"Good." He opened his door wider with his foot. "Come in."

I stayed where I was. "I'm in my bathing suit with a broken flip flop and wet hair. Can you give me a minute to change?"

He cocked his head and did that slow perusal thing he did so very well. "I'll give you ten minutes."

I suppressed my eye roll. I wasn't Marta. I couldn't get away with it. "Thank you for your generosity."

Blocking me from taking a step, he knelt in front of me. His long, tattooed fingers curled around my ankle, lifting my foot like it was weightless, then he hooked his index finger between my toes and slid off my flip flop. His thumb pressed into the arch of my foot before he placed it on the ground again. I was too stupefied by the suddenness of his touch and the roughness of his skin on mine to stop him from doing the same to the other foot. This time when he massaged my arch, I barely suppressed a moan. I caught my bottom lip between my teeth and bit down hard so I didn't react.

Dominic rose with both of my shoes in his clutches.

"Can't have you falling when I'm not there to catch you." He gave me one last look, slapped my flip flops against his palm, and disappeared inside his room.

My brain, heart, and between my thighs all agreed that had been the single most unexpected and sexiest moment of my life. The fact that Dominic was my boss and sixteen years older than me should have dampened the experience, but the truth was, it only made it hotter.

CHAPTER ELEVEN

CLAIRE

I TOOK THE FASTEST, coldest shower I could stand, rubbed lotion all over my sun-sensitive skin, and dressed in a semi-professional pair of jeans and a gray T-shirt that said, "You Got It," a gift from Annaliese. It reminded me I owed her a phone call. She probably thought I was dead in a gutter somewhere since I hadn't been in contact for two days.

Grabbing my laptop and key card, I stuffed my feet in my oxfords and headed to Dominic's room. He opened his door soon after I knocked, holding it wide for me.

"That was sixteen minutes," he said as way of greeting.

"Yes…well, if you wanted me actually wearing clothing, I needed those extra six minutes." I brushed by him to the living area of his suite and set my laptop on a side table.

He nodded at my chest. "Another message tee?"

"Yeah." I traced the letters with a finger. "My sister got me this one before I came on this trip."

He watched the slow journey of my finger over my chest. "Do you often need that reminder?"

I shrugged, dropping my hand when I trailed over a puckered nipple. "I think most people do, from time to time."

"Then it's a kindness, really. To wear those words for everyone to see."

I tugged at the hem, my mouth quirking. "It's just a shirt, Dominic. It's not that deep."

"All right, Claire." He closed some of the distance between us, peering at my face. "You didn't lie about the freckles. I wouldn't have believed if I wasn't seeing it for myself. You actually do have more of them now."

My hand went to my cheek automatically, guarding my warm skin. "I don't generally lie, and especially not about something as trivial as freckles."

"That's a good habit." He reached out and grazed a fingertip across my chin. "I like the freckles."

"Thank you." I stepped back, bumping the coffee table. "Shit." I rubbed the back of my calf, certain I'd be bruised from how hard I'd hit it.

Dominic's brow pinched. "Are you hurt?"

"I'm fine. I swear I'm not usually so bumbling. I don't know what's gotten into me." I carefully walked around the coffee table and picked up my phone. "Did you need to go over the press schedule for tomorrow, or…?"

"Have a seat, Claire. We need to get something straight." Dominic perched on the arm of the couch, one foot braced on the coffee table, the other on the floor. He motioned for me to sit, then clasped his hands together between his spread legs.

"Have I done something wrong?" I sat on the opposite side of the couch, feeling small under his deep, steady gaze and raised position.

"No. Not really. I'm very careful about the information I make public. I know it goes against the grain of being famous, but I am pretty private."

I nodded, still unsure why I was here instead of floating around the pool ten floors down. "That's understandable."

"I looked over the press release you wrote."

My breath caught in my throat. I'd sent it to Marta to proofread and cc'd Dominic as an afterthought, not actually expecting him to read it.

"Did you find an error?" I asked.

"No. It was well-written. The thing is, you mentioned the hospital visit I'm doing in Houston, and that's not something I want publicized. I'm guessing Isabela forgot to mention that."

"Um..." I pressed the back of my hand to my forehead, my thoughts scrambling, "I'll have to go through my files to be sure. I apologize. I saw it on the schedule and just assumed—"

I had assumed because Isabela had told me to include it. She was human and could make mistakes, but it surprised me she would have made this one, considering how long she'd worked for Dominic.

"It's all right. No harm done, huh?"

"No, I guess not." I worried my bottom lip between my fingers, attempting to get my stomach to settle. I could have messed up big, and it was only by chance Dominic stopped me. "I really am sorry. I don't know how I could have overlooked something so important."

"Claire." He spoke my name like warm honey, sticking to the walls of my mind and dripping down into my consciousness. "It's fine. Marta would have caught it if I hadn't. Don't beat yourself up. That's my job."

My eyes flicked to his, and the playful curve of his mouth took me by surprise. I took a deep breath, then leaned forward to grab my laptop from the table.

"I should go fix this," I said.

"You should stay. Do it here."

"Really?"

He lifted a shoulder and ran a finger sideways across his lips. "Might as well. That way I can read it right away and tell you if there should be any other corrections."

"You could do that by email, you know."

"Do you really have to argue about everything?" The corners of his mouth twitched, holding his smile at bay.

"I'm not arguing. I'm just pointing out the flaw in your logic." I opened up my laptop anyway. Doing this on Dominic's couch would be just as easy as in my room.

I clicked on the file in question and started to read through it to figure out how to change the wording. Dominic hadn't moved from his perch, watching me work.

"That's disconcerting, you know."

His head cocked. "What?"

"Being watched while I try to work. Do you think you could be slightly more subtle? Maybe lurk across the room?"

As he stood, I swore I heard him huff a quiet laugh. "I'm going to order something for dinner. What do you want?"

My fingers paused over the keyboard. "For dinner? I'm eating here?"

"Sure." He tossed his cell phone back and forth between his hands. "With the exception of our first night in Miami, I've eaten dinner alone since you've stolen my usual companion. Seems like you owe me the company."

"Do I?" I raised an eyebrow at his audacity. "Is this an order from my boss?"

He slipped his phone in his pocket. "No. Do you have a better offer?"

I had an offer from Adam. Was it better? Probably wiser—no, *definitely* wiser. But I wasn't even tempted to mention our tentative plans. Not when I could stay in this room and maybe get to unlock some of the mystery that was Dominic Cantrell.

"No better offer." I held out my hand. "Is there a menu?"

An hour later, I'd rewritten the press release, gotten Dominic's approval, and our food had arrived. His suite had a dining table, and we sat across from each other with our dinners. He'd gotten a burger, while I had shrimp and grits. It *was* New Orleans after all.

"Have you been to the city before?" he asked.

"New Orleans? Once, a few years ago. It was a week post-Mardi Gras, and there were still beads everywhere." That had been with Derrick, of course, and several of our couple friends. He'd gotten trashed and belligerent with...well, everyone. Aside from the beads, that was what I remembered most about New Orleans.

"You're not disappointed you're not out on Bourbon Street tonight?"

"No, not really. Are you?"

He wiped his mouth and beard with his napkin and spread his arm along the back of the seat beside him. "Even if I wanted to, I don't really have that option."

I motioned to his silver hair. "I guess you're kind of conspicuous."

"Yeah." He smoothed a tattooed hand over his beard. "It's been a while since I flew under the radar."

"If you weren't famous, would you be drinking a hurricane and wearing beads around your neck?"

The heavy exhale from his nose was practically an answer in itself. "No, Claire. That doesn't mean I didn't do a *lot* of stupid shit when I was younger, and I'm no angel now, but my days of sticky drinks and being stupid in front of other drunken idiots are long over." He tipped his chin my way. "What about you? Did you get stupid the last time you were here?"

I got yelled at until sunrise by my husband for taking his friend's side when they said it was time to call it a night.

I hadn't told a soul on this tour I'd been married, but I told Dominic. "I was here with my ex-husband and our other married friends. We were in our early twenties, but we liked to pretend we were sophisticated. Or...they did, and I went along with it. Actually, I don't even know."

A pensive expression swept over Dominic's features, and his jaw worked back and forth. "You're young to be divorced."

"Well, I was young to be married."

"When did you get divorced?" he asked.

I tried to smile to cover how raw this topic was. I'd been the one to introduce it, and I didn't regret it...yet. But I was very aware one wrong move, look, word, and I might bolt—from both the conversation and the room.

"It's still in the process, actually. It's been almost three months since I left."

He balled his fist beneath his chin. "Think you'll go back?"

"To him?" He had no idea how preposterous that suggestion was.

"To your husband," he confirmed.

"No. Never. Absence has made my heart grow harder. And I don't consider him my husband anymore. A piece of paper doesn't make someone a husband."

"That's good." He nodded approvingly. "A harder heart will serve you well."

"That remains to be seen. I don't want to become so hard I can't feel anymore."

"Yeah...well," he shifted in his chair, "you figure that out, let me know."

I picked up a piece of cornbread dipped in grits from my plate. "I'll work on it when I get home. Now's not the time to think about *him*." My teeth tore into the bread with savagery, making Dominic chuckle.

"Are you enjoying this job, Claire?"

"Oh, yes." I licked the crumbs from my lips with a swipe of my tongue. "What's not to enjoy about traveling and music and finally getting to do the thing I went to college for?"

Dominic reached out with his napkin and dabbed the corner of my mouth without making a single comment. While my heart caught in my throat, he continued like he hadn't just taken care of me in an intimate way. Sort of like when he'd taken off my shoes in the hall and sent my body into a tailspin.

"I'd really like you to be at my shows." He folded his napkin on the table and pushed his empty plate forward. "Is there a reason you haven't come to any yet?"

Yes. I was avoiding you because from the second we met, you've made me forget which way is up. Yes, because I work for you and can't feel this way. Yes, because I know nothing good can come from what I'm feeling. Yes, because you do scare me, but you also piss me off pretty constantly. Yes, there are a million reasons.

"No, no reason. I watched the opener, but I didn't know I was expected to watch your show too. I will tomorrow night," I promised.

He scoffed and canted his head slightly away. "Don't you think, to represent me, you need to be familiar with my music?"

"I am familiar with your music. I've been listening to your voice since I was a little girl. I had your poster on the back of my bedroom door when I was in middle school. And when I moved out of the home I shared with my ex into my sister's apartment, I fell asleep in my tiny closet bedroom listening to "Angel Moon" on repeat."

"Middle school, huh?"

I laughed. "That's all you picked up on from that?"

Both dark brows shot up. "Oh, I heard that you're a real big fan of mine, Claire."

I pressed my index finger to the table between us. "Of your music."

The smile he finally allowed to break through was more of a smirk. "Right. Of my music, not the man."

"My opinion of the man is still up in the air. But buying me grits tips the scale heavily in your favor."

"Did you think the grits were free? I'm taking them from your paycheck."

I giggled again. "I have to say, they were worth every penny."

The smile lingered on his mouth for a few moments as his coal eyes raked over me. "Have you had a good day, Claire?"

The way he said my name...

"I have. It's topped my last time in this city by a mile."

"Did you have a nice time with your friends at the pool? With that kid?"

His question gave me pause. "How do you know who I was with?"

He slid his phone across the table toward me, the screen glowing. On it was a picture of Adam and me in the pool, smiling at each other.

"Did Marta take this?" I asked.

He nodded. "Yeah. When I texted her to ask you to come up here, she sent me this."

"And you told her to tell me to come up here anyway?"

"I did," he confirmed.

I should have been mad or at least annoyed Dominic had purposely interrupted my time with Adam, but I wasn't. The truth was, I'd rather be here than anywhere else. Maybe that was sad and a little pathetic, given Dominic was...well, Dominic Cantrell, but I got the impression he was enjoying me as much as I enjoyed him.

"The press release could have waited until later." We both knew that was true, but I felt like pressing him a little, since we were being honest.

"It could have. But I didn't want it to."

"Well..." I pushed back from the table, "I guess I should go. Thank you for dinner."

He pushed back too, standing. "Thank you for the company."

I glanced over my shoulder at him as I gathered my laptop. "All you have to do is ask, you know. You're not the worst to have dinner with."

He sputtered a short laugh. "Got it. I'll work on my manners so next time I'll be a step above 'not the worst.'"

I preened internally for eking a laugh from him, the most contained man in existence. Dominic stayed on my heels all the way to the door, which he held open for me.

"Goodnight, Dominic. I'll see you in the morning."

This crazy part of me wanted to kiss him on his cheek, to feel the brush of his beard on my lips. Luckily, I refrained from embarrassing myself and took a step into the hall.

"See you, Claire."

All the way to my room three doors down, I felt his eyes on me. When I took my key card from my pocket, I chanced a glance back. Dominic leaned in his doorway, his arms across his chest, doing nothing to conceal the way he watched me. He tipped his chin, and I went inside with a warmth coating my insides.

Once I kicked off my shoes, I curled up on my bed and called Annaliese.

"Is this the ransom call?" she answered.

"Yes. Give me five-million and I'll give you your sister back unharmed," I said.

"Meh. That's a little steep for my pockets. You can keep her."

I grinned. "I guess you're angry I haven't called."

"I'm just hoping there's a good excuse, like ill-advised dudes."

That made me snort, which caused her to cackle, setting off a chain reaction that ended in a fit of giggles from us both.

"So, are there dudes?" she asked when she'd calmed.

"There are many dudes. There's one in the opening act named Adam who has been paying me extra attention." I rushed out my next confession. "And then there's Dominic...who I might have a very inappropriate crush on."

"Whoa-ho-ho there, missy. What did you just throw in there at the end?" Annaliese sounded amused rather than admonishing, so I told her about Dominic. The way he said my name, the way he'd touched my feet, how he kept staring and staring, how I liked it.

"It's not like anything would ever happen. He's the man from my posters and my boss," I said.

"Do you *want* something to happen?" There was no judgment from Annaliese. She wasn't that type of sister at all. If anything, I'd always been the more conservative of the two of us, but she hadn't judged me for that either.

"I don't know." I cupped my forehead, thinking about the way he looked at me when I entered my room a bit ago. "No. It would be a terrible decision. The tour just got started, and the last thing I need is an awkward work situation. Besides, I highly doubt *he's* into *me*, you know?"

"Why wouldn't he be into you?"

Because I blend in with the fucking furniture.

"He's famous and a lot older. I work for him, and I—"

"Have a big, juicy ass?" she finished for me. "I know what you were thinking, and like I've told you a hundred times, that *isn't* a negative."

I couldn't wipe the smile off my face. She *had* told me that before, in those exact words. My sister was my very own hype woman, and sometimes I even believed her.

"You're the best. Your ass is really nice too."

She sighed. "Thanks, babe. Speaking of asses, Derrick came by the nursery looking for you. He seemed completely poleaxed when I told him you were out of town for work—and I loved every second of it."

All the lightness from the last few hours crashed onto my shoulders like a heavy shroud. "What did he want?"

"He wanted to talk. I told him you weren't interested."

"I'm definitely not." I'd had my closure with Derrick when he knocked me unconscious. He could seek his somewhere else. He wouldn't be getting one thing more from me.

"Then I'll picture him twitching around in his own crapulence while you have an amazing experience and get chased by rock stars. Deal?"

"Deal."

She could think about Derrick all she wanted. He wasn't the one who was on my mind when I laid down in bed and slipped my hand between my legs. Adam wasn't either. No, my brain wanted the most inappropriate, ill-advised man around, and no one else would do. Not tonight, in my fantasies, anyway.

CHAPTER TWELVE

DOMINIC

THE FIRST VOICE IN my ear this morning wasn't the one I would have chosen. But Isabela knew me, she knew when I woke for the day, so she called then, confident I'd have time and the desire to speak with her.

"Hey," I answered, stepping out on my balcony.

"Hello, Dominic. How is everything?"

"Pretty damn fine, Iz."

"Excellent. All logistics are working out for your shows?"

"Yeah." I rubbed the center of my forehead. "I don't ever have to worry about that. You know I basically just show up and do my thing."

That wasn't strictly true. I knew we had double everything. While a crew was setting up for a concert in one city, another crew was speeding down the highway to set up in our next venue. I was familiar with the sound engineers since I'd worked with a lot of them for a long time, and I knew most of the roadies by name. So yeah, I didn't have to worry, because I'd built up trust with the professionals who did the behind-the-scenes work.

"Oh, I know. You let the little people handle that."

She made it sound like a bad thing, that I wasn't schlepping shit and setting up pyrotechnics, but that was stupid, and Isabela wasn't stupid. She was poking around for something, information probably, and trying to be sly about it.

"Do you want me to run wires?" I asked. "Maybe test out the speakers? Build the sets?"

She sniffed. "I get your point. Tell me how Claire is doing."

There we go.

"She's fine. Seems to be on top of everything. I don't have any complaints."

I had a lot of complaints about Claire Fontana, but none that had anything to do with how she did her job—and none I'd be discussing with my ex-wife.

"Wow, Dom. That was more than I've ever heard you praise any of my PR assistants. I guess there truly is something to be said for hiring a girl you aren't going to be attracted to."

I held back the growl in my chest. "You sound like a cunt when you talk about her like that, Isabela. It's also pretty un-fucking professional. You'd think you would have learned a lesson from the last time you insulted her looks."

She went silent for a beat, obviously unprepared for my admonishment. She shouldn't have been, though. When we were married and she got catty about other women, I always shut that shit down. *That* was what I found unattractive.

"You're right. I'll watch myself." She cleared her throat twice. "I'm just happy Claire is working out and I won't have to fly out to douse any fires."

"No, you won't. It's all under control here."

Her inhale hitched. "All right. Well, I was thinking I might fly out to LA when you're there. You have the gala and—"

"And what? Did you think you'd be my date?"

She sure as hell would *not* be. She knew that. I knew that. She could blame me all day for her not being able to move on, but when push came to shove, Isabela was the one who continued to insinuate herself into my life. We still had good times, but the romantic portion of our relationship ended years ago.

"Well, not a *date*. But I could go with you if you need someone..." She trailed off, and I let the silence blanket the conversation. "It was just a thought."

"I'm good, Iz. You were right about us not seeing each other."

"Yeah," she breathed. "Okay. Well...call me if you need me. And I'll be in touch with Claire as well."

The knock on my door distracted me enough, I barely said goodbye to Isabela. Claire stood on the other side with a white bag in her hands, clear-rimmed glasses perched on her nose.

"I don't know if you eat beignets, but I took a chance and bought you some." She thrust the bag at me. "Here."

"Did you get some for yourself?"

Her nose wrinkled. "They're in the bag. I didn't think that through."

I widened the door. "Come in. We'll eat together."

She entered my room, and after she passed me by, her honeysuckle scent rising above the sugary beignets, she peered back over her shoulder. "Two meals in a row? That sounds like the beginning of a habit, Mr. Cantrell."

"I've had worse habits."

This one was bad, though.

I sat on one end of the couch, and she took the other, propping her shiny shoes in front of her. I tore into the bag, laying it flat on the coffee table, steaming pastries covered in powdered sugar piled on top. Claire had brought us both coffees too.

Powdered sugar snowed down on the hint of cleavage peeking out from Claire's V-neck shirt. Instead of wiping it with a napkin, she wet her thumb with her tongue, swiping the sugar from the slope of her breasts, then sucked her thumb into her mouth, softly moaning.

I'd seen a lot of sexy women in my life. I'd had a lot of them too. Some of their sexiness was contrived and purely for show, some came naturally. Watching Claire suck sugar off her thumb had to be one of the sexiest things I'd ever seen.

It pissed me off. Right the fuck off.

She ate and talked about the upcoming day while I swallowed down the bitter coffee she'd brought me. I had no interest in the beignets or my schedule, and I couldn't feign it—not when there was a swirling dervish gathering in my gut, threatening to tear apart my control.

Touching her foot last night had been a mistake. Asking her to stay for dinner had been another one. All that added to Claire bringing me breakfast and me allowing it. She probably thought we were at the beginning of some beautiful friendship like I had with Marta. But I couldn't be friends with a girl I wanted to fuck —and I couldn't fuck Claire.

Not when she was twenty-six and hurting. Not when she was the kind of girl who believed in love, despite what she said, and the stars in her eyes hadn't been completely snuffed out by the asshole she'd married. Not when I was the worst kind of mistake she could make.

"Hey." She nudged my knee. "You're being quiet and not eating. Did I overstep here?"

"Yes." I turned my cool gaze on her. The smallest dusting of sugar remained on the upper curve of her breast, and my mouth watered at the sight. If I trailed my tongue there, would she let me?

Not now. Not when she was looking at me with her big brown eyes like she was just seeing me for the devil I truly was.

Claire blinked, balling her napkin in her fist. "I did? I overstepped?"

"You did. I probably misled you last night—and that's on me. I'm not really interested in you outside of the work you do for me."

Her breath caught in her throat, those pretty plump lips parting. "Okay. Wow. I apologize." She gathered her trash, squishing several uneaten beignets along with it, and hurried to the door. "I'll meet you at the elevators at ten, sir."

She disappeared as suddenly as she'd arrived, leaving me with a twisting feeling in my stomach and a dick that didn't understand it wasn't allowed to perk up at Claire calling me "sir."

CHAPTER THIRTEEN

CLAIRE

ADAM HANDED ME A beer and slipped his hand behind my back. "Don't go."

"I have to. It's my job."

Last night, I'd been looking forward to watching Dominic perform. I'd laid in bed, thinking about him onstage, the way he'd move, his voice, his nimble fingers dancing over his guitar…

"If I had Dominic Cantrell money, I'd pay you to hang out with me."

He stuck out his bottom lip in a pout, which was completely incongruous with his sweaty, leather-and-denim rocker look. He was so cute and hot, I wanted to feel more than flattery from his attention. And I was so very flattered. Having a guy like Adam so obviously into me gave me a huge boost of confidence.

Clearly too much, considering how much of a fool I'd made of myself by showing up at Dominic's room this morning.

The Seasons Change had already performed their set, and now the second opener was on. Soon, I'd have to make my way to the audience, and I really didn't have a choice about it.

"Unlike Dominic, I'd hang out with you for free." I tipped my beer, taking a deep drink. "You could come watch with us."

He cocked his head, considering my offer. "I might. Gotta finish up some band stuff back here. Save a spot for me, okay?"

"I will."

I strode through the stadium's backstage tunnels with only a vague idea of where I was going. Marta and I planned to meet in the audience at showtime, so I was on my own. I glanced at the signs on the walls, trying to figure out if I was actually on the right path.

I ground to a halt when I slammed right into someone. Strong hands caught my arms, steadying me. With an embarrassed smile on my lips, I looked up, meeting stern, coal-black eyes.

"I'm sorry," I rasped.

"You have to be more careful, Claire."

"I wasn't sure if I was going the right way…" My words trailed off seeing the crowd of people just behind Dominic. His backup band, stage manager, and a few people I didn't know all peered back at me expectantly. "You're going onstage?"

His hands were still on my arms, and he didn't seem like he would be letting go anytime soon. "That's the plan. You're going to watch?"

"That's the plan." I gave him a tight smile. "If I can find my way."

Dominic released one of my arms to snap his fingers. A young guy with a headset on scurried forward. "Ms. Fontana needs an escort to the VIP area."

The guy nodded. "I can take her."

Dominic's attention returned to me. "Are you going to wish me luck?"

"Do you need it?"

From the way he'd eagerly dismissed me this morning and then given me the cold shoulder during his press, I wasn't sure how to behave toward him anymore. I understood, as someone who was famous, Dominic had to set firm boundaries. I just didn't understand exactly where his were.

His palm slid from my bicep to my shoulder, giving it a gentle squeeze. "It's the polite thing to do."

"Well, then good luck, sir." I slipped from under his hold, twisting around to face the guy who'd be taking me to my seat. I glanced back once. Dominic's bottom lip was trapped between his teeth, and the look he gave me was the boundary-smashing kind.

"See you, Claire," he murmured before turning away and continuing on his path.

Marta waited for me in a cordoned-off area at the front of the stage. There were seats, but neither of us took them. Instead, we stood, plastic cups brimming with beer, drinking and chatting until the lights dimmed and excitement pulsed through the thousands of Dominic Cantrell fans surrounding us.

"Are you ready?" she asked beside my ear.

"Twelve-year-old me is pissing her pants." My pulse thundered when Dominic's tall, lithe silhouette became visible through the dim, smoky gray lights.

Marta bumped shoulders with me. "And twenty-six-year-old you?"

A light snapped on, illuminating Dominic in all his glory. Head tipped back, his silver hair sparked, and the expression on his face was rapturous, like he'd been elevated from the dregs of this earthly plane to where he truly belonged.

I whimpered without realizing it, and Marta laughed.

"Girl, he hasn't even started singing. Don't tell me you're a fainter."

I wasn't, but when Dominic's fingers moved over his guitar, my breath caught. I didn't want to miss a single chord.

His backup band joined him, flowing into one of his most popular songs. The stadium filled with cheers, and then we were all singing along. Marta and I held up our drinks and swayed, belting out the words with Dominic and thousands of our closest friends. His eyes met mine once, and I didn't mistake the curve of his lips when he saw me singing with him.

The show was incredible. Dominic never stopped moving, using every inch of the stage and catwalk jutting out in the middle of the audience. There were some pyrotechnics and tricks with lights and video, but for the most part, Dominic was the main attraction.

And what an attraction he was. Offstage, he was gorgeous and dreamy, but so human, sometimes I forgot how famous he was.

Onstage, those words didn't even begin to touch him. He transformed into a rock god, confident and full of swagger, in slim jeans with a chain dangling from his hip and a black T-shirt barely skimming his waistband. Somewhere in the middle of the concert, the T-shirt came off, leaving his golden, tattooed chest bare and shiny with sweat. Dominic breathed his stardom; he proved why he was worshiped and had been for two decades.

I didn't worship him, but I did become swept up in the tidal wave of Dominic Cantrell. Marta and I sang along, drank, danced, and listened. She'd been to dozens of his concerts, but she seemed to be enjoying every second the same way I was.

Dominic strode to the center of the stage and clutched the microphone in both hands. The ends of his eyebrows hooked up, giving him a devilish appeal.

Maybe she wasn't enjoying him exactly the same. The heat pooling in my belly was undeniably lust. The fiery, dangerous kind that would cause a less level-headed woman to become stupid. Luckily, I'd have time to recover from this feeling before I got up close and personal with him again.

"The next song we're going to play is an old one. To be honest, it's a B-side track. But recently, someone told me it got her through some pretty fucking tough times, and I had to wonder, why the hell am I not playing 'Angel Moon' more often?" He plucked at his guitar and huffed a short laugh. "Let's see if I remember how it goes. I might need your help, okay?"

Marta's hand around my shoulders flexed. "I wonder who he's talking about."

I shook my head, not because I didn't know, but because I did. This was the song I told him I listened to in Annaliese's closet in the days and weeks after I left Derrick. It had buoyed me, brought me peace and hope, and now he was playing it for me—*to* me.

Maybe I *was* a fainter. My entire being wobbled. I closed my eyes, allowing the lyrics to steady me the way Dominic had steadied me backstage.

A girl I know likes to walk alone at night
She says that's when the time is right
To look at herself on the inside
And ask the hows and whys
Of how she got here and where she's going

Oooh, wind like wings
Leaves like feathers
Walk along the clouds, girl
I'll be right there too
Don't hide your sad from me
I want to see it all
You go down
We'll both take the fall

Let it go without a fight
Cry those tears and take flight

Let it go without a fight
Cry those tears and take flight

She's never lonely in the light of the moon
Got a smile that lights up the room
Even though those black clouds loom
She says it's all gonna be clear soon
And she keeps dancing down that dark road

Fingers made for weaving
I'm holding on tight
You're not leaving
I'm here beside you, girl
I want you to start believing
We're in this together
If you're bruised and hurt
Then I'll be bleeding

Let it go without a fight
Cry those tears and take flight
Let it go without a fight
Cry those tears and take flight

Nothing is forever
Even if it feels like dying
Lift your broken wings

And start flying
Like an angel over the moon
You'll get there soon

I opened my eyes, finding Dominic's gaze locked on me as his fingers glided over the final chords of the song that had comforted me out of my darkness. My pulse pounded, and I couldn't seem to wrap my head around the torrent of emotions he'd unleashed by singing that to *me*, tonight of all nights.

Strong arms banded around my middle, lifting me off my feet. I squealed, and the moment with Dominic was broken.

"I'm here," Adam announced as he set me down.

I pushed him away playfully. "I noticed."

He kept his arm around my waist as he moved beside me. "Having fun?"

"Yeah. He really knows what he's doing." Vast understatement. Dominic was masterful, both in his showmanship and his musicality. His voice, smooth and low, belted out lyrics like paint on a canvas.

Adam snorted. "He should. He's been doing this since I was a kid. He's like fifty, right?"

"He's not that old and you know it," I argued.

Adam tugged his ear. "Huh? Can't hear you."

I rose on my toes, my mouth beside his ear. "He's not that old!"

He turned before I could move away, and his lips grazed mine. It wasn't a kiss, but from the way he grinned and dragged his tongue over his lips, it might as well have been.

"You're so fucking sweet, Claire. Best vibes ever." He stole my beer from my hand and took a long swig, wriggling his eyebrows over the brim of the cup as he drank.

Marta reached around him, hitting the bottom of the cup, and Adam sputtered as beer spilled over the sides and down his chin. I braced myself for his anger, but he only laughed and wiped the dripping liquid with the hem of his T-shirt.

Marta wagged a finger at him. "We don't steal beer."

"Noted, girl, noted." He chuckled, and I was in awe of his good nature. Derrick would have seethed until we got home, then lectured me about my friend making a fool of him. It took leaving him for me to see how controlling he'd been during our marriage, and I was still getting used to the fact that his behavior wasn't normal.

My attention was pulled back to the stage when Dominic stopped mere feet in front of where we stood, hips thrusting forward as he shredded on his guitar. Again, his eyes found mine, but this time, they were full of thunder.

I raised my arms over my head and moved with him, rolling my hips to the rhythm he set. Adam still held onto me, but I barely felt it. Dominic's music flowed through me like lava in my veins. He moved on, striding across the stage like it was his very own.

Marta danced in front of me, hooking her arm around my waist and pulling me against her and away from Adam. We caught the same beat, moving to the heady, intoxicating sound. When she threw her head back, I did too. The crowd went wild for Dominic, and I screamed right along with them.

By the time the lights went down and Dominic had left the stage, I was sweaty and a little drunk, both on beer and adrenaline. Marta, Adam, and I made our way backstage, flashing our passes to security to bypass lines. At Dominic's dressing room, we stopped.

"You coming back to the hotel?" Adam asked.

"Later. I should probably go in there and check in with the boss man," I said.

"Sure thing." He tugged one of my damp waves. "Hit me up if you're not quite ready to sleep. I'll be around."

Marta and I watched him amble down the corridor, then she shot me a wicked grin. "That boy is lovestruck."

I rolled my eyes. "He isn't. I barely know him."

"Well, he wants to know *you*. And have your babies. And take your last name."

I snorted. "That's so backwardly heteronormative, Mar. I'm surprised at you."

She hung her head. "You're right. I'm ashamed."

Grabbing her hand, I tugged her into the dressing room. Only a few reporters were inside since Dominic had done most of his press earlier. The man himself had his arms crossed, clutching a water bottle in one hand, listening to a pretty woman speak.

Since it was my job to be there for any interviews, I marched up to the two of them, ready to intervene if needed.

The pretty woman with the hourglass figure and long, blonde hair, let out a throaty laugh and touched Dominic's arm. "You have to tell me who you sang 'Angel Moon' for, Dom. There were a few thousand jealous women in the audience wishing it was them."

His dark eyebrow arched. "Were you one of them, Ariana?"

She laughed again. "It would be unprofessional of me to say. Let's just leave it at I've never been serenaded before, but I wouldn't mind it."

Marta mimicked the reporter behind her back, scrunching her face and mouthing the words she'd just said. I had to cover my mouth to hold back a giggle. Dominic's heated gaze landed on us, and it only became more molten.

"Excuse me. You have my assistant's number. Call if you need to ask me any further questions." Dominic pushed off the wall, swerving around Ariana, the pretty reporter, and stopping in front of the two of us. "Are you drunk?"

"No." I shook my head. "We're just having a good time."

Marta jerked her thumb at me. "Claire's beer was stolen, so I know for a fact she isn't drunk. I'm questionable."

"Go home," he growled. "I won't need you anymore tonight."

She saluted him with two fingers. "All right. Good show tonight. I'll see you tomorrow." She held out her hand to me. "Let's hit it, C."

Dominic's fingers curled around my upper arm. "Claire needs to stay. Her job isn't over yet."

Marta left without argument, and I stuck around to watch Dominic give a few casual interviews and meet a fan or two. He didn't need me, but I imagined it wasn't fun to be alone in the middle of all this either.

On her way out, Ariana stopped by Dominic, raised on her toes to whisper to him, and unmistakably slipped a piece of paper in his tight pocket. She gave him a lingering look before leaving with a swing of her curvy hips. Dominic licked his lips as he watched her go, driving an unwarranted spike of jealousy straight through my chest.

In the car to the hotel, we sat across from each other, the glowing lights wrapping around the ceiling the only illumination. Shadows swirled over Dominic's stern face, giving him an even darker, scarier countenance.

"Does that happen often? Reporters slipping you their number?" I asked.

"What do you think?"

"It probably does."

He shifted forward, his palms pressed together between his spread knees. "What you're really wondering is how often I use the number. Right, Claire?"

My teeth bit into my bottom lip to stop myself from reacting. But nothing could halt the goose bumps rising on my flesh. "I would never ask that, sir."

His fingers dug into the sides of his hair, and a deep exhale left his lungs. "Jesus, girl." He shook his head hard, like he was trying to clear something unspeakable from it. "It happens often, and I take them up on it on occasion. I don't really like when details of my private life end up on a blog or in a magazine, so reporters aren't my first choice."

"But she was hot," I pressed, though I wasn't sure why.

"She was."

That was all he said, and I was relieved. This line of conversation made me feel like I had spiders crawling beneath the surface of my skin.

In the elevator to our floor, I sucked in a breath and gathered a bit of courage. "Thank you for playing 'Angel Moon.' I know it wasn't for me, but I loved every second of it."

He nodded, and when the doors slid open, he stepped through them, holding his hand out to keep them from closing on me. I walked ahead of him, and when I reached my room, he paused beside me while I fumbled for my key.

"Who did you think I played it for, if not you?" he asked softly as I pushed open my door.

My head jerked up, meeting his gaze. "I don't—"

"I'm glad you loved it, Claire. It made me happy to see you loving it."

With those knee-liquifying words, Dominic Cantrell casually walked away like he had not a single care in the world.

How had this man—who'd made it crystal clear he wanted nothing to do with me outside of our professional relationship— managed to knock me sideways at every turn? And even more importantly, if he had no desire for anything more from me, *why* did he keep doing it?

CHAPTER FOURTEEN

CLAIRE

DOMINIC DIDN'T PLAY MY song at his second show in New Orleans. I was disappointed, but only slightly. Last night had been special, just for me. Yes, I'd shared it with thousands of other people, but not thousands more tonight.

Marta and I danced to Dominic's music again, singing along until my throat burned. Adam joined us late in the show, wrapping me up in his arms like we were long-lost friends and hadn't just seen each other backstage an hour before.

"Party in our suite tonight," he whisper-shouted into my ear.

"Is that an invitation?" I asked.

"It is. Are you accepting?" He grinned excitedly and bounced on his toes.

"As long as Dominic doesn't need me, I'll be there." I elbowed Marta. "Are you in?"

She paused her singing. "For what?"

"Party in our suite," Adam answered.

She fist-bumped with him. "Hell yes, my friend. It's about time you guys use that suite of yours for good and not evil."

I gasped. "Have you been committing human sacrifices in there?"

Adam's eyes shifted right and left. "I'm innocent, I swear."

My attention was pulled away from him when the audience went wild. I went wild too, even though I hadn't heard what we were cheering for. Dominic made it easy to get caught up in his show, to feel like you were part of it and vital.

When the concert was over, Marta and I went straight to his dressing room to check in and see if he needed us. Only a few people were milling around, but Dominic was alone in a corner, drinking from a water bottle and keeping watch on the door.

He stood when he saw us, leaving the bottle behind. "Let's go."

I caught his arm, which was still a little slick with sweat. "Don't you need to stay and talk to people?"

"No. I've done enough of that." He sounded pissed off, which seemed impossible given the incredible show he'd just put on.

Marta and I flanked him as we made our way through the corridor. "Are you tired?" I asked.

"No." He rubbed his face with both hands and breathed out a long exhale. "Are you?"

"Not really."

"I'm not tired either. Thanks for asking," Marta chimed.

Dominic huffed a short laugh. "If you go out tonight, try not to get too shitfaced. The plane takes off at ten and your ass will get left behind if you're late."

"I'm not going out. Claire and I happen to have been invited to a very elegant soiree in a hotel suite tonight. Try not to be jealous," Marta deadpanned.

Dominic said nothing, but I felt his eyes on the side of my face as we continued walking to the car. He didn't let up on the ride to the hotel, and after a few minutes of allowing him to stare without challenge, I stared back. Neither of us spoke, but tension built in the space between us anyway.

I had no idea what I'd done to make him angry, but there was no denying he was. I couldn't say I wasn't confused by my torrent of feelings for him, but I tried to remain as professional as possible, and he seemed to want to make that difficult.

By the time we were in the elevator to our floor, I felt like I might go insane if I spent one more second in his presence. The way he looked at me, the low, simmering anger just below his surface, what he *wasn't* saying, and what he had said, swirled together in my consciousness. Marta chattered with us both, but I couldn't concentrate—not with Dominic Cantrell across from me in the too-small moving box, frowning and blazing his eyes along my skin.

The doors slid open, and I barely refrained from throwing myself through them. Instead, I calmly followed Marta out with Dominic directly behind me.

"Goodnight, Claire. Marta." That was all he said before he sauntered away like he hadn't just engaged me in eye contact warfare for the last twenty minutes.

Noise, music, and people spilled from the suite at the opposite end of the hall, so it wasn't hard for Marta and me to find the party. The living area wasn't filled, but there were lots of bodies milling around.

"We need drinks," I said.

"Absolutely." Marta clasped my hand, and we wove around the room until we came upon the dining table laden with a surprising array of alcohol.

"Claire, Marta, you're here!" Iris hugged us both with equal fervor, which made me a little sad since Marta desired so much more. "Allow me to be the bartender, ladies. What will you have? Actually, let me surprise you with my signature cocktail."

She ended up making us a concoction from many bottles, which tasted strong and sweet—a dangerous combination.

"Yum." Marta licked her lips after one sip, which made Iris laugh.

"It's terrible. You can say it. I'm like the one musician who never worked as a bartender before signing a record deal." Iris turned her attention to me. "Tell me the truth, Claire."

I swallowed more of my drink and hummed. "It will get me drunk fast."

Iris pumped her fist. "Hell yes, honey bunny. And really, isn't that the goal?"

From behind me, someone slipped a string of beads around my neck. Without checking to see who it was, I said, "I'm not showing you my tits, so you can take your necklace back if you're expecting it."

Adam laughed and hugged me from behind, his arms around my shoulders. "That's a freebie." He kissed the side of my head, then leaned down to whisper in my ear. "And did you mean never, or not right now?"

I couldn't decide how I wanted to answer. Flirt or laugh him off? If I tried to be sexy, it would undoubtedly come out awkward, but I wasn't sure I even wanted to be sexy with him.

So, I tipped my head back, giving him what I hoped was an enigmatic smile, and winked. He grinned back at me, so I must not have looked too ridiculous.

"Where are my beads?" Marta demanded.

Adam broke away from me to pull another string of beads from his pocket and place them around her neck. "There you go, princess. I'm the official beadmaster of this shindig."

Iris nodded. "I dubbed him that when he came back to the suite with a thousand beads from some tourist trap he stumbled into this afternoon."

I gasped. "You have a thousand beads and I got one measly strand?"

He tapped my nose. "Keep being cute and you might find yourself with *two* measly strands."

"So generous," I teased.

As much fun as I was having with Adam, I felt like I was practicing with him. I flexed my dormant flirting skills, basked in his attention, but I still wasn't sure I wanted this to go further than it already had.

The four of us hung out, drinking and singing terribly to the music we could barely hear over the din of voices. Iris made another powerful drink for Marta and me, and it went down even smoother than the first.

The more I drank, the cuter Adam became. I got another two bead necklaces by dancing with Adam and Rodrigo, and a third by taking a shot of something that tasted like Swedish Fish and burned like lava.

Feeling slightly overheated, I broke away from the group and leaned against a cool, floor-to-ceiling window, my head just the right amount of floaty. Adam followed, bracing his hand on the window beside my head, his fingers toying with the ends of my hair.

"You're so pretty when you're tipsy." He dipped down, his face slowly closing in on mine. "So pretty," he murmured.

At the last second, I giggled and turned my head away. I hadn't had a first kiss since I was nineteen, and my nerves had gotten the better of me.

It wasn't that I didn't want to kiss *him*, it was that I wasn't ready at the moment.

That's what I told myself, anyway.

"Adam…" I giggled again, but he straightened and pulled back.

He tugged my hair good-naturedly. "It's all good. I see someone I need to talk to. I'll be back."

Adam wandered off into the crowd, but I didn't have time to dwell on possibly hurting his feelings. Rodrigo brought me another shot, and then we got caught up in a rousing game of rock, paper, scissors. We both kept choosing paper, then high-fiving with our paper hands.

"This game is never gonna end, *preciosa*." He sounded excited about that more than anything.

"What if I do rock next and let you win?" I offered.

"Nope. I don't want a pity win." He bounced on his toes, his eyes wide and wild. "One more, winner takes all."

Neither of us questioned what "all" was. I went for rock this time, and Rodrigo went for scissors. I pounded his scissors until he made an explosion sound with his mouth and his hand went flying into the air.

"Boom, Claire is the goddamn winner!" he cried. "She came in at the last second with the rock and blew her competition apart."

Snorting with laughter, I fell against him. "I still can't believe you went for scissors after I told you I was going for rock."

"Cheaters never win, *preciosa*." His arm curled around my waist. "Let's go tell Adam his girl is the winner."

Without giving me a chance to balk at being called Adam's girl, Rodrigo tugged me through the crowd, weaving around groups and couples. Marta and Iris were together, but unfortunately, not alone. Marta gave me a subtle thumbs down, and I blew her a kiss.

Rodrigo stumbled as we passed one of the open doors to a bedroom and muttered, "Oh shit."

"Oh shit, what?" I tried to peer around him, but he blocked me.

"Let's keep looking." He tried to pull me away from the doorway, but he was drunk and clumsy, while I was drunk and determined. I ducked beneath his arm to see what he hadn't wanted me to.

There was no mistaking Adam's long, lean form stretched out on the bed beside a shirtless woman who had multiple bead necklaces strung around her neck. She writhed against him as they made out like they were running out of time. Desperate, mad, panting, humping. It would have been a turn on to watch if he hadn't just tried to kiss me against his window. Was any man sincere? Adam obviously didn't owe me a single thing, but this made my stomach twist.

"Gross," I whispered, stumbling away from the train wreck.

"He's drunk," Rodrigo said, attempting to defend his boy.

"So am I. I managed to keep my tongue in my mouth."

But why should I? I'd been a good girl for so long. Loyal to a disloyal husband. With one man for seven years, and instead of going wild when it ended, I'd taken time to "heal."

Well, fuck that.

I didn't have to be a good girl anymore. Men did whatever they wanted and enjoyed the hell out of it—it should be the same for me.

"He's going to be sorry tomorrow," Rodrigo said, rubbing my hand between his.

"Aren't they always?" I tried to flip my hair behind my shoulders, but had a feeling the move more resembled swatting a fly.

"Oooh, burn with the truth napalm." He looked me over with lazy, drunk eyes. "What's your move?"

"I'm getting out of here. My buzz is too good to deal with Adam's guilt when he's done hooking up with that girl with the really nice boobs."

He cupped my cheeks with both hands. "Are you good to get back to your room?"

"Yes." I wasn't going there, though. "I know the way."

He gave my cheeks a pat, then spun me toward the door. "Go, fly high, pretty Claire. I'm gonna gloat so hard when I tell my boy you got to witness his fuck up. And I promise to tackle him if he bugs you."

I waved over my shoulder and finally made it into the hall. A few people were still hanging out here, but it was a lot quieter than inside the suite. I took a deep breath, smoothed my palms over my black T-shirt dress, and walked with determination around the corner to another suite.

Dominic Cantrell's suite.

I rapped my knuckles on his door and leaned against the jamb as I waited for him to open it. When he did, I almost stumbled forward—which wasn't seductive at all.

"Claire?"

He wore nothing but a pair of gray sweatpants, and the smell of soap and spice drifted from him into the hallway. His tattooed hands gripped the frame of the door, and the frown pulling at his mouth only served to make me even more committed to my mission.

I leaned into him, taking one step inside his room. "Why are you angry with me?"

He tried to laugh me off, rubbing his mouth as the low sound escaped. "You had to come to my room at one in the morning to ask me that?"

"Yes. If I did something wrong, I want to know. And if you're just an ill-tempered dick, I want to know that too." I took another step, my chest brushing against his, my head tipping back to keep my eyes on his.

"Are you drunk?" he murmured.

"Don't avoid the question." I slid a finger up the center of his chest and tapped on his throat. "Speak, sir."

"Claire," he breathed. "We'll do this in the morning."

"No. This won't keep. Let me in, Dominic."

With a heavy exhale, he gripped me by the waist and tugged me into his room. The air around us snapped, and my control was on the brink of doing the same.

"What do you want tonight?" His palm slid down the curve of my back, splaying at the top of my ass.

My pulse ratcheted, and I reached behind me, moving his hand lower. "I want to know why you're angry. And then I want to be bad."

There. There was no going back now.

CHAPTER FIFTEEN

DOMINIC

ROUND, soft, perfect, Claire's ass filled my hand, and I couldn't stop myself from squeezing once before I pulled away. She was the apple, the snake, the entire damn garden, forbidden for a man like me.

And here she was, temptation in the flesh, offering herself up. If she weren't drunk, I couldn't say I'd be able to resist. But the fact that she was here, letting me touch her, pressing her body against mine when I knew I couldn't have her, pissed me off, and I was already angry to begin with.

"You want to be bad, little girl?" I closed in on her until her back was against the door. "Thought you'd stop by, taste the dark side?"

"That's exactly what I thought." She raised her chin, not even a hint of backing down. "Why are you angry with me?"

"Doesn't matter. Irrelevant."

"Is it because you want to fuck me and think you can't?" She blinked her big eyes, her lashes brushing her rosy, freckled cheeks. The innocent sexiness of her looks combined with her dirty mouth made my cock throb inside my pants. And since I was commando, there was no hiding my reaction to her.

"What are you doing here, Claire?" I practically growled at her.

"You can, you know." Her hands gripped my shoulders to pull her body flush with mine. She felt so fucking good, like a place I could get lost for a long, long time. I rocked my hips, sliding my erection against her stomach. "Dominic."

She nipped at my bottom lip with her teeth, and when I didn't stop her, she sucked my lip between hers and wove her fingers into the back of my hair. The tip of her tongue flirted with the whiskers below my mouth, and then with a sigh, her lips were on mine.

She kissed me like a tornado, touching down and sweeping me up in her storm. I kept my hands braced on the door—my own show of resistance. It took everything in me not to touch her, feel her skin, take this a lot farther than a kiss. Claire didn't make it easy, with her breathy sighs and eager tongue sweeping over mine.

The sweet taste of rum on her lips was enough to keep me contained, though. My dick pulsed angrily in my sweatpants, but it wouldn't be getting any game tonight. Not from this girl—even if she begged for it.

Oh, how I wanted her to beg. Down on her knees, blinking at me the way she did, "sir" spilling from her pouty lips. I'd never desired that from anyone else, but Claire brought out a different side of me.

"Dominic." Her hot breath woke me from the stupor of her lips.

"This isn't happening." I sounded strong, but my words were weakened as I cupped the back of her head and covered her mouth with mine. Her kiss had ended, and mine took over, pushing my tongue between her lips to taste every drop of her night.

She moaned and clawed at my neck, but I didn't let up, showing her what being with me would be like. We wouldn't take strolls in the park. I'd fuck her until she couldn't walk straight. And then I'd do it all over again.

"Sit on the edge of the bed, Claire. Take off your dress."

She moved immediately, tossing her dress behind her on the way into the bedroom. I followed slowly, balancing on a fine line between right and wrong. I had no intention of having sex with this girl, but I also couldn't make her leave. Not now. Not until she understood what she'd started.

Perched on the corner of the bed, her hands stacked in her lap, legs crossed at the ankle, her pose said demure, but the sheer mesh bra barely containing her tits and her kiss-swollen lips told a different story.

I stopped a foot from her, looking down at her offering. "Are you wet?"

Her brown eyes peered up at me, flaming heat in their centers. She bit her lip and nodded. "So wet."

"Is it for me or the boy you're always flirting with when I'm onstage?"

Her breathing hitched, and color rose in her already-pink cheeks. "Only you. Are you hard for only me?"

I palmed my rock-hard erection, pushing the steel length against my belly. "I have been for a solid fucking week now. You drive me crazy. Everything about you. And you show up in my room drunk, coming from another man's room, aching for it? You want trouble, don't you?"

She reached out to touch me, to touch my cock, but I knocked her hand away. "Dominic. Let me."

"Not gonna happen." I wagged my finger at her. "Bad girls don't get what they want."

She slapped the mattress with a pout. "Then why did you tell me to get on the bed?"

"Because, Claire," I nudged my sweatpants down so the head of my cock showed, "I'm not going to get any sleep until I take care of this. So, unless you tell me no, I'm going to jerk my dick while I look at your pretty tits until I come."

She nodded, her tongue sweeping over her bottom lip. "I'd like to see that."

"Then watch." I pushed my pants down far enough for my cock to pop out and slap firm and hot against my belly. Precum beaded at the slit. Using my thumb, I spread it over, sliding my hand down my thick, pulsing length that would much rather be buried inside Claire. Drunk or not. Too young or not. My employee or not.

Claire's eyes roamed from my hand curled around my cock to my face. The air between us crackled like a live wire had been let loose, sparking and sizzling. Her thighs pressed together, rubbing back and forth against each other. The fabric of her bra strained against her tight nipples. The sheets were bunched in her hands, like she had to hold on for dear life to stop herself from touching me.

If she tried again, I might've let her. Seeing her like this, wanting, needing, desperate, made me want to take care of her—to give her what she craved.

That was why she was the apple, the snake, the garden.

My perfect Eden.

"Claire." I was barely restrained now. A trickle of sweat ran down my face and into my beard. I stepped closer, looming over her, and her hands broke free from the sheets to grip the sides of my legs. "Jesus," I gritted out. "I'm going to come."

Immediately, she reached behind her, and a second later, her bra was discarded. Heavy, round breasts capped with light brown nipples and spattered with freckles bared to me, I lost it. My fist jerked my raging cock, the other hand bracing the curve of her neck. My thumb pushed into the underside of her jaw, keeping her head tilted back and her eyes on mine.

"Make me filthy, Dominic. Cover me with it," she mewled.

Every muscle in my body tightened as an orgasm ripped through me, tearing me apart at the seams. Ropy, white streams spurted onto Claire's beautiful breasts and chest, and she sighed like it felt as good to her as it did me.

Panting and relieved, I curled my arm around the back of her head and pulled her face against my stomach for a moment. Without even touching me, she'd satisfied me in a way I hadn't been in a long time. I dipped down to kiss her forehead.

"Such a good girl, Claire." The smile she gave me was tremulous, and her eyelids were heavy. "Stay here. I'll clean you up."

I came back from the bathroom with a wet washcloth, taking care to wash every drop from her soft, pretty skin. She sighed and leaned her cheek against my arm, her eyes barely open.

"Lie down. You look ready for sleep." I ran my palm over her hair and jaw.

"Here? Sleep here?" Her brows pinched, and she tried to stand, but I gently pushed her back down.

"We've gotta get up in a couple hours. Just go to sleep so I don't have to worry about you."

Relenting, she pulled the covers over her and gave me a sloppy, sleepy, drunk grin. "Oh no, don't go catching feels. I'm not into that."

Holding back a laugh, I patted her head. "Go to sleep, Claire."

No surprise, Claire was gone in the morning. The sheets on her side of the bed were cool, so she must've been gone for a while.

That was fine with me. With any luck, we'd both forget last night happened and move back into being solely professional.

Only...the first image that entered my mind when I woke up was Claire covered in my cum, breathy and sweet. And damn if I didn't have to jerk off in the shower to that image.

By the time I got down to the car taking me to the airport, I'd spent my morning thinking about Claire Fontana.

"Morning, sunshine." Marta was already in the car, tapping on her phone. She was alone.

"Where's Claire?" I barked, harsher than I'd intended. "We can't wait for her."

"Already on her way to the airport on the bus. She was too hungover to deal with your foul mood this morning."

"Did she say that?"

Marta huffed and put her phone down on the seat beside her. "No, she didn't say that. I connected the dots. You're always grumpy and mean to her, and it's getting a little tiresome."

"I'm an asshole, Mar. That's nothing new."

"Well, Claire's *not* an asshole, and I want to keep her around." She threw her head back on her seat. "Is it possible not to speak? I'm also hungover and not in the mood to deal."

We stayed quiet for the rest of the drive, which wasn't long. When I boarded the plane, I automatically searched Claire out. Oversized sunglasses covered half her face, and a blanket was wrapped around her body. I stopped in the aisle beside her, mouth quirking.

"Feel like shit?" I asked.

"Don't gloat," she rasped.

"I'm not. Get up and come to the back with me."

She pulled her blanket higher beneath her chin. "I'm good here."

"Come to the back, Claire. You can lie down on the couch back there."

Marta grumbled behind me. "You never let me lie down back there."

I glanced over my shoulder. "Weren't you just telling me to be nicer?"

Claire groaned, but she relented pretty easily, following me to the rear of the plane and curling up on the leather couch across the aisle from my usual seat. She pulled the blanket so high, only the top of her head peeked out.

No awkward conversations would be happening on this plane ride. No need to potentially hurt her by telling her nothing would ever come of whatever this heat was between us. Besides, I had a feeling she already knew.

And I was relieved. Truly.

But I had no explanation for why I spent the entire flight to Dallas on tenterhooks, waiting for Claire to wake up so we could banter or bicker or piss each other off. No explanation at all.

CHAPTER SIXTEEN

CLAIRE

AS SOON AS WE TOUCHED DOWN IN DALLAS, we all went to work. We didn't have the day to acclimate to the new city or take a breath. Dominic's show was tonight, which meant doing press and fan meet-and-greets all afternoon.

I stayed by his side through it all, chugging coffee and Tylenol like it was part of my job description. I hadn't been this hungover in forever, which was probably why I was *this* hungover. My body wasn't used to this kind of abuse. It didn't know how to recuperate.

If I could have crawled into bed for the day, I would have, but the show must go on. I'd survive on caffeine and dreams of cool sheets and black-out curtains.

"Does Marta have my food ready?" Dominic asked.

"Yes. She texted a few minutes ago. It's in your dressing room at the venue," I replied.

"All right." He checked his phone for a second, then slipped it in his pocket and headed to the conference room door. "You can stay at the hotel. I won't need you tonight."

I hurried after him. "What do you mean? You don't want me to go to the venue? To your show?"

"No. It's not necessary." He glanced at me under furrowed brows. "I can tell you're not feeling great, even though you've been working hard to hide it. I'll give you today to rest."

"Why?" I found it hard to believe he would willingly take it easy on me. Dominic wasn't nice—especially not to me.

"Because I don't need you right now." A low rumble vibrated his chest. "Do you want me to find work for you? Is that it?"

"No. You just surprised me and I'm reacting to that. I have things I can do."

I tried to brush by him, but he caught me under the elbow. "Don't work. Nurse your hangover."

This man should have been a mob boss or a king of a small country instead of a rock star. He thought he ruled all he could see. Put a scepter in his hand instead of a guitar, and he'd be right at home.

I took my arm back with a tug. "You're being very weird. More than usual."

Obviously, I knew why things were strained between us and he wanted me out of his sight. I'd thrown myself at him, then he came all over my naked breasts. I hadn't had an orgasm, and he hadn't so much as touched me beyond kissing, but it had still been the hottest moment of my life.

"I thought I was being kind." He shoved his hands in his pockets so hard, I was surprised his jeans didn't rip apart.

I sighed, digging in my reserves for some bravery. "Nothing has to change because of last night. You don't have to treat me with kid gloves."

His brows pinched together. "Are we talking about it?"

"No, we're not." I shook my head, a little grin on my lips. "Because if we do, you might say it can't happen again, and I don't want to hear that."

His breath hitched, and he almost stumbled forward, barely catching himself from falling against me. "What do you mean?"

"It means I liked it a lot and I didn't even get off." I shrugged like I hadn't a care in the world, when in reality, it had been nearly impossible for me to say the words. I only hoped I came off as relaxed as I was trying to portray.

The truth was, I would have never been able to do what I did last night while sober, and I had no intention of getting drunk anytime soon. But if I could have another taste of what happened last night with Dominic, I'd take it.

"Hmmm." His features twisted in confusion. "Okay."

"Okay."

"Go back to your room. Rest."

I nodded. "I will. If you're sure..."

He paused, rubbing the center of his forehead as though he was physically jogging his memory. "I am. Enjoy your time off."

I gave him a half-smile. "Good luck tonight, Dominic."

We parted ways, and I retreated to my room, undressing and slipping into my pajamas even though it was only midday. I took a phone call from Isabela and typed up a press release at her direction, then I called Annaliese, leaving out Dominic jacking off on me for now. I didn't have my head wrapped around the situation enough to talk about it, and she'd want to *talk*.

Finally done with work and catching up with my sister, I curled up in bed and turned on the TV, intent on watching something trashy and consuming. Of course, that was when Adam texted, asking to talk after his show tonight.

I'd been dreading this more than facing Dominic. I didn't have a clue what I'd say, but I guess I could leave that up to him. I told him to come to my room when he got back to the hotel.

A few hours later, Adam tapped on my door. I answered, still in my pajamas, my hair piled on top of my head. He'd obviously showered and changed, with his wet hair and fresh smell.

"How was your show?" I asked once I let him inside.

"Great. Good crowd. We played well." He rocked back on his heels and glanced around my room. "I royally fucked up last night."

I canted my head. "In what way?"

"Claire," he sighed. "I like you a lot, and I acted like such a dick. I was drunk and I did a line, but that's not an excuse."

"Adam, it's fine. You don't owe me anything." I folded my arms around my middle. "Maybe close the door next time you're hooking up, though."

He groaned, scrubbing his hands over his face. "Dammit, I hate that you saw that."

I scrunched up my face at the mental image of the writhing and tongues and...oh, if I could *Eternal-Sunshine-of-the-Spotless-Minded* one memory from my brain, it would be that one. "I kind of do too."

He held his arms out to the side, then let them fall like heavy weights at his side. "Where do we go from here?"

I raised my shoulders. "We're good, Adam. I'm not mad at you. Last night was cringey, but that's all."

He took a step toward me, dipping his head like he always did when he wanted to be on my eye level. "If the situation was reversed, I wouldn't like it very much."

He had no idea how reversed the situation had become. If he knew what I'd let Dominic do to me, he wouldn't be feeling an ounce of remorse. I couldn't really be mad at him anyway. Seeing him last night had awakened something inside me that had made me brave enough to stop holding back.

"We'll be friends, right?" I rubbed my lips together, not to tempt him, but to gather my wits. "I want that."

He brought his hand to the center of his chest, leaning his head away from me a bit. "I kinda thought we might be more. But yeah, guess I flushed that down the drain."

"Sorry that being my friend is such a disappointment." I rolled my eyes and swiveled away, taking two steps toward the bank of windows along the far wall. Adam caught me by the arm and spun me back around, making me laugh.

"See?" He pointed to my grinning mouth. "Those vibes are immaculate. Of fucking course I want to be your friend, Claire. Who wouldn't?"

I wrinkled my nose. "Idiots?"

"Exactly. If we're meant to be friends, I accept that. Maybe I'll get to show you I'm not a gigantic douchebag along the way."

"I don't think you're a gigantic douchebag. Just a minor one."

He squeezed my arm once more before releasing me. "I deserve that. I really do."

"I know you do. You gave that girl way more beads than me. I mean, jeez, Adam, break my heart why don't you."

It was easy to make a joke of it now, but I couldn't lie and say I hadn't been hurt last night. Not heartbroken, but certainly let down. And after everything I'd been through with Derrick, being let down by a man, even in a small way, knocked some wind out of my recovery.

Adam snorted and looked away, scrubbing the corners of his mouth. "God, I'm such a screw-up. I'm really sick over knowing you saw that. Rodrigo has been going after me all day."

That knowledge warmed me like a cozy blanket. Rodrigo was the real deal. Crazy, bouncy, out of his mind, but true to his word, and at this point in my life, a man being true to his word meant a lot.

"Good. He promised he would." I tipped my head to the armchairs on the opposite side of the room. "Can we be done with this conversation and watch TV or something?"

He exhaled in relief and offered a crooked smile. "Hell yes. I'd love that."

We flipped around for a while until settling on a rerun of *The Golden Girls*. Adam's choice, not mine, since I'd never seen it. I was dubious until I met Sophia and Rose for the first time, then I was in love.

"How do you know about this show?" I asked.

"It's kind of iconic." He shot me a bemused glance. "You've really never seen it?"

"Never. My parents were weird and made us play board games and do crafts together. We hardly ever watched TV."

"That is..." His shaggy hair moved with his head shake. "That's really wholesome. But it doesn't surprise me."

I snorted a laugh. "Because I come across as wholesome?"

"Nothing wrong with that. But no, I guess I'd say you come across as whole, more than anything." Again, he shook his head. "God, I'm tired. I don't even know what I'm saying."

He sees me as whole and not broken. I wonder if that means Derrick didn't really shatter me into a million pieces...or maybe I'm just really good at faking it.

"It was something nice, I promise." Even if I didn't exactly believe it to be true, I'd take it.

I walked Adam to the door, and he lingered right outside of it. He raised his hand and cupped the back of my neck, gently squeezing.

"Is it still sore?" he asked.

"Sometimes. But I'm okay right now."

"I'm glad." His hand slipped to my shoulder. "We're gonna hang out again, right?"

"Obviously."

With a happy grin, he ambled off, not noticing the men coming from the other direction. Dominic and his two bodyguards were about to pass my room, so I raised a hand and said, "Goodnight". Before I could even turn to retreat into my room, Dominic took two long strides, slapping his palm against my door.

"Claire." The warm honey of my name became molten on his fevered tongue.

I blinked at him and sucked in a breath. "Sir."

He nodded once at his security, dismissing them, then pushed into my room without another word.

CHAPTER SEVENTEEN

DOMINIC

CLAIRE'S ROOM WAS NEAT AS A PIN. Her bed was only slightly rumpled, and like before, there weren't any clothes tossed around or random tissues on any surfaces.

Her scent was everywhere, though. Honeysuckle invaded my senses, scrambling my synapses. Memories were becoming mixed up with the here and now. I'd always associated honeysuckle with warmth, love, safety. Now, I couldn't seem to separate sex from it. Maybe that was what drew me to Claire. She was sexy as hell in this completely unexpected and really fucking exciting way, but she also reminded me of a time where everything was simple and easy—when life hadn't gotten away from me and pain didn't squeeze at my edges.

Claire folded her arms under her chest. She wore pajama pants with cherries printed on them and a loose White Stripes T-shirt. She wasn't trying to entice me, but now that I knew what she looked like under there, I was fully enticed.

"Did you need something?" She sounded impatient, which she probably was, since I was standing, uninvited, in her hotel room, at midnight.

"I saw you in the hall, thought I'd stop by and make sure you were resting up as ordered."

I saw her in the hall, being touched and caressed by a kid with hearts in his eyes.

Her lips quirked in the corners. "I did, thank you. I haven't left the room all day. I've fully recovered."

"Did you rest with the kid?" I hated myself for asking. I hated myself for wanting to know. A big part of me wanted her to say yes, to say she was fucking him, so I could put her back in the box I'd originally set her in: employee and nothing else.

"We watched *The Golden Girls*, so I don't know, does that count as resting to you?"

"Why?"

Her head tipped to the side. "Why what?"

I shoved my hands into the side of my hair. "Why the hell did you watch *The Golden Girls*?"

"Is that really what you want to ask?" Her throaty voice dropped to a low, soft tone. Once again, she'd made me feel like I was the clueless one here and she was gently prodding me in the right direction.

My gaze snapped to the bed without intention, then back to her. Her tired eyes moved slower, following the trail I'd left behind before returning to mine.

"Why'd you come to my room last night?"

My question took her by surprise. Her hand pressed to her throat, and her eyes widened.

After a long, pregnant pause, she said, "Because I was just drunk enough to lose a lot of my inhibitions."

"I get that." I moved closer, tipping her chin up with my knuckle. "But why *my* room? Why not Adam's? The kid follows you like a fucking puppy."

She didn't jerk away from my touch, but she held so still, I had to wonder if I was scaring her. I uncurled my fingers and dragged them along her soft jaw, then let my hand fall to my side. She breathed easier the moment I stopped touching her.

Claire swallowed hard. "I came to your room for something I knew I'd only be able to get from you."

"What?"

Her eyes flicked to mine, and there was no fear there. Fatigue, yes, but she had fire burning deep inside her. It had probably always been there, waiting to be stoked.

"Something dirty and hard. Something I've never, ever done. Something bad for me." She tugged on her T-shirt, but didn't look away. "I knew I'd get that from you, and in my drunken mind, I thought you'd be willing to give it to me."

"Jesus." Her words had me twisted up and spinning in every direction. The biggest part of me wanted to toss her on the bed and show her last night had been *nothing*. But I was old enough and wise enough to hear everything else she'd said. I'd be bad for her. She'd never been done dirty and hard before. That should have made me hesitant. Take pause. But the shame of it was, her confession had twisted me up even worse.

"I'm sorry." Her lashes lowered to her cheeks. "I know. I'm being wildly inappropriate, and I have no excuse tonight other than a need to be honest."

"You should always be honest." Her lower lip trembled as she took in a deep breath. "Open your eyes."

Her eyelids fluttered open. "Hi," she whispered.

That made my lips twitch. "Hey. You tired?"

"Really tired. You?"

I breathed out a chuckle. "Exhausted to my bones."

"Then we should say goodnight."

"We should." I rarely did what I *should* do, but tonight, I would. Claire followed me to her door, staying a step or two back. I cracked it open, but before I left, I turned back to her. "Wildly inappropriate suits you."

"Does it?"

"Yes." I brought the back of my hand up to her cheek, gliding it over her smooth, silken skin. "I hope to see it again sometime soon."

She leaned into my touch like she was starved for it, not like she feared me. "Dirty and rough suits you, Dominic. But this part is pretty nice too."

My grip on her door tightened to the point I swore I heard the wood cracking. I wanted this girl so bad, I had to get out. This kind of need wasn't me. It wasn't wanted either.

"This shouldn't happen," I choked out. I couldn't bring myself to say that it couldn't, only that it shouldn't.

Her satiny cheek rubbed against my palm one more time, then she backed away. "Goodnight, Dominic."

I rapped my knuckles on her door twice. "Goodnight, Claire."

Marta kicked my knee with her platform shitkickers. "You look so blue. I'm not used to you like this."

I huffed a humorless laugh. "Right. I'm usually a barrel of laughs."

We were on a plane again, this time flying across Texas to Houston. The quiet roar of the engines wasn't enough to block out the oncoming dread filling my head. Marta's presence at the rear of the plane wasn't either.

"You're not, and I know you've got a lot on your mind. This city…"

"Yeah." I peered out the window. "This city."

I had a history with Houston I didn't like to think about. I didn't like it, but there was no avoiding these thoughts. The loss. The helplessness. I couldn't stop myself from reliving it every time I came through, even though it'd been more than half a decade now since…everything.

"Do you want me to come with you tomorrow?" she asked.

"No." Knee-jerk, gut instinct drove me to do this alone. It always did. "I'm good. Once I get this done, I'll be square."

She folded her arms in her lap and pressed her lips together, obviously suppressing a strong opinion. Marta rarely held back, but on this topic, on this city, she tried.

"Say it."

Her arms unfolded so she could rub at her legs. "You don't have to keep doing this. It hurts you, and you don't owe any kind of penance. You could take some time away, not visit the hospital—"

I shook my head and turned back to the window. "I'm doing what I need to do, Mar. If I don't go, it'll be worse. It'll be a failure."

"To who? Not to me. Not to anyone who knows." Her words were a blanket in a cradle. If I let them, they'd lull and comfort me. The thing was, I didn't want comfort. Not now. Not about this.

"I don't really have it in me to argue."

"I'm not arguing, Dom."

I jerked my chin. "Why don't you go sit in the front with Claire? I'm going to close my eyes until we land."

If I could have gone to the front of the plane and sat with Claire, I would have. But the way I felt, on edge and brutal, she wouldn't have appreciated my company. She could say she liked it a little dirty and rough, but that wasn't happening. Not today. Not like this. If I went up there and she gave me that look, the one she gave me whenever we got close, my tenuous control just might snap.

Marta unbuckled herself and scooted forward in her seat. "Fine. I will. My offer stands, no matter how pissy you are or how hard you try to push me away. I'm here, and I'm not going anywhere."

"Hmmm." My brow tightened. "That paycheck *is* pretty sweet."

"Oh, shut up. You're never going to reverse psychology me into working for free." She flicked my ear on her way by me. "I love you like a brother, Dominic. A much, *much* older and annoying brother, obviously."

I squeezed her arm before she could move on. "Back at you, kid."

Her lips twitched into a smirk. "Oh, I know."

I closed my eyes, but I didn't sleep. Instead, I pictured Dylan the last time I saw him healthy. Eight-years-old, freckle-faced, and a demon for music. Try as I might, I couldn't keep the last time I saw him from creeping in. Gaunt and pale, barely conscious, still begging for music, in that Houston hospital that was way too big for a dying eleven-year-old.

My hands fisted so tight, if I'd had longer fingernails, blood would have dripped between my knuckles. I longed for that, a slice of pain to pull my mind away from the very real pain of losing Dylan—a kid who hadn't been my son, but could have been in another life.

One day. All I had to do was get through one day in Houston, then I'd leave this place and these memories behind for another year or two. I could do one day.

CHAPTER EIGHTEEN

CLAIRE

I BUMPED INTO A stony-faced Dominic waiting in the elevator bank with his security detail. We'd arrived late last night, and I'd crashed hard in bed. The past two days, I'd barely spoken to Dominic outside of work, but whenever we were near each other, I was always aware of everything about him. His breath, his scent, the cadence of his words, his moods. I wasn't great at reading men—clearly, since I'd been with a lying bastard for so long without realizing it—but I truly believed Dominic was just as aware of me.

He still scared me, but in a different way now. Now, he made me tremble like I did when a rollercoaster crested the top of the hill. The anticipation both killed me and made me feel alive. I wasn't in a huge rush to see the other side of the drop, but I wouldn't slow it down when it happened either.

"We have to stop meeting like this," I quipped as he steadied me by holding my arms.

His hands lingered. "I'm starting to think maybe you like running into me."

"It isn't the worst place to end up." I pushed back from where I'd braced myself on his chest when he barely reacted to my pitiable attempt at flirtation. "Are you going to the hospital?"

"Yes." His nod was stiff, and the purple shadows beneath his eyes were almost as dark as the mood he appeared to be in. "Where are you headed so early?"

"My parents live right outside the city, so I'm spending the morning with them. I haven't seen them since I left my ex, so I'm not sure how things will be."

"Do you think they're mad at you for leaving?"

"No." I shook my head hard enough my curls slapped my cheeks. "No, definitely not. They're disappointed, but they don't blame me, given the way it ended."

He took that in while we rode the elevator down, so I tapped on my phone to order an Uber.

"What are you doing?" he asked.

"Ordering my ride." I glanced up from my phone to find Dominic leaning over me. "What are you doing?"

"Thinking you should just ride with me. Depending on where you're going, my driver can drop you off first or after they drop me off." He closed his hand over my phone. "I don't want you riding with a stranger."

The soft plea behind his order made me want to say yes, so I did.

It turned out my parents' house was on the way to the hospital, so we drove there first. Dominic spent the ride sitting across from me, staring out his window, one of my feet tucked between his. He hadn't even looked at me when he'd done it. His large, brown leather boots had closed around my rose gold oxford and kept it there the entire way.

Dominic finally looked my way when the car idled at the curb in front of my parents' house. If possible, his eyes were even more black than normal.

"What time will you be ready to go back?" he asked.

"I don't know, but don't worry about it. I'll just order an Uber like I'd planned on." I tried to pull my foot back, but he kept it trapped between his.

"Let me know when you're ready. I'll send the car if I'm not finished."

My first instinct was to argue, but I didn't. For one, it would be silly to decline an offer like that. Moreover, the tightly held together look Dominic gave me made me want to take it easy on him—to give him a win. He seemed to need it.

"Okay. I'll call," I said softly. "You'll have to let go of my foot, though."

My request drew his eyes down to our feet. He stared for a moment, then flicked his eyes back to mine. "I like when you wear these shoes."

"I wear them every day." He finally released my foot, so I slowly drew it back. "But thank you. I'll see you later."

Dominic nodded, then turned back to his window. I watched the car pull away, then faced my parents' house. I hadn't grown up in the modest, brick rancher, but they'd lived here long enough that when I visited, it had started to feel like coming home.

As soon as I started up the path to the front door, my mother threw it open and screeched my name. Their cocker spaniel, Gladys, came flying out, her long ears flapping in the wind. This dog barely knew me, but she acted just as excited to see me as my mom, who'd swooped me into a fierce hug. My dad, tall, stoic, and sweet, followed her, wrapping his long arms around me and holding me against his chest.

"My baby girl's here!" My mom clapped and hopped between two feet while Gladys yipped at her heels.

Dad cupped the back of my head and gave me a long look. "How are you, Claire? You look right as rain."

"I'm doing pretty great. My job is this big adventure everyday—"

Mom sucked in a deep breath. "I saw the limo."

That made me laugh. "Yeah, I've been taking regular limo rides. It's pretty crazy how quickly I've gotten used to it."

"I always knew you were meant for bigger things," she said.

The truth was, my mom had encouraged me to marry Derrick after the first time she met him. That I'd been nineteen and unsure of my own feelings for him hadn't mattered. She saw herself in me—the plump part of herself to be specific—and thought because I'd landed a catch, I needed to hold on to him since there was no telling if another man would ever be attracted to me. And when Derrick wanted me to be a homemaker instead of making my own way with a career, my mom had encouraged that too, to keep him happy and coming home to me.

The funny thing was, my dad looked at my mom like she hung the moon, even now. And from the way he told it, he—the tall and handsome former jock—had done all the chasing to win her over. My mom hadn't wanted anything to do with him, but he'd had his sights set on her. He finally got her to go to their high school senior prom with him, and the rest was history.

I couldn't really explain why she'd been so worried for me. Annaliese said everyone hated at least one part of themselves, and having a fairytale ending didn't erase that hatred, unfortunately.

That was all the past, though. If my mom said I was meant for bigger things, then I'd trust she meant that. I had no idea what I was meant for, just that it wasn't being Derrick's wife, and it certainly wasn't allowing a man to ever control me.

I spent a couple hours working on a puzzle with my parents, then my mom went into the kitchen to make lunch. When she left the room, my dad grew serious, and his normally mild countenance pinched into something grim.

"Claire, I would like you to reconsider pressing charges against Derrick."

I sighed. I should have known this would be an issue. "It's done. If I try now, I'll get in trouble for making a false statement to the police. As long as he's out of my life permanently, I'll be satisfied."

His long fingers curled into a tight ball, which he slammed against his leg. I jumped on impact. My dad rarely raised his voice, and he never got rough. Seeing the color rise in his face and the fist in his lap made me anxious.

"I would kill him if I could. If you'd walked in looking any worse for wear and didn't have that beautiful spark in your eyes, I can't promise I wouldn't have done something extreme."

"Dad." I dropped my forehead to his shoulder. "I'm okay. Please, *please* don't worry about me."

He pressed his lips to my temple and held them there for a few seconds. "My Claire. No woman should ever be hurt by a man, but you—" His voice cracked, and so did my heart. "You have the softest spirit and try to see the best in everyone. For that ghoul—I refuse to call him a man—to take you for granted... well, it makes me spit fire."

We held each other for a solid minute, neither crying, but oh, I was close. I'd done all my sobbing the night I had to call my parents and tell them what had happened. They were such good parents. Great even. I never wanted them to worry about me, but they had, and they still did.

By the time my mom announced lunch would take place on the patio, we had pulled ourselves together. My phone began to ring on our way out, so I grabbed it and told my dad to go ahead.

"Hey," I answered.

"Are you ready to go?" Dominic sounded exhausted, even though it had only been a couple hours since I'd seen him.

"I'm not. But you should go back to the hotel and rest. I'll catch an Uber and meet you at the venue later."

"No. I said I'd give you a ride, and I will."

I pressed two fingers between my eyebrows, willing myself not to argue. "Okay. Well, my mom just set up lunch on the back patio. I'll see if she can wrap my food up and—"

"Take your time, Claire."

I hung up with a promise to be done in twenty minutes, then rushed outside to join my parents. Lunch was laid out on the center of the table—pasta salad, mini sandwiches, fruit skewers, and baby carrots and celery—and my mom was in the middle of attempting to mime a movie title to my dad.

"'*The Princess Bride!*'" I yelled.

She shook her finger at me. "Oh my word, you're a cheater. You can't hop in the game right in the middle."

"Fine, you can have the win." I grabbed a sandwich and a few carrot sticks, crunching down on one. "Sorry, Dad. Mom wins."

Dad grumbled about how put upon he was, but I didn't miss him holding Mom's hand under the table, or her feeding him a strawberry from her plate.

I was in the middle of miming *Blair Witch Project* when my mom yelped, "Oh my word!" and my dad stood from his seat. I followed their gazes and gasped to find Dominic entering our yard from the back gate.

He held up both hands. "I'm sorry to interrupt. Claire isn't answering her phone and I wanted to see if she was ready to leave. I'll wait in the car."

"This is Dominic, my boss," I hurried out to my perplexed parents. My phone was lying facedown on the table. I picked it up, and there were several missed calls. "I'm sorry I didn't hear it ring. We might have been laughing too loud."

Dominic's head cocked slightly. "That's the finest excuse for missing a call I've ever heard."

Dad peered down at me. "Isn't he the one on the posters in your room?"

"Yes." I rubbed my forehead. "Yes, that's him. I'm touring with him, as you well know."

Dominic's soft chuckle brought my eyes to him. Only the corners of his mouth were tipped up, but for him, it was a lot.

My dad crossed the lawn to shake Dominic's hand. "Have you had lunch? My wife made quite a spread, so we've got plenty. I'd rather Claire not rush away, if at all possible."

Dad and Dominic couldn't have looked more different. Dad resembled Bill Nye the Science Guy, and Dominic...well, he was Dominic, alarmingly sexy. But it hit me that they were closer in age than Dominic and me. My parents had Annaliese when they were still in college. They were only fifty-one. I'd never found any of my parents' friends attractive. To me, they were *old*. But they weren't rock stars with golden skin, killer tattoos, and eyes that could burn entire countries to the ground.

"Uh..." Dominic's eyes darted to mine, and I nodded, "if you're sure it's okay. I have some time."

Mom made up a heaping plate of food for Dominic, and Gladys parked herself beside him, nudging his leg with her head until he pet her.

Mom batted her lashes at Dominic. "Do you want to hear embarrassing stories about Claire?"

Dominic wiped his mouth with his stars-and-stripes napkin. "Yes. I'd very much like to hear them. I can't picture Claire doing anything embarrassing. Although, she seems to be prone to stumbling."

The wink he gave me was so subtle, I almost missed it. Thank goodness my mom did.

Dad ruffled my hair with his big palm. "She might stumble, but she always catches herself."

Mom rubbed her hands together. "I have a few up my sleeve. I hope you're ready."

She spent the next half hour telling Dominic about the haircuts I gave myself in middle school, and the time I won every single prize at an awards banquet in high school, the people in charge scrambled to invent new awards to give to the other kids. She also described in great detail how many of his posters I'd once had in my room and how often I'd listened to his music.

Each time Dominic cracked a smile, he covered his mouth, but he couldn't hide the crinkling around his eyes. He seemed especially amused by how big of a fan of his I'd been when I was younger.

The afternoon slipped by quickly, and sooner than I wished, we were saying goodbye to my parents and climbing into the limo. Dominic settled across from me, and when I looked at him, I saw a brute sadness. His day weighed heavy on him. Melancholy filled his limbs.

Why did I want to be the one to lift it? I knew better. A woman couldn't fix a man, especially not one who didn't want to be fixed.

"Your embarrassing stories were really just humble brags," he said out of nowhere.

"Except for the posters."

He nodded. "Not so much embarrassing, more disconcerting for me considering what I think about doing with you."

My breath caught in a knot at the back of my throat. "What do you want to do?"

He muffled his chuckle with his hand, facing his window. "I just met your parents. Doesn't feel right to describe in detail the way I want their daughter's lips wrapped around my cock."

"No, that doesn't seem right." But wrong was what I wanted. Wrong and dirty were what I longed for. "We won't tell them."

That earned me another stifled laugh. "Claire, Claire, what am I going to do with you? I should stay away." He slapped the leather bench beside him. "Seeing you with your parents, how loved you are, how sweet and perfect...the only thing I've got is dirt."

That Dominic Cantrell, one of the most successful and well-known musicians in the world, would call me perfect made me wonder if I'd entered another dimension. I wasn't perfect in any way, but maybe I was different enough from the women Dominic had been with that he saw me as something precious and unsullied.

That pissed me off. I wasn't anybody's sweet little thing anymore.

"Then stay away. I don't want to be a source of frustration for you."

"Claire," he gritted out, "I've never been so fucking frustrated in my life. I have no business looking at you, but you're all I see."

"Do you want me to quit?" The very idea twisted in my gut, but I'd do it if I had to. I had started over once, I could do it again.

"No." He said the word with such vehemence, he nearly shouted. "No, you're not quitting. This is my problem."

If he only knew I'd crawl across the floor of the limo and kneel in front of him if he gave me an opening. I'd suck him just like he wanted, and I'd love every second of it.

"Why is it a problem?" I tucked my hands in my lap, my smile demure. Dominic unleashed desires in me that had been completely dormant my entire life. I would never beg, but I *would* tease until one of us broke.

"Just let it be. I'm on edge already. I can't do this with you." He flexed his fingers again and again, then he patted the seat beside him. "Come over here."

Heat immediately pooled in my belly as I crossed the small space. Dominic tugged me down flush beside him and fisted the back of my hair, tilting my head to the side. He wasn't gentle, and his beard on my neck was even more rough, but my whimpers weren't from pain. He buried his face in the crook of my neck and inhaled so deep, I thought he might swallow me up.

"Claire." He pushed my T-shirt aside and bit into my shoulder. Goose bumps instantly rose on my skin and my thighs clenched tight. One bite, and I was more turned on than I'd been in ages.

He moved his mouth along my shoulder, biting down harder each time, like he was testing me to see if I could handle his need.

My fingers threaded in his silky hair, pulling him closer. Dominic's groan vibrated my skin, sending little electric shocks down my spine.

His teeth ravaged my shoulder and neck, but each time he bit me, he licked away the pain. I'd never been touched this way, and it was a pity. It turned out, this was exactly what I'd been needing.

Dominic drew a line straight up the center of my throat with his warm, wet tongue, and tugged my head so far back, he took my breath away. The rough pads of his fingers caressed the line of my jaw and traced the bite marks he'd undoubtedly left on me. Then he buried his face in my neck again, inhaling my scent like this was his last chance.

His arms circled my middle, nearly pulling me into his lap. He murmured my name each time he kissed and bit me. My underwear was soaked, and I worried my jeans would leave a damp spot on the seat. He had me on edge, and he hadn't even kissed my lips.

Our car came to a rolling stop, and only then did Dominic pull away. His eyes were glazed and unfocused, but his arms remained banded around me.

"Jesus, Claire."

That made me laugh and scratch my nails along the side of his head. "I think that was all you."

He captured my hand from his hair and gently bit the inside of my wrist, then pressed a kiss there. "You see what you do to me?" His head fell back on the seat, arms loosening. "I'm gonna need a minute or two before I get out of the car. You need to go."

"I can wait with you."

He huffed a laugh, slinging his forearm over his eyes. "Do you think my dick's going to go down if you're sitting beside me, smelling as good as you do right now? Fuck, Claire, I can smell how wet you are."

I didn't know whether to be flattered or deeply ashamed. Maybe both. I scooted away, but Dominic caught my hand, stopping me.

"I want you to go to your room and finish yourself. Then text me how long it took."

I nodded once. "Okay. I will."

He sighed, his head falling back again. "Good girl."

I made him wait. Exactly one hour after I left the car, I texted him two words:

Three minutes.

He texted me back immediately:

Two.

CHAPTER NINETEEN

CLAIRE

MARTA LET ME TOSS my things in my hotel room in Denver, then dragged me with her to go "shopping." When she'd learned the last time I'd smoked weed had been my freshman year of college, she'd insisted on treating me to some legal edibles.

Dominic watched us from his doorway while his security checked over his room. His arms were folded across his chest, shoulder leaning on the doorjamb, expression unreadable.

"Plans?" he asked.

"Yep." Marta slipped her arm around my waist. "Claire and I are going to explore Denver. Should we pick you up something?"

He tipped his bearded chin. "Surprise me."

Dominic and I hadn't spent any time alone together since our limo ride. He was holding back, and maybe I was too, but that didn't mean the tension between us had lessened. If anything, it kept building. When we got home from his concert last night in Phoenix, he'd texted me ten minutes after we went into our separate rooms.

Five.

That one word flipped a switch inside me, transforming me into a wanton, frenzied creature who could only think of one thing. When I texted him back with my number—six—he'd replied, "Good girl", which got me going yet again.

But he hadn't touched me, and I hadn't touched him. We were treading a dangerous line, and we both knew it, but I wouldn't stop unless he explicitly told me to.

When we did this, when we played with each other, it made me feel like who I should be: Claire, the young, slightly wild, twenty-six-year-old. Not who I was: Claire, the old for her age, slightly repressed, soon-to-be divorcee.

We crammed into a van provided by the hotel with Iris, Adam, and Rodrigo. I'd come to realize Callum didn't really hang out too often, and when he did, he was quiet and spaced out. Iris said that's just how he'd always been, but he was one hell of a bass player, so they let him be.

Rodrigo squeezed my hand and bounced beside me. "What are we buying, baby Claire?"

"I'm older than you, silly." I pretended to be offended, but I loved this man more than I should have loved anyone I'd only known a couple weeks. I wasn't sure Rodrigo could ever truly offend me.

"That might be true. But you're baby."

Iris turned around from the row in front of us. "It means adorable and loveable. It's pretty much a high compliment."

"Ah." I pinched Rodrigo's dimpled cheek. "You're baby too, then."

He beamed and snuggled up against me. "Now that we're officially best friends, what are we buying you?"

I threw my hands up. "I don't know my options. I smoked weed twice my freshman year of college and that's it. I need guidance."

Adam leaned over the back of our seat. "Rodrigo can definitely be your guide in all things marijuana."

"'Tis true." Rodrigo sat up straight and saluted an imaginary flag. "Lieutenant Colonel Cannabis, reporting for duty."

The dispensary they took me to wasn't anything like I'd pictured. It wasn't seedy or smoke-filled. Instead, it was brightly lit and immaculately clean and reminded me of an old-fashioned pharmacy. I let Rodrigo and Adam pick out my treats, trusting them to do right by me. They picked up a tube of gummies and a roll of taffy. I snagged a package of what looked like Swedish Fish for Dominic after Rodrigo approved of my choice.

Iris and Marta took their pot buying seriously, having a long discussion with one of the workers about different strains. I listened, because it was interesting, but their knowledge was far too advanced for me. I was looking to get high and giggle—that was it.

After we left the dispensary, we had lunch on the patio of a tiny Mexican restaurant and planned our night.

"Anyone up for going out? Upside of high-altitude drinking is getting drunk hella fast," Iris said.

I groaned. "I seriously don't want to be hungover again for a good six months."

Marta tapped her chin, then perked up. "I happen to know Dominic's suite has access to a private rooftop terrace complete with a firepit. Maybe I can bribe him with weed taffy to let us hang out there."

"Sweet." Rodrigo held a tortilla chip loaded with salsa aloft. "Think we can lay our hands on some marshmallows? I want to make Claire some s'mores."

Iris cocked her head back. "I have known you for six years and you've never made me a fucking s'more. Claire is amazing and everything, but where's the love, Roddy?"

He gave me a look while he chewed on his chip. I cleared my throat and leaned in closer to Iris. "The thing is, I've never called him Roddy. That might be a starting point."

Iris cackled and gave my shoulder a playful swat. "Thank you, honey bunny. I love you to pieces."

It was strange and delightful how quickly I'd been welcomed into this group of rockers. They weren't anything like the friends Derrick and I had shared, but I liked them better. They were raw and messy sometimes, but they were true to themselves. Or, in Iris's case, as true as her record label allowed her to be. And even though on the outside I didn't quite fit in with their achingly hip, punk rock aesthetic, it turned out that didn't really matter.

I'd never felt so warm and cozy with people. I hadn't known that was an option, outside of family members. But when Rodrigo cuddled with me or Iris called me honey bunny, I felt genuine affection from them. I would hate when this tour ended, but I'd always be glad to have known them. And hey, maybe it was possible we could be forever-friends, even when their star began to soar—and it would.

Once we finished eating, Adam handed me a piece of taffy. "Start small and see how you feel."

I took the sticky candy, flipping it over in my hand. "I can't believe this is going to get me high."

He waggled his eyebrows. "Just wait."

The high was gradual, but suddenly, everything was just a little bit funnier and my troubles were background noise. Marta and I sat in the rear of the hotel van on our way back, slumped down with our knees on the back of Rodrigo and Adam's bench, whispering secrets to each other like no one else could hear. It was quite possible they either couldn't or didn't care, since everyone else had partaken too.

"What do you think Callum's deal is?" I asked.

Marta sputtered. "He's extremely serious."

I rolled my eyes and stuck out my tongue like a dead man. "The worst. Let's promise to always be unserious. Oh shit, is that a word?" I snickered.

Marta drew her phone from her pocket, holding the screen close to her face. "Score! Dom says we can use his terrace."

I poked at her phone. "He's serious too."

"Yeah, but he likes to be around people who aren't."

"What?"

She grinned at me and cupped my cheek. "Nothing. I think Iris might not be into me."

"Impossible. You're so pretty."

She blinked twice, like she was trying to clear something from her eyes. "Are you hitting on me, Claire?"

I laughed so hard, I fell over into her lap. She stroked my hair and laughed along with me.

Rodrigo turned in his seat and aimed his phone at us, taking our picture. "You're gonna want to remember this, *preciosa*."

I looked up at him with tear-filled eyes, that, for once, weren't caused by sadness, and smiled wide. "I promise you I will."

Our group met back up in the evening. I'd spent time resting in my room, and when the high wore off, I talked to Isabela for a while about the upcoming tour stops. She seemed confounded by how well-behaved Dominic was being, but I was happy about it. I wasn't sure I was quite up for handling a big scandal.

We had to go through Dominic's room to get to the terrace, so we knocked on his door.

He opened quickly, ushering us inside. The others passed by, thanking him for letting us use his space, but I lingered behind, waving his gummies at him.

"A thank you."

He took them from me, examining the package, then looked up, eyebrows raised. "Did you have fun?"

"I really did." I tipped my head in the direction of the steps everyone had climbed. "You should come up and join us."

He shrugged. "I'm good here."

"Haven't you been alone in your room all day?" I pressed.

"I have. I don't mind being alone. Most of the time, I prefer it." He brought his hands to his hips, the plastic of the gummies crinkling. "You should go, find your friends."

"I know I should." I tugged on the ends of the strings on my hoodie. "I will. I just wanted to ask you to come too."

He sighed, sweeping a hand over his short hair. "You asked. You did your duty. Don't feel guilty that I'm sitting down here lonely."

I couldn't seem to be in Dominic's presence without my stomach doing this crazy falling thing. It was impossible to stand two feet away from him and not long to close the distance—to not hope he'd say "fuck it" to his tightly held control and...

I had to stop. My friends were waiting, and from the heat spreading down my cheeks and chest, I was surely blushing.

"Okay. Well...goodnight, then."

I hurried up the stairs to the roof where Adam and Rodrigo were getting a fire going. Lattice walls divided the space, giving it privacy and a cozy feel. There were padded lounge chairs off to the side, and brightly colored Adirondack chairs circled the wide, stone pit. The night was just crisp enough for me to want to lean into the warmth of the fire.

The hotel had provided us with s'mores kits, so we were eating marshmallows and chocolate for dinner tonight. I curled up in an Adirondack chair and tipped my head back to look at the stars.

Marta pushed a gummy into my hand. "You need this, kidlet."

"Thank you, my love." I popped it into my mouth with a grin, chewing slowly. "Did I ever tell you you remind me of my sister?"

She took the chair next to me. "You didn't. Give me more information. Is this sister amazing? Tell me more, tell me more."

"She is. Her name is Annaliese and she's a femme lesbian gardener."

Marta looked down at her button-up shirt, cuffed jeans, and platform boots. "Uh..."

I giggled. "Not on the outside. I meant your personality and how caring you are. Annaliese is hilarious, but she also has this innate sense when she's needed and she's just there, you know?

And you just looked at me, said, 'that girl needs a pot gummy,' and you were exactly right."

Marta snorted. "Okay, well, Annaliese sounds cool as hell, so I'm gonna need to meet her when we go home." She reached across and squeezed my hand. "I've got you, Claire-bear."

I involuntarily jerked back. "Oh, please don't call me that. That was what my ex-husband called me and—"

Rodrigo bounced in front of me. "You were married? Way to keep secrets from me."

"Yeah." Marta smacked the hand she'd just been holding. "What the hell?"

Adam scooted his chair closer. "Claire was married?"

Iris raised her hand. "First I'm hearing about this."

"Actually, I'm going through a really fucking awful divorce right now." I cringed, awaiting their reactions.

Marta immediately climbed out of her chair, plopped her tiny butt on my lap, and bear-hugged me. Then Rodrigo found a space to snuggle in on my side. They both murmured sweet nothings, and since I was a little high from the gummy, I hadn't felt that good...maybe ever.

When they let go, Iris fist-bumped me, and Adam gave me his own hug.

"Okay, okay." I cut my hands through the air. "I'm fine. My ex is awful, and I can't wait to be rid of him, but I'm not broken, promise."

Iris shook her head. "No one thought you were."

Rodrigo sat on my other side, and the firelight glowed on the puppy dog eyes he gave me. "Tell me how to make it better. Let's plan some kind of Claire-is-emancipated-from-the-dragon shindig."

Calling Derrick a dragon tugged at my belly and sent a ripple of giggles through me. Once I got started, I couldn't stop. I laughed so hard, I rolled to my side in my chair, clutching my middle.

When I finally got myself together and opened my eyes, a tall, shadowy figure caught my attention, and my breath wedged in my throat.

"Dominic?" I croaked.

He stepped forward into the light, his lips curving into a rare smile. "Does the offer to join you still stand?"

CHAPTER TWENTY

DOMINIC

CLAIRE'S LAUGHTER HAD BROUGHT ME TO THE ROOF. I'd never heard her laugh so hard and for so long. My gut told me I needed to see her that way for myself.

And what a fucking sight. Her throaty laugh sounded like the devil's church bells calling all the sinners to service. The firelight danced over her cheeks, and when she opened her eyes, they caught the flames like stained glass in the sun.

There was no doubt she was as high as a kite, but I liked seeing her this way. I didn't remember a time I'd ever reached that level of happiness or ease, chemically enhanced or not. It soothed me to know it was possible.

Marta held out her hands. "Get over here, Dom. I have to ask you a question."

I took a seat opposite Claire with the fire at my back. "Ask away."

Marta poked a finger at me. "Did *you* know Claire was married?"

"Uh…" I scrubbed my chin. "Yes…"

Claire giggled again. "Stop it. It wasn't a secret, I just don't want to think about it."

Rodrigo crossed his arms. "I'm betrayed."

Yeah, the whole group was fucking flying. I should've popped an edible before coming up, but there was something to be said for being the only sober one in a group of stoners. That hadn't always been the case, but I wasn't twenty anymore either.

"Oh my god, it just came out when I was talking to Dominic the same way it came out tonight. There's no big conspiracy." Claire ruffled Rodrigo's hair, and he leaned into her hand like a kitten.

"Okay, I forgive you."

"How long?" Iris asked.

"How long was I married?"

Iris nodded.

Claire held up four fingers. *Four years*.

"What? You were a baby!" Iris's mouth hung open for a beat. "Wow. So, how long have you been separated? And is it definitely going to be divorceville?"

"Oh yeah. There's no going back for me." Claire leaned her head on her hand. "It's been three and a half months since I left."

"This is really new," Adam said.

"It is," she confirmed. "But the person I was when I was married feels a thousand miles away. That's old Claire, and she was a submissive bore."

Iris snapped. "I hope you lit all his shit on fire."

I didn't know Claire's ex. I had no idea why they broke up. But I strongly agreed with Iris. I would have been cool with it if she'd lit the whole man on fire.

"I didn't. That's not my style. All I want is to be free, and I am." She wiggled her fingers in the air. "Look at me now, baby."

Rodrigo rubbed his hands together. "Now, let's plan your emancipation celebration. What kind of naughty things can we make Claire do?"

"We're making Claire do things?" Adam waggled his eyebrows at her. I had to stop my hands from balling. This kid was the human equivalent of toothpicks under fingernails. He made me fucking cringe with how obvious and cheesy he was.

"No one makes Claire do anything," Marta declared. "But hypothetically, if we made you do something you've never done before but always sort of wanted to, what would it be?"

Claire bit her lip and hummed to the sky. "Strip club. I've never been, and I've always wanted to go. My ex used to take bro golf trips and they'd always hit up the strip club, but he never wanted me to go with him."

Rodrigo cupped his mouth. "Whaaat? We're getting Claire some booty in the champagne room? Hell yes!"

Iris bobbed her head a few too many times. "I'm in, I'm in. We should go in Vegas. Those girls are stunnas."

Adam slammed his hand down. "It's settled. My girl's getting a lap dance."

My girl? Who the hell did the guy think he was? I highly fucking doubted Claire was timing her orgasms for him. Highly. Fucking. Doubted.

Claire opened her arms. "I'll take one right now if you're offering."

He started to rise, but my arm shot out, blocking him. "Don't. She's high, and if you take advantage of that, you're even more of a twat than I thought."

He sat back in his chair, shooting me a withering look, but I ignored the little shit. I knew I was something of a hypocrite, but that didn't mean I'd let anyone else slide—not with her.

Undeterred, Claire curled her finger at me. "I wouldn't mind a little silver fox in my lap."

"There's nothing little about me," I deadpanned.

She snickered, mouthing, "I know."

The others kept on talking about the strip clubs they'd been to and trading horror stories of some of the worst, most seedy ones. I could've told a hundred stories of my own, but I wasn't much on sharing. Especially not now, when I was caught up in looking at Claire, and she was looking right back.

She gave me a slow, lazy smile, and my lips twitched at how outrageously adorable she was, all mellow, snuggled in her chair in a big hoodie. She made me want to take her in my lap and touch each of her soft places, then bend her over and slap her ass for taking up so much space in my head.

Claire uncurled from her chair and approached the fire. As she passed me, she brushed her hand over my shoulder. "What is going on in your brain?"

I stood too, watching her push a marshmallow onto a metal spear. "A lot of things."

She lowered the metal into the fire. "Are they text-worthy thoughts?"

"Some."

She tipped her face up to me and arched a brow. "Intriguing. You should tell me more."

"I don't think I should. Not with your boy hanging around."

Claire glanced over her shoulder at Adam, then back to me. "I think you know I'm not interested in boys."

Her marshmallow caught fire, so I took her hand, lifting it from the flames, and blew it out. She smiled and put it right back in.

"I like them charred black. You didn't need to rescue my poor little marshmallow." Her elbow nudged my ribs. "Make one for yourself. When was the last time you ate a s'more?"

I allowed a small chuckle to release. "Longer than you've been alive."

"Eat one, Dominic. Get sticky with me." She slid her black marshmallow between two graham crackers and took a bite. White spilled over her lips, and her tongue poked out to catch it. "Yum."

This girl knew exactly what she was doing, and it was working. If we were alone...

"Is it s'mores time now?" Rodrigo bounced between us, pushing Claire and me apart.

"Yes, it is. I was just convincing Dominic to make one."

Rodrigo whirled around on me, his eyes manic. Hell, maybe they were always manic. "You're not making a s'more, dude? What, are you on some dietician-approved, no carb, plant-based, zero fun diet to maintain that smokin' bod?"

"You caught me." Who the hell was this kid? Had he been beamed here from another planet? The weird thing was, I kind of dug him, and I didn't dig many people. No doubt I'd get over it the more I knew him, but for now, I didn't mind his presence.

Rodrigo rubbed his chin, deep in thought. "I won't tell if you want a cheat day. Claire won't tell either." He wrapped his arm around her shoulders. "Will you, boo?"

She shook her head with a solemn expression. "No, sir. I won't tell anyone, even if they torture me."

I pointedly grabbed a marshmallow from the pyramid the kitchen staff had stacked on the tray and jabbed the metal spear through it.

"No one tortures you but me."

"Oooh, yeah. I can see that about you. You like the whips-and-chains lifestyle. Spicy." Rodrigo checked his marshmallow and declared it perfect. He doctored up his s'more, leaving Claire and me by the fire again.

"Having fun?" I reached out, swiped my thumb over her sticky bottom lip, and sucked it into my mouth. "Marshmallow."

She groaned quietly and eased closer to my side. "More fun than I should have while I'm working, I think. I doubt my next job will live up to this one."

"Don't think you'll keep working for Isabela?"

Claire cringed, but not from my question. "Your marshmallow is gone."

I checked my stick, and sure enough, it was empty. "Fuck. I actually wanted that."

She ran her hand up my chest, patting twice. "I'll make you one, and it'll be the best you've ever had."

When her hand lingered on me, I glanced down at it, then up to her eyes. "Are you still scared of me, Claire?"

"Do you still want me to be?" She dropped her hand and went to work on my replacement marshmallow.

I blew out a breath, deciding on full honesty. "I don't know."

"I don't know either." Her eyes slid to mine. "Do you like the whips-and-chains lifestyle?"

That made me laugh. I turned away, letting it out, then angled back to face her again. Her brows were drawn together, pretty lips curving down.

"Why do you always hide your laughs?" she asked.

"Do I?"

"You know you do."

"It's not conscious." I took my s'more from her, backing away. "Don't try to dig into my faults. I'm not looking to be fixed or saved."

Her eyes rolled as she followed me back to the chairs. The one beside her was vacant, so I snagged it and enjoyed the hell out of my s'more. Claire watched with her chin on her hand, seeming to find me amusing.

Need surged in my belly. I wanted a taste of Claire, of what she had—her easy way, how people gravitated to her and the way she let them even through all the hurt she had to be experiencing. If I could have her, her flavor on my tongue, her scent in my nose, the feel of her on my skin, maybe I'd soak up some of it.

She made me want to feel.

She made me want.

"I want you in my bed tonight," I murmured.

She chewed on her bottom lip before answering. "Even though I've had a few edibles?"

"In my bed, Claire."

It wasn't right. She should turn me down and tell me to go to hell. I shouldn't want her, and I sure as hell should be able to resist her.

None of that mattered. Thoughts of her mouth, her scent, her creamy, freckled skin, took up every corner of my thoughts. I needed her out. Out of my system, out of my head. And I thought she really needed it too.

"Okay," she whispered.

My fingers dug into the wooden arms of my chair. "You won't let me kick everyone out, will you?"

The smile she gave me shined brilliant. "No, I very much won't."

By the time everyone cleared out, it was past midnight, and Claire had started drooping in her chair. Marta tried to wait for her, but she was toasted enough to accept that I'd get Claire back to her room myself.

I tugged Claire up, and she stumbled into me, her fire-warmed face nestling in my beard. She stayed there for a long moment, then tipped her head back. Her fingers slid into my hair, nails scratching a shallow path. Her lids were heavy, but it killed me to admit not solely from desire.

I grazed her bottom lip with my teeth. "Come to bed."

We went downstairs together, and I guided her into my bathroom. Claire faced me, waiting for me to make the first move, her eyes shining in the bright lights. I gripped the hem of her hoodie, slowly lifting it over her head. Beneath, she wore a nearly sheer white camisole and black bra. I slid my hand into the cup of her bra, brushing my thumb back and forth over her beaded nipple. Her skin felt as creamy as it looked, like I could sink right into it and disappear.

I fisted her hair at the nape of her neck, and her lips parted, breath stuttering.

"What is it about you?" I gritted out, almost angry with the desire I couldn't seem to keep in check. My cock throbbed from wanting her. There was an ache in me I'd had for weeks.

She slipped her hands under my shirt, tracing the ridges of my abs with her fingertips. "What is it about you?" She sounded breathless, but also like she really didn't know the answer.

I didn't come across that often. Women wanted me because they knew who I was—the rocker, the star, the guy on the screen. They didn't question it or wonder. That they would want me was a given.

Maybe I was getting older and losing my touch, or maybe Claire was just...Claire.

"I don't think I know." My fist tightened in her hair, tilting her head to the side, and I dipped down to taste her like I'd been thinking of doing all night. She moaned when my teeth met her flesh, arching into the bites of pain.

My breaking point was a near-palpable place, and I was fast approaching it. Her breast in my palm and throat in my mouth pushed me to the outer depths of my control.

Violence ran through my blood. Not that I would ever hurt Claire, at least not in a way she wouldn't want. But I had a deep-seated need to unleash with her. To push her, to be real and raw with her. Maybe because I didn't think she'd ever had that.

With the way I felt tonight, the edginess in my veins, holding back would be impossible, and she wasn't there. She had to be fully awake and prepared for what I'd bring.

"Get ready for bed." I yanked my hand out of her bra and reached around her, unclasping it easily. The straps slipped down her arms, then I pulled the whole thing from under her camisole and tossed it on the bathroom floor.

Her hands flew up to her nearly-bare tits, cupping them. I knocked them away with a feral growl. "Don't hide yourself from me, Claire."

"Yes, sir." She swiveled toward the door, but I caught her shoulder, spinning her back around to the sink. "Wha—?"

I unwrapped a new toothbrush, provided by the hotel, drew a line of toothpaste on the bristles, and handed it to her. "Brush."

I did the same with my toothbrush, scrubbing my teeth beside her. When she spit into the sink, I filled a glass with water and handed it to her. "Drink."

She shook her head. "No, I'm not thirsty."

"Fine." I swallowed her water down, placing the glass on the marble countertop. "Come to bed."

I walked behind her, my eyes glued to the sway of her hips and the bounce of her full, round ass. She stopped beside my bed and turned, pressing her chest against mine.

"Now what?" She was a little pissy, just the way I liked her.

My index finger hooked on the waistband of her leggings. "Now, I take these off you."

Her fingers tucked in the waistband of my jeans. "And I take these off you?"

It had been my intention to help her undress, then tuck her into bed. My intentions were shit when Claire was involved, though. Her fingertips grazed the head of my cock as she unzipped my jeans, making me jerk away.

I shoved her onto the bed and swept her pants off, then I kicked mine off and tossed my T-shirt aside. Claire's tired eyes were hungry, even as she wrapped her arms around her middle, again trying to hide from me.

"Lie down for me, beautiful girl. Under the covers."

She did as I asked with a snarl as menacing as a kitten. I climbed into bed beside her, both of us on our sides, facing each other. Her mouth was on mine before I saw her coming, and that hunger was there too.

I slipped my palm into her panties. She opened her legs to let me between them, to feel her slick, wet heat. I only meant to touch her once, to find out if she ached for me the way I ached for her, but once I rolled her swollen clit under the pad of my finger, I couldn't stop. Not until she fell apart for me.

Her mouth stopped moving against mine as little pants escaped her lips. Eyes wide and almost startled, she watched me as I touched her.

"How long is it going to take, Claire?"

Her breathing stuttered when I pushed one finger inside her. "Oh god, not long. I'm already close."

She held my face in her hands, keeping my eyes on her. Like I'd ever look away from this. Her cheeks were bright pink, and her lips were kissed a ruddy red. Her eyes did me in, though. They flashed her emotions like a scrolling billboard. From one second to the next, she went from shy to disbelieving to frantic to overwhelmed.

Her pussy pulsed around my finger. I pressed hard on her clit until she whimpered and dug her nails into my jaw.

"Dominic," she panted. "Oh, please."

Legs scissored back and forth, squeezing my hand between them. Her body arched, shaking and shuddering, then curled in, riding my hand to find every last bit of pleasure she could.

When she stilled, I kept my hand there, the tip of my finger still inside her. Her eyes closed for half a minute, muscles slowly relaxing. They reopened when I brushed a sweaty piece of hair off her forehead.

She reached for me, gripping my length through the fabric of my underwear. "You're so hard." Her voice was so full of wonder, I nearly laughed. But fuck, it was difficult to laugh with a raging hard-on that wouldn't be getting any relief tonight.

"Claire." With reluctance, I removed my hand from her panties and gripped her wrist. "We're going to sleep."

"Oh." Her eyes flicked to mine, then down to the sheet covering our bodies. "Okay."

"Look at me." I nudged her chin with my pussy-soaked knuckle, bringing her gaze back to mine. "I don't have a lot of good in me, but I won't fuck you when you're even a little bit loaded. When you wake up tomorrow and your brain is fully yours, all you have to do is say the word, and I'll fuck us both into oblivion. Right now, I want you here. I want to fall asleep with my dick nestled in your ass, and I sure as hell want to wake up that way too."

Her eyes darted back and forth between mine. One inhale, and another, then she rolled over, pressing her butt into my groin. My arm draped over her waist, pulling her closer until we were flush with each other.

"You're like a dream, Claire." I cupped her breast beneath her shirt, rolling her nipple between two fingers. "Go to sleep."

The moan she let out was soft, but it shot straight to my dick. "I can't fall asleep when you're touching me like that."

I kissed her shoulder and ear. "I think you can. Set your mind to it."

"You're really mean," she whispered.

"I know, baby. Never said I wasn't."

She fell asleep while I inhaled the smoke in her hair and honeysuckle on her neck, wondering how the hell I planned on getting her out of my system when she kept working her way deeper. I fell asleep soon after, draped around her, deciding not to give a shit. At least not tonight.

CHAPTER TWENTY-ONE

CLAIRE

I WOKE UP WET AND HOT. I'd been dreaming of Dominic, his cock between my thighs, rubbing my clit again and again. It was no wonder my panties were soaked.

Last night, I'd been embarrassed and hurt Dominic didn't want to have sex with me once again. Confused too, that he wanted me in his bed anyway. This morning, with my head a little clearer, I remembered how achingly hard he'd been, the struggle in his every move to chain back his reactions to me.

He wanted me as much as I wanted him.

When I moved, the arm around my middle tightened, holding me in place. In his sleep, Dominic shushed me, petting my stomach, then moving to cup my breast.

I couldn't stop myself from whimpering at the feel of his rough fingertips grazing my skin—skin that had only ever been touched this way by one man.

Dominic groaned in his sleep and pressed his growing erection between my ass cheeks. My spine bowed, nestling his cock even closer.

"Claire." His beard scratched my shoulder as my name left his mouth like sandpaper.

"Dominic," I whispered, reaching behind me to cup his tightly muscled ass. "Good morning."

He squeezed my breast, hot breath huffing in my ear. "You make me so fucking hard, even in my sleep."

I laid my hand on his, urging him to keep touching me. "I was dreaming of this."

"Tell me." His teeth caught my earlobe, nipping to the very edge of pain.

It was easy to say what I wanted when I didn't have to face him. I could be the wanton woman in my dreams and not the girl who'd only been with one man in her entire life.

"You pulled my panties off and took your dick out. Then you laid behind me like you are now and slid it between my legs so you hit my clit." My voice wavered, but not from nerves. Dominic plucked my nipples into sharp peaks while I spoke, sending shockwaves directly to my core.

"If I touched you now, would you be wet?" He growled beside my ear.

"Soaked. Completely drenched."

He moved suddenly, no longer laying behind me. The sheet was whipped off my body and my underwear followed. With a gasp, I turned my head. Dominic was kneeling next to me, raking his black eyes over every exposed inch of me.

His gaze snagged with mine, and we were frozen in that one beat of time—the precipice we were going to jump off no matter what—the moment before we lost ourselves in each other.

"Open your legs." His words were commanding, but soft, which made me want to do exactly as I was told. Still on my side, I lifted my knee as he watched. His nostrils flared, and his fingers curled on his knees. "Fuck, baby. *Fuck.*"

Dominic dove between my legs, licking me from top to bottom. The animalistic moan that came from deep within his chest had my hips arching. He held nothing back, not anymore. His teeth clamped down on the tender flesh of my thighs and lips, surely leaving marks. The very idea of walking around with Dominic's marks between my legs was nearly enough to make me come.

"You taste too fucking good, Claire." Dominic sounded feral, and when his eyes found mine, they were so black, I could have disappeared in them.

He circled his arms around my thighs, securing me against his mouth, then he went to work on my clit. I came within seconds, fingers tangling in his hair, my ass leaving the bed completely. But he didn't stop. Not even close. He ate me like he'd never be done, and I wasn't sure I'd *let* him. I kept coming, each orgasm more powerful than the last. My limbs trembled endlessly, and my eyes rolled around in my head like they'd become untethered.

One finger, then two, slid into me, plunging roughly to the beat of Dominic's tongue on my pulsing clit. My hips rose and fell, trying to ride the waves of pleasure so I wouldn't be washed away in them. The third finger drove me crashing over the edge. I screamed his name, cried to the heavens, trying to escape from the sweet torture of his mouth.

"I can't, I can't," I panted, grabbing for his beard. "Come up here."

He hummed against my pussy, dragging his tongue through my folds in a slow, torturous pass. Turning his head to the side, he rubbed his face on my inner thigh. The places he'd bitten sparked to life with each brush of his beard.

He murmured my name as he climbed up my body, pressing my hips to the bed. His chest molded to my back, and his teeth clamped on my neck.

"I need to fuck you, beautiful," he gritted out.

I arched my back, giving him consent without words because my lips couldn't seem to form them at the moment.

Dominic grabbed a condom from somewhere, the wrapper crinkling, then his hips lifted from mine as he rolled it on.

His knees bracketed my sides, and strong hands gripped my hips, pulling me up as far as he could with his body on top of mine. I peered over my shoulder to watch him. His eyes were on me, and when he spread my ass with his fingers, in the back of my mind, it was in me to feel embarrassed, but I didn't. Not with the wild look in Dominic's eyes. Not with the way he licked his lips as though the very sight of me made him hungry. With certainty, I could say I'd never been looked at that way before.

I writhed on the bed, my clit pulsing back to life. Dominic's grip on my hips tightened, and his cock slipped between my thighs, just like my dream. He moved to hover over me, his lips close to my ear.

"I see you. You want this, don't you?" He nipped at my shoulder, and when I nodded, his hips reared back, then drove forward, filling me in one smooth, pounding motion.

My lungs seized up, trapping a scream in my chest. Dominic's cock stretched me well past my limits, but oh, the pain-tinted pleasure he brought was delicious. I could hardly move, but he did. He plunged into me relentlessly, skin slapping skin each time.

"Claire, Claire, Claire, your pussy feels as sweet as it tastes. What the fuck are you doing to me, baby?" His arm slid under mine, palm cupping my cheek to turn my head to the side. His mouth covered mine, consuming me everywhere. Teeth nipped and bit my lips and chin, then kissed away the hurt the next second.

We were messy and untamed, and I held nothing back. Dominic was stripping away my defenses and barreling through my walls. He grunted against my lips, sweeping his tongue inside, claiming my mouth just as sure as he'd planted a flag.

In that moment, I belonged to Dominic Cantrell. There was no one else before or after, only this. The spaces where our skin connected were the only real things in the universe. Not a single thing mattered beyond this bed. The only pain I felt was what he gave me, and I accepted willingly.

"Your pussy is greedy for my cock." He kept my face in his grip, watching what his words did to me. "You feel too good. My mouth got you so slick and hot. I want to stay here all day, but I'm not going to be able to. Not when I'm pounding against your pretty ass and your pussy is clenching my cock like that. I need you to rub your clit so I can feel you come all over me. Do it for me, Claire."

I fit my arm between my body and the mattress, slipping my hand between my spread thighs. I rolled my clit, and Dominic moved faster, fucking me harder. I mewled for him, writhing when another orgasm dragged through me. This one was raw and painful, seizing all my muscles and vibrating my bones.

Dominic gripped my hips with both hands, driving into me so hard, my teeth chattered. My fingers curled into the sheets, holding on for him to use me how he wanted. His rhythm stuttered, then jerked, and my name sounded almost like a curse from his lips. He held himself deep within me, spilling his pleasure. For one crazy second, I wished he was coating my insides instead of the condom.

He fell over me, pressing me into the mattress with his weight. His hands slid up my arms, covering mine. Slowly, I straightened my fingers, and his fitted in the empty spaces between them. Pinned down, I still couldn't move, but I wasn't sure I would have been able to without a sweaty man on top of me either. I focused on the gray and black rose tattooed on Dominic's hand and how his inky skin contrasted with my pale freckles.

Our mingled pants sounded like two lovers whispering filthy secrets to each other.

He chuckled low and soft. "I think you might be a liar."

"Hmmm? Why?"

"Because…" he nuzzled his nose into the side of my neck, "I've seen every inch of you, and I haven't discovered a tattoo."

"Oh." I wiggled beneath him. "You didn't take my top off."

And the night I'd thrown myself at him, when I'd taken my own top off, he'd been too focused on my breasts to notice anything else.

"You're right. Damn." His forehead fell on my shoulder, and with a groan, he pulled out of me. He shifted so he was beside me, gathering my thin cami in his fist. His impatience to find my tattoo made me grin into the pillow.

"Hold on." I rolled over to face him, lifting my cami to expose my ribs. "I hope this doesn't freak you out."

He propped himself on his elbow to examine it closely. I'd gotten this tattoo a month after I left Derrick. He'd never liked them, so getting one was a great act of defiance for me—especially since I'd always wanted one.

Dominic's stony silence worried me. If I'd known I'd one day be working for him—or worse, naked in bed with him—I probably wouldn't have gotten his lyrics inked on my skin.

"I told you I love that song." This man had just seen every intimate part of me, and only now did I feel shy. He traced the watercolor angel wings with his fingertips, then read the words scrawled between them. "I wanted to remind myself what I was going through wouldn't last forever."

"Nothing is forever
Even if it feels like dying
Lift your broken wings
And start flying"

He dipped his head, kissing my inked flesh, then bit along the edges of it. His arm crushed me against him, rough and demanding.

"I'm honored. This is beautiful." He lifted his head, giving me those deep, dark eyes. "I wrote 'Angel Moon' when someone I once knew was going through something unspeakable that would break a lot of people. Not her. Just like you, you're not broken either." He bit my side again, dropping his forehead there as he exhaled a long, slow breath.

"I'm just starting to believe that might be true." I patted his sweaty hair and stared up at the ceiling, unsure of anything. "I should go get dressed."

"Yeah."

For the longest time, neither of us moved. He held me there, and I let myself sink into his arms. Finally, Dominic's alarm got us moving. I threw on my clothes from last night, hoping I wouldn't run into anyone we knew in the hall. When I straightened with my shoes in my hand, Dominic was sitting on the corner of the bed, keeping vigil over me.

I sighed, pushing my hair off my face. "Is this where we have some big talk?"

He opened his hands. "I don't need to have a talk. Do you?"

"No, I'd rather avoid that, thanks."

He stood and closed in on me, cupping my nape. "For the same reason you didn't want to talk about the last time you spent the night in my bed?"

Because you might say it can't happen again, and I don't want to hear that.

"It could be."

Dominic nibbled on my bottom lip, his hold firm on my neck. "Good. Then I'll see you in an hour."

"Mmmhmmm." I leaned into him, taking just a few more of his sweet-like-arsenic kisses for the road. "See you later, sir."

Dominic shoved me away with a smack on the ass and a low, rumbling chuckle from his chest. I ran back to my room like a thief in the night, unseen by anyone I knew.

The first thing I did was call my sister.

"Hello, whore," she answered.

I groaned. "If you only knew."

"You gave it up? What a floozy! Tell me everything." Annaliese sounded as excited as she'd been when I told her I got this job. If she tried to throw me another celebration dinner, I'd have to draw the line.

"I just came from his room."

"Who? I don't even know which gentleman caller you'd decided on. Or...was it both?"

I snickered and fell back on my bed. "There was only one, and I don't think anything we did could constitute as gentlemanly."

"Okay. I'm really proud of you for getting banged dirty. But you still haven't said who you were with."

"Dominic. So inappropriate." But I couldn't find it in myself to regret him.

She sighed, but it didn't sound especially judgmental. "Wow. When you go big, you go *big*."

"*Big*," I concurred.

That made Annaliese laugh. "I am...I am flummoxed. Truly. How old is he again?"

"Forty-two." I cringed because our age difference was also *big*.

"And...? Did it feel weird being with a man who could be your father if he'd had you in high school?"

"Well, now it does." My arm flopped over my head onto my pillow. "No, it didn't feel weird. He was incredible. So much so, I hardly felt self-conscious being naked in front of him. Like, there wasn't even a chance for my brain to formulate those thoughts. They just didn't happen."

A big breath whooshed out of my sister. "That *is* incredible."

"Yeah."

"So, you have sex with an extremely famous rock star who made your brain switch off, and now, you're...what?"

My lips curved up with how good I felt. "Satisfied. I just...I'm not overthinking things. There's not a chance of Dominic and I actually being together outside of this situation, so if it happens again, I won't protest."

"I love that for you, baby. I love it so hard. You deserve a little slice of satisfaction after everything. Are you going to come back to me a brand-new Claire?"

I thought of the friends I'd made, my experiences, and Dominic. Yes, I'd changed already. But I'd already been on this path since my husband knocked me unconscious in our bedroom. I couldn't be that girl anymore. She wasn't an option. I was only finding out who the woman I was becoming would be.

"I think so. Now, tell me, how are you? Did you go out with that chick from Tinder?"

"You mean the psycho who cackled like a damn witch at my, and I quote, "little plant hobby"? Because yes, I went out with her, we had sex, and she ghosted."

Annaliese spilled her dating woes, and I listened with a curl of a smile on my lips and a light heart. I still had battles to fight and walls to climb, but those were far off in the distance. I'd just had ridiculously hot sex this morning, and it deserved one whole day to be the center of my thoughts. Tomorrow, I might allow thoughts of Derrick and my divorce and my lack of home to slip in, but there was every possibility I might not.

CHAPTER TWENTY-TWO

CLAIRE

DOMINIC FELL OVER ME, sweaty and panting. His full weight crushed me into the bed, and I wrapped my legs around his waist to keep him there. Not that he seemed to be going anywhere. His arms were banded around my shoulders, and his cock was still firmly planted inside me. We were both shaking. He tried to catch his breath while I tried to catch reality.

But this was real.

We'd arrived at our Salt Lake City hotel an hour ago. It took five minutes for Dominic to barge into my room. Another couple for him to rid me of my clothes. And a few after that for me to come.

"Jesus." He groaned, lifting his head from my neck to peer down at me. "Pretty sure you're going to kill me." His hand came up to my jaw, cupping me roughly. "How is my dick still hard when I just came? What magic spell do you have inside you?"

I grinned, clenching around him. The smile was wiped from my lips when he thrust forward, swelling against my sensitive walls.

"Claire…" He smacked the side of my thigh. "No more."

With a sigh, I let my legs fall to the mattress so Dominic could pull out. He stayed for another half a minute longer, dragging his teeth over the bite marks he'd left around my nipples, then he shifted to lay beside me. He took care of the condom, tying it off in a tight knot and wrapping it in a tissue, then he captured my jaw in his hand, his mouth coming down hard on mine. His tongue swept into my mouth, tasting me until I couldn't breathe, but I didn't give a damn.

He yanked his lips from mine and looked like he was angry at me for making him kiss me again. His eyebrows pinched tight over inky black pools. Fingers curled in my hair. Breath grazed my cheek.

"Let's go to dinner."

My lips parted, but no words came out. He'd surprised me. Having dinner together was the last thing I'd expected him to suggest.

"Come on. There's a place I want to go that I think you'll like. I'll have my security make the arrangements." Dominic squeezed my breast, dipping his head to suck my nipple into his mouth. "Or I could fuck you again."

Heat throbbed between my legs. "We should probably eat first." The anticipation of what would happen when we returned to the hotel would be so crazy hot, I was willing to press pause. "But wait. *Can* you go out to dinner? At a regular restaurant?"

He chuckled against my skin. "Yes, Claire. I'm able to go to dinner."

I slapped his shoulder. "Fuck you, Dominic." The growl he emitted had me laughing. "I meant, won't you be mobbed? Your fans know you're in town…"

"Don't worry about it. My guys will handle it. People might show up, take some pictures if they get a chance, but the place I want to take you is pretty private."

"All right." I scratched the skin under his beard, then tugged him down for another quick kiss. "I'm convinced."

His hand came down on my thigh again. "Good girl. I'm gonna head to my room and clean up. Is an hour enough time for you to get ready?"

In my past life, I would have needed more than that. Derrick only liked my hair straight, but I embraced the curls these days, my makeup routine had been pared down, and my clothes were simple. Still, it was sort of sweet for Dominic to think I put a lot of time into getting ready.

"That's plenty," I answered.

I saw him on his way, took a quick shower since I smelled too much like sex to be fit for the public, then dug through my clothes, settling on a kelly green jersey dress that nipped my waist so tight, *I* actually found myself hot, which wasn't a common occurrence.

Only a half hour had gone by when there was a knock on the door. I opened it with bare feet and no lipstick, but otherwise ready. It wasn't Dominic standing on the other side, though.

"Look at you, C." Marta gave me an exaggerated once-over. "Pretty, pretty."

"Well, thanks, M. With the shape this dress gives me, I should have bought fifty of them."

She reached out and gave my waist a pinch. "I've seen you in a bikini, woman. Don't be shy."

I should have invited her in, but even though I'd made the bed, there had to be sex pheromones in the air. I wasn't at all prepared to answer any questions—especially not from Marta.

"You're making me blush. Stop it." One foot pressed on top of the other, and I leaned my head on the edge of the door. "What's up?"

"I wanted to see if you wanted to go grab dinner. Did I send you a psychic message that I was going to ask so you got dressed up for me?"

"Actually," I glanced down at my bare toes, "Dominic and I are going to grab a bite."

"Oh." Marta's slitted brow rose, then she backed up a step. "I see."

I reached for her arm, but she backed up another step. "It's not like that. Please. He just wanted company, and I happened to be the first person he saw."

"I got it. I'll just go check in with Iris and friends. One of them is bound to be hungry." She slinked off down the hall before I could say another word, which made me feel sick.

I should have known this would happen. We didn't live in a vacuum where only Dominic and I existed. We were traveling in close quarters with a lot of people who would notice us hanging out...if that was what we were doing.

I texted Marta, hoping she'd forgive me.

Come to dinner with us! Don't be mad at me.

It took her a few minutes, but she finally texted me back.

It's all good. I'm with Iris and Callum. Maybe we'll both get laid tonight.

Me: *It's not like that, M.*

Marta: *C, please. It's so like that. I know Dominic. He doesn't take women out to dinner if he's not banging them too. Just don't let yourself get wrapped up. He won't.*

Me: *Have fun tonight. Breakfast?*

Marta: *Yeah, let's do that. But if I show up at your room and see Dominic's naked ass, I won't be thrilled.*

Me: *I will make sure no asses are naked. Xoxo*

Marta: *xxx *wink**

Dominic showed up just as I was dissolving into a pit of self-hatred. I tried not to show it, but he grabbed me by the jaw and examined my face like a soothsayer reading tea leaves.

"What's wrong?" he demanded.

"Marta asked me to have dinner with her. She put two and two together pretty quickly when I told her you and I had plans." I tapped his open lips. "And no, I am not quick enough on my feet to come up with a plausible lie. So, there you go. She knows."

He took my finger between his teeth and growled, but not angrily. "Marta knows everything. There's no sense in even attempting to hide from her." He gave my butt a smack. "Let's go."

I shoved my feet into brown leather sandals that had a short heel and grabbed a small purse that only fit my phone and lipstick. Dominic's two bodyguards accompanied us in the elevator. He didn't touch me at all, but I didn't mind. We weren't a couple. We weren't going to walk around holding hands while staring into each other's eyes.

In the car, Dominic took his usual position across from me, and only then did he really take me in. My knees were tucked to the side, skirt flowing over them. Normally when I wore this dress, I put a camisole beneath, but not tonight. The deep V left the upper swells of my breasts exposed. In the hotel, I felt somewhat daring. In this car, I had become unsure.

Dominic said nothing. His expression remained stoic. He never stopped drinking me in, but he always did that.

My insecurity was a deep-rooted thing that had been carefully tended to over the years. My husband had complimented me, but only when I was absolutely perfect. If he were here, he would take one look at me and ask me if I wanted to be confused with trash, because that was what I looked like. I could almost hear his voice, but I shook it off.

I liked compliments as much as the next woman, and I'd gotten an epic one from Marta earlier, so I really didn't need one from Dominic. I sure wouldn't be telling him how sexy his arms were peeking out from the sleeves of his button-up shirt. Or how I wondered if the heavy silver watch on his wrist would feel cool on my heated skin if he touched me. No, I'd keep that to myself.

The car pulled up to the side of a nondescript restaurant, and we were escorted inside to a small, partitioned area near the back. The interior of the restaurant was just as plain as the outside, but the Mason jar of wildflowers surrounded by fairy lights in the middle of the table gave me a fuzzy feeling about the place.

"This is awfully cute for you." I gestured to the lights and flowers and gauzy white fabric draping from the screen separating us from the rest of the restaurant. "I'm surprised this is your spot."

Taking the seat beside me instead of across, he straightened his collar and arched a midnight brow. "This isn't my spot. I've been here a few times and thought you might like it."

"How thoughtful." I picked up my menu, blocking my view of him. I hated that I was annoyed with him. It wasn't entirely his fault. Marta finding out about us already had me on edge before he even showed up.

"Claire—" He pushed down the top of my menu, but whatever he had intended to say was interrupted by our waitress.

"Hi, I'm Layla. How are you tonight?"

Dominic murmured that he was fine, which made her beam pearly white teeth at him. His eyes flicked to her and held for a beat before returning to the menu.

"I'd love to answer any questions you have about the menu or make a drink suggestion if you'd like." She placed her hand on the table directly beside where Dominic's rested.

Layla was pretty, in a very obvious way. I didn't have to study her or examine her features to find what made her special. One glance and—*boom!*—pretty. I didn't fault her for that, since prettiness was mostly an accident of birth and she couldn't help it any more than I could help that I sometimes blended into furniture until someone got to know me.

What I didn't love about Layla was that she only addressed Dominic. I might as well have not been at the table. That made her both a shitty waitress and crappy human.

Dominic didn't look at her again. His eyes found mine, and a flare of amusement lit in the black depths of his gaze. He knew exactly what she was doing, and he found it funny.

We ordered drinks, and then dinner when she returned minutes later. Dominic didn't try to address me again until after she'd retreated a second time.

He leveled me with a heavy, black stare that read trouble. With no menu to hide behind, I had to face him. Taking a deep breath, I waited for him to say what he needed to, hoping it wasn't more than I could handle.

CHAPTER TWENTY-THREE

DOMINIC

CLAIRE WAS...maddening.

Not that it was her fault. Not really.

Seeing her neatly made bed when I picked her up for dinner had sent me deep into my own head—a place I never liked spending much time.

"Claire." Despite the shitstorm taking up residence in my skull, the pissed off woman across from me had me fighting off a smile.

"Dominic." She had no idea how stunning she looked right now, her cheeks full of color, traveling all the way down the dip in her dress. The shape of her breasts caught me up, distracting me. My fingers twitched to take them in hand.

Then I remembered how she'd smoothed out her sheets and fluffed up her pillows, erasing the time we'd spent in her bed earlier. Something about that image stabbed a place in my gut I'd forgotten existed.

"Did you make your bed after I left?"

She straightened in her chair, unintentionally pushing her breasts out. "I did. Why?"

"Do you always do that?"

"I do. It's a reflex at this point." She shifted in her seat uncomfortably. "What makes you ask?"

"It surprised me. I couldn't even tell I'd been there."

"Is that really a problem?" She'd stiffened, her shoulders drawing inward—*all of her* drawing inward.

"No." I raked my fingers over my hair. "No, fuck. Of course it's not. Your bed, you keep it how you like."

She toyed with one of the lights in the center of the table, rubbing her thumb over the glowing bulb, letting silence descend over the table. It gave me time to think of how I would phrase the proposition I'd been mulling over for several days.

"Claire."

"Hmmm?" She ran the tip of her finger over the delicate petal of a daisy, not bothering to glance up.

"I can't get you out of my head."

That got her attention. Her eyes shot up to mine, startled. "What?"

I grabbed the back of her neck, tugging her closer to run my nose over her collarbone and throat. Beneath her curls were my marks. She carefully hid them, but just thinking about them being there got me hard.

"When I walked into your room tonight and that bed was made like no one had been in it, I kept thinking about the times Adam had been in your room before me. Was he in your bed? It's none of my fucking business, and I don't want you to tell me."

She steadied herself on my chest, her breath stuttering, but she didn't speak. I guess I hadn't really asked a question.

I plowed on. "The thing is, Claire, I don't want him in your bed—or anyone else."

"You don't?" Her words held surprise and an edge of mistrust, which I didn't understand.

"No. We've got four more weeks on this tour, and I want you to be mine for the duration. Every night, you're mine. In my bed or yours, it doesn't matter. I've thought this out, and I really believe this is the only way I'm going to be able to get you out of my head."

I dipped my head to lick the fluttering pulse in her neck. There would be a point when I tired of her scent and the feel of her skin, but we were nowhere near it.

She curled her fingers in the back of my hair, yanking me away. "Do I get any kind of say?"

"Of course." I settled back in my chair, immediately regretting the loss of her under my hand. "Tell me what you think."

Her hands were busy on the table, straightening silverware and smoothing the cloth. "What if four weeks is too long?"

Her question was a tree trunk to the chest, solid and unexpected, knocking me out. "Too long? For who?"

Her gleaming eyes flicked to mine. "Me. Or you. That's basically a month, which is longer than I've known you."

This girl...this fucking girl. She'd been throwing me off my game since the second she stumbled onto my airplane. I couldn't say what I'd been expecting with this proposition, but it hadn't been this. To be honest, I'd almost entirely been considering myself, fairly assured Claire's agreement was a given.

Our conversation paused when our waitress reappeared with our dinner. She set down our plates, brushing against me unnecessarily. Her hand rested on the back of my chair as she bent forward next to me.

"Is there anything else I can get you?" she purred.

"There's nothing. You can go."

She straightened quickly, murmuring to let her know if we needed her as she hurried away. Claire shook her head like she disapproved of me.

"You don't like how I spoke to her?" I asked.

"Not much." She picked up her fork and poked around at her dinner.

"Did you enjoy her hitting on me in front of you?"

Unbothered still, she scooped up some of her eggplant souffle. "I didn't enjoy it, but it didn't make me want to fly into a jealous rage. I imagine that happens often. Actually, I've seen it happen everywhere I go with you. People want to be near you and be with you because of who you are. I understand that."

Her lips wrapped around her fork, eyelids fluttering at the taste on her tongue. A little moan escaped her, landing directly in my lap. I'd already fucked her seven ways from Sunday, but my cock ached to be inside her again.

I didn't like this, wanting her but not being certain I could have her. If she'd just agree to my proposition, I could relax and enjoy this fucking dinner.

"Is that why you won't agree to the four weeks? Do you think I'll be sleeping around?" I asked.

One shoulder lifted. "You have to admit you sprung this on me without warning."

"Maybe. It's been weighing on my mind for a while now, but I see that doesn't mean it's been weighing on yours too."

She wiped her mouth with her napkin. "It honestly hasn't. You're the first man I've slept with since my separation. The last thing I'm thinking of is 'what next.' I'm taking everything moment by moment, and then you want me to agree to almost an entire month. That's a lot for me."

What she said made sense, but her words tangled together, making them hard for me to swallow. I needed her to say yes. I couldn't walk around occupied with thoughts of her day in and day out.

"Claire, you have to know when I say four weeks, I mean four weeks. We'll both walk away at the end of this with our memories, but that's it. I'm not proposing marriage, I'm talking about four weeks of really explosive sex and maybe a few dinners if we happen to be hungry at the same time."

This was the only way we could work. Claire wasn't looking for anything more than sex. I sure as hell wasn't either. But over the last few days since we'd started sleeping together, I found I needed a guarantee. Not just that I could have her for the rest of the tour, but that we both were firm in our end date.

She tucked her hair behind her ear. "Can I think about it?"

"Do you need to?"

"Yes, I do. And I'd like to eat my dinner without you staring a hole in my skull." She nudged me under the table with her toes. "You too. Eat, please."

"Claire—"

Her hand covered mine. "Did you bring me here for this, or because you thought I'd like the food here?"

I flipped my hand over to lock our fingers together. "I didn't bring you here for this."

"I know you're used to having your every whim catered to right when you want it, but I need time. If you can't give it to me, then the answer will be no."

My fingers flexed around hers, pulse skyrocketing. "No?"

"I don't like to feel pressured or controlled. It's something I'm just learning about myself, and right now, I'm feeling both from you."

I released her hand immediately and sat back in my chair with a heavy exhale. "I apologize. I never purposely want to make you feel that way."

"I know that," she said simply. "So, let's eat dinner. This souffle is too delicious for me to let it get cold."

My chicken tasted like sawdust through no fault to the chef. My mind was far too occupied with pinning Claire down to have space left over to register the flavor of the food I kept shoveling into my mouth.

"How did you meet Marta?" Claire asked.

I tossed down my fork, giving up on eating for now. "Seems like she's always been around."

"But she hasn't."

"Nah, she hasn't." My finger tapped the table, itching to touch Claire again. "I was in a bad mindset. I'd fired pretty much everyone who worked for me except my housekeeper, Milagros. One day, she brought her smart-ass daughter with her to help her clean, and she somehow convinced me to hire her to be my assistant. It was a whole lot of being in the right place at the right time."

Claire's foot touched mine, and when she left it there, I had no doubt it was on purpose.

"Did she make you laugh?"

"In a way." I rubbed my forehead, wishing I didn't have to tell Claire this part of the story. But if I didn't, Marta would, and I liked my version better. "I was out on my patio with my guitar while they cleaned. Marta marched up to me with rubber gloves on, swinging a used condom. She called me a pig for leaving it on the floor in my room, and she wasn't wrong. I just...didn't care about much back then, but Milagros deserved more respect than that, and Marta fucking told me."

Claire pressed her hands to her cheeks. "God, I love Marta more than all the stars in the sky."

That made me chuckle even though I didn't have a lot of humor in me tonight. "She has a way about her."

"I don't suppose you'll tell me why you were so miserable." There was no question in her statement. Claire didn't know me well, but it was obvious to most people who had a couple conversations with me I was closed off.

"You're right."

She took another bite and let her foot slide alongside mine until our calves touched.

"That's fine. I don't need to know anything else about you. I bet you're boring beyond the brooding and the fame and the tattoos and—"

I had her neck in my hand and my mouth covering hers before she could say another word. If she wanted to play, I'd play right back. Only, my version had her coming before we left this restaurant.

"Go to the bathroom, Claire."

She shook her head. "I don't need to."

"You do. I'll meet you there in one minute. Have your panties off when I get there."

She hesitated for a handful of seconds, then she was out of her seat, gracefully walking through the restaurant. I counted in my head, my knees bouncing as I waited.

At exactly sixty, I followed the path Claire took. She stood in the middle of the single stall bathroom, black panties draping from her finger. "What now?" she breathed.

I gripped her waist, backing her into the counter. "Now, you spread your legs for me."

"People will hear…" Even as she protested, she lifted her dress.

I snagged her panties and held them up to her mouth. "You don't want anyone to hear, then you'll have to be quiet. If you don't think you can, open those pretty lips for me."

Gliding my hand up the inside of her silky-soft thigh, I squeezed and pinched until I found her heated center. Two fingers dipping into her wetness was all it took for her to moan, opening those lips for me just like I'd asked. I stuffed the lacy fabric into her mouth, then fell to my knees in front of her.

Claire had been driving me crazy all night, so this wasn't for her. I'd eat her pussy out, have her moaning my name, and it would be all for me. She could come, but it would be *my* orgasm.

With a tight hold on her thighs, I dipped my head to sink my teeth into the underside of her ass. She shook from one touch of my mouth, that was how much she wanted this. One long drag of my tongue through her folds tasted like my ticket to damnation.

I threw Claire's legs over my shoulders and buried my face between them. My beard and lips were soaked with her. She writhed under my ministrations, muffled groans still echoing off the tiled walls. Sharp fingernails dug into the back of my head as she drew me closer and pushed me away at the same time.

Another bite in the crease of her thigh reined in her fight, but she didn't stop moving with my tongue.

My shy, sweet Claire couldn't get enough of my mouth on her sex. Her hips rolled, dragging her slick folds along my tongue. This woman turned me on like no one ever had, and I couldn't even say why. A thousand reasons maybe. She turned my cock to steel and strained the fabric of my pants. My skin felt tight everywhere, like I'd explode out of it in seconds.

The torture was sweet.

I reveled in the pain of pleasuring Claire for no other reason than I wanted it.

She came hard, jerking hips and tossed hair. Her nails scrabbled for purchase on the counter, thighs clenching around my head. Her panties fell from her mouth onto the floor beside me, and I swiped them up, stuffing them in my pocket for later.

Freeing myself from the steel trap of Claire's thighs, I stood, pulling her pliant body flush with mine. "What's your answer now?" I licked along the seam of her puffy lips. "Did that change your mind?"

Claire's eyes flew open, the clouds parting immediately. "You made me come so I'd say yes? You asshole."

My lips twitched. "I made you come because I love the taste of you, Claire. I made you come because I can't get enough of it. It would be a side benefit if having an orgasm made you more amenable to my offer."

"Well..." she gave my beard a hard, mean tug, "it didn't." She shoved away from me, throwing open the bathroom door and stalking out.

On the ride back to the hotel, I kept Claire's foot between mine. She didn't fight me on that, but when we arrived at her room, she did. I tried to follow her inside, but she blocked her doorway.

"I'm not in the mood, Dominic. Go to your own room."

"I'm sleeping with you." Hands under her elbows, I backed her into her room, kicking the door closed behind me. "I want in your bed."

She folded her arms, pushing her breasts together. They were so close to spilling out of her dress, I had to force myself not to hold my breath.

"I'm angry with you. I want you to go."

"No." I closed in on her and slipped my hand inside her dress to cup her breast. "You don't. You don't want to answer me, that's fine. Be angry. I'll give you space for that. We don't have to have sex, but I am sleeping with you tonight."

"I'd be more convinced if your hand wasn't down my dress." Some of the edge had left her voice, and her lips parted with a pant when my thumb brushed over her pebbled nipple.

"I promise, Claire." I slid my hand out of her dress and held her jaw gently. "I'll watch *The* fucking *Golden Girls* with you if you want."

Brown eyes moved back and forth between mine, checking for my sincerity, I guessed. Finally, she huffed, relenting. "Okay. You can stay. I'm going to get out of this dress."

I kept her in my arms when she tried to move. "Let me have another look at you before you take it off."

She swallowed hard. "Do you like the way I look in this?"

"Claire." I pinched her chin between two fingers. "I just kneeled down on the floor of a public bathroom to eat your cunt because of how insanely beautiful you are and how goddamn hot you looked sitting beside me."

"You didn't say."

"I didn't?" I scratched my head, rifling through my memories of the night. "My thoughts were screaming so loud, I must've thought you could hear them. My mistake."

Taking her hand, I twirled her in a tight circle in front of me, whistling softly. "Beauty," I murmured.

"Thank you. That's nice to hear." She tugged away from me and disappeared into the bathroom to change into pajamas. While she was gone, I took off my shirt and dress pants, laid them across a chair, then climbed into bed.

A few minutes later, Claire crawled in beside me, smelling like mint and honey. She tried to stay on her side, but I wrapped my arms around her middle and brought her to me. She settled against me, her round ass cradled in my pelvis. I nuzzled the back of her neck, making goose bumps rise on her freckled skin.

"What if one of us doesn't like this arrangement in a week or two? Will I lose my job?" she asked.

"I don't see that happening."

"I need you to tell me what if." Her fingers traced the black lines of the tattoos on my hand.

"You won't lose your job. If this isn't working for you, then you tell me, and that'll be that."

"And if this isn't working for you?" she pressed.

"I'm not going to be an issue."

"You sound so sure."

"I know my own mind. I want you, and that won't change until the tour is over and we walk away."

She twisted her head to look at me. "What if you fall for me?"

"I won't." I took her face in my hand to make sure she heard what I was saying. "Four weeks is all I have in me. I like you, Claire. I want to be around you and inside you, but I'm not going to be in a relationship with you. Not beyond this tour. I don't think you want that either."

"I don't. You're right."

"Say yes." I kissed her smooth cheek twice, then the underside of her bottom lip. "Say yes, Claire."

She shivered in my arms, but still resisted. "Will you really be in my bed every night?"

"That's right."

"I'll probably be annoyed with you and kick you out within a week."

I had her, so I allowed a small smile to slip out. "Probably. Say yes anyway so I can watch some TV and go to sleep."

"Yes," she whispered. "You have to leave early, though. Marta's coming for breakfast and I really don't need her seeing you in my room."

A startling amount of relief flooded my veins. I kissed her supple lips hard, sucking and biting them until they were rosy and swollen, marking where I'd been and where I'd keep going. This girl was mine. Not forever, but for as long as I wanted.

"We'll see."

She kicked back, but I caught her foot with mine and trapped her leg between my legs. "Stay still, Claire."

When she finally relaxed in my arms, I breathed easier. Now that I had her, I could spend the next four weeks working her out of my system. When the last day came, we'd both be ready to walk away for good. Of that, I had no doubt.

CHAPTER TWENTY-FOUR

CLAIRE

DOMINIC TOOK HIS SWEET TIME LEAVING MY ROOM. He'd barely pulled up his pants by the time Marta showed up. I tried to shove him in the bathroom, but he opened the door for her like nothing out of the ordinary was happening.

"Morning, Mar."

He backed away to let her inside. She had a slight sneer on her face, but when she looked at me, she smiled.

"Good morning to Claire and Claire only." She gave him an appraising once-over. "At least I didn't have to see your ass."

He hooked his arm around her shoulders and kissed the side of her head. "You would have enjoyed it if you had."

She elbowed him off her. "Mmmhmmm. That's why I've been working for you all these years. Just biding my time until I could catch a peek."

Dominic actually laughed. It wasn't loud, and it didn't last, but it was a true laugh he didn't cover. My stomach flipped at the sight of the crinkles around his eyes and the flash of his white teeth. Not because he was gorgeous—he was—but because I often thought Dominic carried sorrow with him like a flak jacket, and for just a few seconds, he'd let down his guard, allowing a bit of happiness to seep in.

"Are we cool, Mar?" He shrugged on his shirt, eyebrow raised as he buttoned it.

She waved him off. "I thought my girl had better taste, but yeah, we're cool. Now, go away so C and I can have breakfast. We see enough of you at work."

"No breakfast for me?"

She narrowed her eyes on him. "Being delivered to your room momentarily, as always. Go before it gets cold."

He shoved his shoes on and gave me the barest of smiles. "All right. I'll head out. We're gonna have to rethink the breakfast situation, though. I'm not going to be kicked out of bed for the rest of this tour so you can hang out with Claire." He took my hand and clamped his teeth on the meaty part of my palm by my thumb. "You drive me crazy," he murmured.

"I'm innocent," I whispered back through the flutters his teeth on my flesh never failed to induce.

"I know. Which is exactly why I'm going out of my mind." He laid one hard kiss on the inside of my wrist, then headed for the door, tossing a wave over his shoulder.

Once he was gone, I dug into the bag Marta brought with her while she made coffee. After doctoring up a bagel, I settled against the headboard of my bed.

Marta handed me a paper cup full of steaming coffee. It probably tasted like piss, but I'd take it. She sat cross-legged on my padded desk chair, swiveling in my direction. I swallowed down the bite of bagel in my mouth.

"Are you thoroughly disappointed in me?" I asked.

She grinned, shaking her head. "No. Dominic did what Dominic always does." She sipped her coffee with a grimace. "But what the hell did he mean by the rest of the tour? This isn't a hit-it-and-quit-it situation?"

"Well, we've been messing around for a couple weeks and—"

She sat up straight, slamming her empty hand down on the arm of her chair. "A couple *weeks*? Where the hell have I been?"

"I guess we've been discreet. I certainly didn't want anyone to know. It's just sex, so it's not like we're going to be walking around holding hands to announce we're a thing."

Her head tilted. "But *are* you a thing?"

"We're a thing for the rest of the tour, then we'll both walk away. Believe me, when Dominic brought it up last night, I was skeptical. And I still am. But we'll see how it goes."

Marta knocked on her forehead like she was trying to physically push my words inside. "This does not compute with the man I know. Besides Izzy, he doesn't have regular lays. I mean…" she made an hourglass shape with her hands, "I get it. You're fine as hell and undemanding and probably not looking to be tied down since you're going through a divorce…"

"First, thank you for the compliment. It means so much. Second, Dominic and Isabela still hook up?"

Marta winced. "Yeah. I don't know when the last time was, but she's always slithering around. The woman cheated on him and left him in the middle of a tour. She's a ridiculous creature. I can't stand that he keeps allowing her back into his life in any capacity."

It was my turn to rub my head. "That's a lot of brand-new information."

I'd known Isabela and Dominic had been married several years ago, but I had no idea they were still *something* to each other. That made this whole thing…uncomfortable. More untoward. I certainly didn't want to get in between their entanglement. I would never be that girl—the man poacher, the toe stepper.

The smile Marta gave me was apologetic. "Sorry, I normally don't run my mouth, but I'm so thrown off by everything."

"Thanks for being cool about this. I was really worried last night."

She shook her head. "Nah, girl. Sometimes it takes me a while to process surprises, but I'm not mad at you for getting while the getting's good. Honestly, Dominic's probably the ideal post-divorce hookup. He locked away his heart a long time ago. It's probably all withered and dry like a raisin at this point. You know he won't catch feels and it can just be an uncomplicated fling. Any other man, I'd be worried, because you're immensely loveable." The wink she gave me softened the truth of who Dominic was.

"You really do know all the right things to say." I crossed the space between us, bending down to give her a tight hug. In the short time I'd known her, I'd formed a kinship with her I didn't see ending after the tour. "Now, you have to tell me about your night. I need all the tea to be spilled."

I sat down in front of her on the edge of my bed. She set her coffee on the desk and wiped her palms on her jeans.

"So...we went out to dinner. Rodrigo, Iris, and me. Some Mexican joint, good chips, terrible everything else. Anyway, they had a live band, so obviously we danced. Roddy went to the bathroom at some point, and Iris took the opportunity to kiss me."

I squealed and kicked my feet. "Oh my god! How was it?"

She flattened her hand and wobbled it back and forth. "We were both two margaritas deep, so it was a little sloppy. There weren't the fireworks I was hoping for, but she has *nice* lips."

"Okay, I can work with that. So, she's gay?"

Marta bit the corner of her lip. "Not confirmed."

That made me laugh. "I guess sloppy margarita kisses aren't confirmation. Are you going to pursue or just see what happens?"

"I don't even know. I've had a crush on her forever. Now that it might actually happen, I can't decide if I'm more into the idea of her or *her*. I mean, she's like this hardcore goddess. Do I really want to be another one of her worshippers?"

"Sounds like cold feet, lady."

Her eyes rolled, but she grinned. "I know. I'm never like this with women, but Iris..."

"She's something else," I finished.

"She is. Anyway, *she* didn't pursue me after the kiss, so it might have just been the margs talking."

I groaned. "Is this seriously what dating's going to be like? Do people not just talk to each other?"

Marta chuckled. "Oh, girl. I don't know what straight dating's like, but shit ain't easy out there. You'd think cutting men out of the equation would make things easier, but it doesn't. Women still play games, cheat, fall in and out of love in a blink. I'm not saying I'm innocent either."

"God, I thought I'd really lucked out. Derrick and I were just *together*, you know? Pretty much from the start, we were a couple. We said we liked each other, and that was it. Granted, we were nineteen…" I knotted my T-shirt around my fingers. "I can't believe I'm here. Being single again, starting from scratch… it's just the last place I ever imagined myself."

I could have kicked myself for the tears welling in my eyes, but I refused to let them fall.

"Baby," Marta soothed. "You're so upbeat, I keep forgetting you're going through it right now." She sat beside me on the bed, circling her arm around my shoulders. "Can I ask what ended your marriage or is that off-limits?"

Releasing a heavy breath, I let my head fall on her shoulder for a moment, then I gathered myself and twisted to face her. "I figured out he'd been cheating on me. He admitted it had been going on for over a year, then begged me to stay. The second I knew he'd cheated, my mind was made up. I was leaving, no matter how hard he tried to fight me."

Marta looked ready to throw down, and she didn't even know the half of it. "Fuck him. I already know this guy is a total fucking waste of space. I'm glad you're done with him, C."

"Me too. He got rough with me when I told him I was leaving, and I'd like to say I saw the monster he was then, but when I think back, he'd always been a monster. He hid it most of the time, and he'd never physically hurt me before, but he's awful. Controlling and angry. I didn't work because he wanted me home. He presented it as loving me so much, he wanted me to always be there when he came home in the evenings, but looking back, it's so easy to see it for what it was."

I hadn't intended on telling Marta any of this, but once I started, it was like an avalanche, each secret picked up another, then another, tumbling out until I was wiped clean. For her part, Marta listened intently, holding my hand in hers.

"Did that asshole go to jail?" she asked, her tone much milder than her words.

"No. I didn't report him. I just wanted to be done with him." I waved thoughts of Derrick away. "I've figured out I settled with him. I thought he was as good as I could get, so I settled. Next time, if there *is* a next time, I won't. I'll wait for the man who sees me as his equal."

Marta tipped her chin, giving me a pointed look. "And one who worships you like a fucking warrior queen, Claire."

"Right." I grinned at her. "A warrior queen. I'll remember that."

She hugged me tight, gently stroking the back of my hair. "I'm so sorry he hurt you, baby. My deadbeat dad used to beat on my mom, and since he was a U.S. citizen and she wasn't, she felt like she couldn't leave. She waited until she was a permanent resident, then got my brother and me out of there." Marta pulled back, patting my cheeks twice. "Being hurt by the man who's supposed to love you doesn't mean you're not a strong woman. It means the man is weak."

Nodding, I swallowed down the lump in my throat. I'd have to remember that too. Derrick's abuse would never mean I was a weak woman. He was the weak one. My only fault was not seeing it sooner.

"Thank you, M. I'm really glad I met you."

"Me too, C." She took me by the shoulders, giving me a shake. "Now, I'm going to be rooting for you to get all the no-strings dick you can on this tour. Obviously, I'll train my brain to forget it's Dominic's dick you'll be getting, but..."

Laughing hard, I fell back on the bed. "By the way, he told me about the condom that forged the start of your friendship."

Marta flopped down beside me. "Wow, Dominic actually told you something personal? And he wants you all to himself for the rest of the tour? That's practically a marriage proposal."

"Oh, no, don't say that. I'll have to end it right now."

"No, don't do that. I take it back"

It worried me, just a little, that the idea of ending this crazy, outlandish thing with Dominic early filled me with bubbles of panic. I pushed it away. It didn't matter when it ended. We both knew it would, and that was the important thing to hang on to.

CHAPTER TWENTY-FIVE

CLAIRE

ISABELA CALLED ME THE DAY AFTER WE LEFT UTAH FOR BOISE, Idaho. She caught me in a rare moment alone in my hotel room while Dominic was at the gym and Marta was off doing something for him.

"Hello," I answered.

"Claire. How is the tour going?"

We'd kept in constant contact, emailing every other day. She'd called a couple times, but not often. She wasn't especially chatty, so I doubted she was really calling to have a friendly conversation.

"Really well. I'm surprised by how fast it's breezing by."

Isabela took a deep breath. "Good, good. Have you checked Dominic's socials today?"

Part of my job was to be on top of Dominic's social media. I scanned for his name over all the platforms, checking for any stories we needed to spin or pictures we could use. He had people who ran his accounts, but I flagged anything for them I thought they should give special attention to.

"No, not yet. We flew in late last night, so I—"

Isabela cut me off. "That's fine. One of my interns—you remember Marley, right?—alerted me to a picture posted on a young woman's Instagram account. She's a waitress in Salt Lake City." She paused, and my stomach sank. "You see where I'm going with this?"

"Am I in the picture?" I asked.

"I didn't notice you at first—not until Marley pointed you out." *So much for loyalty among underlings.* "Do you remember why I hired you for this job, Claire?"

I sighed. "Nothing inappropriate has happened. Dominic wanted company, Marta was out with other people, so I went along with him."

None of that was a lie. Technically. I shouldn't be sleeping with Dominic, but I'd already made that choice, so I couldn't take it back. I'd found I was perfectly capable of doing my job anyway. I wasn't a jealous woman, clinging to him when I should have been working. So far, I'd been able to compartmentalize and keep each side of our relationship separate.

Dominic was the one who kept grabbing my ass and biting my neck the second we were alone. Maybe I should have Isabela call him.

"I want you to know you're nothing special," Isabela said without venom. In fact, her tone was soft, almost comforting. "That restaurant Dominic took you to? He took me there before we slept together the first time. It's where he takes women he has to work a little bit harder to get. Of course, I didn't know that at the time. I thought it was a sweet little place, with the Ball jars and twinkle lights. So, if you truly haven't slept with Dominic yet, don't. It would be a colossal mistake for you and mean absolutely nothing to him. Don't spoil your potential for a man who will never care for you."

I sat down on my neatly made bed, slack-jawed. I couldn't quite figure out what to say. Isabela was so far out of line, but in a way, she wasn't. She probably thought she was doing me a favor, as awful as her delivery was.

So, I said the only thing I could think of. "Thank you, Isabela. I'll keep that in mind."

"You should." The clicks of her pen echoed in my ear. "I know this entire arrangement has been unconventional, but I really am looking out for you, Claire."

After a few more awkward niceties and platitudes, Isabela rushed off the phone with barely a goodbye, and I scrolled through Instagram to find the pretty waitress's picture of us.

My breath caught. It had clearly been taken from afar, but Dominic's expression was illuminated by the lights on the table. He'd been looking at me, frustration pulling on his mouth, fierceness pinching his brow. I was in the corner of the picture, smiling back at him with my fork at my lips.

If I hadn't been there, I wouldn't have even noticed me in the picture. I was surprised Marley had. The caption—"Guess who was a lucky girl and had the silver fox himself, Dominic Cantrell, seated in my section tonight? Total Daddy vibes"—didn't mention me either.

I scrolled through the comments, laughing to myself. There were so many "Daddy" references. Dominic would probably hate the hell out of that. I only felt a twinge of jealousy and possessiveness. Dominic wasn't mine, but he kind of was mine for right now. More than anything, I got a kick out of how many girls claimed they would dump their boyfriends for him, and maybe a sliver of pride for being the one he had chosen.

Dominic barged into my room, kicking the door shut behind him. His silver hair was dark from showering and his eyes were black with hunger. He took my mouth before I could say one word and had me stripped and facedown on the bed within minutes. I didn't have a second to feel self-conscious at being so exposed with the morning light streaming through my sheer curtains.

Rough hands clamped down on my thighs, spreading them. His warm, wet tongue pressed against my clit from behind. He growled and sucked at my flesh like I was his favorite flavor.

Sometimes I thought he got off on going down on me almost as much as I did. Knowing he loved it, wanted it, craved it, only made me wetter. I writhed in the sheets, clinging on like they were my only tether to this plane.

His thumbs spread my cheeks apart so he could get to every part of me. He laved me all over, from end to end. The wet, sucking sounds his lips made were so obscene and carnal, I could have flown off the bed had Dominic not been holding me down.

He hummed as he sucked my clit, and the pure pleasure in that sound rocked me out of my head and into a soul-shaking orgasm. I pressed my pussy against his face, needing more, less, everything. Dominic gave it to me, riding out one wave and bringing me over again, this time with his fingers thrusting deep inside me.

"Dominic," I cooed desperately.

His teeth clamped down on my ass, sending a jolt of the sweetest pain down my spine. Then he slapped me in the same spot, making me cry out his name again.

"One more," he rasped.

His hand came down between my thighs, connecting solidly with my clit. I bucked beneath him, mewling. In that moment, I couldn't decide if I liked what he did or hated it. Dominic didn't give me time to think. He hauled me to the head of the bed, flipping me onto my back. Sheathing himself with a condom, he sank into me in one slow, fluid thrust.

His body moved at that languorous pace, sliding in so deep, I saw stars, then pulling almost all the way out. Some of the desperation he'd had in the beginning had burned off, and now, he took his time.

"Claire." He brushed sweaty hair off my forehead, eyeing me everywhere. The fire in his gaze hadn't gone out. It was there, flickering, waiting for a chance to rage.

Once he'd gotten his fill of looking at me, his mouth left trails of bites and kisses everywhere he could reach. I wrapped my legs around his narrow waist, arching into his movements, letting him dictate our pace.

I was getting addicted to this. The weight of him pressing me into the bed. The rapture in his expression when he finally got inside me. The explosive chemistry and wildfire passion between us. How he worked my body like he'd known me for years, like he'd studied me and knew without asking what got me going faster than anything else.

More than anything, I couldn't get enough of the way he took control. He allowed me to shut my brain off and *feel*. When he cuffed my wrists with his long fingers, I let go of everything except the slide of his cock against every one of my singing nerve endings.

Fingers closed around my jaw, tilting my face up to meet his searing gaze. No words were spoken between us, but a thousand things were said.

You're mine.

I own you.

How can this be so fucking mind blowing?

Why can't I get enough of you?

I'm going to break you, and you're going to love it.

I'll put you back together better than before.

This'll be over so fast.

I'll miss it when it's gone.

I came with a sigh, and Dominic followed me over with a growl from deep inside his chest. The fingers cuffing my wrists tightened to the point of pain. His eyes ignited with black fire, burning into mine as he spilled his pleasure in my body.

He stayed like that, panting, holding me down until I squirmed beneath him. He snapped back from the far-off place he'd fallen into, looking down at me like he hadn't seen me in a while.

His mouth twitched, almost turning into a smile, but my flexing fingers distracted him. With a grunt of surprise, he released his hold on me, placing his hot palm on my cheek.

"Such a good fucking girl, Claire." He lowered his face into the crook of my neck, his breath warm against my already-heated skin. "We're in Idaho."

That made me laugh. "We are. You're also inside my pussy."

I felt his slow chuckle rather than heard it. "I like when you talk dirty. Seems so wrong, yet so right coming out of your sweet mouth."

"You're a bad influence." I rubbed my feet along the backs of his thighs, telling him without words that I liked where he was right now and he could stay for as long as he wanted. "Was there a point to your Idaho declaration?"

"Just thought you knew Idaho is the state where I stay in bed all day fucking my PR assistant named Claire. It's an age-old tradition." His teeth scraped along my skin, teasing the places he'd no doubt left his mark.

"I think Marta forgot to put that on the schedule." My nails scratched along the sides of his head, which made him sigh and his bunched muscles loosen slightly. "I do like tradition, though."

He nodded. "It's important to keep it up."

"I do have some work to do, so you might have to entertain yourself for a while, but I don't think I have to leave this room or this bed until tomorrow."

Dominic finally lifted his head. The smile on his face wasn't in full bloom, but it was enough to send my pulse racing. Sometimes I wanted to ask why his smiles were so precious and rare, but I knew he wouldn't tell me. If we were something more, or even had the potential to become something more, I'd ask him directly. But since this was all we'd ever have, I'd eat up those few smiles he gave me and live in the moment like I had promised myself at the beginning of the tour.

CHAPTER TWENTY-SIX

DOMINIC

WE MOVED TO MY room so Claire could do her work at the desk in the living room of my suite. That lasted for an hour before I had her on her back again, fucking her so hard, she ripped the sheets off the bed. She'd just looked too goddamn sexy in her little glasses, chewing on the end of a pen, her legs tucked under her in the big, leather desk chair.

Now, she had her tablet in bed, tapping out an email. I was supposed to be working on writing music for my next album, but that wasn't happening. Not when I had this little filthy angel beside me in nothing but lacy black panties and a T-shirt. She was on her stomach and the freckled cheeks of her ass were looking like a nice place to lay my head.

With a groan, I rolled onto her, nuzzling against her impossibly soft skin. My arms slid between her stomach and the mattress, holding her close.

I'd never felt anything better than this girl. She was sexy without trying, and when she did try, she blew me the fuck away. No woman had ever staggered me this way.

"What are you doing back there?" She sounded bemused, but not unhappy.

"Mmm." I pressed my face into her. God, she smelled like sex and honey. We'd already had sex twice today, and somehow, my dick was getting hard again.

"Are you cuddling my butt right now?" Claire let out a little wheezing giggle-snort that sent a wave of delight through my bones. "That's adorable."

"I don't cuddle." My arms banded tighter around her.

"I think you do. I fall asleep to you wrapped around me every night. That's cuddling."

I lifted my head. "Are you telling me you don't like it?"

She twisted enough for me to see the smile on her lips. "I would tell you if I didn't like something."

I grunted, dropping back down onto my resting place.

"So, what *are* you doing back there, if not cuddling?"

"Thinking about how good your ass would look covered in my cum."

"You already *know* how good it looks, silly."

I licked one of my favorite freckles. "True. But I forget easily, so I'm going to need a reminder."

She wiggled her hips a little, moaning softly. "Aren't you supposed to be slowing down at your age? How can you possibly want it again so soon? I won't be able to walk."

I swatted her ass for mouthing off, momentarily mesmerized by the way her flesh moved under my hand. "I can admit this isn't exactly usual for me. Our time is limited, though, so I'm taking all I can get from you."

She tried to roll to her side, but I held her down. "Dominic..."

"I'm comfortable here, Claire. I'll let you do your work."

"Actually, I need to talk to you."

Those words were like nails on a fucking chalkboard. Nothing good ever came after them. I immediately hated that Claire's mouth was even capable of forming them.

Resigned, I shifted off her to lie on my back beside her. She sat up, cross-legged, her tablet in her lap. She turned on the screen and handed it to me.

"Isabela called me this morning while you were at the gym to tell me one of the interns had spotted us together in this picture."

The screen showed a whole lot of me and a little bit of Claire at the restaurant I took her to in Salt Lake City. Having my picture taken by random people was an everyday occurrence for me, but not for Claire. If I could have protected her from this, if there was any way, I would have.

I switched the screen off and tossed the tablet onto the bed beside Claire. "What'd Iz have to say?" Her shoulders jumped, but it was so quick, if I hadn't been looking, I wouldn't have noticed. "You okay?"

She shook her head. "Sorry, it was weird hearing you call her that. I forget my boss is your ex-wife."

"That's because *I'm* your boss." I curled my fingers around her ankle and tugged, sending her falling over me. She pushed up from my chest, her glasses crooked and hair over her face. I pushed a curl off her forehead, tucking it behind her ear. "Tell me what she said."

She scrunched her nose. "I told her nothing inappropriate was going on—which was a stretch of the truth—and she reminded me I'm nothing special. I shouldn't throw away my career on a man who would take me to the restaurant he takes all the women who require a little extra effort to coax into bed."

Heat blanketed me from head to toe. I was angry, but not just at Isabela. I hadn't given one iota of thought to the implications of taking Claire somewhere I'd taken other women. Just because we had a hard and fast end date didn't mean I wouldn't treat her right while I had her.

"She didn't lie. I *have* taken more than one woman there."

Claire sat up again, tugging her shirt over her bare thighs. Her eyes darted around the room before settling on my hand gripping her foot. "Well, that...sucks. And taints that memory for me. How many women have you gone down on in the bathroom there? Do they keep a special stall just for you?"

I raised an eyebrow at the dulcet, steady tone of her voice. She didn't sound angry or enraged with jealousy. Not for the first time, she spoke to me like *I* was the younger, inexperienced one in our arrangement.

"Only you, Claire." I snagged her hand, bringing her fingertips to my lips. "I like that place and thought you'd enjoy it, just like I told you. No one else was on my mind when I took you there. I can see it makes me look like a jackass, though."

"It kind of does," she agreed. "I don't need to be seduced by you, and I really don't enjoy knowing I'm getting the 'Dominic Cantrell treatment.'"

"I apologize." I nibbled each of her fingers while keeping my eyes locked on hers. "It won't happen again."

"I know it won't. No more dinners out. I don't want to lose my job because flirty waitresses can't stop taking pictures of you." She gestured around my hotel room. "This is it."

"We'll see."

She ripped her hand away from me, swatting my chest. "No 'we'll see.' This doesn't work if I'm fired, Dominic. I'm not going to trail behind you as your concubine for the rest of the tour. We don't have to leave your hotel room to follow through on the arrangement we made."

"That's not what this is. I thought I made it clear I *like* you."

"You like fucking me." Her fingers stroked my cheek and beard gently, softening her harsh words. I knew I was damned weeks ago, so I didn't hesitate to lean into her touch.

"I do. I love it. But I also enjoy the hell out of your company. We can be discrete, more so than we were, but if I want to take you out, I'm going to take you out."

I had no idea why I was pressing this issue. We weren't dating. I *didn't* date—not anymore. And she was right, I didn't need to seduce her. But I had this undeniable need to be around her, and I couldn't live the next few weeks in hotel rooms. If I went out, Claire would be coming with me.

"I don't like feeling like I'm being controlled." Her nails scratched light trails along my jaw. "My ex didn't want me to work. I built my life around him. Now I'm building my life for myself. Right now, that means I am indulging in discovering a different side of myself with you. But it also means I'm just starting my career. That's important to me, and I would like you not to dismiss it as something small and easily tossed aside. I'm not a rock star, but I *am* something other than a wife."

"Claire." I went to her, laying my head in her lap and banding my arms around her middle. "I would never dismiss you. I don't know shit about your marriage or how you were treated, but now that you've told me, I'll try to keep my tendency to steamroll at a low simmer."

Her hands glided down my bare back, still as gentle as she was. "You know, you might actually be sweet. One day, some woman's going to crack you open and get to see that side of you all the time."

I huffed a humorless laugh against her soft stomach. "It hasn't happened yet. I'm not that guy."

"Well…" one fingernail dragged the length of my spine, "luckily I won't be waiting around for it to happen. But if I open up a magazine ten years from now and see you with your blushing bride, my wedding gift to you will be a silver platter engraved with 'I told you so.'"

"That doesn't sound like something I'd register for."

She giggled. "I like to be a rebel and go off-registry."

With a growl, I got on my hands and knees and crawled over her until she had to lean back against the pillows. I gripped her jaw, brushing my lips over hers.

"I'm not the guy who gets a happy ending, Claire. That's not me."

Her brown eyes held something that looked so close to pity, I had to squeeze mine shut.

"Life is so unpredictable. I thought I had my happy ending, but I was only at the beginning. I refuse to shut myself off to experiences. You shouldn't either."

My eyes opened again, holding hers. "I'm brutally aware of the unpredictability of life. I didn't get to be forty-two without seeing that for myself. This is where our age difference shines bright. I'm not shut off, I just know what life holds for me, and a happy ending isn't it. I get moments, brief reprieves, and that's it."

"But why?" She raised her head, kissing me slowly, sliding her tongue into my mouth to gently curl with mine. She held onto the back of my neck, keeping me in her tender kiss.

I never answered her, and she didn't ask again.

When we reached Seattle, Claire, Marta, and I took a car to the rental house we'd be staying in for the next week. Claire tried to sit in her normal place across from me, but I snagged her around the waist, pulling her down beside me.

"What is happening right now?" she squeaked.

"You're sitting here," I answered.

Marta was held up talking to one of the crew, so I covered Claire's mouth with mine, sliding my tongue between her lips. She melted against me, her confusion and fight forgotten. I pushed my luck and her boundaries by snaking a hand up her shirt, thumbing her beaded nipple.

"Dominic…" Forehead to forehead, her eyes fluttered open. "Not here. I don't want Marta to feel weird."

"I have no intention of making her uncomfortable, but she's not here right now." I backed away, though, adjusting my half-hard dick in my jeans. "I hear you."

She squeezed my knee, her plump lips turning into a grin. "Thank you for listening."

When Marta finally climbed into the car, she did a double take at our seating arrangements, but kept her opinion to herself —which didn't happen often.

The car started the drive to the rental house, and Marta pumped her fist. "Oh my god, I can't wait to live out of more than one room for an entire fucking week."

"I know. I think I'll wander aimlessly." Claire raised a questioning brow. "I'm assuming the house is big enough for wandering."

"It is." I laid my hand on Claire's thigh, tucking my fingers around the curve. "You can get some wandering in."

Her eyes darted to my hand, then up to mine, giving a subtle shake of her head. I'd conceded on not kissing her in front of Marta, but goddamn, I would not back down on putting my hand on my girl's leg. It wasn't like I was fingering her for all the world to see.

I held on tighter.

She spent the rest of the drive ignoring me, every so often attempting to dislodge my hold. Marta shot me a smug little look, letting me know she was enjoying our silent show. By the time the car pulled to a stop on the gated grounds of our house, Claire had given up, but she didn't hesitate to dart away to freedom.

Before I could follow her, Marta finally spoke up. "That looked a lot like coupledom, Dom."

I shrugged. It felt like that too. Didn't mean anything changed. "It is what it is."

Her eyes narrowed at my lackadaisical response. "Don't fuck her over. We both know your hard little heart is impervious to feels, but I'm not so sure Claire's is. She's been broken far too recently to be broken again by you."

I scrubbed my face hard, groaning with frustration. "Shit, Marta, you act like I'm a monster, but the truth is, you don't know anything about what goes down between us. She needs something I've got, I give it to her. And yeah, maybe I need something she has too. We're slaking each other's needs, but that's as far as it goes." I jabbed a finger in her direction. "For both of us."

She held her hands up. "Fine. I'm sorry. I was thrown off by seeing you being affectionate, that's all."

I rubbed a hand over the short sides of my hair. "Can't help how good Claire feels to touch."

Marta didn't need to say anything to that. She slid out of the car with a shit-eating grin on her face, like she'd caught me in something. She hadn't caught anything, though. I'd never once denied being attracted to and fascinated by Claire. I would've been an idiot to try.

I'd stayed at this house a few times before, so I was familiar with the views of the bay and lush, green trees surrounding the grounds. Marta and I both had bedrooms we always slept in, but Claire didn't know. I found her in one of the smaller ones, her bag on the bed as she took in the view from the wall of windows.

My arms circled her waist, and I scratched her shoulder with my beard. "What are you doing in here?"

She jumped a little, then leaned back against my chest. "I call dibs on this room."

"Wrong pick. My room is down the hall. That's where you'll be too."

"So…" She turned in my arms, tapping lightly on my chest. "My period just showed up. I'll just sleep in here."

I blinked at her, impassive. "Why?"

She exhaled through her nose, her palm flattening on the side of my neck. "Really?"

"Yeah, really. I want you in my bed. I thought we already covered this."

"I know you like the post-sex cuddles, but—"

"I don't cuddle." I covered her mouth with mine, kissing her hard and fast. "But if I did, it would not be limited to post-sex. When you agreed to be mine, I meant the entire four weeks."

Her mouth opened—to object, no doubt—so I kissed her again.

"Another thing, Claire. If you don't like it, fine, but some blood doesn't scare me. I'm not a little boy."

Her eyes went wide, and she gasped, her chest rising and pressing against mine. "Let's put a pin in that idea."

"For now." I kissed her one more time, then grabbed her bag and her hand. "Let's get you where you belong—in my room and my bed."

CHAPTER TWENTY-SEVEN

CLAIRE

I WONDERED IF ROCK star wives ever became immune to the sexiness of their men getting sweaty and intense, baring their soul for thousands. For a split second, I imagined myself with Dominic ten years down the road, and I couldn't fathom ever not wanting to lick the beads of sweat off his chest and fit his hips between my thighs.

When Dominic left the stage in Seattle, I was there, waiting in the shadows. He homed in on me immediately, moving into the darkness with me, his body pinning mine to a cinder block wall. We didn't speak. There was no need. Throughout the concert, we'd spoken through eye contact. He sang "Angel Moon" to me, and I danced for him. When his mouth finally moved over mine, it felt like it had been a thousand years coming.

He cupped my cheeks with hot hands, sliding his even hotter tongue between my lips to meet mine. His body aligned with mine, so flush, not even a ray of light could come between us.

I wanted him. I wanted him so badly, I ached from it. But I still had my period, and as adventurous as I was becoming, I didn't think I was there yet.

He pulled away first, exhaling through his nose. "I like when I see you in my audience. Especially when you're by yourself, no one distracting you."

My teeth dug into my bottom lip, biting back a smile. I knew exactly what he was saying, even though he'd never come out and really say it. He didn't like when Adam joined me to watch his shows. He especially didn't like when Adam danced with me or talked to me, so I gave him my attention instead of Dominic.

"I like *being* in your audience, especially when you play 'Angel Moon' for me. I do wish you'd tell me the story behind my favorite song."

His forehead dropped to mine while his fingers toyed with my hair. "Maybe someday."

Which meant never, since we wouldn't have a someday.

We went back to the house without Marta. She was going out with Iris and the others. I'd been invited, and while I'd been tempted, soaking up all the Dominic time I could had won out.

Showered, Dominic stood in the center of the glass-walled living room, rubbing his flat stomach. "I'm fucking starved."

I curled my arms around his middle from behind, resting my head between his shoulder blades. "Should we order something? It's midnight, but I'm sure something's still open."

He brought my hands up to his mouth, taking his time to nibble each fingertip. "I want to cook."

"When you say that while biting my fingers, I think you want to cook me."

I felt his low chuckle through his back. For once, he didn't try to hide it, but then again, I couldn't see his face. "When I eat you, I like you raw."

My thighs instantly clenched. It had only been two days since we were last together, but my body had become accustomed to having him multiple times a day. I missed his weight covering me and the way he stretched me so perfectly when he slid deep inside me.

"I know you do. But since that's off-limits, let's cook together. As it happens, I'm kind of amazing in the kitchen."

He brushed his lips along my knuckles. "I didn't know that about you."

"Well…" I circled around him so we were face-to-face, "this is probably your only chance to get to know that part of me. What do you want me to make you?"

"Pancakes."

His response was so immediate, a laugh popped out of me. "Okay, I can do that. What are you going to make me?"

His dark brow lifted. "I'm making you something?"

I shoved his chest. "Weren't you the one who suggested cooking?"

"Yeah. Guess I was." He tugged at one of my curls. "Your wish is my command."

"I'd like an omelet please. With a lot of cheese."

He gave my ass a resounding smack, which caused me to jump closer to him rather than away. My instincts were rat bastards when it came to Dominic.

"Get in the kitchen, woman."

I slapped his tight ass right back. "As long as you're in there with me."

Cooking with Dominic was maddening, but in the best way. I'd been trained over the years living with an overly fastidious husband to clean up behind myself, never allowing countertops to be anything but shiny, even in the middle of preparing a meal.

Dominic didn't play that. He tossed flour around like confetti, wasted utensils and bowls, and copped a feel whenever he got near me—which was a lot, even in the spacious kitchen.

I had to stop myself from cleaning up after him and live in the moment like I'd promised myself. Playful Dominic didn't come out too often, so I didn't want to miss a second of him that way.

We ended up sharing the massive omelet he made, and the chocolate chip pancakes I made. We took them out to the deck, which was surrounded by lush forest, the lights of the city twinkling in the near distance.

He watched me take a bite of his omelet. I took my time chewing, moaning faintly.

"Yum. It's about fifty-percent cheese. The perfect ratio."

He huffed a laugh. "My girl wants cheese, she gets cheese." Then he shoved a forkful of pancake into his mouth, groaning with pleasure.

"My man wants chocolate chips, he gets chocolate chips." I waggled my eyebrows, ignoring the stab to my chest at calling Dominic my man. That was an entirely new feeling, and I really didn't like it. To drive it away, I added, "Too bad you'll never get to experience the extent of my culinary skills."

That hadn't felt much better.

"Too bad," he murmured, his black-as-night eyes searing into mine for a beat. Then he glanced down at his plate, pointing to it with his fork. "My grandmother would have appreciated these pancakes. She was always trying to up her 'cake game.'"

That made me laugh, instantly lightening the slow wave of melancholy that had threatened to take me under.

"Did she cook a lot?"

"Oh yeah." He leaned his head back, face up to the sky. "She was a true southern lady. She made biscuits and fried chicken like it was her religion. Sweet tea pumped through her veins. I spent my summer mornings singing along to Joni Mitchell—wait, are you too young to know her?"

"I know who Joni Mitchell is." I resisted the urge to roll my eyes.

The cocky curve of his lips made my belly flip.

"I should've known, music girl." He shook his head, escaping back into his memory of his grandmother. "We'd sing to Joni Mitchell while she baked. She was ahead of her time concerning gender roles. She taught me how to make pie and shared all her secret family recipes."

"Are you telling me you could make me an apple pie?" I asked.

"I don't know." He ran his thumb along the edge of his bottom lip. "I'm rusty, but I could probably do it. For you."

"You'll have to send me one in the mail one day." I ate another bite of omelet, ignoring the pang in my chest yet again. "So, every summer in Georgia, huh?"

"That's right."

"My sister, Annaliese, and I went to Girl Scout camp for half the summer from the age of eight onward, and the other half we'd take some crazy family road trip in a rented RV. I was always jealous of other kids who went to Europe or the islands, but not anymore."

"I get that. The best things that ever happened to me came from simple, human connection. Even my music, it connects me to souls I'll never meet, but I feel."

My hand went to my chest, which had grown warm from that little piece of Dominic.

"When I was lying in my tiny room after I left my ex, listening to 'Angel Moon' a thousand times, I felt connected to those words like I never have before. It's pretty wild the way life brought me to you."

"Yeah." His voice turned to gravel. "Wild."

We ate in silence for a bit, and it wasn't quite comfortable, but it wasn't bad either. I had too many thoughts and questions whirling around in my head to relax. Curiosity got the better of me, so I finally asked, "Why don't you ever go inside their house? When you took me there, I thought maybe the house held some dark, tragic memories you didn't want to relive. It doesn't sound like that's the case, though."

"No, nothing dark ever happened there." He set his fork down and pushed his plate away. "Maybe that's why I don't want to go back. I've never really thought about it, except that I have no desire to step foot in that house. I'm not the kid I was then. I'm not even the man I was the last time I visited them. And I think...I think who I am now will sully some of the only good memories I still have. Every other good thing has already been dirtied by me. But not them. Not those summers, not that house. That is still pure, and if I have my way, it always will be."

This was the sorrow I saw in Dominic. He had demons he'd never dealt with. Deep wells of sadness I knew nothing about. He didn't see himself the way I did. Or Marta did. I couldn't fix him or heal him—even if I had all the time in the world with him, it wasn't something I was capable of—but damn if I didn't wish I could.

He slapped his legs. "Come here."

As a woman who had never been tiny, sitting on boy's laps wasn't something I'd ever been comfortable with. But the first time Dominic pulled me into his lap and I tried to protest, he very quickly reminded me he was a *man*. So now when he made the request, I readily complied, scooting in close, burrowing my face beneath his beard.

He stroked my hair and breathed some of that hot sorrow onto my cheek. "Don't feel sorry for me, Claire."

"You really shouldn't tell me how to feel."

"I'm not. I just don't need pity. It's a waste on me. Some things are fact and not a thing will change that. I shouldn't have said as much as I did."

I picked my head up and pressed my hands to his cheeks. "I've seen you from the beginning. I might not know where you grew up or who your best friend was, but I do know you hate to let yourself laugh. You are drawn to happy, funny people. You surround yourself in their laughter, but don't allow yourself to have it."

He sucked in a breath, his hands curling around my wrists. "Claire—"

I went on, because I wanted him to know what I saw. "You're intensely private, but when a reporter from a small website wants to interview you, you always give them your time. You never flirt unless you mean it. Sometimes when you don't know anyone is looking, you seem to fade away from everything. I know something terrible happened in Houston, but I don't expect you to ever tell me, because I also know when you gave us an end date, there was no wiggle room. So, while I'm here, before we fade on each other, I would like to be as real as we can."

He fisted the back of my hair, jerking my head. "I really need you to stop speaking."

He kissed me like his life depended on it. And maybe it did. Maybe opening up any more than he already had would be like spilling his own blood. I had pushed down my own sadness, doubts, fear, for years during my marriage, until they hit me over the head—literally—and I couldn't ignore them anymore. I had no idea what Dominic had gone through, but I did know a man who hadn't yet walked through the pain when I saw one.

I kissed him back. If all I could be was his brief reprieve and he could be mine, that was what we'd be. His mouth tasted like chocolate, and his tongue pushed away my questions and curiosities.

His hands were all over me, beneath my shirt, kneading my ass, rubbing between my thighs. I squirmed in his lap, wanting more, always wanting more.

"I need inside you." He sounded desperate, like he really did *need* me.

"I have to shower first. My period..."

He was up and out of his chair before I could finish my sentence, pulling me through the house wordlessly.

In the master bath, he flicked on the water and tossed his shirt aside. He looked at me like he was angry, but I wasn't afraid. Not of Dominic. The only thing I feared was how much my heart had begun to ache.

Despite his anger and desperation, when we stepped into the shower together, he gave me space to wash myself. He'd just showered a couple hours ago, but he went through the motions again too.

When he got to his swollen cock, I took over, gliding my soapy hand over his length. He grunted, rocking with my rhythm, his hands exploring every part of my slick body. This man made me feel sexy like I never had. He touched me like he was the lucky one for getting his hands on something so rare and prized. Because of that, I'd never once tried to hide what I used to see as imperfections. Not from him.

His fingers slid through my folds, and for a split second, I thought of objecting. Period sex had never interested me. But the heat in his eyes, the hold he had on my nape, the shakiness of his muscles, all had me forgetting why I'd ever say no.

Dominic turned me, pushing me to the back wall of the shower. He cuffed my hands, raising them above my head to the stainless steel towel rack.

"Don't let go," he gritted out. "I'm not going to go easy on you."

You never do.

The head of his cock nudged between the valley of my thighs, sliding through my folds a few times, then he angled my hips just right and pushed inside me.

Dominic's hips were pistons, need powering every thrust. He held onto my sides, the rough tips of his fingers digging into my flesh. Water sprayed wildly each time our bodies collided.

Teeth clamped on my neck, biting down hard—hard enough to bruise, in a spot high enough it would be difficult to cover. I tossed my head back anyway, giving him more access. I loved carrying his marks all over my body. My inner thighs, breasts, and neck were never without his signature.

My fingers curled around the metal rack as I rocked between pleasure and pain. Dominic grunted in my ear, whispering filthy nothings. He talked about my body and all he wanted to do with it. He told me it was his, that I was his. He claimed his position as the owner of my pleasure.

If he was trying to prove this was all we were—physical, sex, desire, and nothing else—then he failed. There was nothing casual about the unwavering pull between us. When we were together, everything else fell away.

Dominic brought me over with his fingers, and then again with his cock. He rubbed the place inside me that caused my knees to go weak, but held me up.

One arm banded around my torso, his other holding my head against his shoulder. His breath was heavy and hot in my ear, and his filthy words had morphed into frantic grunts.

"Claire." My name had never sounded more like a plea.

He groaned so loud, it echoed off the tiled walls, then he pulled out of me, spilling his liquid heat between my ass cheeks and on my lower back.

When I finally let go of the towel rack, my fingers were sore from holding on so tight. I reached behind me, clutching his sides. He hadn't let me touch him at all, but I needed to, if only for a moment.

His chest rose and fell against my back. "Did I hurt you?" he murmured.

"Not in a way I didn't like or want."

His head fell against my shoulder. "You're just...I'll let you have some space to get cleaned up."

He left me in the hot shower, and when I stepped out a minute or two later, my folded pajamas were waiting for me on the counter. The simple thoughtfulness of that gesture, after he'd just fucked me so hard I'd be sore tomorrow, had me leaning against the wall, slightly overwhelmed.

Not just from Dominic, but from everything I'd missed out on by settling for Derrick. When I had my period, I was practically untouchable. He never would have brought me my pajamas or made me a cheesy omelet at midnight. Was this what most men did for women they cared for? My dad did for my mom, but I had always thought they were the exception.

I hated that I thought that. Regret threatened to take over, so I left the bathroom, snug in my pajamas. Dominic pulled back the covers for me, and I climbed into bed beside him. He didn't hesitate to wrap his body around mine and lay his head on my damp hair.

"Promise me you'll never be with another fucked-up man like me. You are too good for this, Claire." His warm palm pressed against my chest, right above my heart. "You have to be a lot pickier with who you allow to be close to you."

"I don't want to talk about that, Dominic." My fingers toyed with the darker hair that grew from his chin. "Stop it."

"Promise me and I won't bring it up again." He cupped my cheek, his eyes searching mine.

"I promise," I whispered.

He released a long, slow breath, his heavy gaze still on me. "You do see me. But I see you too. I'm thinking it was better back when you were scared of me."

"Who says I'm not?"

His lips parted, like he wanted to say something, but he gave a sharp shake of his head. "Goodnight, Claire."

Dominic held me close as he fell asleep. It took me longer, my head filled with questions that would never be answered, aches that would eventually fade, and worry I had already fallen for a broken man who wouldn't be there to catch me.

CHAPTER TWENTY-EIGHT

DOMINIC

I WATCHED CLAIRE AS SHE WAS BENT FORWARD, buckling a strap around her ankle. I hadn't seen her wear shoes like this before, strappy and dangerous. I had to stop myself from tossing her on the bed and fucking the notion of going out without me right out of her.

"I'm coming."

Claire's head whipped up. "You can't. Public place, Vegas, celebrity—doesn't mix." She smoothed her dress over her hips. "I didn't think you had any interest in strip clubs."

"I have an interest in you, in that dress, wherever you plan on being."

Time had slowed down while we'd stayed in the house in Seattle. We *wandered*, cooked together, hung out with Marta and watched movies, and kind of just lived. I had concerts of course, but in between, I'd settled in. I'd gotten used to the comfort of having Claire everywhere I looked and Marta to talk to whenever I wanted.

The moment we'd boarded my plane, time sped up again. Claire sat in front, while I was in the back, alone. She was adamant about keeping our relationship a secret, and I had no choice but to respect that.

Except, I couldn't seem to wrap my head around her going out with *Adam* to an innately sexual place while I stayed behind.

True, Marta, Iris, and Rodrigo were going too, but that did nothing to appease me.

"Don't be difficult." She ran her finger along the collar of my shirt. "I'll come back here and tell you everything."

"I think I'll go. My security will arrange privacy. If press happens to find me there, we'll be with a group. You'll be safe." I gripped her waist, keeping her at arm's length so I could look her over again. Her champagne dress spilled over her curves like liquid. The front wrapped under her tits, dipping low between them. There was no room for a bra in this dress, and the longer I looked at her, the more obvious that became. Her nipples strained against the silky fabric, and it was all I could do not to take them in my mouth.

"Do you really want to go, or are you jealous?" Claire never beat around the bush. Normally, I appreciated that about her, but not when she was calling me out.

"I'm boiling with jealousy, but I also want to go." My hand splayed across her back, pressing her against me. "If you say no, I'll accept it."

Her eyes rolled, but the twitch of her lips said she wasn't as annoyed with me as she wanted to be. "Fine, yes. Of course I want you there. I'm just worried about...well, I'm worried."

"I've got you. There's no need to worry."

Her palms flattened on my chest. "All right. If you're coming, I'm going to need you to dress your fine ass up and look hot for me."

There was no holding back my laugh. "Again, I've got you."

All it took was a call from my security and our group had a private area at the Red Velvet. I hadn't been to this spot before, but I'd been no stranger to places exactly like it in my early years.

Smoky lights illuminated multiple stages, leaving the rest of the club dim. Black club chairs surrounded low glass tables now covered with drinks. Claire sat beside me, but her eyes never left the stage.

Marta leaned over from my other side. "I think Claire likes it here."

I nodded. "She looks like she either wants to get up on that stage or pull the girl off of it and into her lap."

Claire's plump lips were parted as she watched the curvy, dark-haired woman writhe on the stage. Her hand covered her throat when the dancer ran her own hand down the length of her body with sensual slowness. Claire swallowed hard, shifting in her seat.

I didn't dare interrupt her show, but I found myself unable to take my eyes off Claire, despite the beautiful women dancing feet away from me. I wasn't blind, or a fucking saint, so of course I'd taken a long look, but Claire was where my true interest lay. There was something addictive about seeing her enthralled and turned on by this experience previously denied to her.

When the dancer left the stage, Claire released a long exhale and faced me. Her cheeks were stained red, eyes alight.

"Wow. I wish I could move like that." Her voice sounded throaty and strained.

"You *do* move like that. I've seen it in my bed."

Her hand covered her cheek. "Shut up. That can't be true."

Rodrigo appeared in front of Claire, grinding his hips in the air. "Want a lap dance, lady? I'll rock your world with my moves."

Laughing, Claire held out her arms. "Let me see what you've got, big boy."

He plopped down on her lap, circling his hips in an exaggerated way that made her laugh even harder and *didn't* make me want to murder him. I reached over, a twenty-dollar bill between my fingers.

"You earned this." Rodrigo bent forward so I could drop the cash down the neck of his shirt, then he raised his arms over his head and gave Claire one last grind before hopping up.

She clapped for him, still giggling. "You've been hiding your true talent all this time, honey."

"I was holding out for that Cantrell cash." He rubbed his fingers together. "He's got the big bucks."

Claire stage-whispered to me, "It was nice of you to give charity to this hideous stripper who will never make it in the business."

"I'm all about charity work," I deadpanned back.

Adam joined Rodrigo, tossing his arm over his shoulders. "Claaaire...can I buy you a *real* lap dance?"

Rodrigo pushed him aside. "My girl just got the best lap dance of her life."

Claire raised a finger. "True. Since that was my first and only, it also qualifies as my best."

Rodrigo pointed at her. "Your words are daggers, girl. I'm not happy with you."

Adam seemed undeterred. "So, for real, let me buy you a lap dance. I'd love to see that."

She shook her head, blushing hard. "I don't think I'm ready for that yet. Too many people watching."

He rubbed the back of his neck. "Ah, if I was making bank, I'd get a private room for you, but alas, I'm not there yet."

"Don't worry about it. I'm thoroughly enjoying my first strip club experience without any extras."

And there was not a fucking chance she'd be going into a private room with any man other than me. Adam sure as hell kept shooting his shot, though. I wondered if she had any idea how that boy looked at her.

He jerked his head toward his chair. "Come sit by me and Roddy. Help us pick a girl to dance for us."

Her smile was pinched. "Yeah, maybe in a bit." She picked up her full drink. "Let me down this first. I need a little liquid lube."

Rodrigo dragged Adam back to their seats, giving Claire a wink that said he got her vibe and would take care of the kid who didn't seem to want to take a hint.

"I almost feel bad for him."

She burst out laughing. "You don't at all."

"I said almost." It was dark enough, I took a chance and smoothed my palm along her bare thigh. "Tell me if you want me to arrange a private dance."

Her eyebrow arched. "You want to watch?"

"That's up to you. If you want to do it by yourself, or with Marta and Iris, that's fine too."

She pressed her legs together, trapping my hand. "I'll think about it, okay?"

"Yeah." My thumb dragged back and forth over her smooth skin. "I want you to enjoy yourself however you'd like."

Claire had fun watching the boys get their dances and seemed to enjoy the other strippers who took the stage in front of us, but when the first dark-haired woman performed again, she reacted the same as the first time.

"You want her?" I murmured.

Her breath caught. "I—yes. I do."

"Do you want me to come with you? Or Marta?"

"You," she breathed.

My gut clenched from her blown out pupils and her teeth digging into her bottom lip. I couldn't get enough of my sweet Claire letting herself be sensual and a little dirty.

I spoke to my security, asking them to arrange a private dance for us. A few minutes later, a man with an impassive expression showed up to escort us. I tapped Marta on the shoulder.

"I'm taking Claire home."

She glanced at the man waiting for us. "Oh really? That's your story?"

"If anyone asks."

She sipped her drink, grinning around the glass. "I've got it, boss. You're definitely not going into a back room with your girlfriend."

I smirked. "Exactly."

Once we were away from our group, I wrapped my arm around Claire's waist and kissed her shoulder. "Are you excited?"

She nodded. "And so nervous."

"Don't worry about a thing. I'll make sure you're taken care of."

"What about you?"

"Me?"

She tipped her face up to mine, her fingers curling under my beard. "Are you excited?"

"To watch you? Hell yes. But this is all about you. Only you."

We were shown into a small room with a mirrored back wall, a small platform with a pole, and a tufted leather bench. Claire and I sat down together, and a moment later, the door opened.

"Hello." Claire's dancer walked in, closing the door behind her. "I'm Raquel. What a beautiful couple you are."

Her accent was soft and lilting. She sounded like her native language was Spanish or Portuguese.

I shifted away from Claire, giving her room. "You're here for her and only her. This is her first time."

Raquel walked up to Claire, squatting in front of her. "Hi, beauty. I'd love to take care of you. Do you mind if I touch you?"

Claire shook her head. "No. I don't mind."

Raquel hit a button behind the bench, turning on a Nine Inch Nails song. She rose to her feet, rotating her body in a slow circle while undulating to the heavy beat. She made eye contact with Claire, giving her a hungry smile, and my girl gave her one back.

Raquel approached her again, raising one knee onto the bench, and then the other, straddling Claire's legs.

"You're really beautiful," Claire rasped.

Raquel lowered her ass onto Claire's knees, her hands braced on the back of the bench. "You are too. Your breasts are amazing. Does your man love them?"

Claire nodded while Raquel rolled her hips. "He does."

"He's a lucky man." She slid forward, grinding her core against Claire, then ran the back of her fingers along Claire's cheek. "Your skin is so fine. He must touch you constantly."

Claire reached for my hand, threading her fingers with mine. "He never stops."

"Lucky him," she cooed.

Raquel went on, moving over my girl in a languid rhythm. My cock strained in my pants, pulsing from the two beautiful women caught up in each other beside me. They admired each other's bodies and hair, complimented scents and makeup, but underneath their quiet murmurings was a heady sexuality impossible to ignore.

"Are you wet for him, beautiful?" Raquel ran her hands along Claire's sides, skimming her breasts.

"Yes," she answered.

"Mmm...he'll fuck you so hard when you leave here."

"He will."

Raquel flipped her hair over one shoulder to whisper in Claire's ear, and Claire's fingers flexed between mine.

For three songs, Raquel gave Claire her undivided attention. Her hands slid along Claire's legs, pushing her dress up so their skin there could meet. Claire whimpered, but made no move to protest or stop her. She seemed to melt beneath Raquel, while I sat rigid, straining for control.

When the last song ended, I was close to losing it—to hauling Claire over my shoulder and dragging her out of the room so I could sink myself inside her.

"Thank you so much, beautiful." Raquel kissed Claire's cheek. "This has been my pleasure. Now, go have some fun with your man."

She winked at me as I handed her a generous tip, then gathered her discarded clothes and made her way out of the room.

Claire shot me a shy smile. "Thank you, Dominic."

I shook my head at her, more than pleased with this woman beside me. "You fucking loved that."

She nodded at the bulge in my pants. "You did too."

I pulled her into my lap, her ass pressing against my erection. "This is all for you. Your reactions, the way you were squirming when she touched you, how you let go of your inhibitions and allowed yourself to enjoy every second of it. I am so hard for you, Claire. Only you."

Her hips rolled one torturous time. "Then I think you should take me back to the hotel so we can do something about it."

CHAPTER TWENTY-NINE

CLAIRE

MY SKIN FELT SUNBURNED, and my core was molten. Having a sexy, gorgeous woman writhe all over me had turned me on, but she wasn't who set me on fire.

Dominic did.

It started with the way he encouraged me to enjoy myself. He never once tried to rein me in or mold my experience into the shape he wanted. I knew it killed him not to touch me in front of the others, but he held back because I had asked, and that in itself made me want him more than ever.

The private dance had only fanned the flames. He made me the center of both his and Raquel's attention. The thinner, sexier, more conventionally beautiful woman had barely turned his head.

The ride back to the hotel was interminable. I kept apart from Dominic, because once we got started, I knew I wouldn't be able to stop, and I wanted more than a quick fuck in the back of a limo.

When we were finally back in my room, tension and lust stood so thick between us, it was almost impossible to move through it.

He took a seat on the end of my bed. "Will you dance for me?"

"Really?" My heart skipped a beat from both excitement and nerves. "Would that make you happy?"

His fingers tapped one at a time on his thighs. "A dream come true."

Not giving myself time to get nervous or overthink it, I took my phone from my purse and switched on one of my playlists. "Electric Love" cut through the air, and I kicked off my heels, bouncing to the beat as I made my way to Dominic.

Draping my arms over his shoulders, I rotated my hips in languid circles. He captured me in his gaze, but what he didn't understand was I was willing. He didn't have to cuff me or tie me down with some four-week contract. I wanted him, and I wasn't running—even if I'd never danced like this for anyone and doing so took me away from my comfort zone.

He trailed his knuckles down my sides as I moved with the song. Leaning forward, I dusted a kiss across his lips, but he was quicker than me. Long fingers threaded in my hair, keeping me in place to devour my mouth like a starved man.

Breathless, I pulled back. "You're distracting me from my dance."

Dominic licked his bottom lip and held out his palms. "By all means, continue."

Swiveling away from him, I gave a sharp rock of my hips so my dress shimmied around my legs. Dominic's hands were on me again, gliding up the outline of my curves, following my movements. He kneaded my breasts, then made a path along my stomach with his fingers. I watched him touch me in the full-length mirror facing the bed. The rough tattoos on his skin contrasted with the smooth fabric of my dress so beautifully, I shivered.

He could tear me apart, but instead, he was reverent. Careful. Worshipful in his gaze and touch. I didn't shy away from seeing how we looked together in the reflection. When his fingers toyed with the clasp of my dress just under my bust, I helped him open it to reveal my cream, silk thong and miles of freckled, bare skin.

I cupped my breasts as I sat down in his lap, gently grinding on his erection. Dominic's gaze met mine in the mirror, just as entranced at watching us together as I was.

Turning my head, I nuzzled my mouth into his beard. "Take your shirt off so I can feel you."

He released my waist to unbutton his shirt, his nimble fingers flying, and tossed it aside. His touch immediately returned to glide the rough pads of his fingers along my lust-drenched skin.

I tipped my head back to rest on his shoulder, rolling my hips to the new, dream-like song that had begun playing. Dominic kissed along my collarbone and neck—everywhere his lips could reach—and took over cupping my breasts for me. He plucked at my nipples, eliciting whimpers of pleasure from deep inside me.

"Open your eyes, Claire." His words were low and commanding, and my compliance was automatic. He squeezed my breasts together, then let them fall as his hands splayed on my stomach. "Do you see what I see?"

I spoke around the knot in my throat. "Tell me what you see."

"This stunning woman," one hand dipped into my panties, teasing my slit with a fingertip, "owning her power."

"What power?" I whispered as he tapped on my clit.

"You wield all the power. Every day, I drop to my knees for you." He gripped my pussy in his palm like he owned it. "Your cunt drives me out of my mind. Your whole fucking *being* does."

"It's mutual." Although, I didn't know if I had lost my mind or only just come to my senses. This thing between us was crazy, but it made more sense than anything had in a long time.

I reached up to wrap my hand around the nape of his neck, arching my back in the process. Dominic growled, plunging two fingers inside me to the hilt.

"It's outrageous. Fucking criminal, Claire."

His fingers moved with expert precision, thrusting and playing with my clit at the same time. I tried to keep moving to the beat of the music, but I got lost in Dominic's rhythm, riding his hand and the thick erection prodding my ass.

I came so fast and hard, I saw stars. My breath evaporated, and when Dominic ordered me to open my eyes, the reflection showed a lust-filled woman, plump lips parted, nipples in tight peaks, lush hips and thick thighs, spread for the man beneath me —the man with midnight eyes who held me by the throat and pussy with tremulous hands.

"Dominic," I rasped.

He told me to stand, and when I did, he stood at my back, removing his pants and my panties. He was a dark tower behind me, keeping his secrets in the shadows he shrouded himself with. Dominic was beautiful in the same way as a rolling storm— fascinating to watch, and almost impossible to look away from, but equally dangerous.

For a brief moment, when our gazes clashed in the mirror, his guard collapsed. There, in his stern brow and tight jaw, behind the stardom and fame, was a man on the precipice. That split-second showed me how unsure he was. About what? I would never know, because he pulled me back down to the bed, onto his lap, and thrust inside me.

My legs hung on either side of his knees, giving him full control—what he needed after that accidental slip of vulnerability. He spread me wide, and the sight of my slick pussy molding around his thick length as he moved inside me held both of our attention. He went slow and deep, dragging along my inner walls with that same precision his fingers had.

My nails dug into his corded arms. "This makes me scared."

He nibbled on my earlobe, breathing hot and heavy from his nose. "You have nothing to fear from me, Claire. I told you, you have all the power here." He jerked his chin at our image. "I can't even look at you for very long or I'll lose it."

"I've never seen myself like this." I barely recognized my own voice. It had gone mellow and raspy, my tongue curling each word with sensuality.

His beard scratched my neck and cheek as he pressed his face next to mine. "And I am never going to forget you looking like this."

"My body." I trailed my hand to where his was spread wide on my curved stomach. When he touched me like this, I couldn't even be bothered to hate any part of me. "I don't know this body."

"*I* know your body. If I could live inside you and feel every one of your soft places, I would." His fingers flexed, pushing into my flesh. "You are Eden and damnation, Claire."

That hurt, but I couldn't really explain why. Not with my mind overloaded with pleasure and lust, every corner filled to the brim with Dominic's name, face, his teeth on my skin, his voice...

I twisted my head to kiss him and relieve some of the ache his words had caused. He took control of my mouth too, his lips moving over mine sensually while he held my throat. He slipped his tongue into my mouth, tasting me and laving mine. Everywhere he touched seemed to have developed a direct connection to my core.

Dominic raised his hips, hitting an even deeper place inside me. I gasped, my inner muscles clenching hard around him. We wrenched our mouths apart to face the mirror as I came. My limbs and belly trembled like leaves from the storm Dominic had stirred within me.

"Beauty," he growled. "So perfect."

Some of his carefully crafted control fell away, and his grip on me tightened. Fingers dug into either side of my waist as he plunged into me from below. I rolled my hips again and again, my channel a live wire. Each pass of his cock sent shocks of electricity down my spine.

"Dominic...oh, that feels so good." My hands covered his again, fingers locking between his like puzzle pieces.

"Yeah?" His eyes found mine in the mirror. He jerked his hips, making me shake like he'd hit a raw nerve. "Like this?"

"Yes, yes, just like that."

We kissed again, our mouths moving together just as languidly as our bodies. I'd felt frantic with need when we'd arrived at the hotel, but now, I wondered if it was possible to keep doing this forever.

If the devil appeared at this moment and asked for my soul, I might have signed it over so I could stay here making slow love to Dominic Cantrell for the rest of my life.

My pleasure mounted again, this time from Dominic's fingers circling my swollen clit. When I came, tears welled in my eyes, and he saw. He saw everything. He wouldn't allow me to hide—and I didn't want to.

His hips jerked, and then he started bucking beneath me in earnest. My ass slapped against his pelvis, skin connecting with skin. He grunted my name, called me sweet, told me I smelled like honeysuckle, then he clamped down on my shoulder, our eyes staying locked.

My receptors were set to pleasure only. The dig of his teeth in my skin and his cock pounding me so thoroughly I had to will my eyes not to roll back, felt like I'd been transported to paradise. Eden.

We showered together after, both of us moving slow. I laughed when I dropped my washcloth for the second time.

"Crap. I'm weak." My arms fell limp by my sides.

He held up his big, soapy hand. "I've got you."

Dominic rubbed soap all over me, not missing a spot. For some reason, I'd expected him to pull away after the intensity we'd just shared, but he hadn't at all. I had been close to crying while he was inside me from how exposed and raw he made me feel.

I leaned into him, circling my arms around his waist. "You always seem to have me."

He planted a kiss on my temple. "Tonight was good, huh?"

Warm water sluiced down my face as I pressed my cheek to his chest. "Mmm…yes."

"You were going to tell me all about it."

"I was." My fingers drummed the rose tattoo on his chest. "But then you forced your way in."

He squeezed my butt. "Are you trying to tell me you really had a problem with me being there?"

"I am not. I liked you being there. A lot."

"Then tell me about it. Come to bed with me and tell me all about your night."

We dried off, I threw on a T-shirt, Dominic a pair of briefs, then I climbed into bed, and he wrapped his arms around me.

"Tell me."

My lips curved into a soft smile. I didn't quite understand why he wanted me to tell him about the night since he'd been there too, other than he wanted to know exactly what I'd experienced.

"Well, it started with my man dressing up and looking really fine for me. He's older, and kind of grumpy, but I like him."

Dominic growled, giving my ass a quick smack.

"Then we met up with these people who've become my friends so quickly, I sometimes can't believe it. Especially Marta. I love Marta."

He kissed my chin. "She likes to go and make unwilling people love her."

"True, except I wasn't unwilling." Our legs tangled together under the sheets, and my chest panged, but I shook it off quickly. I'd gotten way too used to this.

"After that, we went to this...den of iniquity. Beautiful, naked women everywhere. One in particular caught my attention. I liked her hair and her crazy curves. My friends tried to buy me a lap dance, but I wasn't into it. I really loved when the man I was with stood down and didn't try to impose any restrictions on my behavior or reactions."

I wove my fingers through the side of Dominic's hair, letting my eyes close as his warmth seeped into me. He brought me even closer to him and nibbled on my bottom lip.

"And then?"

My lids lifted, and we were face-to-face, almost nose to nose. "And then my man bought me a dance with that beautiful woman. She kept whispering how hot he and I were together. She told me my man looked like he worshiped me like a queen. I got so hot from everything she said, I thought I would combust."

"But then," I brushed my lips over his, "we got back to this room and you opened me up."

His lips curved into a small, naughty smirk. I tapped them with my fingertips, a tired laugh slipping from me.

"Stop that. You opened me in every way. I can't remember very many times I've been as vulnerable as I was stripped and raw in front of that mirror. But with you, I felt safe to lean into my vulnerability and explore the raw parts of me. And I think...I think once this is over, I won't go back inside my shell ever again. *That's* what I meant by being opened up."

Dominic was still, the rise and fall of his chest his only movement. I mirrored him, waiting to see if I'd gone too far, shared too much.

He finally blinked and brought my mouth to his, moving his lips over mine in a slow, tender slide. When we separated, his forehead rested on mine so I couldn't see his expression.

"It's a fucking honor to be part of your journey, Claire."

I couldn't think of anything to say to that. The tight ball in my throat made it impossible to speak anyway, so I kissed him again.

We fell asleep like that, embracing and kissing like it was the end of the world. Truly, it was almost the end of the world we'd created just for us.

CHAPTER THIRTY

CLAIRE

MY PHONE RUDELY SNAPPED ME OUT OF SLEEP. I rolled out from under the hot weight of Dominic's arms to snatch it from where I'd plugged it in to the charger the night before.

Isabela.

I cleared my throat to rid myself of early morning croakiness. "Hello?"

"Hello, Claire. How are you today?"

"Um..." I rubbed the crust from my eyes, walking into the bathroom so I didn't wake Dominic.

"Didn't we talk about saying 'um.' It's unprofessional, and as women, we have to work harder than men to be seen as respectable."

I wasn't buying her women supporting women schtick anymore, but she wasn't wrong either.

"Yes, I'm sorry. It was a late night and your phone call woke me up."

We'd flown in from Las Vegas last night and were now in Dominic's Los Angeles house. It was beautiful, set in the hills, with walls of windows and a pool that went on to infinity. Neither of us had made any pretense about separate rooms, even though Marta was just down the hall. I'd spent the last few hours in Dominic's low, king-size bed, making love, and then sleeping in his arms.

But dammit, I hadn't gotten nearly enough sleep, and now I was cranky as hell.

A short, humorless laugh came through the phone. "Oh my. I've forgotten about the time difference. It's only six in LA, isn't it? No wonder you were still in bed."

She paused, perhaps for me to tell her it was okay, but I didn't fill in her silence, finding it truly hard to believe she hadn't remembered we were three hours behind the east coast.

"Well, now that you're awake, let's chat. How are things?"

"The same. A lot easier than when I first started. I've gotten the hang of my tasks. Marta is—"

Isabela hissed. "Marta is a nuisance. I don't know why Dominic keeps her on."

"That's funny. I've had the opposite experience with her. I was going to say what a big help she's been."

Isabela tsked as if I was a fool for going against her. "That's nice. Maybe Marta has finally grown up. Anyway, enough about her. I trust you've seen Dominic has the evening after next blacked out on his schedule."

"Yes, I noticed. I didn't ask what he'll be doing since he's made it clear how private he is."

I didn't know what Dominic had planned, but I *did* know a designer would be stopping by his house later today to fit him for a suit. Dominic wasn't much of a suit guy, so I'd concluded he would be wearing it to the mystery event.

I couldn't say it didn't sting that he wouldn't tell me where he was going, but we had one week left together. Every time I thought of our grains of sand slipping through the hourglass, my insides twisted into knots. I had no intention of spending the time we *did* have left arguing with Dominic or doing something that would make him push me away.

"You're right. Dominic is extremely private, but this gala will be teeming with press, and I want you to attend. It's black tie, so you'll need a gown, but I'm assuming you can sort yourself out. Although, it's probably not as easy for you—"

"I can find a dress," I blurted, not waiting for whatever sideways insult she was about to dish out.

"Great. This particular gala is a fundraiser for a nonprofit supporting pediatric brain cancer research. Dominic attends every year and supports the foundation. I've gone with him in the past, which is how I know it's important for you to be there to field any questions the press might have for him. I'll send you information on the foundation, but as far as Dominic's involvement, our answer is always that someone dear to him lost a child to brain cancer, so he'll do anything he can to help. This isn't something you'll be discussing with Dominic, of course. Simply let him know I told you to attend, and keep to yourself as much as possible while you're there. He's always in a mood at these galas, so give him space. It shouldn't be too difficult otherwise, but I'll be available by cell if you need anything."

Flummoxed by all the information Isabela had unloaded, I told her I understood and I'd be looking for her email, then we hung up. And the timing couldn't have been better since Dominic knocked on the door once before walking right in.

He glowered at the phone in my hand. "Why are you out of bed in the middle of the night taking phone calls in the bathroom?"

I rolled my eyes at the blatant accusation in his question and brushed by him to plug my phone back in. Then I crawled into bed, pulling the covers over my head. Naturally, he yanked them off and scooted my body over with his until we were all tangled in each other again.

I shoved at his chest, but there was no heat to it. "Isabela called. She pretended she didn't know it was only six here."

He laughed. "She can be a real cunt when she wants to be."

"It seems she wants to be quite often when it comes to me." I tugged on his beard. "Why were you married to her? I don't see it."

The humor drained from his features. "We met at a time in my life when I was pretty decimated. She was there when I needed someone. I learned too late it's easy to mistake love and need. I pulled back from her, she cheated to get my attention, then when I couldn't bring myself to give a shit, she left. The divorce was a relief, but we keep circling back to each other." He kissed me softly. "That's done now, and I'm even more relieved to have her completely out of my life. It's better for her too. I think I make her crazy."

I snorted under my breath. "You do have that way about you." My eyes lifted to his. "My ex cheated too. For over a year before I found out. Although, I think I knew and was lying to myself so I didn't have to make the decision to leave. Like you said, love and need are two sides of the same coin. I thought I needed him, but it turns out, I really didn't."

Shadows of wrath passed over Dominic's eyes, and his brow pulled into a taut line. "Fucking dick. Damn right you don't need that shit, baby. If you're going to be with someone, it has to be because of *want*—and cheaters should all burn in hell."

I threaded my hand through his under the covers. "No redemption?"

"Not with me. I don't forgive easily. It takes a lot for me to let someone in, so when I do, and they cross me, I'm pretty much done."

"Before Derrick, I would have said I was a forgiving person. But once I found out about his affair, I shut him out of my heart without looking back. So maybe we're alike in that way."

"No reason to forgive someone who steps out on you."

"Yeah," I whispered. "By the way, Isabela has commanded I attend the gala with you, so I'll need a couple hours to find a dress today and—"

He gripped my chin. "She what?"

"She said there will be a lot of press there, and she usually goes, so she felt I should be there."

His hand shook, but he didn't hurt me. "What did she say?"

My fingers curled around his wrist. "She didn't tell me anything personal."

His nostrils flared. "Did I tell you where I am going that night?"

He gave nothing away in his flat, detached tone. I couldn't tell if he was angry, worried, or something else.

"No, you didn't."

"Then she told you something I did not give her permission to reveal."

"I would never repeat a word she said, Dominic."

He stared at me hard, his eyes pinning me in place. "I know you wouldn't. Your NDA is ironclad."

I slapped his hand off me and shoved myself to the other side of the bed. When that didn't feel far enough, I clambered to my feet and made it as far as the door before Dominic was on me, banding his arm around my waist.

"Get back in bed," he growled.

"I'm done sleeping." I jabbed my elbow behind me, hitting him in the ribs. "Let go of me. You're scaring me."

His arm dropped, and the heat of his chest on my back disappeared. I looked over my shoulder to see him leaning against the wall, hitting his forehead with the heel of his hand.

"I'm sorry." He said it so quietly, I barely heard. "I trust you. I'm pissed at Isabela, but that isn't in any way your fault."

I leaned against the opposite wall, sliding my bare foot next to his. "Don't ever touch me in anger again."

He lifted his head, remorse burning sharp in his gaze. "I won't." He straightened and took a tentative step toward me. When I didn't stop him, he took another and reached out to cup my face. "I don't give interviews about the charity. I go to support a friend and having my name listed as a donor pulls in more money for the foundation."

"I'll be working, Dominic. I won't be your date, and you won't have to worry about me. I'm capable of being professional, even around you."

"You're amazing at your job. I'm being a reactionary asshole right now." He bent to kiss me. "Come back to bed. It's too early and I can't sleep without you."

"I'm a little bit mad at you."

"I know, baby." He gathered me to his chest, holding me tight. When he didn't try to talk me out of my anger, I forgave him.

"Fine," I mumbled.

Instead of allowing me to walk like a normal man, Dominic swooped me up in his arms with barely a grunt—and I wasn't a featherweight—and carried me to our bed, depositing me in my spot. Flushed with pleasure from being carried, I kissed him hard, then settled back in his arms.

"Gorgeous girl," he murmured into my hair as he stroked it, lulling me right back to sleep.

Marta and I went dress shopping together, and it hadn't been as soul-sucking as I had expected. She called ahead to a high-end department store, securing a personal shopper for me. I had given them my measurements, so when we arrived, there were two racks of dresses to choose from.

I'd gravitated to a black dress, while Marta had tried to steer me to a flaming red number. My personal shopper had convinced me to try on one I wouldn't have without a nudge, and that was the dress I'd bought.

Now, with my hair and makeup done, and my dress and heels on, I had my doubts.

"It isn't too much? Shouldn't I fade into the background?"

Marta rolled her eyes. "No, kidlet. That should never be your goal, no matter the circumstance. You look amazing, and Dominic will piss his pants."

Smoothing my hands over the sequined flowers on my skirt, I exhaled. "Okay. I believe you. Will you go tell Dominic I'll be ready in a couple minutes?"

"Of course." She stood in front of me, running her palms down my bare arms. "He's probably going to be in a dour mood all night. Don't take it personally, okay?"

I nodded. "I'll be working. I'm not expecting the red-carpet treatment from him."

She hesitated before tipping her chin, giving me a wink, and heading out the door.

I took one more look at myself in the mirror. The bodice of my dress was black, off the shoulder, and simple. The skirt was anything but. Cream, with big, burnt orange and yellow flowers, accented by sequins in the centers, it wasn't made to blend in with a crowd. Old me would have hated it, but the woman I was now was beginning to believe Marta was right.

I should never desire to be invisible. That wasn't me anymore.

CHAPTER THIRTY-ONE

DOMINIC

MARTA STRAIGHTENED MY TIE. "YOU LOOK SLICK, Dom. How do you feel?"

"Less than slick."

"Well…" she patted my chest hard, "your girl looks like an angel, so I hope you find it in your cold, black heart to treat her like one."

"I always do, Mar."

"Mmmhmmm. You do, and I'm proud of you for that. However, we both know tonight isn't like other nights."

I'd like to think if I had the chance, I would have found the words to refute her, but the click of high heels drawing near averted my attention elsewhere. Claire strode toward us, her shiny plum-colored lips curving into a smile.

"Beauty." I took her hands in mine, holding her at arm's length so I could take a long look at her. Her dress was unexpected, and at first glance, not blatantly sexy, but gorgeous nonetheless. Her breasts were pushed up high, swelling round and firm above the top of her bodice. When she moved, the subtle slit in her skirt revealed a pale, freckled leg, all the way up to mid-thigh.

Her breath caught when our eyes finally met. "You're in a suit." She shook her head. "I'm not sure you should be allowed out of the house like this. Danger, danger."

I chuckled as I pressed a kiss to the side of her neck. "You're incredible, Claire. If I forget my manners while we're at this thing, remember me telling you this now—you are stunning, and I'm really proud to have you with me."

Marta clapped. "All right, all right. The car is here. Time to go, peeps."

Claire caught her hand. "Have fun on your date with Iris."

"Not a date," Marta singsonged. "Not when those cunt-blockers Roddy and Adam are going to be there too."

As we passed, Marta smacked me on the ass. "Be good to her, Dom, or I swear to god..."

She didn't finish her threat, but she didn't have to. I had no intention of treating Claire poorly tonight, no matter how badly I wanted to sink into a dark hole. I wouldn't. For her.

And for Dylan.

Tonight wasn't about me. It was about raising money so other kids wouldn't suffer like Dylan had. I had no idea if they'd ever find a cure, but if there was any sense to this fucked up world we lived in, there had to be a way that children didn't suffer through surgeries, chemo, radiation, *pain after pain after pain*, only to die before they even had a chance to live.

In the limo, I tucked Claire beside me, burying my face in her neck. Her scent never failed to ground me, to give me that safe, cared-for feeling I'd had during my long, hot summers in Georgia.

"Is there anything I should know before we arrive?" she asked.

I straightened, tracing my eyes over her serious expression. "Is this work-mode Claire already?"

"It is. It's easier for me to compartmentalize this way. You can go off and do your thing and I won't be hurt or neglected." She tugged on my tie. "So, is there anything?"

There were a million things. Shit I should say, should tell her, wanted her to know, but I had no clue where to begin, or if she'd even want that baggage when she was walking away from me in less than a week.

When we were walking away from each other.

"No, baby. Have a drink or two and keep the wolves at bay. Maybe strut by me every so often so I can watch and be distracted by your tits and ass."

She let out a light snort. "Oh, you and your way with words."

We arrived at the venue without fanfare, entering through a side door. Claire trailed beside me into the museum, which had been transformed into an event space. Bars bracketed the wide-open space with perfectly set tables dotted around the center.

I headed straight for the bar, although I felt eyes on me from every direction.

My beer was ready first, so while we waited for Claire's cocktail, I surveyed the room. I recognized many of these people from attending this gala the past several years, but none whose name I remembered.

None except *her.* Chelsea Watson.

From across the room, our eyes met, and she waved me over with a grin. Claire moved beside me with her drink in hand. I touched her shoulder.

"I see someone I know. Would you mind if I...?" I nodded toward the direction I intended on going.

She straightened, following my gaze. "Oh. Sure. I'll be fine. I wanted to wander around and look at the paintings anyway."

I forced a half-smile out. "The wandering queen."

"CEO of Wandering. That's me." She nudged me forward. "Go, please."

I peered down at my girl one more time. "I'll find you. Don't wander too far."

As I walked away from her, I swore I heard her whisper, "I'll try," but when I turned around, she was already gone.

CHAPTER THIRTY-TWO

CLAIRE

I DID WANDER. I sat in front of paintings, studying them as I sipped on my vodka cran. This museum was a bit too modern for my taste, but I studied the art like I was going to be quizzed on it. Otherwise, I would have to watch Dominic in an intimate huddle with a willowy blonde goddess. Seeing them embrace, the way he'd cupped the back of her head and held her against his chest, had been enough.

For the first time since I'd known him, daggers of jealousy stabbed at my gut. I'd waded through groupies and women he'd been intimate with. I'd seen reporters flirt and basically shared a naked stripper with him, and I'd never once felt possessive or concerned about my place with him.

Not until her. Even from across the room, their expressions of shared pain and love were so clear, I could have been standing in front of them.

I didn't allow myself to wallow for long. I skirted the room, listening for press or anything else I should have been aware of. But it seemed I didn't really have much of a job to do here. There weren't any obvious reporters, no paparazzi clambering outside. I took notes on my phone in case Isabela wanted me to write up a press release or something for social media tomorrow, but I doubted I'd need them.

I went to the bar for another drink as dinner service was called. Since we hadn't discussed it, I navigated around the tables to where Dominic was seated beside the blonde, still deep in conversation.

She saw me first, lifting a brow when I hovered beside the table, my drink sweating on my hand. Dominic turned to see who his friend was looking at, and when we locked eyes, his expression became guarded and flat.

"Claire," he practically growled.

I sucked in a breath, painting on a smile. "Do you know if I'll be sitting with you for dinner, or is there another place for... employees?"

The blonde woman stood, towering over me in a sleek, black dress. She offered her hand and a bright smile. "I don't believe we've met. I'm Chelsea."

We shook, and I returned her smile, though mine was decidedly less bright. "I'm Claire, Dominic's PR assistant."

"Lovely to meet you. Your dress is exquisite. I always wear black, but seeing you in all this color makes me want to go for it. Next year, it's game on." She winked. "*And*, since I organized this little event, please let me show you to your table."

She steered me back across the room, pointing out donors and doctors who worked with the foundation. I really wanted to hate this woman who had been putting her hands all over Dominic, but I couldn't—not when she bled sincerity and had such a gentle way about her, I wasn't sure she'd ever even hurt a fly.

"Normally, Isabela sits with Dom, but obviously she's not here. You were added at the last minute, so I had to sneak you into a table with an extra seat. Don't worry, it's not for B-listers. I happen to know there's a single cardiothoracic surgeon, a neurosurgeon, *and* an artist at your table."

I had to laugh. She was so off base, it was funny. "Thank you, Chelsea."

"Of course. Thank you for coming and supporting the foundation."

Dinner was fine. My tablemates were lovely. I made great efforts to engage in conversation and learn about the foundation. I made even greater efforts not to give my attention to the man on the other side of the room.

My efforts were in vain, though. I kept finding myself glancing his way. For the most part, he sat stiff in his chair, but every once in a while, I'd see Chelsea touch the back of his neck or lean her head on his shoulder, and he made no move to stop her.

I imagined this was why Isabela had insisted I come tonight. Despite my denial, she probably guessed something was going on between Dominic and me and this had been her way of once again hammering home I was nothing special.

I certainly felt like a pile of scraps, unwanted and soon to be tossed aside. I hated myself for allowing one night to drive me so low, but the reality was, I hadn't fully healed from my marriage. Foundation already cracked, all it took was one light hit and I fell apart.

Speeches began during dessert, finally capturing my full attention. I learned a lot about the research efforts funded through donations and the advances doctors were making. Nothing was fast enough, no matter how much urgency everyone involved felt. Children were suffering and dying and it just...it wasn't fair.

The man beside me—the neurosurgeon with a smile that could light up any room—tapped my arm when the speeches ended and the music started again. "How do you feel about dancing?" he asked.

"I feel great about it, but I'm afraid I'm going to have to decline. I didn't bring my dancing shoes."

I excused myself from the table, needing a little room to breathe. As I made my way toward the terrace, I saw through the floor-to-ceiling windows that it was already occupied by a few people, but one pair drew my eye.

Dominic and Chelsea were face-to-face, in profile to me. His hands were on her waist, hers clutching his arms. She nodded at something he said, and after a pause, he dipped his head to her shoulder.

Swirling away from them, I strode in the opposite direction to the bathrooms, flinging myself inside, shooting up a thanks to everything holy the room was blessedly empty.

Was it possible to be numb and searing with pain at the same time?

Because I was.

My mind scrambled, and I was unable to catch a single thought as they zipped around my skull. I felt betrayed, but I didn't even know if I had been. Dominic and I weren't together. We weren't a couple. We had sex and spent time with each other. We had an expiration date—and it was fast approaching. Perhaps he was lining up his next arrangement already.

I rubbed my chest, watching my reflection in the little mirror over the sink. Sadness hung around me like an accessory, clashing with my pretty dress.

This wouldn't do. I couldn't allow another man to ruin me. I had to suck it up, push my emotions aside, and finish my job.

After applying a fresh coat of lip gloss, I pushed through the door into the long hallway leading back to the gallery. I only took two steps before Dominic appeared at the end of the hall, the light from the gala glowing around his dark form.

He took long, assured strides toward me, eating the distance in seconds.

"I looked everywhere for you." He sounded more gruff than normal, and almost accusatory.

"Did you? I guess you missed the restroom." I brushed by him, unwilling to participate in anything other than work-related conversation.

He caught my arm, bringing me to a stop. "Can you stay here with me for a minute?"

I shook him off. "Actually, no. I need to get back out there. If someone saw us here together, they might get the wrong idea."

I tried to move around him, but he wouldn't let go. "Claire."

My eyes flicked from his to the hand clamped around my arm. "Dominic, please let go of me. I'd like to leave this hallway now."

He dropped my arm, but kept my path blocked with his body. "Are you angry with me?"

"I'm not anything with you." I folded my arms under my breasts. "I'm working."

He slammed his hand on the wall beside him. "This is bullshit," he hissed. "Tell me what's going on. Talk to me, Claire."

My eyes flared. "*Now* you want to talk to me? That's funny, because I want the exact opposite." I pushed past him, and this time, he let me. Right before I left the hall to rejoin the gala, I turned back. "Let me know when you're ready to leave."

In my head, I made a dramatic exit, running down a grand set of marble steps like Cinderella with my prince chasing after me. Reality didn't look like fairy tales, though. For one, I wasn't much of a runner, and I couldn't be certain Dominic would chase me. But more importantly, I wouldn't upend my burgeoning career for a relationship that was nothing but temporary.

An hour later, Dominic found me at my table, chatting with my new doctor friends.

"It's time to go, Claire." He stood over me with his hand out for me to take. I allowed him to help me up after I said my goodbyes to everyone and tucked away the business card Dr. Neurosurgeon gave me.

In the limo, I tried to sit on my own side, but Dominic just parked himself beside me.

"Did that guy actually give you his phone number in front of me? And you took it?" He sounded flat, devoid of any emotion.

"It doesn't matter." I scooted over as far as I could, my head turned to the window.

Deep grumbles vibrated his chest. "I can't fight with you tonight. I just can't."

"I'm not fighting you, Dominic. I promise."

We rode home in silence, though Dominic didn't allow me to have any physical space from him. He practically sat on top of me with a possessive hand gripping high on my thigh. The tension riding with us as a third passenger wasn't anything like what we normally had. It wasn't lust-filled and explosive. Sorrow and disappointment clung to the thick edges of the air. When we pulled up to Dominic's house, I couldn't get out of the car fast enough.

I went straight to his bedroom, digging through my neatly packed bag for pajamas. Dominic followed me into the room, pensive and careful. He removed his tie and jacket, laying them on the back of a chair, then unbuttoned the top of his shirt.

"Can I unzip your dress for you?" he asked.

"Yes, thank you."

He came up to me, spinning me around to face away from him. His knuckles dragged along my shoulders, then the center of my back until he reached my zipper. He tugged it slowly, letting his fingers touch my skin as he lowered it. When he reached the bottom, he pressed a kiss to my shoulder blade.

"Beauty," he murmured.

I stayed rooted there, trembling, until the bathroom door closed. Then I grabbed my things, taking them with me to the guest bedroom down the hall. I hung my dress in the closet, threw on my pajamas, then washed my face in the attached bath.

Dominic was sitting on the end of the bed when I came out, his dark eyes thunderous.

"What the hell are you doing, Claire? Explain yourself."

"I'm sleeping in here tonight. I thought that was plainly obvious."

He approached me and cupped my jaw. "You're angry at me."

"How astute of you to notice." I jerked my face away. "Get out."

He had the nerve to laugh and throw his hands in the air like I was the exasperating one. "I've had a hell of a night. I need you to get back in our room and stop pushing me. You're not going to win."

I wasn't quick to anger, and I had more patience than most, but I'd run out of both. If he just left me alone, I could have cooled down. In the morning, I could have had a level-headed conversation.

Not now, though. I went off like a shot, almost hissing my words. "You had your hands all over another woman tonight. I *saw* you on the terrace. I saw how you were touching her, and from my vantage point, there was nothing innocent about it. You may not think you owe me fidelity, and maybe you're right, but I won't be in your fucking bed when you're hard for another woman. You can go, Dominic."

When he didn't move, I pushed his shoulders. "Please go."

He caught my wrists, cuffing them at my sides with surprising gentleness given how rigid he was. "I haven't looked at another woman since you showed up on my plane. Tonight wasn't about that, and the last thing I was at that gala was aroused."

I lifted my chin, unwilling to yield. "You ignored me all night. You ignored me, and you held that woman in your arms." I broke away from him, striding to the door. "I don't even understand why you're here. Why aren't you with her?"

I opened the bedroom door, but he didn't budge. His head hung like the weight of whatever was going on inside it was too heavy to hold.

"I'm sorry." His voice broke, and I nearly did too. What the hell?

His eyes lifted to mine. They were black pools of sadness, tempting me to dive in.

"I'm not good with emotions. I know I fucked up tonight, but it wasn't about her."

"That's not how it looked to me."

He moved closer, and when I didn't protest, he closed most of the distance between us. His brows were angry lightning bolts, slashing through the landscape of his beautiful, livid face. "You have to see I'm all about you. Every second is you."

"Are you actually mad at me?" My hands balled into fists. I was seriously considering socking this infuriating man right in the jaw. "Really, Dominic?"

His hand snapped out, grasping the nape of my neck and pulling me against him. "I'm angry at the fucking world, Claire."

"I know," I whispered. That much had become quite clear to me.

The crazy thing was, I wasn't afraid of the trembling, barely-controlled man whose hands were on me. When his mouth closed over mine in a desperate kiss, I returned it with equal fervor. I clawed at his bare chest, quietly raging against him and my reaction to him.

"I need you, Claire," he gritted out.

Dominic backed me into the wall beside the door, kissing me so hard, if lips could bruise, mine surely would be when he was finished with me.

His thick erection prodded my stomach, and I couldn't stop myself from rubbing against it. That earned me a growl, and my shirt torn off me. His hands were everywhere, rough and insistent. Touching my skin like if he didn't, it would disappear.

My nails raked ribbons down his sides and back, slipping under the waistband of his sweatpants to draw red lines on his tight ass. There was nothing loving or affectionate about the way we were going at each other. This was need and frenzied desire.

Dominic spun me by my shoulders, leaning his full weight against my back as he used one hand to tug my shorts off. His cock wedged in the valley of my ass as he reached between my legs to drag his fingers through my folds.

"Wet, baby."

"It seems being pissed off at you turns me on." He circled my clit as I spoke, so my voice faded out on the last half of my sentence. My back arched, opening me to Dominic's cock. He kept circling my clit even as he positioned himself at my entrance.

My breath slammed out of my body when he entered me in a merciless thrust. My ass slapped against his taut pelvis as he took me with brutal force. Grunts and huffs were loud in my ear until his hot lips closed around the tendon in my neck, sucking hard enough to bruise.

A violent, soul-shaking orgasm crashed through me. My belly tightened, and my skin vibrated, each nerve ending alive and flaring. Dominic never slowed his relentless pace, plunging into me like if he fucked me hard enough, he'd wipe my memory clean.

"I hate you," I panted.

"I know, baby," he answered back. "I hate me too."

His sweat dripped on my shoulder, and then his mouth was there to lick it up. Goose bumps rose on my heated skin, but Dominic scraped them away with his teeth.

I pressed my hips back, grinding against him. "I need it so much harder."

Dominic went harder. He slammed into me again and again, grunting and slapping. I tried to keep up with him, but he was in charge, drilling into me like he was trying to fit his entire being inside me.

"You don't walk away from me." He gripped my jaw, turning my face to the side. "You don't sleep in another room. We had a deal." His eyes were wild, but still so needy and mournful, tears pricked behind mine.

"You broke our deal first." I kissed him hard, not wanting excuses. This was madness, this thing between us. Reason had no place here.

Dominic tipped my head back as far as it would go, drowning me with his lips and tongue.

"You're mine, Claire. *Mine.*"

None of this made sense. We were done in five days. I wasn't his, and he wasn't mine. The boiling jealousy raging inside me wasn't mine. It was borrowed, and the expiration date was fast approaching.

But still, I clawed at the wall as my pussy gripped Dominic's thick cock. He kissed me through my second orgasm, which left me shattered and weak.

A sharp bite on my shoulder preceded him pushing into me as deep as he could and holding there. He opened his mouth, bellowing my name like a cry for help as he filled me with hot, liquid pleasure.

After a minute or two, he slowly pulled out, and I winced, suddenly aware of how raw I now was between my legs.

He murmured my name, stroking my cheek with his knuckles. It was too tender, too sweet, and I wasn't ready for that. I couldn't deal with nice Dominic.

I managed to slide from between the sweaty, panting man on my back and the wall at my front, and snag my T-shirt and shorts. Even though cum dripped down my thigh, I quickly dressed, distancing myself from what we'd just done, then closed myself in the bathroom to clean up.

I took my time, staring at the strange girl in the mirror, with bruises on her neck and swollen lips. This girl was almost unrecognizable, and in some ways, that was a relief. I'd gotten so used to living internally, that when I'd arrived on this tour, I hadn't remembered how to live out loud. That wasn't a problem anymore, but in moments like this, I sort of wished to be my old self. If I were, I'd curl tonight up in a tight ball and stuff it away in the recesses of my mind.

The woman I was now washed her face, brushed her teeth and hair, and calmly walked back into the bedroom. Déjà vu hit me when I found Dominic waiting on the end of the bed again.

"Come to our room," he said immediately.

I shook my head, my lips pressed tight.

He sighed, looking tired and every bit his age, with deep lines around his mouth and etched across his forehead. Then he came to me and wrapped his arms around me, pressing a feather-soft kiss to my temple.

"Please. I need to tell you about Dylan. My boy." He cleared his throat, then pressed another kiss on my head. "My son."

CHAPTER THIRTY-THREE

DOMINIC

I'D NEVER HAD A SINGLE INTENTION OF TELLING CLAIRE ABOUT DYLAN. It didn't make sense to lay my trauma and grief at her feet. But I couldn't let her fall asleep tonight without at least explaining why I'd behaved the way I had.

She refused to come back to our room, and as much as every fiber of my being wanted to haul her over my shoulder and force her, I didn't. She was pissed, and I had to respect that, so I pulled her down beside me on the end of the guest bed.

"For what it's worth, I *did* check on you. Every time I looked over, you were talking and laughing with the people at your table." I scrubbed at the side of my head. "You seemed okay, and...I don't know. I'm not used to having someone I even *want* to check up on."

Claire wasn't interested in hearing that. She barely acknowledged me with a twitch of her lips.

"Chelsea is Dylan's mother." I hadn't told anyone this story, about my past, my kid, any of it, since I met Marta. And even then, it only came out over a blunt and a bottle of tequila. It could be said I wasn't much of a talker anyway, but about this, I barely knew how to formulate the words.

"I met her back when I was coming up, just getting famous. Back in my The Hype days. We were friends who sometimes slept together, but we weren't ever more than that." Leaning forward, I steepled my hands under my chin. "I was only twenty-four when she told me she was pregnant. She wasn't one-hundred-percent the kid was mine, but she was pretty sure."

Claire sat as still as a statue, her gaze stuck somewhere around my knees.

"I was basically a kid myself. Didn't want to be a dad. But once he was born, he was mine. I looked at that wrinkled old man baby face and knew. I had two weeks with him. Chelsea got really overwhelmed at first, so it was just me and the kid a lot of the time. Then she came home one day and told me Dylan wasn't mine after all. He was my bandmate, Eric's. They were going to be a family."

"She took him?" Claire whispered.

"She took him, and I let her. The Hype broke up, I checked out of life, cut everyone off. It was over three years before I pulled my head out of my ass and saw him again. When it came down to it, Eric wasn't very interested in being a father, but Chelsea stepped up the mom game. Dylan was cool as hell. He called me Dom, I called him kid. I taught him how to play guitar, and we wrote songs together."

Her fingertip trailed along my knuckles. "You loved him."

"Of course I did." I pounded the heel of my hand into my forehead. "I loved that boy like he was mine. He *was* mine. Though, it took me years to acknowledge that, until he got sick and we knew he wasn't going to get better."

"The hospital...in Houston?" Her index finger hooked with mine.

"Yeah," I breathed. "Chels took him there to be treated by a specialist. She moved there with him. My denial was so fucking thick, I kept working, doing concerts, putting out albums instead of soaking up every last minute I could with him. I failed my boy."

"How old was he when he...?"

"Eleven. He'd be eighteen this year, but I can't picture him that way. All I see when I think about him are his first breaths and his last. It's like..." I stabbed at my chest, "everything else became eviscerated the moment he died."

"I'm sorry." She wrapped her soft arms around my middle, resting her head on my shoulder. "I'm so, so sorry."

Honeysuckle enveloped me, thawing some of the hollow ice in my chest.

"Yeah." I kissed her hair, nuzzling my face in her waves. "Chels and I don't have much in common anymore. Our kid was the one thing tying us together. Grief sent us on our separate ways. We see each other once a year at the gala. What you saw between us was two parents missing their boy. And on the terrace—" I had to stop, breathe, figure out how to say the words.

"You don't have to tell me anything else, Dominic. This is so much." Her palm flattened on my cheek. "I don't want you to hurt."

What she didn't understand was I deserved the pain. I had loved that baby, but the second I was presented with an out, I took it and walked away from him. Chelsea would have shared Dylan with me. She wasn't a monster. But it was easier for me to walk away entirely than deal with my heart being cracked in two again and again seeing him with his *real* dad.

My selfish decisions cost me years with my boy. If I could relive any choice I'd ever made, it would be that one. I'd still be a grieving, broken man, but at least I'd know I did right by him.

I inhaled more of Claire's goodness, breathing out the black, black tar of regret filling my chest.

"Chels is pregnant. She's only twelve weeks, but she did all the testing and knows it's a boy. That's what she was telling me on the terrace. And I'm fucking sorry I touched her that way. I'm sorry you saw it and—"

Claire cut me off with a tender press of her lips. She hummed, stroking my hair and holding me. I hadn't cried since Dylan died. That part of me had been shut off. But being held by this sweet, entirely too young and too *good* woman, had me on the edge. Claire made me want in every way. For a crazy second, I thought about what it would be like to heal this gaping wound in my soul so I could really, truly have her.

But even the thought of trying to keep her threatened to send me spiraling. I didn't *keep*. Life was too fleeting for me to consider anything as more than temporary. No matter how much I wanted it. Or how utterly vital it became.

"I don't understand how she can want to go through it again."

"Through what?" Claire asked.

"Loving someone, loving her new baby, while knowing what it's like to have that kind of love ripped from her." I shook my head. "I could never. *Never.*"

"I don't know." She rubbed my shoulders and kissed my cheek. "I guess she weighed the risks and decided it was worth it to have that kind of love again. She's brave, but that doesn't mean you aren't because you don't want to take the same risk."

I sucked in a ragged breath, reaching for Claire like a drowning man. Even considering what it would mean to let myself feel, to allow myself to love someone the way I'd loved Dylan, pulled me under like a pair of lead boots.

My fingers tangled in the back of her hair, firmly gripping her so we were face-to-face. "I need to know you're okay. I hurt you, I know that, but I didn't want to."

"I'm okay." Her big brown eyes were wet with tears I'd put there, but they were open and true, so I believed her. "I wish you would have told me what I was walking into, but that doesn't matter anymore. Thank you for telling me about Dylan. I'm so sorry he's not here anymore. I know you took the best care of him, though. It's who you are."

Panic swirled in a cyclone inside me, and the only way to squelch it was to shut down. If Claire kept saying things like that...no. I couldn't do this anymore.

I leaned my forehead on hers. "Will you come to our room now?"

"Of course I will."

We left her bag there to deal with tomorrow. Once we were back in my bedroom, I breathed easier, then easier still when tangled up under the covers. We caressed bare, warm skin, and though I was hard, there wasn't anything sexual about it. We were finding our way back to each other—back to where we so easily fit—where our lives outside of this tour didn't exist. It was only us, only this.

"I have Chelsea's song tattooed on me, don't I?" she asked with a hint of a grin.

My mouth ached to smile with her, but my muscles didn't cooperate. "I wrote it with her in mind, but it's about picking up when it seems impossible. I think it's your song now too."

She snuggled against my chest, yawning. "I don't mind sharing a song with her. She liked my dress."

"*I* liked your dress."

"I like you." Sleep weighed down each word.

"I like you too, Claire." *Too damn much.*

If I could have, I would've put some space between us. Instead, I stood in the middle of the tracks, a train barreling straight for me, with full knowledge I'd be flattened on impact. That was an ending I knew.

It was the unknown endings I wouldn't stick around for. Because nothing lasted forever, no matter how much I wished it wasn't true. I'd done my share of hoping for forever, and those days were done for me.

CHAPTER THIRTY-FOUR

CLAIRE

SOMEHOW, we'd made it to our last stop of the tour. Nearly two months had gone by since I'd staggered onto Dominic Cantrell's plane. Annaliese had joked about me coming home a different woman, and I *felt* different. Somewhere along the way, I'd found my confidence again, and my youth. Life didn't have to be serious or about achieving goals. It was too short not to be enjoyed.

I had enjoyed the hell out of my life over the last two months. Dominic had been the centerpiece of that, sure, but it wasn't all about him. Marta was never getting rid of me. The Seasons Change had a fan for life. Rodrigo was the brother I'd never had, nor wanted, but I loved him more than I thought possible. Tomorrow night was the last show, then we'd be packing up and heading home.

So, it was natural for me to be sad this was all coming to an end. Even if I saw them again—and I really thought I would—we'd never be able to recapture this exact magic. The Seasons Change were going to blow up and join the big leagues any second, and...well, Dominic and I were parting ways for good.

Marta slapped me on the shoulder. "No frownies, kidlet. I disapprove."

"But I'm sad. I'm not allowed to be sad?" I stuck out my bottom lip so she'd take pity on me.

"Save it for when you go home. Tonight is about drinking with friends and making really stupid memories that'll make you giggle every time you think back on them."

"Fine. That actually does sound better than moping around here." Even though *here* was a stunning penthouse in Chicago with views of Lake Michigan from the walls of windows spanning the length of the condo.

"The old man still has no plans of joining us, right?" Marta asked, referring to Dominic.

"No, he's staying home to putter. You know how the olds like to putter."

She snorted so loud, we both froze, eyes wide, then fell into a fit of giggles.

"No you didn't, girl. He will murder you," she said through laughter.

Once we straightened ourselves out, I went to find my old man, who had just gotten back from working out in the building's gym.

Dominic was pulling on a pair of jeans when I walked into the bedroom. My stomach clenched both from how unfairly handsome he was and how much I already missed him. After he told me about Dylan, I'd half expected him to pull away, but instead, he'd held me even closer.

Ending things wasn't my choice anymore. If I could keep this man I'd fallen for so wholly, I would. But he made it clear again and again our time was finite, and I had to believe him, even though it felt like he never planned on letting me go either.

"Hi." I paused at the door. "Can I come in?"

He crossed the hardwood floor to where I stood, slipped his hand around my waist, and tugged me inside. "I always want you where I am. That shouldn't be a question at this point."

"You never want to be alone?"

A line formed in the center of his forehead as his eyebrows pressed inward. "I want to be alone with you."

I snorted a laugh. "That's not alone."

"If I have the choice between stewing in my own thoughts and spending every waking second with you, it's going to be you every single time."

"Whoa." My heart flipped and lodged in the back of my throat. "That was incredibly sweet."

He shrugged like he hadn't said something big. "It's just the truth." He dipped his head to nibble on my neck. "Can I watch you get ready?"

"Only if you promise not to derail me by luring me into bed."

Marta and I were going out with The Seasons Change to Adam's favorite dive bar. He'd grown up in Chicago, so some of his friends were coming out too. I'd invited Dominic, but to my surprise, he declined. Then he reminded me he was *Dominic Cantrell* and couldn't just hang out at dive bars at this stage in his life. He didn't really blend, and neither did his two brick-wall bodyguards.

Dominic sat in the bathroom, talking to me while I took a shower. When I told him how amazing the acoustics were, he took the hint and sang a few songs. I hadn't taken enough advantage of having my own rock star at my beck and call, and now, it was almost too late.

Wrapped in a towel, I searched through my clothes and picked a dress. I tossed it on the bed, and Dominic picked it up, sliding the fabric between his fingers.

"I like this one," he murmured.

"You haven't even seen me in it."

"But I can tell how good you'll feel wearing it." He cocked his head, raking his eyes over me. "Wear something else."

I tugged his beard. "Not a chance in the world."

A half-smile ruined his attempt at being stern. "I didn't think so. You'll just have to let me get my hands all over you before you go. And after."

"Always."

If always meant the next forty-eight hours...

I dressed with my audience of one, my own personal fan club who never failed to remind me how *goddamn hot* I was. Before I slid on my heels, I climbed onto the bed, straddling Dominic. I ran my thumb over the crease between his dark brows, then touched my lips to his. A wave of wistfulness hit me so hard, I clung to Dominic's neck so I didn't get knocked down.

I'd miss this when it was gone.

"What are you doing tonight?" I asked.

He squeezed my ass, growling against my neck. "Thinking about you in this dress."

"Do something productive. At least write a song about me in this dress." I was purely joking, but the way Dominic's eyes lit up, he liked the idea.

"Stay with me, Claire," he crooned. "Your lips are like honey, your smile is my air."

My eyelids fluttered, and a corset tightened around my chest. "I'd stay, you know. If you asked me tomorrow, I'd stay."

I hadn't meant to say that, but how could I not? If I walked away without bringing up the possibility of us being together after the tour, I'd regret it forever.

Dominic's arms flexed around my middle, and he buried his face in my neck, but he didn't say a single word. And that was answer enough.

I finally tore myself from him, and Marta and I hopped in an Uber to the bar. Adam leaned by the entrance, waiting for us. When our car pulled up, he opened the door, helping Marta and me out.

"Immaculate, Claire." He let out a low whistle, looking me over.

"And what about me?" Marta demanded.

Adam grinned wide. "Fucking hot. Gorgeous. If I wore glasses, they'd be steamed up."

Marta flipped him off. "Way too much, lover boy."

The inside of the bar was a true dive, but in a hip, gentrified way. The wood floors were scuffed from being trod on for decades by combat boots, and the walls were decorated in old neon beer signs with Sharpie scribbles in between. Loud rock music only added to the vibe. '

Perched on the end of the bar was Rodrigo, sitting cross-legged with his beer in the air. If he were anyone else, I would have said he was already drunk, but he wasn't anyone else.

I stopped in front of him. "What are you doing up there, silly?"

He booped my nose. "Waiting for you, *preciosa*. What are you doing down there?"

I pointed to my feet. "I thought this was where the booze was. Am I wrong?"

From behind him, the bartender handed him a light pink drink in a glass, and Rodrigo held it out to me. "Here you go. Vodka cran, light on the ice, just like you like it."

I took a sip, a smile splitting my lips. "My man. What would I do without you?"

He shrugged. "You'd be so damn thirsty."

He hopped off the bar, and we joined the rest of the group. Adam's friends were a loud bunch of dude-bros and a few really hot women. Introductions went around, but I was more interested in talking to Iris, Marta, and Roddy than making new friends I'd never see again.

"What happens when you get back to New York?" I asked Iris.

She held up two fingers. "We have a couple weeks at home, then we're off to Europe. When we come back, we're doing a music festival. I don't think we'll be home for longer than a month until next year."

Rodrigo bounced in his chair. "It's gonna be so lit."

Adam swooped down on me, bending over so he could hug me from behind. "Are you ready for another drink? I'm the drink fairy tonight."

I swirled my half-full vodka cranberry. "I'm still good, but I'll sprinkle some pixie dust in the air when I'm ready for a refill."

He kissed my temple before I knew it was coming. "All right. When you get a chance, I want to talk to you for a minute."

I shifted away from his hot beer breath. I really didn't want to have a private conversation with Adam, but he'd been decent to me through the tour, so I'd listen to what he had to say. I'd also put it off as long as possible.

"Find me in a little bit," I said.

He let go of his hold on me and squeezed my shoulders. "Don't run away."

I smiled. "Don't worry, I won't."

He moved back to his friends and flirty girls, and I refocused on mine. Rodrigo challenged me to another round of Rock, Paper, Scissors, and I once again trounced him.

Despite Adam's claim of being the drink fairy, Roddy turned out to be my supplier. I never got thirsty when he was around, and neither did Marta or Iris. The night wore on, and we line danced to rock music and played darts with a picture of a rat with a mohawk as the target.

On my third drink, I finally got the dirt on Callum, the ever-absent band member.

Iris shook her head. "Callum is…"

"Shy," Rodrigo supplied.

"He's shy and not very good with people." Iris stretched an arm behind her head, revealing a wide swatch of tight, tattooed stomach. Marta barely looked for more than a second or two. Even *I* looked longer than a second or two.

Roddy nodded vehemently. "He's a good, sweet kid, though."

Marta slung her arm around my shoulders. "So, he doesn't hate Claire and me? He hasn't been actively avoiding us this whole tour?"

Iris laughed. "Oh, he's actively avoiding you, just like he's actively avoiding the rest of the world. That's just Callum."

I put my drink down on the table and snagged Marta, dragging her to the restroom with me. She gave me crazy eyes once I shut us inside.

"Are you over Iris or what?" I demanded.

Marta tucked her hands in her pockets and casually leaned against the wall. "She's a friend."

I wagged my finger at her. To be fair, I was half-drunk. "More information needed. Don't even try to escape my inquisition."

She shrugged. "We messed around again, but the spark wasn't there. It's sad because she's hot as hell, but on the sexuality spectrum, I think she leans more toward men. Another loss for the team."

"Boo. I'm glad you're not heartbroken at least."

"No, because you're going to hook me up with your sister." Her eyebrows shot up and down.

"Come see me when we get back and I'll make it happen. Annaliese will give you a run for your money, girl."

Marta rubbed her hands together. "Why do I like her already?"

We spent a few more minutes in the bathroom, then headed back out. Adam was hovering just outside the door with an expectant look on his face.

"Can we have that talk?" he asked, holding up a drink for me. It had too much ice, but I took it without complaint.

"Sure." I told Marta I'd catch up with her, and the face she made behind Adam's back was nearly my undoing, but I kept it together.

I leaned against the back wall of the bar, Adam beside me. His eyes were heavy-lidded, the aroma of beer was strong on his breath. "We haven't hung out much lately," he said.

"I know. I think because we haven't been staying in the same place lately—"

He reached out and tugged one of my curls. "I like you."

"I like you too. We're friends."

Shit, I was terrible at this. I'd never been faced with rejecting a man before. I'd been with Derrick so long, it had never been an issue. But I had a dreadful feeling that was where this was going.

"Yeah, we are." He inched closer, turning so his chest brushed my arm. "But we vibe when we're together. I'm not the only one who sees it. Even my friends feel it."

I glanced at Adam's overgrown frat-boy friends. They were nudging each other, red faced and laughing as they watched us together.

"They're laughing at us," I said.

"At me. They're laughing at what a fucking pussy I am. I've been into you for two months and I'm too chickenshit to make a move." His hot, damp hand slid over my jaw. "Well, I'm not throwing away my shot."

"Stop." I pressed a hand to his chest. "You're drunk, Adam."

He leaned in, running his nose along mine. "Come on, Claire-bear. I *like* you."

Derrick's nickname coming from Adam was like nails on a chalkboard. It made me want to curl into a ball and cover my ears so I never had to hear it again.

"You're making me really uncomfortable. That's not what you do to someone you like." My heart pounded like a wild beast in my chest. Adam had me caged in, both hands bracketing my head. He'd reduced my voice to a squeak and my fight to a mere scrap.

"I'm just tryna show you how good we could be." His hot breath pummeled at my lips, then his mouth took over, smashing against mine with no grace or finesse. He was sloppy, his tongue licking all over my lips and chin, alcohol dimming his aiming ability. His arms banded around my shoulders, molding me against him so tight, all I could do was squirm.

He lifted his head to meet my eyes, and I saw realization there. "Claire-bear?"

If he said it one more time, I'd scream the shaky walls of this dive down.

"Get off me, Adam," I rasped.

"I'm not gonna hurt you," he cooed.

"I don't want you to touch me." Tears welled in my eyes as panic surged through my veins. We were in a public place. My friends were just around the corner. This wasn't anything like the night Derrick knocked me unconscious, but telling myself that didn't help—not when I was trapped and afraid. My body froze as fear rooted me in place.

He brought his hand up to touch me, hit me, I didn't know, because he never got to do it.

Suddenly, I was free, and Adam had disappeared. I blinked, and Dominic was there, holding Adam by the back of his shirt. Dominic shook Adam hard, shoving him into a wooden high-top table and chairs.

Adam turned around with his hands raised, but Dominic didn't give him a chance to defend himself. His fist slammed into Adam's face. The music was too loud to hear, but I *felt* the crunch of Adam's nose.

"You don't get to touch her," Dominic roared. His fist met Adam's stomach, bending him in half, then Dominic brought his knee up, connecting to his chin, sending him back again.

Adam's friends came running over, surrounding us, yelling for Dominic to stop. Marta tried to intervene, but Dominic didn't see anything but blood. He got two more hits in on Adam before the bartender and bouncer were able to pull him off.

I couldn't breathe. Couldn't stand still. Couldn't be surrounded by the stench of beer, sweat, and blood one second longer. Mostly, I couldn't look at Dominic raging violently. His face was so contorted, I barely recognized him.

Was every man really a monster waiting to be unleashed?

Iris was the one who got me out. She rode with me back to the condo, assuring me Marta was taking care of Dominic. She rubbed my cold, shaking hands, promising everything would look better in the morning. She cursed alcohol and testosterone. I appreciated she was trying to comfort me, but I barely heard a word she said.

When I finally got back to the condo in the sky and had my first moment of silence, I slid down to the floor and sobbed. Adrenaline fled my body as fast as my tears flowed, leaving me listless.

How could Adam have put me in this position—back in the place where I was let down and hurt by yet another man, after spending months clawing my way back to the surface? Was this how it was? How it would be? Trusting someone new was difficult enough without being on edge all the time, waiting for their mask to fall. I didn't know if I could do this again.

It took the rest of my energy to stumble into the first bedroom I passed. It wasn't the one I'd been sharing with Dominic, but that didn't give me a second of pause. Still in my dress and makeup, I curled up under the covers, exhausted to my very core.

Before I fell asleep, I had enough presence of mind to text Isabela.

Dominic was involved in a fight at a bar here in Chicago tonight. I can't be sure it wasn't caught on film. If this becomes public, I don't think I'm capable of handling this situation alone. I'll be in touch in the morning. I'm sorry.

CHAPTER THIRTY-FIVE

DOMINIC

"CLAIRE!"

Marta tugged at my arm. "Shut up, Dom. Stop yelling."

Panic stabbed at my gut with a dull blade. All the lights were off in the condo. The only noises were Marta's shoes squeaking on the floor as she dragged her heels, attempting to slow me down. I was a bull, and the stark absence of Claire Fontana was my red flag. I charged through the sprawling space into our bedroom.

Empty.

"Where is she?"

"I'll check the other rooms. Iris said she came back here so she's somewhere." Marta headed toward her room while I went in the opposite direction.

The door to one of the guestrooms was closed. Instinct told me Claire was in there and if I went barreling in like I had the urge to, I'd make everything worse.

Carefully opening the door, the hall light illuminated a sliver of the dark room and the top of Claire's head peeking out from the covers. Needing to see her more than I needed to take another breath, I kneeled beside the bed, finding my sleeping girl.

Her nose was still red, and mascara tracked down her cheeks from crying. I almost reached out to touch her, to stroke her cheek until she opened her eyes, but I didn't. What the fuck would I even say?

That I couldn't stand spending one night away from her, especially after she said she'd stay if I asked, so I took a chance and showed up at the bar?

That seeing that kid, that asshole touching her, sent me into a blind rage?

And then, when I realized she'd left, my heart hammered in my chest so hard from fear, I'd considered the very real possibility I'd been on the edge of stroking out?

I couldn't say any of those things. My insides were disfigured so hideously, I wouldn't wish seeing them on my worst enemy. Instead, I looked at her for as long as I could bear, then retreated to the living room.

Marta was waiting for me with a bottle of water, quiet music playing over the speakers.

"She's asleep?" she asked.

"Yep. Out cold. In the guest room."

"I'm surprised you didn't demand she wake up and get her ass in your bed."

Marta knew me too damn well. It was exactly what I wanted to do.

I shrugged, sinking down onto the sofa. "Sometimes, I'm actually able to fight off the devil on my shoulder."

Marta took a seat on the ottoman in front of me. She rubbed her hands on her jeans, lifting her head to look me in the eye. "You scared me tonight."

"I know. I scared myself."

"No, listen to me." She jabbed a finger at me. "Violence has no place in my life. I survived loving a violent man, but that's done now. You don't get to react however you want with no thought of the consequences. This isn't just your life, Dom."

"He was touching her, and she was trying to push him off! Where were you?" I hissed.

"I couldn't see them. If I had, I would have kicked him in the dick. But you sent him to the motherfucking hospital. He won't be playing tomorrow night. I'm pretty sure you broke a few bones in his face. You went crazy, and for what? What the hell did you accomplish? Terrifying your girl and your best friend?"

I whimpered at that on the inside. "I'd never hurt you in a million years, Mar."

"But don't you see? A violent man is a violent man. You're a volcano waiting to erupt."

"I know I overreacted, but I will not stand by while a man touches a woman who doesn't want to be touched. Especially not a woman who is mine."

She blew out a long breath. "A woman who's yours? Who the hell are you kidding? Your little *entanglement* is over in a day. That woman isn't yours, and now she gets to walk away from another man who used brute force to express his feelings rather than...I don't know, words."

She brought me to a halt. "What do you mean another man?"

Marta flicked her fingers dismissively. "Claire's angel of an ex-husband left her with a concussion as a parting gift."

"*What?*" Fury shot me to my feet. "*What* did you say?"

"Sit down, please. I've had enough of your rage for one night. It's giving me a headache."

I looked down at Marta, her hand pressed to her forehead. Guilt sapped my strength. My legs folded, sending me back down to the cushions.

"She never told me," I said.

"I would have thought, with the way you've had her locked away with you for the last month, you'd know everything."

"Fuck." I scrubbed at my face, frustrated and uneasy. "No, she said he was controlling, but never said a word about physical abuse. *Claire...*"

Marta leveled me with an assessing glare. "You were thinking about keeping her, weren't you? Dominic, were you going to ask her to be with you after the tour?"

"Does it matter now?"

Her glare hardened. "You tell me. Does it?"

I hadn't gone to the bar with an answer. I only knew when Claire said she wanted to stay together, I felt such a powerful sense of relief, I'd been silenced by it.

My hands shook as I stared down at them. Nothing about me had changed. I'd let this beautiful woman in, to an extent, but I was still this deeply chaotic, damaged, unfit-for-human-companionship man. If I kept her, I'd ruin her. I'd hurt her and break her heart. Not because I would stop wanting her, but because I wasn't any good at loving.

Not even myself.

Everything about Claire was good, including my memories. I'd like to think she had collected some good ones of me. If we cut this off now, we wouldn't sully them. I'd leave her sweet, freckled face pure in my mind, like my grandparents' house back in Georgia.

She'd move on, get her life together, find someone else—someone her age who wasn't emotionally stunted and unable to give her everything she deserved.

The knife already lodged inside me twisted, stirring my guts into a mass of knots.

I opened my palms on my knees. "We had an agreement. Four weeks and we'd walk away."

Marta nodded slowly. "So, nothing's changed."

She meant *I* hadn't changed. Maybe I had, I didn't know, but it wasn't enough.

My phone started buzzing in my pocket. Not many people had the number, so I took it out, checking the screen. Isabela had texted.

Claire informed me of the incident tonight. I'm flying out tomorrow morning to handle everything. Try not to burn down the world or punch a grandpa before I get there.

"Iz is coming."

Marta rolled her eyes. "Wonderful. What a perfect cherry on top of this shit sundae. What are you going to do, Dom?"

Groaning, I shoved my hands into my hair. "I'm going to do the right thing for once."

It might possibly kill me, but I was going to do right by Claire, no matter what.

CHAPTER THIRTY-SIX

CLAIRE

WHEN MY BEDROOM DOOR OPENED AND DOMINIC QUIETLY STEPPED INSIDE, I'd been awake for a while, even though the sun had barely risen. He didn't approach my bed like I'd braced myself for. Instead, in the dim light of dawn, he set down my suitcase and carry-on bag next to the door.

"Hey."

His head jerked in my direction. "I didn't mean to wake you. Sorry."

"I was awake when you snuck in like a thief in the night."

He ran his hand over the top of his head and blew out a puff of breath. "Bad night, huh?"

I sat up and swung my legs over the side of the bed. "It was. For you too?"

He stayed right by the door, folding his arms over his chest. "I didn't do a lot of sleeping."

"Why not?"

Part of me wanted him to say he couldn't sleep without me. That he was miserable over his behavior last night. He'd been too worried about me to close his eyes even for a second. Another part of me, maybe the bigger part, feared he *would* say exactly that and what it would mean.

He shook his head. "It doesn't matter. I brought your things in here. Isabela's coming, so I didn't want her to see your clothes in my bedroom."

A ton of bricks hit me square in the chest. I recognized Dominic's flat, detached tone from when we first met. I understood his aloof demeanor and the context beneath what he was saying.

I stood up beside the bed, facing Dominic fully in my wrinkled dress and smeared makeup. "Will Isabela be spending time in your bedroom?"

He shrugged. "She goes where she wants. I don't want our temporary arrangement to have lasting repercussions on your career."

I moved closer, to the foot of the bed. "So, you and I are done now?"

One second went by, then he nodded, his eyes unreadable in this light. "With everything that happened…"

"What happened? Was it me telling you I want to keep seeing you, or you attacking Adam because he tried to kiss me? Or was it before that? Was it when you told me about Dylan and let me inside?"

He straightened, his body tightening. "Claire, you knew what this was. You're not even divorced and you think you want something more with me? I'm an old, broken man, baby. This isn't your stop. You have to keep riding on."

I knew he was right, but he pissed me off. I wasn't ready, and neither was he, but I also wasn't closed off to something more. The difference between us was I saw myself as a work in progress, and he viewed himself as a factory reject, destined to be tossed aside as imperfect and unworthy.

I stepped up to him so he could look me in the eye when he told me he didn't want me anymore. I wouldn't put up a fight or yell or scream, but I expected honesty, just as he'd demanded from me all along.

"You know, I kept thinking you were the right person, but our timing was off."

Dominic's nostrils flared, but he kept every other reaction tightly locked down.

I laid my hand on his taut forearm. "You once told me it was easy to mistake need for love, and I'm beginning to think that's what I've done with you. You came into my life when I *needed* what you offered, and I thought I was falling. I see how easy it would be to confuse the two feelings." I slid my hand down his arm to rest on top of his. "Thank you for giving me what I needed. And thank you even more for reminding me never to settle. When I *do* fall in love, it will be with someone who unquestioningly loves me back in every way."

He opened his rough palm and squeezed my fingers. "You deserve that. The moon and the stars and the whole fucking universe."

I gently shoved him away from me. "I know."

His exhale was heavy. "You're going, aren't you?"

"I don't think I'm needed here anymore. Isabela will take care of you."

I'd said the last part with more venom than necessary, but as hurt as I was, I was also pissed. Dominic Cantrell was a coward, and I was getting really tired of cowardly men.

He backed up to the doorway. "This isn't how I pictured us ending. I'm sorry it has to go like this."

The funny thing was, I'd never pictured our ending. Not that I was naive enough to think we'd last forever, but the ending was never the thing I'd concentrated on.

"It didn't *have* to go like this. Life doesn't just happen to you." I kneeled beside my bags, searching for something to wear other than this dress. I'd burn this dress if I had access to an open flame. I certainly wouldn't be wearing it again.

"You're right." He tapped on the doorframe. "I'm sorry anyway."

When I looked up from my bag, he was gone. If I stopped moving, I'd fall apart, and that wasn't an option. Not here. So, I booked a last-minute flight home, then I showered, dressed, and slipped my feet into my favorite rose gold oxfords.

The condo was quiet and empty when I wheeled my suitcase through. My steps didn't stutter even once when I left, pulling the door shut behind me.

When my plane lifted off and the city of Chicago lay beneath me, I gave it the middle finger as a last goodbye. My husband's affair in this city had shattered me. Silly me, a few months later, I came back to be kicked in the teeth by Dominic Cantrell. My lesson had been well and truly learned this time. Chicago and I were officially through. No more men who couldn't find it within themselves to rise up and be better. No more settling for lukewarm. Once my bruises healed, *I'd* rise up and be better.

I needed just a little Annaliese time before any of that happened. She waited at the airport for me with open arms, which I fell into with a deep sigh of relief.

"You're going to be so good," she murmured into my hair.

"I know."

Even though I ached all over from missing him, I wouldn't let myself stumble. Never, ever again.

Annaliese took my bag on her shoulder and my hand in hers. "Let's go home, baby."

CHAPTER THIRTY-SEVEN

CLAIRE

I WALKED DOWN A row of evergreens with a hose in hand, giving them a gentle shower. The Seasons Change played on my earbuds, and the sun shined through the open roof of my sister's nursery.

This gig wasn't so bad. I'd been working here a week and hadn't killed a plant yet. And Annaliese kept me so busy, I didn't have time to focus on the ache in my chest.

That happened at night, when I curled up in my closet-room, alone in my little bed. That was when I missed Dominic so badly, it took my breath away. A week's absence had done nothing to lessen the intensity of my loss. I wasn't falling apart like I had when I left Derrick. This was different. This was heartbreak.

A tap on my shoulder startled me into dropping my hose, which got back at me by spraying me in the face. Shrieking, I snatched it off the ground, pointing it away from me, and whirled around to find Marta cracking up.

I turned the hose off and yanked out my earbuds, both stupefied and thrilled.

"What?" I screeched.

"Did you really think you could walk outta my life forever, kidlet?" Without hesitation, she gathered me into a tight hug. "I missed your freaking face."

"Missed you too." Tears of relief pricked my eyes.

She pulled back, giving me a long once-over. "I know you said you needed a little room, but I'm a self-centered bitch, okay? I needed to see you."

Marta had texted me by the time I got to the airport, frantic to find me gone from the condo. I had told her I needed to go quiet for a while, but that she hadn't done anything wrong.

"I'm glad you're a self-centered bitch because I needed to see you too." I spread my arms. "My new boss cracks the whip, but it's not such a bad place to work, is it?"

Marta tucked her hands in the pockets of her jeans. "If you're happy, then I am too."

I sighed, my shoulders rolling forward. "I'm not happy, but I do like working here."

"Aw, Claire. Shit, I'm sorry. Does it help to know he's a miserable fuck right now? Like, more miserable than usual?"

Pressing my lips in a tight line, I shook my head. Knowing that didn't help at all.

Marta knocked on her forehead. "I'm stupid and terrible at consoling apparently. That topic is closed. I get it."

I tried to laugh instead of cry. "Who could have predicted I'd become attached to the man I spent every waking and sleeping moment with for almost two months?"

"I could have."

Marta and I turned at the sound of my sister's voice. She stepped closer, that same sympathetic expression she'd been giving me all week plastered on her face. Annaliese could be funny and sarcastic, but when it came down to it, she was a soft place to land for anyone who needed it—especially me.

"And you didn't warn me?" I asked.

Annaliese curled her arm around my shoulders. "Are you going to introduce me to your friend?"

"This is Marta. Marta, my sister, Annaliese."

Marta gave me an eyebrow raise, then she leaned in and gave Annaliese a quick hug.

"So, you're the sister Claire said I reminded her of."

Annaliese glanced at her, then at me with a purely skeptical expression. Marta had on her signature all-black clothes with platform boots and dramatic makeup while Annaliese wore cargo pants, a T-shirt that said, "Garden Gangster," and a pink bandana in her hair.

"Not looks. Personality," I clarified.

Her arm tightened around me. "It's lovely to meet you. You were the person Claire mentioned second most often when she was away."

Marta grinned at both of us. "That is one of the many reasons why Claire is my favorite person. Also, the two of you are more than adorable together. It feels all sistah-power up in here all of the sudden."

My sister had the audacity to wink at Marta. "We can be a terrible twosome or a dream team. Depends on the day." She glanced at me again. "Is Marta coming to dinner with us?"

I bumped her with my hip. "I don't know. I haven't asked her."

Marta gave an exaggerated nod. "Yes, Marta is down for dinner."

Dinner was at the little Mexican hole-in-the-wall down the street from Annaliese's apartment. We sat on the patio, drinking margaritas and catching up on what life was like outside of the madness of touring.

"No more public relations for you? You're a gardener now?" Marta teased.

I laughed around the sip of margarita in my mouth. "Annaliese was kind enough to hire me, but it's a temporary thing. I actually have an interview next week, but I'm keeping quiet for now."

When I got home from Chicago, I'd tendered my resignation with Isabela. I couldn't picture being able to work for her, and I had a feeling she'd fire me anyway since I'd left without notice. The following day, she'd emailed, assuring me she'd provide a stellar recommendation to my next employer. I hadn't expected that, and knew Dominic was behind it, which only broke my heart further. He was still taking care of me, even after giving me up without a backward glance.

What was I supposed to do with that? How was I supposed to get over a man like that?

Annaliese knocked on the wooden table. "My Claire isn't meant for manual labor. She's an office and adorable shoes kind of girl."

Marta peeked at my muddy sneakers under the table. "I miss the shiny pink shoes."

I sighed. "Me too. They're going to make a comeback soon."

"I'm relieved to hear that. Really relieved." Marta held my gaze. "He's my best friend, like my ride or die, but I've been so angry at him, thinking he might have torn you apart because he has chosen to be a disaster."

"He broke my heart." I lifted a shoulder. "But nothing is unfixable."

"I wish he understood that." She sounded as frustrated with Dominic as I had been.

Annaliese touched my arm. "When Claire was twelve, we fostered a kitten. My parents made it clear to all of us we weren't keeping it. We had a dog already, and we were only taking care of the kitten until it had a permanent home. Claire swore up and down she didn't even like cats. But every day, she fell more in love with that kitten, until she begged our parents to let her keep it. By then, they'd already found a family to take it. There was no chance for the cat to be ours, but even knowing that, she still snuggled with that kitten every night. The day it went to live with its new family, Claire's heart was broken into little bits."

I shook my head. "I still miss Floofs. He was the sweetest kitten, and I really *don't* like cats. But I don't see the point of reliving this story."

She took my hand in hers. "My point is you're incapable of closing your heart, even when you want to. You aren't made that way. You, baby girl, were built to fall. It's just who you are."

I groaned. "So, I'm destined to wind up here again? And where was this little piece of knowledge when you were advising me on the ill-advised dick?"

Annaliese threw her hands up. "I didn't realize you didn't understand the concept of a quick fling! You had to go and cohabitate with him..."

The only thing I could do was laugh. "Oh god, I'm terrible at this. What type of woman leaves the only man she's ever been with and falls in love with her rebound?"

Annaliese pointedly raised her eyebrows. "You, babe."

Marta leaned forward, resting her elbows on the table. "You fell in love with him?"

"I don't think I'd ache this way for something less than love," I answered. "But please don't say anything to him."

She pressed a hand to her chest. "I won't. I'm just...I'm sorry he couldn't be better."

"Me too. But it's probably for the best. I have to deal with my ex, get a new job, land on my own two feet. As much as I'm hurting, I *need* this time."

And still, the thought *right person, wrong time* echoed in my mind.

Marta drummed her hands on the table. "I, for one, cannot wait to watch you take flight. I will be doing that watching from the couch while I take two weeks' vacay. There will most likely be a lot of chip crumbs all over me too, but that won't stop me from cheering you on."

Annaliese burst out laughing like Marta was the funniest person she'd ever met, and my belly warmed, especially when

Marta's cheeks pinkened so furiously, she pretended to look at something fascinating off to the side.

Eventually, Annaliese excused herself to use the restroom, and Marta pounced.

"Okay, your sister is gorgeous. Is it going to be weird for me to ask her for her number?"

I shook my head, happier in that moment than I'd been in ages. "It won't be weird in any way. I'd be disappointed if you didn't."

"All right, all right. This is why you'll always be my favorite." She tossed a chip at me. "I have one other thing to say about Dominic, then I'll drop it."

I tossed the chip back. "Fine. Go for it."

"I met him right after Dylan passed. At first, I thought he was this gigantic asshole—and he was—but he was also an angry man wracked with guilt. He didn't want to enjoy life since Dylan wasn't here to enjoy his own. The shit with Isabela only made it worse. He just disappeared behind her for a while." She shuddered. "He's been crawling out of that hole. It's slow, so slow, I don't even think he knows he's doing it, but I see it."

A sharp pain stabbed at my chest. "Why are you telling me this?"

"Because I want you to know you did nothing wrong. Your picker isn't off. Dominic is a deeply wonderful man. If he could, he'd rip his heart out to replace your broken one. He thinks he did right by you in breaking up with you. And maybe he's right, even though the way he did it sucked. Because I think you're a deeply wonderful woman, Claire, but I don't think you're in a place to be what Dominic needs. Not right now."

"Right person, wrong time," I whispered.

Marta got up from her chair and bent down to hug me tight. "Maybe. But you both have some work to do if that's true."

Two nights later, while Annaliese and Marta were out on their first date, I received a text from Dominic. And in a way, I wasn't surprised.

He'd forwarded me the picture Marta had texted him of her and my sister, their rosy cheeks pressed together, smiles dancing in their eyes.

Dominic: *Marta hasn't spoken to me in days, then this. Is she defecting? I don't blame her.*

As soon as my hands stopped shaking, I texted back.

Me: *I didn't realize we were enemies.*

Dominic: *No. Never that. How are you?*

Me: *Oh, just grand. And you?*

Dominic: *It's all sunshine and roses here. I've been thinking about going to Georgia.*

Me: *You should. You should go in the house.*

Dominic: *Funny thing is, when I see that honeysuckle bush, it's going to remind me of you now.*

Me: *I'm going to go now. Good luck with Georgia.*

Dominic: *Claire...I'm sorry.*

I threw my phone down, sadness leaking in through my cracks. It hadn't been long enough for me to talk to him again. I wasn't prepared. One short conversation, and all I wanted to do was lock myself in my closet-room and cry.

Maybe I was getting better, though. Instead of dwelling, I walked outside to the shared courtyard and sat in the grass. Annaliese had told me touching the earth every day was grounding, so I spread my fingers out and let the soil do its work.

In a few days, I had a job interview. In two weeks, I'd be going to my divorce hearing. In a month, maybe two, I hoped to be able to move to my own place. Yes, my chest still felt caved in, but I wasn't staying in this place of pain.

Dominic had been right about one thing: I did deserve the moon and the stars and the entire fucking universe, and I'd work my ass off to get them.

CHAPTER THIRTY-EIGHT

DOMINIC

IT TOOK ME THREE weeks of staring at my apartment walls to finally fly down to Georgia. I'd done some work too, like once and for all severing my ties with Isabela's PR firm, after I made sure she'd do the right thing when it came to Claire. Once that was taken care of, I wrote. I wrote like I'd never written before. Most of it would never see the light of day, but purging my brain onto paper had been a relief.

Now, I was here, in my grandparents' hometown. For two days, I sat at the end of their driveway, next to the honeysuckle bush that now reminded me more of Claire than all the years I spent suckling honey from it as a kid. For two days, panic wormed in my gut whenever I told myself to get out of the car. To suck it up and go inside.

What got me to open the door was Claire. When I thought about her leaving a husband who'd been her whole world to make her own way. To go on tour with strangers who could barely give a shit after she'd been in a car accident. How she'd confronted me on that last day when I would have done anything to avoid it. The way she held my feet to the fire in the end, telling me it didn't have to be that way.

I'd never met a braver woman. She was quiet about it. So quiet, it was easy to miss. Maybe most people did, but I'd seen her. She'd seen me too. She saw me for the coward I was.

So, it was Claire I channeled on that first step into my grandmother's kitchen. Morning light shone through the window over the farmhouse sink. Nothing had changed, but everything was different. It didn't smell like I remembered, and somehow, the room felt smaller.

I ran my fingers along the Formica counter, a smile tugging at the corners of my mouth. I couldn't think of a single bad memory that had happened here. Why the hell had I waited so many years to come back?

Snapping a picture, I texted Claire. She was the reason I was here, and I wanted her to know.

It took me two days, but I finally came inside.

My phone rang almost immediately. I stared at it, too stunned to answer right away. We'd texted a couple times, but I hadn't heard her speak in weeks.

"Hello?"

"Hey," she answered. "Tell me about it."

Her husky voice cut me off at the knees. I sank to the floor with my head in my hand. "Give me a second."

She let out a faint laugh. "I have about five minutes before I have to go back to work. But you can have a second."

"I don't know where to start. The last time I was here—" A lump lodged in my throat, so thick, it cut off my words.

"Was Dylan with you?" she asked.

I nodded even though she couldn't see. "He was five or six. My grandparents were enamored by him, even though their blood didn't run through his veins."

"Because he was yours and you were theirs." Like it was that simple. And I guess it was.

"Yeah. That's right."

"Did you bake?"

"Grandma's arthritis had gotten pretty bad, but nothing stopped her from baking with Dyl. We sang Joni Mitchell and baked a pie. My grandpa taught him how to pick honeysuckle,

like I showed you." I pressed on the aching place in my chest.
"My grandmother died a year later, and granddad followed soon
after. And then Dylan. Nothing's *ever* been the same. Nothing."

"What do you want to do now?"

I huffed a laugh. "I don't know."

"Say the first thing that comes to your mind."

"Bake."

"So bake, Dominic. Why not?"

Someone on Claire's end said her name, then Claire said
she'd be right there.

"Listen, I have to go now. I'm really glad you went inside,"
she said.

"I'm really glad you called," I replied. "Can I call you another
day? Tell you more about the house?"

She hesitated for a beat before she replied. "This is where I
should say no, but I won't. Don't ask me why."

She said she had to go again, and I let her. It seemed like I had
a habit of letting her go when all I really wanted to do was hold
on as tight as I could.

I still had too much shit to deal with to even consider that,
though. I climbed up off the floor, tracing the same steps Dylan's
little feet had. Up the stairs to the bedroom he'd slept in—the
same one I'd spent my nights in as a kid. To the bathroom and
the clawfoot tub where we'd both bathed. All of it aged and
unused, gutting me straight to my core.

This house had once held the lives of the people I'd loved
most in the world, and now, it only held ghosts.

I wanted to tear it down.

But I *needed* to build it back up. To shed some blood and
sweat and bring this place back to life. I hadn't held a power tool
in years, but my hands twitched to get dirty.

The words weren't there yet. The why of it all. But I knew,
deep down in my bones, I was right where I was supposed to be.

"Tell me what you did today," Claire said.

I sat out back on the crumbling patio behind my grandparents' house, drinking a cold beer and listening to the crickets chirp. Everything hurt, except my soul.

"Tore the kitchen apart. I saved the sink, though. It's farmhouse style, original to the house. It just needs some TLC."

"Did you use a sledgehammer?"

I chuckled. "I did. There's nothing like swinging a sledgehammer through a wall or cracking a cabinet."

It'd been a few days since I'd last heard her voice. I hadn't been sure she'd pick up tonight, but when she did, relief coursed through my veins like a drug.

"Mmm...that's not something I've experienced yet. I'll make it a point to do it once in my life."

"You've got time."

She asked me my plans for the kitchen, so I told her I was mostly in the destruction phase, but I'd be bringing in professionals to help soon. It felt normal, yet unlike any conversation we'd ever had.

"Are you ever going to tell me about your job?" I asked.

Claire guffawed. "Were you ever going to ask?"

"This is me asking. Marta won't tell me jack, and I know she's spending every second she can with your sister, so she's privy, but her lips are sealed when it comes to you."

"To be fair, she doesn't tell me anything about you either."

"I have a feeling that's at your request."

Her sigh was so heavy, I felt the weight of it. "Last week, I was hired to do PR and fundraising at a nonprofit that supports battered women. They don't have enough to pay me to work full-time, so I'm also working at Anneliese's nursery. I'm busy all the time, which helps. And I did tell Marta not to talk about you, because when I hear you're not doing well, it makes me want to drop everything to make it all better for you. But I won't do that because right now, I need to make it all better for me."

We released twin exhales. "I'm doing okay. Better than when we last talked. Being here is more right than any place else. At least for now. And, Claire?"

"Yeah?"

"I'm really fucking proud of you. If you're up for it, I'd like to hear about the nonprofit."

She paused before speaking. "I won't tell you the name. You can't write a big check so they'll hire me full-time."

I had to smile. "You know me better than I thought."

"I'll tell you about it, though. If you actually want to know."

"I wouldn't have asked if I didn't."

Marta showed up when I'd been down in Georgia for a little over two weeks, wearing steel-toed boots, an empty tool belt hanging from her waist.

I nodded to it. "Planning on doing a lot of work?"

She took the hammer from my hand and tucked it in her belt. "I knew you'd have tools for me. I travel light, baby."

She glanced around the trashed kitchen of my childhood. "You've been busy, huh?"

I rubbed the back of my sweaty neck. "I'm still in destruction mode, but I've been taking it slow so I don't knock the whole house down." I tapped the farmhouse sink with the toe of my boot where it now rested on the floor. "I'm saving this. Dale knows a guy who can reglaze it."

Marta mimed gagging with her finger down her throat. "How's good old Dale Misogynist Lemon?"

Chuckling, I slung my arm around Marta's shoulders, pulling her close. We hadn't done much talking since the tour ended. She'd been pretty angry with me, and I'd been wrapped up in my own world of self-hate. I'd finally asked her to come down, prepared to be rejected, but she'd jumped at my invitation.

"Missed you, Mar. Like whoa."

She let her head fall on my shoulder. "I missed you too, Dom. If you hadn't invited me here, I would have forced my way in pretty soon. You can only disappear on me so long before it becomes unacceptable."

"I'll remember that."

She slugged my bicep. "You're not doing it again. We're going to work on this house and you at the same time."

I scratched my head, raking my gaze over the piled cabinets and drywall dust everywhere. "I don't have a solid plan...for any of it."

"You don't have to. The point is you're working on it. And I'll be here, working with you." She nudged me with her shoulder. "Show me everything."

I took her on a tour of the place—it wasn't big, so it didn't take long—then we settled in my nightly spot with beers in hand.

"How long are you here?" I asked.

"Until you send me away."

"Is your girlfriend cool with that?"

Marta tipped her head back, resting on the chair's cushion, her mouth tugging up at the corners. "My girlfriend...she gets it. I'm going to be FaceTiming the hell out of her, but I'm here with you and she understands that."

"Look at that smile. You're fucking happy, Mar."

Marta had been pretty single for as long as I'd known her. She always fell for the wrong girl, got dragged along, then spit out. I hadn't seen her like this before. Her happiness was a warm blanket for me.

"I am. I mean, it's new, but Annaliese is a prize." She shook her head, still grinning. "The Fontanas know how to make them."

"Yep." I took a swallow of my beer while my gut dropped.

Quiet settled between us. It was pretty obvious where our minds went. It'd been over a month since I last saw Claire, and a week since she responded to a text. Her last message said she needed space and to focus on herself, and I couldn't really argue with that. That didn't mean I hadn't taken the sledgehammer to the bathroom mirror after.

It didn't help. But that was something I was learning. Reacting before thinking got me nothing but a bigger mess than before.

"We hung out with The Seasons Change crowd a couple nights ago," Marta said.

"Oh yeah? How's Adam's face?"

She smirked, playing with the label on her bottle. "Healed. He's back to being as cute as ever."

I'd gotten lucky and no one had recorded me beating the shit out of the kid. I'd gotten even luckier when he didn't press charges and let the whole thing go. I had a feeling that was more for Claire than me, but I wouldn't say it wasn't a relief not to be facing a court date.

"Was Claire there too?" I didn't really want to know. I had no right to her life, so I shouldn't have asked. But when it came to Claire, I had a lot of trouble doing the right thing.

She nodded. "Yeah. It was a big group thing. She and Adam got to talk. She forgave him when he basically bowed down at her feet. Then Claire and Rodrigo snuck away together and got matching best friend tattoos."

"What?"

She snorted a laugh. "I'm not even shitting you. Those two kill me."

I gripped the arm of her chair, dragging it closer. "You're not going to tell me what they got?"

Her lips pressed in a tight line. "I'm not. One day, if you ever work your way back to her, you can ask yourself."

I rubbed hard at my gritty face. "You're holding out hope for that?"

She raised her beer, toasting to the night sky. "I'm holding out hope for you to accept that you can have good in this life. You can laugh without feeling guilty. You're allowed to stop tying yourself to the whipping post every damn day. Right now, I see a man half-alive, and frankly, you're doing a disservice to Dylan."

Thunder rolled through my veins, a storm brewing behind my gaze. "Don't bring me that shit. You don't know anything about Dylan."

"No. Dammit, I've danced around this for years with you, but I can't stand watching you destroy every possibility of having something good. You miss him. He should be alive, and it isn't fair that he's not. All of that is true, and it will never be untrue. I might not have known Dylan, but I know you. You screwed up, and so did Chelsea, but you were *there*. You loved that boy, despite life, despite everything thrown your way. You loved him completely. And now, it's time to find a way for you to keep living."

My chest rattled as I sucked in a shuddering breath. Anger would have been the easiest response. Sending Marta away and closing myself off in this rubble of a house was on the tip of my tongue. But I came here for a reason. Standing still had gotten me nowhere. I'd gotten grayer, added a few more wrinkles, but I was still that same lost, raging-at-the-world man I'd been when I walked out of the hospital seven years ago. For a while, for a long while, that had worked for me.

Now, not much was working.

"You're right."

Marta sat up straight so fast, her beer sloshed out of her bottle. "No shit?"

"No shit. I'm tired, Mar. Tired of being angry. Tired of working so hard at being a miserable fuck. I've let myself fade into this ghost of a person, and now..." I shook my head, "I just know I'm no good for Claire or anyone like this."

She hit my leg. "I'm not talking about Claire. She shouldn't even be on your radar, not yet."

I opened my fists in my lap. "So, I just let her go?"

"Wasn't that your intention? Isn't that what you did in Chicago?"

"My intention, yeah. I couldn't seem to follow through."

Marta's brow pinched. "I love you, Dom. And I love her. I think you could be great together, but you were both hiding in each other. You know that, right?"

Heaving a sigh, I nodded. "When'd you get so wise?"

She shot me a smug look. "When I turned thirty, it all became clear."

"A year ago? And you didn't want to smack me around back then?"

She swatted the back of my head. "I always want to smack you around."

The boulder on my chest cracked and splintered. I'd been filled with sorrow and anger for so long, moving on into something lighter seemed nearly impossible. Then again, setting foot in this house again had too, yet here I was.

Nothing is forever,
even if it feels like dying

In my mind, I marked this as the night I decided to really live. I had no idea what that looked like yet, and I couldn't say I wouldn't sometimes rage against it, but this was it: the moment, the turning point—my chance to finally get it right.

CHAPTER THIRTY-NINE

CLAIRE

I RUSHED AROUND MARTA AND ANNALIESE'S NEW APARTMENT, lighting candles and making sure everything was in place. They'd hired two servers to do this type of thing, but I couldn't sit still—not when thirty guests would be arriving any minute for their housewarming and everything wasn't just right.

"Claire!" Marta barked.

I startled, nearly jumping out of my skin. Marta yanked the lighter from my hands, a frown pulling at her lips.

"Chill out, kidlet. The place is perf and you're a guest. No more working."

I shook my hands in front of me, scanning the spacious, immaculately decorated apartment. Annaliese and Marta had been together for three months and moved in here last week when I finally got my own place.

They were deliriously happy, and so was I. Happy for them. As for me, I was...content.

"I'll try. Being busy soothes my nerves," I said.

She tugged at one of my curls. "Don't be nervous. I really don't know if he's coming, and if he does...well, you can avoid him if that's what you want."

Annaliese came up behind me, slipping her arm around my waist. "You know Mar will cut a bitch if it comes down to it."

I snorted. "And Dominic is the bitch in this scenario?"

Marta grinned wickedly. "Always. Now, let's ply you with alcohol so you forget your troubles."

Guests began arriving by the time I had one of Marta and Annaliese's signature cocktails in my hand. The fact that they had a signature cocktail was so saccharine sweet, had they been any other couple, I would have hated it. But not them. Not my two favorite people in the world. They were *hardcore meets cottagecore*, and the way they blended was simply beautiful.

So, I drank their cocktail and forced myself to mingle and not watch the door. If Dominic *did* show up, I had no idea how I would feel...or if he'd even have any desire to speak to me—and vice versa. After all, I'd been the one to ask for space two months ago, and he'd given it to me willingly. So much time had gone by at this point, I wondered if I had imagined the deep connection I'd felt with him. And if it had been real, had it faded away by now?

The night wore on, and it became clear Dominic wasn't showing. Needing air, I excused myself from a group of Annaliese's friends to step out on the terrace spanning the length of the apartment. Summer had come and gone, and fall had settled over the city. Luckily, I wore a leather jacket over my gauzy pink dress, so I wasn't too chilled in the crisp evening breeze.

I had no idea how long I stood there, leaning on the railing, staring out at the twinkling city lights, but when the door opened behind me, I didn't bother turning around. There was plenty of room on this terrace for another person.

When that person came to stand right beside me, I did turn my head. Endless black pools beneath slanted ebony brows stared back at me. My heart leapt into my throat, lodging there so I couldn't get a single word out.

"Hi, Claire."

I straightened, giving my heart more room to dance wildly in its cage. "I thought you weren't coming."

Dominic rested one elbow on the railing, his body facing mine. I'd let myself forget how devastatingly beautiful he was. How looking at him like this, so close I'd barely have to reach out to touch him, impacted me.

I backed up a step, needing to. His brows drew tight, telling me he hadn't missed my retreat.

"I was always coming. I just got held up at the house." He tipped his chin, examining me. "How are you?"

I nodded too many times. "Really, really good. You?"

"Better. The house is almost done." He gazed at the view. "This is my first time back here."

"What do you think?"

His mouth quirked into a half-smile. "It's loud."

"Are you giving up your city boy ways permanently?"

"I don't think I could."

"Why not?"

His foot slid forward until the toe of his boot touched mine. My heart hammered so hard, I wondered if he could hear it.

"I've got a lot of unfinished business here. Marta's here. And you—you're here."

I sucked in a breath, unsure of how to respond. Our gazes caught, and then his foot slid next to mine, his pants brushing my knee.

"Where are you living, Claire? Not here, right?" he asked.

"No. Not here. I moved into a studio not much bigger than my closet-room. It's my first time living alone."

I loved it so much. I'd hung prints of my favorite bands, put a thousand fluffy pillows on my bed that doubled as a couch, and had pink and gold accents all over. I paid a fortune for my four-hundred-square-feet of freedom, but it was more than worth it.

"What do you think?" he echoed my question.

I bit my lip, deciding my answer. "It's quiet."

"Do you like that? The quiet?"

"Mmmhmmm. For now I do."

He cocked his head, then chuckled in a way I'd never heard. It tumbled out of him, but he didn't fight to hold it back.

"You're not giving me much to work with, Claire."

"I'm not really sure how much I should be giving you. The last time I saw you, you told me to keep on riding."

His lids lowered to half-mast. "That was right back then. For both of us."

"And it's not now?"

His knee pressed into my leg. "I wouldn't have come tonight if I didn't have every intention of having you back. You asked for space, and I gave it to you. But make no mistake, I never once stopped thinking about you."

Blinking, I retreated again. "I'm not...I wasn't expecting you to say that."

He ran his fingers through the side of his hair. "To be honest, I wasn't planning on saying that. It's just...you're standing here, taking my breath away all over again. You look beautiful tonight. Just beautiful."

"You look beautiful too," I whispered. "But I'm—"

"No, you don't have to say anything." He threw up his hand. "You could have a boyfriend for all I know. Or maybe you're really done with me. I'm making a mess of this."

I giggled at how flustered he had become. "I don't have a boyfriend. As for the other thing—"

"Let me take you to dinner."

My nose wrinkled, cringing at the memory of the last time we went out to dinner in Utah. "I don't really want to have my picture taken with you. I'm sorry."

The door burst open beside us before he could say anything else. We both twisted as Marta came out with her arms raised, Annaliese trailing right behind.

"Dominic, in the flesh! You don't have a MartAnna cocktail, and that's just a crime," she squealed, pulling him inside with her.

Annaliese cocked a brow. "That was her subtle way of giving you room if you needed it. You looked like you needed it."

I tucked my hair behind my ear. "I don't know. I think I did. That was much more than I was ready for."

"He had some things to say?"

"A lot of things." I leaned my forehead against hers. "Would you kill me if I left? I need to think, and I don't think I'll be able to do that with him here."

"You can go, but don't you sneak out without saying goodbye to him."

"That's not my style."

We drifted inside together, finding Dominic and Marta in the kitchen, grabbing drinks. I caught his attention, tipping my head to the front door. He came with me to the empty entryway.

"I know you just got here, but I'm leaving now."

He scanned me carefully. "Running away?"

"Nope." I fought the urge to smile. "If I were, I'd have snuck past you without saying goodbye. If you're not leaving town right away—"

"I'll stay as long as you want me to."

"I'll text you tomorrow. I'm working at the nursery, so it'll be evening." I tucked a curl behind my ear, heat creeping up my face for no reason at all. "You look different, and it's disconcerting, so I'm going to go now."

His laughter trailed behind me out the door.

―――――――――――

Chris, Annaliese's business partner and my other boss, wheeled over to where I was wiping down shelves. "Hey, Claire. It looks like the sky's about to open up any minute. Do you think you can go outside and bring everything in? I'll close things out inside."

I turned to the front windows of the shop. The sky had gone gray and dreary. Luckily, we were set to close in fifteen minutes, so I doubted we'd have many more customers, especially if it rained.

"No problem."

Chris got around really well in her wheelchair, but carrying some of the larger lawn decor we kept outside during business hours was easier for me to do.

As soon as I stepped outside, a raindrop hit my head. The air had cooled enough, I wasn't looking forward to getting soaked. Hurrying, I bent down to pick up a pair of kitschy lawn gnomes and carried them to the locked storage area on the side of the building. Whirling around to grab the next thing, I ran into a wall.

Warm, familiar hands steadied my shoulders. "I feel like we've done this before."

Sucking in a breath, I looked up at Dominic. "It does seem like I have a habit of running into you."

"And me catching you."

"But maybe you keep putting yourself in my way."

His hands slid slowly down my arms. "Maybe you're right."

Thunder cracked in the distance, and the rain began falling in earnest. Big, fat drops landed on both of us.

"I have to put all this stuff away."

He followed me back to the front of the store, helping without being asked. We hurried, running back and forth while getting drenched. I had to admit, it was nice having him there, working with me.

I locked up the storage shed once we'd put everything away and turned to find Dominic right beside me. His dark T-shirt clung to the solid muscles in his chest. Rain dripped from his lips, beading in his beard. He made my heart hurt.

We stared at each other, ignoring the rain and everything else. After an eternity, he reached for me, gripping the back of my neck and pulling me against him. I rose on my toes as he bent, and our mouths collided in the sweetest reunion. His lips moved over mine like they'd never stopped, kissing me breathless, then breathing me back to life again.

My fingers curled into his chest, digging in hard enough for him to grunt into my mouth, but he never stopped kissing me. Dominic's touch remained gentle and controlled, even as I clawed at him. Tears fell from my closed eyes, mixing with the rain pouring down on us.

"Claire! Are you out there?" Chris called from around front.

We broke apart, but I couldn't look at him. My knees were shaky, but I managed to walk around the corner and tell Chris I'd be right there. Of course, Dominic was right behind me, his solid front skimming my back.

He cupped the side of my neck. "Can I come to your place? Or will you come to mine? I can order dinner so there's no danger of pictures."

My heart flipped, but I nodded. "My place." I covered his hand with mine, leaning into his touch. "I have to finish up here…"

His lips pressed against my cheek. "Text me the address. I'll meet you there." He shifted to stand in front of me, dipping down to meet my eyes. "Okay?"

I nodded again, my mouth flattened into a straight line as I willed my emotions to stop roiling inside me. "I'll see you soon."

An hour later, I was showered and dressed in a sweatshirt and leggings, opening the door to Dominic Cantrell. He carried a paper bag filled with Chinese takeout, wearing fresh, dry clothes too.

The first thing he did after kicking my door shut and setting down the takeout was gather me in his arms and bury his face in my neck. He breathed me in like this was the first full breath he'd taken in a long time.

"You still smell just as good as I remembered," he murmured as he straightened, looking me over. "I brought you something, besides dinner."

"You did?"

Below the bag of takeout was a small cardboard box. Dominic placed it on my narrow kitchen counter and opened the lid. I peered inside, and immediately covered my mouth with my hands when I saw the contents.

"Did you make this?" I rasped.

He smiled wider than I'd ever seen. I had to grip the counter, my knees went so weak at the sight of him that way. Happy, lighter, open, present.

"I don't know if it's as good as my grandmother's, and it's not fresh from the oven..."

I poked the top of his creation. "You made me a pie."

"I did."

My eyes narrowed. God, how I wanted to give in and fall into his arms like nothing had ever driven us apart. It couldn't be that simple, though, not if he was going to push me away again as soon as we got close.

"You're here and kissing me and telling me you have every intention of having me back and making me a pie and that's adorable and sweet and I really, really love it, but I'm not sure I'm done being mad at you. Tell me what's changed between then and now. I need words."

"I know." He kneaded the back of his neck. "I met you and wanted everything with you. It was instant and powerful, and it freaked me the fuck out. Giving us that solid end date was the only way I could allow myself to enjoy you. I opened up to you *because* you wouldn't be around very long. But when you said you'd stay with me...I panicked. I wanted that too, but I couldn't do that to you. I couldn't let you tie yourself to a sinking ship."

My eyes burned. This man had been so broken, more than I'd even understood at the time. "If you could have said that—said anything besides making me feel like it was like nothing for you to let me walk away…"

"It wasn't nothing, Claire. It ripped me apart, but I had myself convinced I was being selfless."

"You hurt me badly. And you *scared* me, more than once. Your anger, the violence…it's a nonstarter for me. I can't be with you if I have to be on edge all the time."

His face crumpled with shame. "I'm so fucking sorry, Claire. I would never hurt you, but I get that seeing me hurt someone else isn't okay either. All I can tell you is I'm not in that dark place anymore, and the place I'm in now makes me want to be better. Not just for you, but for me. For Dyl."

He tucked his hands in the pockets of his joggers, glancing around my apartment. "This is nice. Looks like you."

I had to laugh at how absurd it was that he could say all that, then compliment me on my apartment. "Thanks. I used a chunk of my divorce settlement to furnish it."

He let out a long exhale. "That's final?"

"It is. Marta and Annaliese convinced me to take the settlement from him. Now, I'm single like a Pringle, as Marta says." I folded my arms over my stomach. "I think we're getting away from the topic."

He squeezed his eyes shut and pinched the bridge of his nose. "I've been seeing someone—"

"What?" I breathed.

His eyes flew open. "A therapist. I've been seeing a grief therapist."

"Oh." I slumped against the wall. "Your phrasing needs some work."

He chuckled, leaning against the wall across from me. "I'm sorry. I'm trying to get this right and bumbling around like a fucking teenager."

"Just talk to me," I pleaded, desperate to hear more.

The toe of his shoe touched my bare foot, whipping butterflies into a whirlwind in my stomach. This man had put his tongue on every square inch of my body, yet his toes against mine were what made me blush.

"My therapist has pointed out, just as Marta has, I had done shit-all to grieve and work through my loss. I've been locked down for so long, I didn't know how to turn the key, even when I wanted to."

Hope entered my heart like sunshine through a crack. "But you do now?"

"Claire, I wouldn't be here if I didn't. I'm still too old for you. I have more baggage than you rightly deserve to deal with. I'm a grumpy asshole, and yeah, it's hard to go out to dinner with me and not have your picture taken. The thing is, I'm really hoping you'll look past all that."

I closed my eyes, letting his words settle over me. God, they felt good. In truth, I'd been waiting for him to come back. I'd been working, building my own life, making new friends, but in the back of my mind, Dominic was always there. And this, having him here in front of me, saying more than I could have ever hoped for, was like the last puzzle piece of my new life clicking into place.

"Why?" I whispered.

When he spoke, he moved closer. "You don't know?" My eyelids fluttered open, peering up into his crow-black eyes. He was completely unguarded, letting his emotions dance across his features. "I'm in love with you. I've weighed the risks, and loving you is worth it."

I'd said the same thing to him when he'd asked how Chelsea could take a chance having another baby. To know he'd listened and truly taken my words to heart overwhelmed me. He'd changed so much, yet he was still my larger-than-life, rough, brooding rocker. He was just more than that now.

"So, you told two lies?" I whispered.

He stopped moving, cocking his head. "What do you mean?"

"In the game, in Miami, you said you didn't believe love was real and lasting."

He breathed heavy through his nose as realization dawned on him. "No. I didn't lie. I'd never loved you before. If you asked me again, my answer wouldn't be the same. Nothing's been the same since I let you in, and I never want to go back to the empty shell I was. The way I love you is so fucking real, Claire. And I intend to love you like hell for the rest of my life. Even if you send me away right now, I'll love you."

"Dominic…" I sighed his name, laying my head on his chest. His arms came around me, holding me with great care.

"I'm asking for a chance, Claire—however that looks to you. I know I have penance to pay, and I'm willing. I'm here."

A sob shook me, and his arm tightened. He held me close, swaying slightly, then he sang my song under his breath.

"I love you," I said through tears. "I do love you. And I've missed you more than I can say. I'm glad we weren't together, though."

He nodded, swiping tears from my cheeks. "Glad isn't the word I'd use, but we both *needed* this time."

Smoothing my hands over his beard, I sucked in a shaky breath. "I'm ready now. But I need you to know I have to keep standing on my own feet. You don't owe me penance. I only need you, to be here, to love me aggressively."

He sniffed, bemused. "Aggressively?"

"Mmmhmmm. Love me out loud, so I never question it. No lukewarm. No half measures. I'll do the same back."

"That's something I can do. I don't think I'll be able to help myself with you."

I pressed up on my feet and touched my lips to his. "Okay."

He caught my nape when I went to pull away. "Okay?"

"You're worth the risk, Dominic."

A laugh of pure joy rolled from his chest. "I think that's the first time anyone's ever said that to me. Fuck, Claire, do I love you."

I laughed with him. "That was a really good start on the aggressive love thing."

He nuzzled my neck, smiling into my skin. "Just wait, baby. Just wait."

I knew what it was like to settle for lukewarm. Stooping down for a man who refused to rise once had been second nature to me. This didn't feel like that at all.

We were starting over, building something fresh on the ashes of our pasts. I was under no illusions it would always be easy or perfect, but I didn't want easy. I wanted Dominic.

And if we fell, we'd fall together.

DOMINIC

I TRACED THE OUTLINE of the sun tattooed on the inside of Claire's wrist, then lifted it to press a kiss to the filled-in crescent moon.

"Still can't believe you and Rodrigo have matching tattoos." I bit into her tiny sun until she yelped, swatting me away. "When are we getting our matching tattoos?"

Claire laughed, tossing her head back on her pillow. "I think that's considered bad luck for married couples."

"That's only if we get each other's names."

She pulled her head back, studying me. "Are you serious?"

I grinned, stroking her freckled cheek with my thumb. "No. Not really. I'm pretty content with you wearing my ring every day."

She raised an eyebrow. "Content, huh?"

Gripping her jaw, I tipped her face up to mine. "Aggressively happy. Madly in love with my wife. Deliriously into you, baby."

"That's the spirit, sir." She giggled and kissed me hard.

We'd been married for six months now, living mostly in New York, but around Claire's work schedule, we'd found time to spend long weekends and some holidays in Georgia too. I was taking a hiatus from touring for a while. The road and my career had been my sole focus for two decades, I figured I was due for an extended leave.

"It's just as well you don't want my name tattooed on you." I splayed my hand on Claire's abdomen. She hummed, laying her hand on top of mine.

"Mmm...yeah. They frown upon pregnant women getting inked."

When my hand inched up beneath her T-shirt, itching to touch her swollen tits, she swatted me away again. "We have to get out of bed today. We have guests—and you have baking to do."

I lowered my head, kissing her stomach. She was halfway through the second trimester, only really beginning to show. But god *damn* was she sexy like this, carrying our little girl.

Claire squirmed beneath me, reaching for me even though she'd been protesting a minute ago. We did have plans, but that would never stop me from fucking my wife—not when she wanted it as much as I did.

I sank into her from behind, spooning her body with mine. We went slow, gentle, touching and kissing while I slid in and out of her. It wasn't always like that. Claire still wore my marks on her thighs and tits, and her ass was too tempting not to smack. But sometimes, like lazy Sundays in bed, we made love because that's what we both needed.

The truth was, I'd been extra needy lately. The baby in Claire's belly had been planned and was very much wanted, but I couldn't say I wasn't terrified. The reality of having another child nearly sent me into a fresh grief spiral. But I had my level-headed girl by my side and a therapist who walked me through my emotions. We weren't replacing Dylan. That was impossible.

We were creating someone entirely new, and she'd be Dylan's sister. She'd know about him, we'd tell her all about him. This baby wouldn't look like him, but maybe she would *be* like him. She might demand music always be playing, or love the feel of mud between her toes. Or maybe she'd be her own little person.

I might have still been terrified. This probably wouldn't ever go away. But a big part of me couldn't fucking wait to breathe this little girl in and hold her little body on my chest while she slept.

Claire and I came together, shuddering, moaning, holding each other. And when she turned her head and smiled at me, I fell in love with her all over again.

Eventually, we got up, got dressed, made coffee and toast and ate on our terrace. Then Claire cracked the whip and put me to work.

"You have a pie to bake, love." She perched on one of the stools at our kitchen counter with her laptop open in front of her. "And I'm going to watch you in between sending emails."

Claire still worked at the nonprofit for battered women, technically part-time, but she put in full-time hours. Since her salary wasn't an issue anymore, she insisted on not receiving a raise. She really loved her job, though, and they depended on her. She made me proud, but most importantly, she made herself proud.

I'd been honing my baking skills over the last year. I wasn't anywhere near my grandmother's level, but I was getting there. I found rolling dough to be a hit of serotonin straight to my brain. My therapist *and* my wife wholeheartedly supported my hobby.

After I slid my pie into the oven, Claire joined me in the kitchen, helping me clean up. I didn't bother telling her not to help anymore. I'd come to realize cleaning was her serotonin hit.

Once it was sparkling, I pinned her to the counter, covering her mouth with mine. I kissed her breathless, then moved down her neck to sink my teeth into my favorite spot. She moaned and rocked her hips into mine, pushing at my chest at the same time.

"Annaliese and Marta will be here any minute." Her protests were weak, but I listened. Her sister had seen my bare ass once, and that was enough for both of us.

"Fine. I'll let you go." I gave her butt a smack as she ran away from me, grinning wide at the way she screeched and bounced.

My wife, forever drawing me into her lush, vibrant garden of Eden. She was still the tempting serpent and the vital, fresh apple, luring me, but also giving me life. Instead of casting me out, Claire held me closer.

Looking back now, I didn't know why I ever tried to fight against this. When it came to Claire, my life, my paradise, there had never been a chance I wasn't going to fall.

JOIN MY SUBLIME READERS:
   https://www.facebook.com/groups/JuliaWolfReaders
   We're a fun, laidback group. When we're not talking books—
which, let's face it, books are seventy-five percent of our convos
and I'm not mad about it—we're talking about life, TV, music,
and funny shit. Come join us!

Sign up for my newsletter to find out my latest release news:
https://www.subscribepage.com/t7m4u4

Find me on TikTok
https://www.tiktok.com/@authorjuliawolf
   This is where I hang out most these days. I'd love for you to
follow me and say hi!

PLAYLIST

"GUYS MY AGE" HEY VIOLET
 "Circles" Post Malone
 "Heartbreak Hotel" Abigail Barlow
 "Daddy Issues" The Neighborhood
 "Playdate" Melanie Martinez
 "Where We're Going" Gerry Cinnamon
 "Aeroplane" Leon of Athens
 "Mystery of Love" Sufjan Stevens
 "Honey and Glass" Peyton Cardoza
 "I Believe in a Thing Called Love" The Darkness
 "Heavy" Birdtalker
 "feel something" Bea Miller
 "make daddy proud" blackbear
 "Fade Into You" The Moth & The Flame
 "Electric Love" Borns
 "Come & Go" Juice WRLD and Marshmello
 "I Wasted You" flora cash
 "Exile" Taylor Swift, Bon Iver
 "Still Don't Know My Name" Labrinth
 "Elastic Heart" Sia
 "July" Noah Cyrus
 "I Need My Girl" The National
 "The One I Love" David Gray
 "Don't Dream It's Over" Lauren Daigle

"Patience" Chris Cornell
"Mind Over Matter" Young The Giant
Listen to the playlist on Spotify:
https://open.spotify.com/playlist/7MTkFqz8UfAdNuLFCg
w8Ma

ACKNOWLEDGEMENTS

IN MARCH 2020, the world changed for everyone in one way or another. As a full-time writer with school age children, my schedule got flipped on its head. Writing became something I did at night, when the house was finally still again and I could think. So what did I do to fill the time between helping my kids with their distance learning?

I downloaded TikTok. I went looking for a way to entertain myself, and I did, but I also found inspiration.

The silver fox on the cover? That's Carlos (@capereiv on TikTok). Never in my wildest dreams did I think the actual inspiration for Dominic Cantrell's appearance would agree to be on my cover, but he said yes! The fact that he's a sweet, funny, awesome guy makes it even better.

I fell in love with a lot of couples and their sweet, cute, sexy stories. The couple that really struck a chord with me was this witty, beautiful, plus-size woman named Alicia and her stoic, buff husband, Scott. She's the sunshine to his grump. He loves her body (and booty), as he rightly should. And she isn't afraid to ask to be loved aggressively, which he delivers on. Their relationship and her self-love were huge inspirations for this story. (@aliciamccarvell on TikTok)

So, yes, this book wouldn't have happened had I not downloaded TikTok. Peeking into others' lives stirred my creativity like nothing else. I haven't danced on there, and I never will, but I like to think I make some fun content too. (@authorjuliawolf).

Thank you to my betas, Jennifer and Janet. You guys rock, as always.

My cover designer, Amy Queau always rocks my world. I wanted stars, and you gave them to me!

ABOUT THE AUTHOR

Julia Wolf is a lover of all things romance. From steamy, to sweet, to funny, to so dirty you'll be blushing for days, she loves it all.

Formerly a hair stylist, she spent years collecting stories her clients couldn't wait to spill. And now that she's writing full time, she's putting those stories to use, although all identifying characteristics have been changed to protect the not-so-innocent!

Julia lives in Maryland with her three crazy, beautiful kids and her patient husband who she's slowly converting to a romance reader, one book at a time.

Visit my website:

http://www.juliawolfwrites.com

ALSO BY JULIA WOLF

Unrequited Series

Unrequited

Misconception

Rocked

Dissonance

Blue is the Color

Times Like These

Watch Me Unravel

Such Great Heights

Under the Bridge

The Never Blue Duet

Never Lasting

Never Again

The Sublime

One Day Guy

The Very Worst

Want You Bad

Fix Her Up

Eight Cozy Nights